Murderous Pursuit

PUBLISHING

First Edition published 2022 by

2QT Publishing

Stockport, United Kingdom. SK5 9BL

Cover Design by Charlotte Mouncey with illustrations from istockphoto.com and Unsplash.com

Printed in Great Britain by Amazon UK

A CIP catalogue record for this book is available from the British Library

ISBN 978-1-914083-64-8

THE WISSTINGHAM MYSTERIES

A CRIME SERIES

BOOK 2

Murderous
Pursuit

NIGEL HANSON

To Gwyeth
with best wishes
Ne H.

LIST OF MAIN CHARACTERS

Commander Selwyn Fitzgerald: Owner of Wisstingham Hall Estate

Sebastian Monaghan: Selwyn's nephew

Amanda Sheppard: Librarian & Sebastian's fiancée

Miriam Cheyney: Wisstingham mayor and councillor

Karl Tyson: Wisstingham council leader

Archie Fox: Tradesail director

Doug Cutler: Tradesail investor

Mrs Soames: Wisstingham Hall housekeeper

Martin Brightside: Friend of Amanda

Lucian Fitzgerald/Jack Cavannagh: Half-brother of Selwyn

Vincent Monaghan: Wisstingham Hall estate manager

Harry Gaverty: Criminal gang leader

Ronnie Slade: Gaverty's second-in-command

Detective Inspector Stone: Hopestanding CID

Jorge Berensen: Professional hitman

MINOR CHARACTERS

Clifford Caines: Teacher

Jeremy Sinclair: Tradesail Director

Detective Sergeant McBride: Hopestanding CID

DCI Nelson: Hopestanding CID

Fred Ferris: Acting estate manager

Jock Cameron: Gang member

Mac Bilton: Wisstingham Hall quarry manager

Jean-Louis Gaudin: French villager

Xavier Dumas: French villager

PREFACE

A criminal racket operated right under his nose by those he trusted, treacherous intrigue and a trail of murder centred on the discovery of an old deed and map, have brought Commander Selwyn Fitzgerald and his ancestral residence, Wisstingham Hall, to virtual ruin. The documents have also spawned a dispute over land ownership that threatens to further imperil the estate.

The commander's dreams of locating the whereabouts of his family's long-lost treasure are now in tatters, as are the plans he'd agreed with the local mayor, Miriam Cheyney, to open Wisstingham Hall to the general public.

Desperate to recover the estate's stolen money, Selwyn now heads to France accompanied by his protégé Sebastian and a reformed miscreant, Clifford Caines, the man who is to lead them to their destination.

Chapter 1

4TH JANUARY 2011

Ronnie 'the Hammer' Slade felt the fan's warm blast on his short-cropped head as he pushed through the glass doors. His ears were instantly assailed by the familiar cacophony of bells, pings and tinny background music. Heading to the offices, he gave an habitual glance around the arcade, on the lookout for the usual barred scrotes and troublemakers. A security guard chatting with the cashier straightened quickly and broke away from their conversation, but did not escape Ronnie's notice and scowl.

Slade punched in the code on the security lock and passed into the quietness of the corridor to the boss's office. His knock on the door was greeted with a harsh command to enter.

Behind a large mahogany desk inside the ill-lit room sat Harry Gaverty, staring through the rain-spattered window. He'd lost weight following Vincent Monaghan's death, so the ornate gold rings turned easily on his fingers as he pensively rotated them in turn. Gaverty's humour, such as it had ever been, had worsened since the loss of his old friend and partner in crime the previous month; now he lived under a permanent cloud of thinly veiled anger.

'Mornin', Harry.' Ronnie's greeting was met with a mere grunt. 'You said you'd decided about Taylor.'

Harry turned his reptilian eyes on the enforcer. 'Yeah. Take him out. Give 'im some sea air.'

Nonplussed, Ronnie stared back for a moment. 'That's a bit under the arm, innit? I thought you'd just want me to give him a good smackin'. He's been payin' yer back, ain't he?'

Harry sniffed. 'Not enough. Missed a payment. Says he's brassic, but I reckon he's havin' a laugh.'

Ronnie scratched at his greying beard. 'Won't be laughin' much longer, then, eh?'

'Nah, he won't, will he?' Harry turned his gaze back to the window.

'It's gonna cost,' warned Ronnie.

His already thin lips compressed to a tight line, Harry slowly swivelled his head to face Ronnie, who swallowed under the gaze of those slitted, unblinking eyes. The boss inclined his head and frowned. 'Ronnie, you've been in this business long enough now to know it ain't always a matter of money. Got to set an example, right? I ain't gonna be fucked about by anyone and they all needs to know it.'

Ronnie dutifully lowered his head. 'I understand. You also mentioned Bilton.'

'Yeah. Heard anything from the toerag?'

Ronnie shook his head. 'Nah, not since Vincent went.'

'He's supposed to be keepin' us informed. One of Taylor's friends, ain't he?'

'Yeah.'

'Then make sure Bilton knows what he can expect if he doesn't get 'is finger out.' Harry held the stare for several moments before cutting his eyes dismissively to the door, a cue Ronnie was only too eager to take.

***

That same night, through howling winds and sheets of driving rain, the small, shabby fishing boat pitched its way through the rough sea. From the sparse shelter of the wheelhouse, Ronnie peered at the drenched and heavily chained figure huddled in the prow. Taylor repeatedly called out, but the wind and throb of the boat's engine drowned out his pleas.

'Here should be OK,' the skipper shouted to Ronnie, as he throttled back the engine and scanned the swell for signs of any other vessels.

Swaying with the motion of the boat, the Hammer lurched unsteadily towards the prow while the skipper turned to look away. On Ronnie's approach, a fresh cry went up from the victim, who'd been sick.

'Shut it!' Ronnie brought out the hammer from the bespoke pocket inside his large coat.

'Please,' begged the pallid wretch, 'there's gotta be a mistake! Phone Harry, for the love of God. Please. Just let me speak to him.'

'No mistake,' Ronnie muttered. 'Harry says bye-bye.'

With a malevolent grin, he raised the hammer as the vomit-stained Taylor screamed and tried to squirm away from the blow. There was a sickening crack and a piercing cry, then only the roar of the wind and rain as Ronnie dragged the lifeless corpse to the side of the boat, heaved it overboard, then flung the hammer out to sea.

***

His eyes narrowed against the sun's afternoon glare reflecting off the white walls and marble floor tiles, Archie Fox checked the caller's number before he answered. The clink of ice cubes in his glass put up the briefest of contests against the background noise of another Spanish apartment block under construction. This was his third gin and tonic, and he'd certainly needed them.

'Hi, Archie, sorry I missed you,' came Jeremy Sinclair's anxious voice. 'What's happening? What have you found out?'

Archie took a sip of his drink. Reluctant to break the news, he painstakingly positioned the glass squarely on the coaster, took out a packet of cigarillos, lit one, and tossed the packet onto the table.

'You there?' prompted Jeremy.

'Yes, I'm still here, my dear chap. Frightfully sorry. It's wretched news, I'm afraid. Both the Javea and Alicante offices are empty and to let, and there's not a soul to be found or contacted. It's like the flaming *Marie Celeste*.'

'What about the site?' Jeremy sounded frantic.

'Nothing. No one there, either. Looks like the developer's gone bust. There are no machines or materials to be seen, and the villas are no further on than when we last saw them.' Archie took another puff and toyed with the glass.

'Then we're well and truly buggered! What's worse, the press here are onto us. Some of the clients have got together and bleated to them. A snotty little reporter was on the phone for half an hour this morning. Couldn't get rid of the little sod. And Doug Cutler wants a meeting tonight.'

Archie frowned, took a draw and exhaled slowly. The blue smoke curled lazily upwards. 'Don't go.'

'But I've got to. With all he's got invested, we've got to keep him onside otherwise we really are up the Swanee.'

Archie slowly shook his head. He felt he should warn

his partner about Cutler's background and deadly associates, but it was too late for that now. Jeremy would go to pieces if he told him; he would never have joined and invested in the company if he'd known the colour of Cutler's money. He'd have to wait until he could see Jeremy face to face and get a few drinks into him before he broke *that* news.

'Mind you, I think he knows Tradesail's finished,' Jeremy continued. 'From what he let slip, I think he's been doing his own digging.'

'Then for God's sake don't go, my dear fellow. Just get out of there, fast. Grab the files, lock the offices and… '

Archie's desire to see his partner safe began to weaken under the pressure of his instinct for self-preservation. Perhaps he should just leave Jeremy to sink or swim. The shit was going to hit the fan anyway, and he for one had no intention of facing the authorities, let alone Cutler's wrath and vengeance. Would Jeremy prove a liability if Archie threw him a lifeline? Then again, if he didn't help Jeremy, the authorities would have chapter and verse from a disgruntled partner – that's if Cutler didn't get to him first.

'Archie, are you there?'

'I… I was thinking. Get the first flight you can to Montpellier. Text me the flight details and I'll meet you at the airport. I'll talk to Cutler from here, once I know you're on your way.'

'Montpellier? Why there?'

'Because I'm going to Versain, so that's the nearest airport. I'll fill you in when I see you.'

'There's something you're not telling me, isn't there? What is it?'

'I'll tell you everything when I see you,' Archie insisted. 'Just get out as quickly as you can. Nothing to the press. OK?'

Jeremy agreed and hung up.

Archie stroked his beard and stared across the terrace at the swimming pool beyond. Even with the injection of Cutler's and Jeremy's money, he'd harboured doubts as to whether he could pull things round. Now, with the developer gone, there was no hope. The day of reckoning was imminent. God help them both when the police and Cutler discovered Tradesail's true finances and the vanished deposits paid for villas yet unbuilt.

***

It was a cloudy day for the start of the journey from Wisstingham Hall to the south of France. A taxi had deposited their fellow traveller, Clifford Caines, who'd seated himself on the bench near the foot of the stone staircase where he waited patiently.

Standing at the front door, a twinkle in his eye, Commander Selwyn Fitzgerald turned to his nephew, Sebastian, and quickly looked him up and down. 'That shirt you're wearing – it's not for a bet, is it?'

Sebastian glanced down. 'What do you mean? What's wrong with it?'

His uncle smiled. 'Well, I'm glad I remembered my sunglasses, that's all I'll say.'

'So rude!' Sebastian returned the commander's grin.

Any further badinage was cut short as the housekeeper bustled towards them, tears glistening in the corners of her eyes. Nevertheless, to both men's concealed amusement, Mrs Soames embarked on an accusation that they'd deliberately chosen this day to depart just to escape the taking down of the Christmas decorations.

'It 'appens every year – you always 'ave one excuse or another for not being 'ere to do it,' she complained, quite incorrectly. 'I suppose I'll 'ave to drag my Reggie out of 'is workshop to give a hand. *And* he won't do it right, I'll be bound.'

For all that, she'd packed enough sandwiches and delicacies for the journey to rival a royal garden party and sustain an army. With tears now streaming down her cheeks, and after repeated admonitions for their safety, she energetically waved her hanky as the car drove off.

Selwyn and Sebastian were to share the driving, Sebastian opening the journey with the drive to the tunnel. Caines would be no help in that respect. Though he had graduated from a wheelchair to walking sticks, he was still recovering from injuries sustained weeks earlier at the hands of the commander's deceased estate manager. Caines' role was to lead his fellow travellers to Vincent Monaghan's French hideaway and, they hoped, the commander's embezzled money.

As the Jaguar's tyres ate up the miles to Folkestone, Sebastian's thoughts turned once more to the task ahead: the search for Monaghan's papers, bank account and the missing money, as well as the stolen goods the villain had squirrelled away in France during his years of clandestine criminality. He had more than a few matters of his own to settle; for years he'd believed that Monaghan was his real father, only to find that his paternity actually lay with the commander's late brother, Lucian Fitzgerald. He still hadn't come to terms with that.

Trying not to let gloom carry him away, Sebastian

turned his thoughts to his fiancée, Amanda. He pictured those large, oval, come-to-bed eyes and the Cleopatra hairstyle, the flash of white teeth and her wicked smile. Theirs had been a roller-coaster romance, and he still entertained fears over her fondness for that wretched Martin Brightside, despite her protestations that he was only a good friend. All in all, Sebastian felt he had much to gain but also possibly much to lose with this present quest.

***

By the time Jeremy had booked his Montpellier flight from Stansted, hastily packed his bags and set off to collect the files, the afternoon was well advanced. In the office, he liberated a large whisky from the drinks cabinet. The cabinet only usually came into play for celebratory drinks when a client signed up to buy one of Tradesail's Spanish properties.

He set the glass and whisky bottle on the coffee table, perched on the edge of the sofa, and contemplated the three desks located in the suite's office area: his, Archie's, and that of the elderly secretary who'd suddenly quit and walked out earlier that week.

'It's all the hassle from the customers,' she'd complained as she stuffed her possessions into a carrier bag. 'I'm sorry, Jeremy, but I just can't take it any more,' she'd mumbled through tears. 'I'm supposed to avoid stress.' Then, before he could reply, the distraught woman had fled the office.

Jeremy took a swig and looked at the photo on the far wall of himself and Archie, taken in 2007 when they'd received an annual business award sponsored by the local newspaper. That was a year after he'd joined, Jeremy mused, remembering how pleased he'd been when Archie had poached him from one of Tradesail's main competitors. Jeremy had thought his investment in the company a smart move at the time. The company had branched out into the lucrative market of selling off-plan Spanish villas, and Archie had introduced Doug Cutler, a sleeping partner who had made a substantial injection of funds.

The rattle of the door handle brought Jeremy back to the present. Through the glazed glass panel, he saw the silhouette of a tall, slim man.

'Hello, Mr Sinclair,' came a youthful voice. 'It's Jamie Dawson from the *Echo*. Can I have a few words with you, please?'

Oh, not that little shit again! Jeremy glared at the door and remained seated, his only movement to raise the glass to his mouth.

'I know you're in there, Mr Sinclair. I need a quote for the piece we're running in tomorrow's edition about customer deposits and villas still not built. I need to get your point of view and comment.'

Jeremy waited until eventually the silhouette disappeared. He resisted the temptation to creep over to the door and check if the reporter had really gone, refreshed his drink and stepped out onto the balcony. From seven floors below came the drone of the Hillingden traffic heading to and from Hopestanding. Above him, the cloudless blue sky was criss-crossed by vapour trails. He dearly wished he were at the business end of one of them right now. *Better get on with it.* He returned to the office.

He was on the second drawer of files when raised voices came from the corridor, followed by approaching footsteps. The door handle rattled once more, accompanied by a sharp knock on the glass. Simultaneously, a deep, hard voice demanded, 'Mr Sinclair, open up. It's Damian Slater, Mr Cutler's associate.'

Jeremy grudgingly unlocked the door, which was rapidly pushed open by a man whose stature rather resembled that of a large wardrobe.

'I've just had a word with that little tyke who was lurking down the corridor. He won't give you any more bother,' Slater announced. He produced a mobile, which was dwarfed by his large, muscular hands, and his fat fingers tapped out a message. 'Mr Cutler will be here shortly,' he said. The backward rake of his head and the way he unsmilingly looked down his nose at Jeremy brooked no argument.

'But our meeting's not until this evening.'

Framed in the doorway, Slater stared silently at the disconcerted detainee, who backed away and reached for the comfort of the whisky glass. Jeremy immediately dismissed any thought of offering him a drink. The man's gaze appeared to be fixed on some point in the distance, his face expressionless.

Should be standing outside Buckingham Palace, thought Sinclair.

Conscious he was running out of time, Jeremy rose to start work on the files, whereupon Slater coughed and slowly shook his head. Jeremy reclaimed his seat.

After several more minutes, footsteps approached down the corridor. Slater leaned back slightly from the open doorway to see who it was, allowed his boss to enter then closed the door and stationed himself with his back to it.

'Good afternoon, Jeremy,' the newcomer greeted him

18

from the doorway. Short in stature, Cutler was tanned, muscular and smartly dressed in cords and a cashmere sweater. His square face, set with hooded eyes, featured an aquiline nose and small, round mouth. He approached with his hand extended. 'I decided to pull our meeting forward and have it here. I hope that's not inconvenient.'

Jeremy offered him a whisky, which was refused. The two men sat down.

'I thought we should have a little chat,' opened Cutler. 'I have the impression things aren't going all that well with our company.'

Jeremy frowned. 'What makes you say that?'

'Just things I've been hearing. I understand Archie is in Spain. What would that be for?' The smile had vanished, the lips now tightened.

Jeremy cleared his throat. 'He's gone to check on progress and the completions for this next month.'

'Oh, I don't think there'll be any of those. I reckon nothing's happened out there since November.'

Jeremy realised any further pretence was pointless. 'You seem to be remarkably well informed.'

'I think we should get down to some straight talking here. I've got a lot invested in Tradesail, as well you know, so let's not fuck about any more, shall we?'

Jeremy took a lingering sip of his drink. 'Alright,' he admitted, 'things aren't good. The developer's offices are closed down, as is the site. At least, that's what Archie's found.'

Cutler sat forward, elbows on his knees. 'And how about our finances?'

Jeremy cleared his throat. 'Er... '

'Come on, man. *You're* in charge of the finances, aren't

you? Well?'

'Not just me. Archie's involved himself in them recently,' Jeremy floundered. 'There's not as much in the accounts as I thought there should be. I'm sure there's a good reason for it – probably just cash flow. I need to go through the figures with him when he gets back. The more pressing problem we've got is that some clients have been complaining to the local press.'

Cutler's eyes widened, his lips forming a tight O. This nugget of news clearly upset him. He rose, walked to the window and gazed out. After a lengthy silence, he returned to his seat. 'You two have fucked me over, haven't you?'

The malevolence in his tone scared Jeremy even more. He opened his mouth to respond but stopped as Cutler stood in front of him and placed his forefinger across his lips.

'Shut it!' he whispered. He walked over to the cabinet and began to rifle through the files. Jeremy stood to join him but Cutler spun round, his eyes mere slits. 'Sit the fuck down. Don't say anything and don't move.' He spied the stack of files Jeremy had set aside earlier and quickly browsed through them.

Several minutes later, a handful of papers clutched under his arm, Cutler gave Sinclair one more vicious glance, then passed into the corridor. 'Torch it,' he whispered to Slater.

'And him?'

Cutler drew his finger across his throat, turned and started down the corridor towards the lift.

***

Except for the heavy traffic through Lyon, the relative quietness of the *autoroutes* proved a welcome change from the congested English motorways. From the slate skies and chilly gloom of Dover and Normandy, their 700-mile journey had gradually yielded improved weather and temperatures as they neared warmer sunshine, vineyards and sleepy villages close to the Mediterranean.

From the last *autoroute*, the satnav talked them along the *route nationale* that was bustling with lorries and heavy traffic. Eventually, the car was guided onto narrow country roads where the landscape was dominated by a tapestry of vineyards. The vines themselves resembled short, knobbly walking sticks thrust into the ground at precise intervals, each regimented row lined with wires onto which the spring growth would be trained.

From Caines' occasional dour comments, the journey and surroundings held no pleasure, dredging up dark memories of when he'd been blackmailed by Monaghan to courier stolen goods to his French hideaway.

Selwyn nodded with moderate sympathy, his thoughts repeatedly drawn back to the perilous state of his estate's finances thanks to the disappearance of nearly half a million pounds stolen by Monaghan, whom he'd trusted implicitly. The estate was now on the verge of bankruptcy, held precariously afloat by the occasional success of Selwyn's racehorses and his income from the stables and quarry. Even the prospect of finding the family's long-lost treasure, which might have been the estate's salvation, had faded into the far distance.

'Versain's just round the next bend,' Caines' voice cut in.

'You'll get a good view of the village from there. Follow the road straight along and you'll come to the place de la Concorde, the main square alongside the *mairie*. There's a car park next to it and a bar on the opposite side. With a bit of luck, it'll still be open.'

At the corner, Selwyn brought the Jaguar to a stop. He and Sebastian got out to admire the view. Immediately in front of them stretched the village, bathed in the pale glow of the fading winter sun. Houses rose up the hillside, clustered as if some gigantic child had packed them together with no sense of order or uniformity. Façades of cream, beige, sand and discoloured grey were all topped with gently sloping terracotta-tiled rooves. Crowning the scene stood the church. Built in a light sandstone, its round bell tower rose from one corner, giving out to a conical roof.

Selwyn turned to Caines, who was leaning out of the open rear window cigarette in hand. 'You've got to admire the place.'

Caines exhaled a cloud of smoke. 'Not if it holds the memories it does for me.'

Within minutes they'd parked in the town square and were seated round a battered Formica-topped table in the large and unpretentious Café Bar Olivier. By the time they'd been served welcome beers, the general hubbub had resumed following the silence of curiosity that had fallen when they'd entered.

Round the bar, which was liberally spread with glasses of pastis, beer, wine and the occasional coffee, were groups of the establishment's regular clientele. Some were sitting on bar stools deep in conversation, others were watching the PMU racing on the large screen in the far corner, while three more lively customers were competing in friendly banter with the barmaid.

Selwyn drank in contented silence for a while as they took in their surroundings.

Caines, who'd been studying one of the large oil paintings that hung incongruously on the walls, sniffed and passed nicotine-stained fingers through his long, unkempt hair. 'So what now?'

'We should try and get the house keys before we check into the hotel,' suggested Selwyn. 'Then we know we can make an early start in the morning.'

Caines plonked down his empty glass and nodded agreement. Wiping his mouth with the back of his sleeve, he rose with painful difficulty and reached for his walking sticks. 'I'll find Xavier.'

Concerned, Selwyn offered a steadying hand. 'We'll all go.'

'No, best not to go mob-handed. He's a suspicious bugger and can be awkward if the mood takes him. He wouldn't welcome a group of strangers standing outside his door. He'd probably want to make a real issue of handing over the keys. For all I know, he might not even know Monaghan's dead – in which case I won't enlighten him. We can do that later, once we're in the place. Anyway, it's not far.' He pocketed his cigarettes and lighter then shuffled off, his progress watched slyly by the locals while Sebastian and Selwyn exchanged glances.

'I sure hope we're doing the right thing trusting him,' Sebastian muttered as he scanned the room and its occupants.

'It's a bit late in the day to worry about that, dear boy. Anyway, we've not much choice – and he's got everything to lose and nothing to gain if he crosses us. We'll just have to keep a close eye on him.' They lapsed into the silence of their own thoughts.

Twenty minutes later, Caines hobbled back in, a wan smile testimony to his success. He dropped the keys in front of Sebastian. 'No problem. There we are – 27, Chemin du Moulin. As far as Xavier's aware, Monaghan's still in the land of the living.'

Sebastian regarded the keys with a moment's hesitation, glanced at the commander, then stuffed them in his pocket and asked if the others could manage another beer.

***

'Hello, old thing.' Selwyn was speaking into his mobile as he sat in the garden of the Reynard d'Or hotel. 'We've arrived and it's incredibly warm, considering it's January.'

Miriam gave an exaggerated huff. 'Hello, my love. How typically British of you, Selwyn. No "I love you" or "I'm missing you", just the weather.'

'Of course I do, and of course I am. That goes without saying. How are you?'

'I'm fine but missing you. Where are you up to?'

'Well, we've got the keys and seen the house from outside. Tomorrow we'll search for Monaghan's papers and whatever else he stashed away here. Then, if we find his bank details, Sebastian will go and register his claim as his son. I've no doubt we'll probably have to visit a *notaire* and jump through some legal hoops before the bank will accept a claim, particularly as we're not French. Anyway, how are things there? How stands my reputation with the council?'

'Oh, they've totally accepted that Monaghan framed

you for his stolen antiques' racket.'

'Oh, thank God. About time.'

'Indeed. It makes for easier meetings, for sure.'

'Don't they listen to their formidable mayor?'

'Not always, alas. Anyway, some good news for you – some councillors are even talking about giving you access to the recreation land to search for that long-lost family treasure of yours.'

Selwyn grimaced as the weight of a heavily procrastinated conversation crashed down upon him. Though the estate had always leased the land to the village to use, it had recently transpired that it might not belong to the estate at all. Dropping this ruinous detail into conversation would be tricky, to say the least. 'That's … good news.'

'We can discuss it when you get back. You know I'll support you totally with the council.'

'Yes … thank you. I appreciate that, dearest.'

'Don't sound too enthusiastic.'

Selwyn chuckled in spite of himself. 'How's your internet business going?'

'Splendidly. Sales are on the increase and I'm thinking of branching out into homeware. What do you reckon?'

'Oh, it's no good asking me. You know what a duffer I am when it comes to technology. I'm in awe of what you've already achieved. But women's fashion and homeware? Yes, I suppose it sits together quite well…' Selwyn glanced up to see his nephew's shadow falling over him. 'I'd better go now, Miriam. Sebastian's here. We're just about to go out for a meal.'

'Then *bon appétit*. Do take care, and ring me tomorrow. I love you.'

'I love you too.' After a brisk exchange of goodbyes, he asked Selwyn, 'Where's Clifford?'

Sebastian shrugged. 'He's not feeling too good so he won't be joining us.'

'Poor chap. I hope it's nothing serious.'

'He said he'd have an early night.'

The two men strolled to a restaurant that came highly recommended by their host. Despite the beauty of the early evening, anxiety continued to gnaw at Selwyn.

'Did you get through to Miriam?' Sebastian asked, once they were seated.

'Yes.'

'You don't sound very chipper about it.'

'She said the council seem minded to let me excavate the recreation park.'

'What? Even though that document of yours shows that the land really belongs to them and not the estate?'

'She … she doesn't know about that yet. Also, the situation's a mite more complicated than that.'

'Not *that* complicated. Why haven't you told her?'

Selwyn looked at him indignantly. 'I was rather busy, you know, what with the heart attack and being hauled over the coals for mass antiques' fraud. Plus, there was that small matter of Vincent trying to kill us both.'

He sighed, knowing full well he'd had his own part to play in delaying the painful conversation with Miriam. 'I tried to distance myself from her so that she wouldn't get swept up in my ruination, then the light of your life handed me the original copy of that blasted document. We'd only just got back together when we set off for here.' He sipped his drink. 'If I'd told Miriam, she'd have been duty-bound to inform the council and they'd have been baying for the land – and probably my blood.'

Sebastian shrugged. 'At least you have the original document now. You can tell people about it when you're good and ready.'

'Hmm.'

'And it wasn't all bad news, was it? It's not as if you have to hand over a load of land and say goodbye to some of the estate. There's always a chance of finding the reciprocal agreement document that goes with it.'

Selwyn groaned. He'd had limited time to inspect the terms of the land transfer agreement properly after Sebastian's lovely librarian had so obligingly handed over the original document, but it did appear that he was entitled to some of Wisstingham's common land in return for releasing the area that the recreation land sat upon. That would have been excellent news, except he didn't know where the reciprocal agreement document was. He prayed every night that the life-saving parchment would be found among the papers stored in the trunk that had been dug out of his quarry the previous year, but if he couldn't find it among his current mass of ancient papers … he wouldn't even know where to start looking.

'Have you gone to sleep on me again?'

Selwyn smiled. 'Just mulling, my dear boy. You're quite right about the reciprocal agreement, but those documents haven't seen the light of day yet. Unless the two sets of documents are taken together, the estate transfer papers dedicating the recreation land to the village have no meaning. At least … I don't think they have.'

'So there's no real problem, then?'

Selwyn felt that the lad was rather missing the point. 'It's not as easy as that. I've deceived Miriam by omission and that doesn't sit well with me. Not at all. Especially with the way I feel about her.' He sighed. 'It's been hell keeping all of this quiet.'

Sebastian shook his head wearily. 'Why didn't you tell me?'

'You'd more than enough on your plate. I wasn't going to burden you with any of that.'

'Well, there's no reason why she should know, is there? Not yet, at least.'

'I suppose not, but *I* know and it weighs heavily on my conscience.' Even worse, Selwyn reflected gloomily, he was well aware that he was a terrible liar.

***

Later that evening, after Selwyn had retired to his room, Sebastian sat by the log-burning stove in the hotel's small, toasty lounge and tapped out Amanda's number on the mobile.

'Hi, we've arrived. I couldn't get through earlier, the Wi-Fi's lousy here. How are you?'

'Oh, you've been eating garlic,' came the cheery reply.

Sebastian frowned, despite his natural inclination to smile at the sound of that chocolatey voice he loved so much. 'How can you tell?'

'I can smell it.'

He broke into a grin. 'Course you can't, you minx.'

'It was almost a racing certainty that you would have done, knowing where you are. How are you, my love? What was the last leg of your journey like? How's your hotel? What's—'

'Whoa, whoa! I'm fine. The journey was long but very interesting. We stayed at a hotel in Langres last night. It's a beautiful place – I'll take you there one day. The hotel here's OK. More of a B&B with lots of creaky wooden floors. I've got a pillow shaped like a long sausage.'

Amanda chuckled. 'Well, take a snack to bed with you, then you won't take a bite out of it in the middle of the night. Have you been in the house yet?'

'No, that's first thing tomorrow. How's your nan?'

'Difficult as ever. I'm hoping there'll be a place for her in the home before too long. It's touch and go each day whether the carer walks out on her. The old dear can't help her moods, poor thing.'

'And how's your little empire at the library?'

'I'm thinking of installing stocks for those who make too much noise or bring back books late. We could make some money with a side line of rotten tomatoes. What's the village like?'

'We've not seen much of it, but the bar's quite interesting. It's got huge classical paintings on the walls, all painted yonks ago by a local artist as barter for his wine and food bill.'

'You little culture vulture. You'll be telling me that's the only reason you went into the place. Perhaps you should buy a load of painting-by-numbers sets in case it takes longer to sort things out than you'd planned.'

'Ha ha. You'll cut yourself on that wit of yours one day. I'm not intending to be here that long – I've only got two weeks' leave. Anyway, I don't want to be away from you any longer than necessary. Don't know what you'll get up to while I'm not there… '

Sebastian's smile faded as he thought again of the competition he faced from his nemesis, Martin. Despite their engagement, all Amanda's protests had failed to convince him that there was nothing to worry about regarding her feelings for her 'good friend'.

'Now, Sebastian, don't start giving way to unfounded suspicions,' Amanda purred. 'It's you I love, and you only.'

He brightened, soothed by the sincerity of her tone. He pictured those hazel eyes, her slender figure and the straight chestnut hair. His own Cleopatra. 'And I love you. I suppose I'd better go and get some sleep. We've an early start tomorrow.'

After a lengthy exchange of endearments, he rose, turned out the lights and made his way up the creaking stairs to his room.

Chapter 2

The French rural habit of greeting a passer-by in the street, whether acquainted or not, was something the Wisstingham visitors to Versain were unaware of. Selwyn's British reserve permitted an acknowledgement of such greetings with a nod and a grunt, while Caines said and did nothing. There were some locals who didn't say hello, either believing the strangers wouldn't respond or not wanting them in their village anyway; this complicated matters only for Sebastian, who attempted to enter into the spirit of things with enthusiasm.

So, as they walked down the narrow, cobbled rue de Quatre Poules, it was only he who properly responded to the curt '*Bonjour*' offered by the heavily laden Frenchman who overtook them.

Jean-Louis Gaudin was on his way home from the *boulangerie* and *tabac*, bearing two baguettes and a packet of Gauloises. That he'd even offered the greeting ran somewhat against the grain for him, since he was already aware that these *Anglais* were in some way connected with Xavier Dumas, which, in his book, was no good thing. However, curiosity prompted the greeting as perhaps an introduction to discovering the reason for their visit.

He and Dumas had been neighbours for many years, though by no means close friends. In Jean-Louis' opinion, Dumas was tight-fisted, lazy and something of a conman. He'd avoid work at any cost and do almost anything for easy money. His house was a pigsty, mainly through lack of maintenance and decoration. The man often abused his wife, and his children, now grown, only returned occasionally to visit *Maman*. But in a village, you did your best to tolerate such neighbours in the interests of harmony.

Jean-Louis was aware of a connection between *les Anglais* and Dumas in that general, mysterious way of everyone seeming to know everyone else's business in a French village, doubtless attributable to the *boulangeries*, bars, markets and other popular meeting places where gossip flourishes like a virus. Certainly Jean-Louis had been aware of Xavier's connection with Vincent Monaghan. Though he hadn't known that particular *Anglais* personally, he'd never liked the look of him, nor the odd rumour that he'd heard about him.

From the Juliet balcony of his house with its scrolled cast-iron railing, Jean-Louis could look diagonally across to the unprepossessing – indeed somewhat dilapidated – frontage of what had been Monaghan's house further down the steep incline. This he immediately went to do on his arrival home.

'If they're friends of Dumas, they're up to no good,' he muttered to his wife, who'd just returned from a walk to take their aged dog Malcolm for *pee-pee*.

Jean-Louis watched as the youngest of the Englishmen struggled with the locks of the old wooden door before he finally gained access. About to step over the threshold, the eldest man glanced back up the street and straight up at Jean-Louis, as if a sixth sense had told him he was being spied upon. Jean-Louis gave a nod and the briefest of smiles, then pretended to busy himself with a task that required his presence on the balcony.

'Nosy blighter,' Selwyn muttered as he entered the house.

Despite the bright sunshine, it was in darkness thanks to closed shutters that were almost bare of their original paintwork. The place smelled damp, the thick stone walls that kept the place cool in the summer now seeming determined to maintain the temperature near freezing.

Located in the old quarter of the village, 27 chemin du Moulin was a typical terraced dwelling of three storeys with a sturdy wooden front door that opened straight onto the narrow cobbled street. This arrangement provided both shade from the hot summer sun and for any breezes to be channelled up the street and through the open windows. Here and there at ground level was an integral garage, though the narrowness of the street appeared to prohibit the manoeuvre of cars into them.

Caines immediately switched on the water and electricity supplies, then hobbled upstairs to throw open the shutters and crack open the windows.

'So,' he said, when they'd gathered in the sparsely furnished upstairs lounge to formulate a plan, 'there's a bedroom and attic on the top floor, a bedroom through there that Monaghan used, then the kitchen and bathroom downstairs, which you've seen. There's also a small courtyard to the rear. Everything I brought here had to be stored in the attic.'

'I suppose we should start from the top,' Sebastian proposed. 'I'll take the attic if you two do the bedrooms.'

'We should take photos of each of the rooms before we disturb anything,' Selwyn suggested. 'Particularly the attic. Then we'll have a visual inventory. Also, we'll need a detailed list of all the items we come across, cross-referenced with individual photos. Make sure you're wearing the latex gloves at all times. Clifford, if you come across any cash, bank statements, passport, credit cards or important correspondence, give us both a shout. We'll leave to one side any of the loot you brought here or any other valuables, and categorise them together.'

'Sounds like a plan,' Sebastian agreed, upon which the three of them set to work.

***

Archie gazed out unseeingly at the green, well-manicured garden. The view, cloudless sky and breakfast laid out in front of him failed to register. What had totally captured his attention was the morning's news on the laptop screen. He sighed and re-read the item.

> *The police and fire services were called out early yesterday evening to an incident in Hillingden town centre, where the body of a man was discovered outside a multistorey office block. Streets were cordoned off while the fire service tackled a blaze in one of the offices. The deceased was later identified as Mr Jeremy Sinclair, a director of Tradesail, a local travel and development company in whose offices the fire had started. The police are treating Mr Sinclair's death as suspicious and are anxious to trace and speak to Mr Archie Fox, Mr Sinclair's co-director. A spokesman for the fire brigade confirmed that arson could not be ruled out.*

Archie leaned back in his chair and stared at a palm tree, on whose jagged leaves shimmered the reflection of ripples from the nearby swimming pool. This diversion lasted for several moments until the noise of the gardener's hedge clippers jolted him back to his unhappy reality.

'Oh God,' he muttered, and glanced once more at the screen's headline. 'Why the hell did he leave it so late?'

Remorseful that he had not warned Jeremy about their silent partner's background, Archie had no doubt that Cutler was involved. Despite his warning to Jeremy to get out, it seemed that either Jeremy had conducted the meeting with Cutler, or Cutler had caught up with him before Jeremy had the chance to get away. Either way, it had cost Jeremy dearly.

With the Hillingden police now after Archie – and most likely Cutler, too – it was time to escape to the French house that he and his deceased brother Maurice had invested in many years earlier. There he'd garage the Spanish VW, reassume his brother's identity, since everything was registered in Maurice's name, and use his old French Peugeot.

At least they won't find that house in the company accounts, Archie reflected, enjoying a slight improvement in his humour. He should be able to hole up there until all the hullabaloo had died down. Maybe by then Cutler would be in a more receptive frame of mind, particularly if something could be salvaged from the business.

Gloom returned as his thoughts turned to who else might be searching for him, perhaps the Fraud Squad or maybe even Interpol.

He glanced at the pool and wondered if he had time for one last swim. On balance, probably not. With a regretful sigh, he started to clear the breakfast table and turned his thoughts to what he should pack to take with him.

***

The package had lain in the dark recesses of Harry Gaverty's safe for a few weeks. It should have been opened long before now, but Harry had been very busy and out of the country for some of that time. There'd been a lot to do when his and Vincent's stolen antiques enterprise at Wisstingham Hall had to be abruptly wound up. Fortunately that had happened in the nick of time. He'd been lucky, but not so Vincent.

Yes, there'd been several opportunities to open the package but Harry had held back, dreading the emotions it would release. He'd gone through hell in the days following Vincent's death. Harry had always known his feelings would never be reciprocated, but that hadn't mattered; the pain had been no less intense for that.

With the afternoon light fading fast, Harry switched on the standard lamp, took the package from the safe and placed it reverently on the desk. He frowned once again at the standard Royal Mail sticker that apologised for the package having been damaged and torn open in transit.

Before he sat down, he poured a generous stiffener of single malt and took a swallow. He stared at the battered package for several moments as images of Vincent and the times they'd shared assailed him. Finally, he cut carefully around the stickered apology and pulled out two sealed envelopes: one addressed to the leader of Wisstingham Council, the other to himself.

After another drink, he began to read.

Dear Harry,

I'm writing this on the run. I'm at Mole End Cottage at Alstherham, where I used to live as a boy. I'm waiting and hoping you can get me out of the country to France. If you can, I'll be in touch from there. If you can't, or if I don't speak to you from France, you can assume either the police have got me or I'm dead. If I'm in custody, I'll get word to you somehow. If I'm dead, it's more than likely you'll read about it.

We had some good times together and, though I could never return the feelings you had for me, I always counted you as a true and close friend. My closest.

I hope I can rely on our friendship for you to do two things for me.

As the page started to blur, Harry sniffed and glanced away for a moment. He blinked, took another drink, then read on.

Firstly, there's an old document and map which show some land on the Wisstingham estate that was supposed to have been given to the village long ago. That never happened. Fitzgerald was after the documents and may have got them by now. I managed to get copies, which are in the envelope to the council. Only if I'm dead, I want you to send

the letter off and make sure it arrives safely.
And I mean only if I'm dead. In better days,
that old sod said he'd leave everything to
my family, courtesy of his love for that little
bastard, Sebastian. If I'm still able to inherit
the estate, that letter will do me no favours.

That brings me to my second request. If they
are still alive, I want you to do for them
both. You can arrange it easier, specially if
I am inside. I'll cover all the costs. If I am
inside or dead it'll be because of them and I
really want revenge, even if it's from beyond
the grave.

Will you please do these things for me,
Harry?

'Course I will.' Harry sniffed again and took another
swig.

On finding that Sebastian was not my son
(and, let's face it, I never thought he was), I
changed my will and left everything to you.
But I had to leave Wisstingham in a rush, so
you'll find it taped under one of the drawers
in the filing cabinet in the stable block on the
estate. Keys for the cabinet and stables are
taped under my cistern in my old cottage on
the estate. Bilton can get you into the place.

There's another document with the will that
should be of interest to you. What I never

*told anyone was that I got myself a place in a
village called Versain, in the south of France.
You'll find the keys enclosed in this package.*

*All the details are enclosed in the letter you'll
find with my will, like where I've hidden a
stash of stuff you can fence, the details of my
French bank account and the lawyer who
drew up the will for me. There's a guy in the
village called Xavier Dumas who you'll need
to meet. He has spare keys for the house and
will get you anything you need if you bung
him a few euros.*

*Sebastian won't know anything about the
French house and the rest of the stuff, so you
should be able to go to France and claim it,
easy.*

*When you get it all sorted out, raise a glass
to me, old friend. My very best wishes
to you. I hope to be in touch, one way or
another.*

Vincent.

'But there ain't no fucking keys in here, Vincent,' Harry
protested after he'd frantically checked every corner of
the packaging. Clearly they'd dropped out in transit.
'Why is it only the useful shit that has to disappear?'

Distracted by a sound at the door, he rose and went to
open it. In strolled a large grey long-haired cat. 'Come
on, Jasper.'

Harry sat back down and began to stroke the cat, which had jumped onto his lap. 'A right two-and-eight we're gettin' into here. My poor Vincent gone, and now this.' The cat mewed. 'Yeah, course I knew 'e was creamin' off some stuff, but he was Vincent, right? I didn't mind, and I reckon 'e probably guessed that. Silly sod could've had anythin' he wanted from me. But now he's gone, I want it all back – *and* more.'

He bared his teeth and crashed his fist on the empty packaging, whereupon Jasper sprang down and lay on the floor. Harry glared through the darkened window as he mulled over the situation. He'd have to send Ronnie up to Wisstingham straight away. He could only hope to God that neither Fitzgerald nor the police had examined the filing cabinet too closely.

Come to think of it, there'd still been no news or reports from Bilton, their eyes and ears at the estate. What the fuck was the bastard doing, and why wasn't Ronnie on top of things? He'd a good mind to top Bilton, but the man was needed now.

Harry refilled his glass, turned on the laptop and Googled Versain. There was a fair amount of work and thinking to be done, as well as some arses to be kicked the next day.

***

7TH JANUARY

'It's superb!' Suzie Lathom exclaimed, her eye pressed against the viewfinder. 'The zoom's incredible.'

'I'm glad you like it,' her lover replied and stroked her back as she continued to focus through the open car window. 'Happy birthday, babe.'

'It's lovely, but you shouldn't have bought it,' she protested feebly. 'How am I going to explain it to Oliver?'

'Just tell him you bought it for yourself as a birthday treat.'

'Oh, I don't know about that. I don't normally do that sort of thing.'

'Always a first time.' He started to unzip the back of her dress. There was a buzz as the lens retracted, then Suzie replaced the camera in its box on the dashboard. The couple leaned into one another and started to kiss.

The bra was just about to part company with its occupants when the prospects of any further action were halted by the sound of an approaching vehicle. They froze for a moment before Suzie made to hastily adjust her dress.

'They won't be able to see us,' Lover Boy tried to reassure her, which was true.

They'd used this secluded spot on the estate many times before. From where they were, they had a great hidden vantage point. Through the corner of her window, Suzie spotted a black Lexus, out of which stepped three men who cast furtive glances around them as they emerged. 'Hello, hello, what's all this about?' she asked.

'What do you mean?' queried Romeo, warily.

Suzie was now totally engrossed with what was going on. 'Well, that's Geoffrey Hirst, the undertaker, then there's Russell McKaye – he's the council's chief engineer and planner – and that's the council leader, Karl Tyson. A despicable man, if ever there was one. Now what on earth are they doing here, I wonder?'

Romeo slumped back resignedly in his seat as Suzie

wound down her window and reached for the camera. Sensing his pique, she briefly puckered her lips into an air kiss before turning back to the window.

The camera lens buzzed into action once more and captured McKaye as he took a plan from the rear seat of the car and unfolded it on the bonnet. The three men huddled over it as Hirst explained something. They looked around them to translate the information onto their surroundings as Hirst pointed out various locations. All the while, Suzie clicked away, occasionally muttering compliments on the camera's focus and zoom while her frustrated lover picked grumpily at the steering wheel.

When the group had concluded their discussion and inspection, McKaye refolded the map and Hirst reached into his inside pocket. He withdrew two manilla envelopes and handed them out. McKaye and Tyson opened their envelopes and withdrew wads of banknotes, which were quickly replaced, the envelopes pocketed smilingly.

Suzie had shifted the camera to video mode. 'Ooh, I don't believe this. This is too good to be true.'

'That's a matter of opinion,' muttered Romeo.

Once the Lexus had driven away, the couple resumed where they'd left off, though Suzie's mind wasn't really on the job. She couldn't stop thinking about what sort of scoop this could turn out to be for her cousin, Kathy.

Chapter 3

'So how's tricks, Mac? How are things at King Solomon's mines?' asked The Happy Rat's smirking manager.

Mac Bilton drummed his grimy, chipped fingernails impatiently on the highly polished bar top as he watched his Guinness being poured. 'Same old, Clive, same old. And less of the sarcasm, if you don't mind. Wisstingham'd be the much the poorer without the estate's quarry.' He counted out some coins onto the bar towel and picked up his drink. 'Why's the snooker table covered? Is it bust?'

'No, the electrician's rewiring the light.' Clive turned, his attention now back on the televised golf match.

'Blast!' Mac glared at the table. Once he'd thrown off his donkey jacket and claimed his usual seat, he palmed what precious little hair he had left at the sides of his head and took a generous slurp of the Guinness. The foam coated his ginger moustache; he wiped it away then dried his hand on his jeans. From the jacket's inside pocket, he retrieved a folded newspaper and spread it out on the table.

'Oh, I forgot to tell you,' Clive called across, 'a bloke's been in looking for you.'

Mac shrugged as he dived back into the pocket for his reading glasses. *Probably someone after a job.* He took another mouthful of his drink and was ogling the page-three model when he was startled by the scraping of a chair.

''Allo, chrome dome,' the visitor said, smiling at Mac's discomfort.

Mac froze for an instant before his hand shot defensively to his shiny bald head, hovered there for a second, then dropped. He gulped. Seated across the table was Slade, clad as usual in his black Crombie. *You'd need chloroform to get him out of that,* Mac couldn't help but muse.

'Bleedin' hell, Hammer!' he gasped, with a hasty glance round the room. 'What are you doing here?'

'The boss and I ain't 'eard from yer for a while now, Mac, not since Vincent went. Now seein' that Vincent got you the job 'ere, Harry reckons you're not only neglectin' yer duty but also being ungrateful and disrespectful to Vincent's memory. And you know what he thought of Vincent, don'cha?'

Mac's hand moved shakily to his glass. Beads of sweat were now forming on his brow. Unblinking eyes stared back at him. He'd thought he was free. He'd been saving money, planning to move away. He gulped. 'But it's all finished now, isn't it? I'm not on the payroll any more.'

'You're missin' the point. Even though the operation's bin closed down, *your* job here is to keep yer eyes open and report anythin' of note. And by that, I mean *anythin'.* This ain't a job you just quit when you want, pay or no pay. Only the boss decides when you quit, then that's the time to worry. Meantime, he'll pay you when 'e gets results.'

'What kind of results?'

'Not complicated – he wants a close watch kept on who does what, where and when up at the hall. Understood?' Slade leaned back in his chair. His eyes were still boring into Mac's.

Mac shifted uncomfortably, took a deep breath and nodded. 'Of course, Hammer.' He averted his gaze to the

Guinness. 'I won't let you down, I promise. I'll let you know everything that goes on. Don't worry.'

'Oh, *I'm* not the one who needs to worry.' Hammer leaned forward and described in explicit detail how Taylor had died.

When he'd finished, Mac swallowed hard as the enforcer raised his forefinger and ran it through the beads of perspiration on Mac's brow. He studied his moist fingertip for a moment, evidently relishing how he'd been able to make the man cringe and quail, then wiped the finger on Mac's sleeve. Point made, he gave an intimidating smile. 'So what *is* 'appening up there?'

'The commander, Sebastian and a guy called Caines have gone away.'

'When?'

'They set off three days ago.'

Ronnie nodded, pleased. At least that'd keep them out of his way while he searched Vincent's estate cottage and the stables for the stuff Harry was after. 'Where've they gone to?'

'Not sure, exactly. Somewhere in France. It seems Vincent had a house there.'

'What?' Ronnie thundered. 'You said there was nothin' to report, you tosser!' So much for the Fitzgeralds being oblivious to Monaghan's bolthole. He dreaded passing the news along to Harry. 'How long they gone for?'

'I dunno. I don't think even they know. They've allowed at least a couple of days to drive there, so it must be somewhere well down in the south, I reckon.'

That was pretty bloody vague; what Ronnie needed were extra sources of info. He remembered that the bastard Sebastian had a girl on the scene at one point.

'What about Sebastian Monaghan's bird? Did she go with them?'

'Amanda? No, not as far as I know.'

For several moments Ronnie studied Mac, whose eyes were huge pools of fright. He considered smacking Mac's stupid ginger mug on the tabletop to wallop any further information out of him, but the bloke was already scared enough to blurt out everything as quickly as possible.

It was exasperating to be a step behind the Wisstingham lot, but at least he could put Mac to good use as a lookout. Then a thought struck him: best to check out just how reliable all this was. Harry would be sure to ask. 'So where do you get all this info from, Mac?'

'Mostly the housekeeper. I reckon she's got a bit of a soft spot for me because I'm living on my own. Makes me pies and stuff, and I suppose she thinks I need the company and conversation. So I play on it.'

Ronnie nodded. 'Very well, but if I 'ave to come 'ere again to find things out, I will not be an 'appy bunny. Nor will Harry.'

'You won't need to. I won't let you down, I promise.'

'Better fuckin' not. Right, we've got work to do. Finish yer pint.'

'What's happening?'

'I need to get into Vincent's place and the stables.'

Bilton frowned. 'I ain't got the keys. Anyway, we can't go to the stables. Not tonight.'

'Why not?'

'Conrad the stable manager will be in there, probably Fred Ferris, too. One of the horses is having problems, so they could be there all night.'

'Shit!' Ronnie's exclamation was loud enough for a

courting couple to glance round briefly. He glared at them and they quickly looked away. 'Who the fuck's Ferris?'

'He's the acting estate manager. More likely than not they'll be finished tonight, from what Fred said. Well, he was hoping so.'

'OK, I'll meet you by the barn tomorrow night. I'll text you the time. You'll be able to get me into the cottage, right?'

'Yes, but I haven't got any keys for the stables.'

'Don't you worry about that.' Ronnie rose and glanced down at the page-three model. 'Nice pair, eh?' He was feeling a tad more relaxed. 'OK, tomorrow then. Keep that old bonce shone up, eh?'

**

Caines' efforts to assist Sebastian and Selwyn in the search of Monaghan's house yielded little result. His evident unease at being in the house struck a chord with Selwyn, who'd also suffered at the hands of that monster, Monaghan.

Selwyn eventually suggested that Caines took himself off to the *tabac* to buy an English newspaper, then settle down in the café bar to read it. 'We'll join you later,' he called out as Clifford willingly made to leave.

An hour later, the disappointed duo joined him. Sebastian threw the keys onto the table. 'Not a sausage,' he exclaimed, after Clifford had folded the *Daily Mail* and given him a questioning look. 'Unless there's a hidey-hole somewhere, there's nowhere else to look. No bank statements, cards or passbook, and no money other than a few notes and coins in a drawer. They've got to be somewhere.'

'Let's grab a bite to eat and resume the search this afternoon,' suggested Selwyn.

He watched as Sebastian selected one of the keys and showed it to Caines. 'Do you know what this one's for? It doesn't fit anything in the house.'

Clifford inspected it. "Fraid not – I never needed to use it. I did ask Xavier about it when I picked them up this time, but he said he didn't know. Either that or he didn't want *me* to know.'

'There's also what looks like a car key but, if it is, it's an old car. Did you ever come across one?'

Caines shook his head.

Selwyn cleared his throat, needing to deal with a matter that had been bothering him. 'So far, we've not spoken about what we should do with what we find.'

There was a moment's silence before Sebastian spoke. 'We've got to assume that anything other than the money he embezzled from you was the proceeds of crime. As such, it should be handed over to the UK police.'

'My fear is that DI Stone will want to pin something on us, as sure as little apples,' replied Selwyn. 'He'll go through everything with a fine-tooth comb, then accuse us of withholding information and being accessories to crime, I shouldn't wonder. More importantly, if he gets wind of any recovered money he'll also want to claim that as proceeds of crime. After what's happened, we're certainly not his golden boys. He'll be blasted certain not to give us the benefit of any doubt.' He noted Caines' look of consternation. 'Don't worry, Clifford, we'll keep you out of this.'

As silence descended, the other two men no doubt reflecting on the possible consequences, Selwyn's thoughts returned to his additional dilemma of when and how to confess the existence of that damning document and map to Miriam.

Suddenly the background hum of noise abated, prompting him to look up. At the bar's entrance stood a man in a distinctive straw hat that had seen better days. His round face bore a full salt-and-pepper beard, and he had deep-set eyes with which he briefly scanned the room before making his way to the bar. His lack of interest in the surroundings suggested to Selwyn that he was no stranger to the place.

'*Bonjour,* Giselle,' the man called and gave a beaming smile to the barmaid. She instantly broke away from the customers she was chatting to and air-kissed him over the bar.

'*Une pression, ma chérie, s'il te plait.*' His voice was deep and gravelly, travelled well and commanded attention. After several moments of conversation with Giselle, he paid for the beer and seated himself at the table adjacent to the Wisstingham group. '*Bonjour,* or should I say hello?'

'Hello's just fine,' replied Selwyn. 'I'm still struggling to recall my O-level French.'

They exchanged polite smiles. The man took a mouthful of his drink then turned to wave to a new arrival. During a lull in the conversation at the Wisstingham table, he casually enquired, 'Are you staying here or just passing through?'

'We're here for a little while. Do you live here?' Selwyn replied.

'Not exactly. I stay from time to time. Got a little house in the old quarter. I live in a village called Cusham.'

'You're kidding!' exclaimed Sebastian. 'That's only about thirty miles from us. We're from Wisstingham, on the other side of Hopestanding.'

The man's face registered what looked like a momentary flicker of unease. 'Bless my soul, what a dashed small world it is. The name's Maurice Fox.' He rose and, in true British fashion, the four of them shook hands as they introduced themselves, much to the amusement of some of the locals who looked on with curiosity at the performance.

'I see you appear to speak the lingo well,' Selwyn complimented Maurice.

'I get by.'

'Is the bar always as busy as this?' asked Sebastian.

'Only on market day, although it's always pretty brisk first thing in the morning. The usual barflies drift in for a coffee, then mooch off to the other bar down the road to exchange news and gossip.'

For several minutes, the conversation batted between the tables. Maurice became even more animated upon confessing a love of cricket. 'I was quite a decent player in my time, even though I say so myself.'

Selwyn eagerly moved to sit across from this new acquaintance and the two older men immersed themselves in the world of cricket, leaving the other two to chat among themselves.

'So what made you choose this particular village to buy a place in?' asked Selwyn.

'Well, there's the Mediterranean climate, the easy autoroute access both from the north and across the country, and two cities in close proximity for business connections. But mainly, I suppose, Versain is close to some rattling good racecourses. You'd be surprised how many of the British racing fraternity have chosen to settle here.'

'Hmm, very interesting. Very interesting indeed.' Selwyn pondered this. A good nugget of information to have, should he fall on desperate times. 'So you're keen on racing?'

'I am indeed. And you?'

'Well, well, well,' Selwyn enthused, and the conversation continued earnestly in that direction until Maurice finished his drink and rose to go.

As he bade them farewell, he gave them his mobile number and offered translation services, should the party find itself in need of them.

'Seems a good chap,' observed Selwyn as he watched him leave. 'He could prove to be a useful contact.'

'Plays a straight bat, you reckon?' Sebastian teased, his comment and smirk rewarded with a dirty look.

'You've got some serious gaps in your upbringing, young Sebastian,' Selwyn said. 'And cricket's one of them.'

***

Jorge Berensen's gaze rested for several seconds on the envelope that had been pushed across the desk towards him. He eyeballed Doug Cutler for several moments before speaking. 'So, where do I find this Archie Fox?'

'Last heard of in Javea, but he'll no doubt have left there by now. In all probability, he's either in a place called Versain in France,' Cutler paused to spell the name, 'or he's on his way there. That's what my man managed to get out of his partner before he … uh… '

Berensen opened the envelope and withdrew a bundle

of banknotes, a sheet of typed notes and a photograph. He flicked through the edges of the banknotes with his thumb then studied the photo. Staring up at him was a short-haired man, short and stocky in stature, perhaps in his late fifties, sporting a grey-and-black moustache. He held a shabby straw hat. Above the cuff of the linen jacket, the man's wrist displayed a substantial gold watch.

Berensen homed in on the face, which looked back at him with hooded, calculating eyes. The smile was an unconvincing one, as if the man were politely acknowledging a poor joke. He put aside the photo and turned to the notes, which he read carefully. 'What is he like as a person?' he asked eventually.

'Definitely more brain than brawn. He's shrewd, wily, can spin a good tale and is very convincing. Don't let him fool you.'

Berensen smiled, gave a dismissive shrug and smoothed back some of his long blond locks. 'Any habits, characteristics and, how you say … pastimes?'

'He walks with a limp, right leg, likes a drink and almost chain smokes cigarillos. Cricket and horse racing are his main passions. There's more info in the other notes. There's one other thing. He should be wearing a Rolex. *My* Rolex, engraved with my name. I want it back.'

Berensen gave him a quizzical frown.

'He won it on a bet at the races. He'd fed me too much champagne.' Cutler sounded uncomfortable and resentful.

Berensen pocketed the money and neatly slotted the notes and photo back into the envelope. 'I take the contract.'

'I want a clean kill, Berensen. No loose ends. Above all,

the police must not catch up with him. Not alive, anyway.'

The hitman nodded slightly. 'That is why you ask for Berensen. He does not make mistakes.'

***

Amanda toyed with a strand of her long hair as she waited for Martin to pick up. It had been several weeks since they'd last spoken. She broke into a smile when at last he answered.

'Hi, lovely lady, what a nice surprise. To what do I owe the pleasure? Everything's OK?'

'Yes, your Aunty Hilda's fine. Going on as well as she can in the home. The good news is that I've finally managed to get a place for Nan in there.'

'Ah, that's great news. It must be a load off your mind. I don't know how you've managed to cope, what with your job, looking after her *and* running the farm. I bet your brother will be relieved.'

'Yes, it's been pretty stressful. Stevie doesn't know about her placement yet. He was just about to go on stage when I rang the cruise ship. I'll try him later – that's if his mobile's not run out of charge, which would be a change.'

'Wouldn't you be better selling the farm?'

Amanda sighed. 'Don't you start. Sebastian says I'm crazy for hanging onto it. Says there's no money in it. But it's my inheritance from Hector, God rest him. It means something to me.'

'Sorry, I was forgetting about your cousin. I was going to ring you anyway. I'm thinking of coming up next weekend.'

'Oh, that's great, it'll be good to see you again. We can meet up and have a spot of lunch, if you like.'

'Are you sure your fiancé won't mind? You know how jealous he gets.'

Amanda groaned inwardly. It was bad enough continually reassuring Sebastian that he had nothing to fear from Martin without continually reassuring Martin that Sebastian wasn't about to pull off his arms and legs. 'He's in France at the moment. And anyway, he's no reason to see you as a rival any more.'

'Hmmm.'

She rolled her eyes. 'Are you getting cold feet?'

'No, not at all. I'll give you a call nearer the time. Can't wait to see you.'

The conversation ended. Amanda stood rooted to the spot, gently nibbling on her fingernail. The exhausting rollercoaster of being pursued by both Sebastian and Martin was supposed to be over. Poor Martin had indeed harboured and pursued romantic aspirations for her but had eventually accepted they could only ever be good friends, which indeed they were. This, however, was something Sebastian could not come to terms with, despite her seemingly endless protests that she loved only him.

***

The council leader's secretary tapped on the office door and entered hesitantly, a large envelope clutched rather too tightly in her hand. The office was sumptuous, with walls clad in polished mahogany panelling for the most part lined with bookshelves crammed with old tomes. The desk was a picture of neatness: a diary and matching notebook located on each side of a desk tidy set in front of a carriage clock. Only a few papers, which the leader was working on, broke the symmetry. The leader himself was slim and immaculately dressed, his perfectly white hair almost a match for his teeth.

'Councillor Tyson,' the secretary said, for the leader always insisted on being addressed formally, 'there's a letter and some papers that have arrived, which I think you should see immediately.'

Tyson looked up, momentarily closed his eyes then gave her a withering look. 'I do hope it's important, Marjory. I've a lot to get through this morning.' He held out his hand, into which she placed the envelope. With a mumbled apology for the disturbance, she pitter-pattered her way across the parquet floor and out of the room.

Tyson set aside Mayor Cheyney's memo, from which it appeared that the habitually meddlesome woman was again about to frustrate his plans to slim down her portfolio by sharing her responsibilities with more amenable colleagues.

'Damn the interfering bitch,' he murmured, extracting the contents of this mysterious new envelope. He positioned the covering letter precisely and squarely on the desk in front of him, ironed out a crease with his thumb and started to read.

'What the hell?' he exclaimed when he'd finished. He studied the accompanying pages for several minutes, trying to take in the letter's implications. Then he bent to re-read the bombshell.

   Dear Sir,

   I am writing to tell you about an old

*document and map that transfers land
from the Wisstingham estate to the village.
I enclose photocopies. As you will see, the
land not only includes the recreation area
currently leased to the council but also other
land inside the estate boundary.*

*As far as I know, the late historian,
Alexander Penn, found the estate's originals
and these documents are now in the hands
of the hall's owner, Commander Fitzgerald. I
assume the council also has its own original
copies somewhere.*

*I wish you luck in trying to find your
documents and hope you will be able
to restore the land to the people of
Wisstingham.*

Yours faithfully,

Vincent Monaghan

Tyson pored over the copied documents for several
minutes before a grim smile played across his lips. Given
her relationship with Fitzgerald, it seemed highly likely
that Madame Mayor knew of the commander's possession of the original papers, papers which indicated that
the council had been deprived of the ownership of some
of the estate land for *years*. Centuries!

'At last, I just might have the bitch where I want her.'

***

The secretary's tap on the door later that day was to announce the arrival of Miriam Cheyney, a few minutes late for the meeting to which Tyson had summoned her.

Unsmiling, Tyson rose from his chair and gestured at the conference table. 'Miriam, do sit down.'

'Good afternoon, Karl. To what do I owe the pleasure of this invitation?'

He sat opposite and, by way of reply, slid across the letter and documents. Miriam read, her tongue playing along the upper edge of her lip as she did so. She perused the documents, and when she'd finished she stared at them for some moments before pushing them back. 'This is all new to me. I can't help you there.'

Tyson stared at her in silence for several seconds. The casualness of her voice had been betrayed by a frown. 'So you're saying you've never heard of, or seen, these documents?'

'Just so.' Miriam examined her fingernails.

Tyson leaned forward, planted his elbows on the table and rested his chin on clasped hands. 'I wish I could believe you, Miriam. I know how sensitive this must be for you.' Understanding and compassion oozed into his tone. 'Assuming this isn't all an elaborate hoax, and conscious of your relationship with Commander Fitzgerald, I do feel there's a clear conflict of interest for you. I know what high standards you expect of people in public office, so... Do you not think it would perhaps be appropriate for you to consider your position with the council? What do you think?'

'What I think is that you're talking a load of rot, Karl,' she bridled. By now, the mayor's eyes were nearly as fiery as her lipstick. 'Let me make my position quite clear. I have no previous knowledge of these documents and, irrespective of my relationship with Commander Fitzgerald, I would never do anything that was not in the interests of the council and the people I serve.'

'Oh, I don't think we can just leave it at that.' Tyson smiled, drawing enjoyment from Miriam's annoyance.

She rose and placed her hands squarely on the table. 'If you want to make more of this, you go ahead. I'll fight you every step of the way. Just what have you got, Karl? I'll tell you what you've got – photocopies of a so-called document and a map that wouldn't stand up in court without the originals, together with the word of a dead murderer and thief clearly out to cause trouble. I'd make a laughing stock of you.' Miriam crossed to the door. Before she left, she added, 'I trust I've made myself clear.'

The slam she gave the door on her way out barely exorcised a smidgen of her wrath.

Tears welled up as she strode down the corridor, which further fuelled her anger. Not so much anger at the weasel Tyson, but at the possibility that she'd been betrayed by the man she was in love with and who'd claimed to love her.

If those documents aren't fakes – and much as she wanted to believe they were, Miriam feared otherwise – *Selwyn's played me for a fool, all along.* That was all she could think with growing bitterness as, piece by piece, the jigsaw of their earlier negotiations and the emerging background reasoning behind them fell into place. *Was he really only ever interested in getting access to that land for his wretched treasure hunt?* It was a question she was scared to have answered.

She marched out of the council building and headed

in the direction of the Mazawat café, badly in need of a latte over which to order her thoughts. However, when she passed the library, she recalled an occasion not long ago when Amanda Sheppard had come to her office with documents concerning the Wisstingham estate. At the time, she'd thought the librarian was offering them for the ill-fated exhibition. What if they'd been the documents that Tyson now had copies of? *Oh God! And I told her to do what she wanted with them!*

Feeling quite beleaguered now, her immediate inclination was to storm into the building and confront Miss Sheppard, but she needed no mirror to realise what sort of a spectacle she'd present. Nor was she in the rational frame of mind necessary to deal with the situation. Instead she used her mobile to summon Amanda to a meeting in her office first thing on Monday morning, then sniffed away more budding tears and marched on towards the Mazawat, still in desperate need of that coffee and the opportunity to think how she would deal with Selwyn.

***

Mere moments after Miriam had stormed out of Tyson's office, Marcia Pincher, head of Wisstingham Council's leisure and tourism department, arrived in response to his summons.

Marcia had risen through the ranks not so much through her ability but through an unerring knack of being in the right place at the right time, knowing the right things to say, and having a willingness to pander to male egos and vanity where necessary.

Single at the age of thirty-seven, she was still on the

lookout for the right partner, her desire for money and status having already ruled out many potential applicants. Tyson flinched as she approached. With piggy eyes, a wide mouth, a nose that was a touch too long and a prominent chin, she looked rather like her face had been assembled from a box of left-over parts. However, she did have a captivating smile when she infrequently chose to use it, and was intelligent, determined and ruthless when necessary. Thus the leader was slightly more at ease as she squeezed her ample frame into the chair opposite and offered him her most ingratiating smile.

Over the half-moon reading glasses perched on his nose, Tyson gave Marcia a fleeting smile and casually pushed aside the report he'd been reading. 'Miss Pincher, what I have to say to you is in the strictest confidence and must under no circumstances be conveyed to the Councillor Cheyney. Do you understand?'

Marcia frowned but nevertheless nodded her agreement vigorously.

Tyson showed her the copies of the estate land transfer document and map. 'So, your task is to locate the council's originals in our archives as a matter of extreme urgency.'

'I'll get our librarian onto it immediately.'

'You'll do no such thing – I said "in the strictest confidence". I understand Miss Sheppard has close links with Commander Fitzgerald. Under no circumstances is she to be involved in the search, or even made aware of it.'

Clearly taken aback, Marcia subsided in her chair as far as the little remaining space allowed. 'That'll be rather difficult. I'm afraid Amanda's knowledge of these matters is much greater than mine, and the archives are located in the library building. Only she has access to them.'

In no mood for excuses, Tyson applied his best narrowed stare and sighed. Loudly.

'But of course,' she added quickly, 'I'm sure there'll be ways and means to make it happen.'

Tyson smiled. 'That's right, Miss Pincher. Make it happen. Perhaps our librarian needs to go on a course somewhere, or maybe she has leave that needs to be taken before the end of the year. I know you'll find a way to get round any problems.'

'Can I take these copies with me to help identify the originals?'

'Most certainly not. They're far too precious and sensitive to leave this office. Just remember that the document you seek bears two seals and is dated 1642. I assume the map will be with it. Gather together whatever fits into that category and bring it here for comparison.'

'Yes, just leave it to me.'

'That's my intention. Good day, Miss Pincher.' As Marcia was about to step out of the office, he added, 'Don't forget, time is of the essence and much rides on your success or *failure*.'

If the sudden unsettled look on departing woman's face was anything to go by, his emphasis had not been lost on her.

***

8TH JANUARY

On the hotel owner's advice, Selwyn walked to the nearby café to sign in to their wi-fi for a reliable signal. Once his cappuccino had been served, he rang Miriam.

She launched into a frosty greeting as soon as the call connected. 'Hello, Selwyn. Are you having a good time? A pleasant day?'

'Well, er yes—'

'I'm so glad for you,' she interrupted. 'So when were you going to tell me about the estate land transfer documents, eh? Next month? Next year? Or would it have been after you'd hoodwinked the council into giving you permission to dig up the village's only recreation park and snaffled your family treasure from land that's not even yours?'

Selwyn was aghast. 'Who told you about that?'

'Monaghan somehow got a letter to the council leader with a copy of the documents.'

'The bastard! Miriam, I never had the chance to tell you about it. Not about getting hold of the documents—'

'Given to you by your nephew's fiancée, the council's own librarian, yes?'

'Yes, but—'

'Well, we know what sort of a reception she's going to get from me, don't we? And don't give me that bullshit about "no chance". At the very least, you knew the gist of those documents when we were negotiating over the access you wanted to excavate the land.'

Selwyn swallowed. 'That's true, I did. But remember, at that time you were acting solely for the council and I for the estate. And, in case you're not aware of it, that land transfer is a reciprocal one for village land that's due to be transferred to the esta—'

'Irrespective of what you say, you deceived me, Selwyn. You used me. I don't believe you had any intention to open the hall to the public—'

'I did! It was your passion for it that made me fall for you.'

Miriam scoffed, 'You've a funny way of showing it. My reputation with the council is about to be ruined, then there'll be public condemnation. I'm finished.'

'Oh Miriam, of course I loved you. I still do. Nothing could change that. You have to understand that I had to protect the estate, just as you kept the council's interests at heart. If I'd told you about it, what would you have done?'

'Well, we won't know now, will we? I don't think I want to see you again.'

'Miriam, my love, please don't say that. I know it was bad form, but don't end things like this. Not over the phone. Let's at least discuss it in person when I get back. Please?'

'No, I don't think so. I've lost faith in you, Selwyn, and I'm not going to get hurt again in another relationship that's built on distrust. I had quite enough of that with Gerald. Goodbye.'

Selwyn was left holding a silent phone.

He was aware of being poor company when he, Sebastian and Maurice dined that evening in the hotel. The *carte du jour* offered starters of *rillette de thon*, *pâté de campagne* or *carpaccio du boeuf*, followed by a choice of *escalope de porc* in a Calvados cream sauce, *steak frites* or *gambas* flamed in Pernod, the selection rounded off by a tempting choice of desserts or *plat de fromages*. All his favourites in one place, yet his appetite was sadly absent.

Selwyn chose and ate without enthusiasm, declined to join the others for a final *digestif* in the bar and retired early to his room. There he poured himself an immoderately large malt, sat on the edge of the bed and set his iPad to play Dave Brubeck's 'Blue Shadows in the Street'.

All appreciation of the drink and music was leached away as Miriam's words echoed over and over again in his mind.

Chapter 4

On the old quarry road, Mac Bilton nervously fingered the key in his pocket as he paced up and down in front of the barn that had featured so prominently in Vincent's stolen antiques' racket. On seeing approaching headlights, he ducked behind the side of the building and waited. The car slowed, came to a stop in the layby opposite, and out stepped Ronnie the Hammer.

'I thought you weren't coming,' Mac greeted him as he crossed to the car.

Ronnie groused about the heavy traffic, grabbed a torch from the glove compartment, locked the car and took stock of his surroundings. 'Let's get to it, then.'

They set off through the copse of trees, heading across the wildflower meadow that bounded woods and the stable courtyard beyond. There, at what was once Monaghan's cottage, Mac unlocked the door and prepared to enter.

'No. I'll look round on my own,' insisted Ronnie. 'You keep watch on the path. I'll come and get you when I'm done.'

'I don't reckon you'll find anything. Either the commander or the police will have removed anything of interest.'

'We'll see.'

Mac shrugged and went to take up his position at the side of the cottage.

Ronnie started with the ground floor on the off-chance there might be something to interest Harry, but all the cupboards and drawers had been virtually cleared out. Upstairs in the bathroom he swept the room with his torch, then knelt to search under the cistern. He located the stable-block keys but, as he did so, a heavy door banged shut somewhere. Probably at the stables.

Footsteps sounded on the cobbled path. Ronnie moved quickly into the adjacent bedroom and crouched down by the front window. In the moonlight he could see the outline of a man approaching the cottage. Ronnie expected the footsteps to continue past towards the hall, on the same path where Bilton was on lookout, but they stopped close by. He froze as he heard the creak of the porch door being swung open.

'Anyone there?' a voice called out.

Bastard must have seen the torchlight. Ronnie cursed his carelessness. He edged towards the door and felt his way onto the landing.

At the bottom of the stairs, framed in the moonlight from the kitchen window, stood a man who was now starting slowly upwards. 'Is there anyone there?' he repeated. He advanced slowly and cautiously, the stairs creaking as he did so.

The Hammer watched in silence, his breathing rapid. When the man neared the top step, he stepped forward.

'Jesus Christ!' the startled man exclaimed.

Ronnie lunged forward and pushed him. The cry as the man fell must have been audible outside because, moments later, Bilton hurtled through the open front door, dashed through the lobby and came to an abrupt halt at the bottom of the stairs. There, picked out in the moonlight, lay an open-eyed, crumpled form, its life now stilled.

'Oh my God!' Bilton exclaimed as he stared down at the body.

'Religious lot, ain't yer?' Ronnie descended the stairs. 'Who the fuck is it?' He stepped over the body and leaned down to feel for any sign of life. He looked up at Bilton and shook his head.

His mouth agape, Bilton stared at the corpse.

'Come on, pull your fuckin' self together,' said Ronnie.

Bilton stared at Ronnie. 'It's Fred Ferris. What did you do? What have you got us into?'

'Calm down, Mac.' Ronnie's tone was milder now. 'It was just an accident. Lost his footin' on the stairs in the dark. Could 'appen to anyone.' He gripped Mac's arm and led him away towards the lobby. As he did so, they heard the sound of a car engine. 'Who's that?' Ronnie whispered.

'Dunno, probably Conrad come to check on the horse.' They faced each other in silence. Bilton couldn't stop shaking. 'What are we going to do?'

'Shut it, I'm thinkin'. Go an' shut the door. Quietly.'

Bilton complied, numb. When he returned, they stood in silence and waited. From the direction of the body, a mobile started to ring. Bilton gasped, then cried out as Ronnie gripped his arm. 'That'll be his wife,' Bilton whispered. 'Never lets him alone, always on his case. If she doesn't get a reply, she'll probably ring Conrad. So what are we going to do with him?'

'Leave 'im here.'

'But there's no reason why he'd be in here. The police'll get suspicious.'

Ronnie massaged his beard as he watched through the windows. 'What's the stables layout? Is there some stairs?'

'Yes.' The ringing stopped and Bilton allowed himself to breathe.

'Where do they lead?'

'The office and some storage rooms.'

'Would he be likely to go up there?'

'Dunno, probably.'

'Can you see 'em from the rest of the stables? Would anyone who'd gone to see the 'orses see the stairs or need to use 'em?'

Bilton thought about the view from the main entrance. 'Er, no. I don't reckon so.'

'Then we'll dump him at the bottom of those stairs. People'll think 'e just fell down.'

Bilton remained rooted to the spot, focused only on the body, until the spell was broken by the sound of footsteps outside. Ronnie instantly crouched and dragged him down.

Barely discernible in the moonlight that filtered through the hazy cloud, a man walked past the cottage towards the stable block. He tried both doors, then stepped back to take in the whole building. 'Fred, are you in there?' he shouted. After a minute, he turned and retraced his steps.

Mac and Ronnie remained motionless as the figure passed the cottage again. Moments later an engine started and its noise gradually faded away.

Ronnie glared at Bilton who, still crouching by the body, was now rocking gently backwards and forwards, his jaw quivering. 'For fuck's sake, get a grip of yerself.'

Bilton's baleful eyes turned to him, his jaw still in motion, then he closed his eyes, nodded rapidly and rose.

'You drag 'im outside. Look in his pockets for the key to the stables,' Ronnie ordered. 'I'll lock up.'

Minutes later, the cottage locked and the body left in position at the foot of the stable stairs, Ronnie went in search of the filing cabinet. He scoured the office and storage rooms then called to Bilton to check downstairs.

'Where the fuck is it?' Ronnie eventually exclaimed. 'Bastards must 'ave moved it. Let's get the fuck out of here.' Once outside the building, he paused to think. 'Better leave this door unlocked. That geezer found 'em both locked, so now it'll look like the stiff came back after he'd gone and fell downstairs.'

An owl swooped silently on its prey in a darkness penetrated only by the light of Bilton's torch.

As they walked back through the woods to the old quarry road, Ronnie ordered Bilton to get a copy of the filing cabinet key made. He was then to search the hall for a cabinet the key would fit and to inform him as soon as he'd done so. 'And don't fanny about. Get onto it immediately. The boss won't tolerate any delays, right?'

As the Hammer's car departed, Bilton trudged wearily along the quarry road to his cottage. Not only was he burdened by the death of Ferris, a man he'd liked, but also by the problem of how the hell he was going to search the hall without attracting the attention of the ever-vigilant Mrs Soames.

***

Lucian Fitzgerald narrowed his eyes against the sun's glare as he stepped through the open iron gates from the gloomy corridor into the imposing, high-walled square. At its four corners, armed security guards were watching from observation towers that bristled with floodlights and cameras.

The Chinese guards, standing rigidly to attention on either side of the entrance, appeared oblivious to Lucian's departure. Those that flanked him marched in step as they crossed the square towards the steel-barred gates, the prison's first line of security fencing.

As he walked, Lucian inhaled the humid air to clear his lungs of the stale, fetid prison atmosphere, though he feared the memory of it would linger forever. The sun glinted off the coils of razor wire spanning the walls.

Without a word, a guard at the second fence unlocked and swung open one of the gates and Lucian stepped into freedom.

Outside the prison, he paused to hitch onto his shoulder the small rucksack that contained the few personal possessions taken from him eleven years earlier. It was a strange feeling to think that he was a nobody, that apart from one man – whom Lucian hoped would have someone waiting for him nearby – the rest of the world believed Lucian Fitzgerald was long-since dead, drowned after a fall or jump from a ferry.

He waited for several minutes then started to walk along a grimy street almost devoid of other pedestrians but alive with the constant blare of traffic. Lucian thought how incongruous the small café nearby looked with its tables, chairs and white parasols cheek by jowl with the prison wall. Large, bright yellow Chinese characters stood out against equally bright red paintwork, a stark contrast to the grey drabness of the prison. Lucian grimaced at the memory of his recent surroundings made predominantly of steel, a material he'd come to loathe.

Only a few of the café's tables were occupied, mainly by men and women who, from the small parcels that accompanied them, were presumably waiting for visiting time at the prison.

He'd almost reached the end of the street when a

battered grey Fukang drew up alongside him. The window lowered as the car screeched to a halt. 'Lucian, get in,' a voice called.

As the ex-prisoner settled his gaunt frame into the passenger seat, the driver turned and offered a brief smile. The small, sallow Eurasian's forehead bore an old scar that ran across to the edge of his eyebrow. He patted Lucian's arm before they drove off; it was the first sympathetic physical contact Lucian had received in eleven years.

'I nearly not recognise you, but it sure good to see you, my friend,' the driver said. 'Sorry I no come visit but you understand, yes?'

Lucian nodded; he did indeed. 'I'm surprised to see you in person, Macky, though I did hope you'd send someone.'

'For you, I come myself. You very special, Lucian.' Macky gave him a quick sideways grin. 'You take rap for me and save my life. I never forget.'

'If I hadn't, we'd probably both have been killed. How have you been? You've changed your Mercedes.'

Macky gave a short, dry laugh. 'I come in … how you say? In-cognition. Yes, I still alive, so that good.' He threw Lucian another smile and narrowly missed a cyclist.

'Where are we going?'

'To my place. I have your things from old apartment. Wang Wei, he re-let it in an hour after he hear you dead. Bastard. I sort him out after, for sure.' He winked at his passenger then turned his attention back to the road in the nick of time.

Out of the side window, Lucian took in the dirty brick façade of a four-storey apartment block, its upper walls dotted with air-conditioning units. The concrete, almost blackened by pollution, contrasted sharply with the bright colours of randomly strung washing. Below, some of the artisan's shops were shuttered closed. *Yet more steel.* The open shops resembled rectangular, darkened caves with dim lights that glowed from deep inside.

Lucian wound down the window to hear the discordant street noise, the chorus of car horns and the buzz of scooters as they wove through the heavy traffic and swerved round clusters of bicycles. He wallowed in the faint yammer of pedestrians and the background din of industry and construction. Further along, they came to a more affluent area with never-ending shop signs in a rich palette of reds, yellows and greens, which Lucian had missed so much through the years of stark greyness.

They drove on in silence for several minutes.

'I think I not able to stop you talk, Lucian,' Macky commented eventually.

'After eleven years of virtual silence, it's not going to come easy. My Chinese was never very good.'

Macky nodded. 'So what you do now? Even after so long, it not safe for you here very long.'

'Maybe I'll try Singapore.'

'I get you new identity for that. You no worry. I arrange it all. I owe you.'

'OK.' Lucian lapsed into another silence, in which his thoughts turned to the events that had forged and shaped their strange friendship. He and Macky had fallen foul of the local Tong with one of the schemes that Macky had instigated. Lucian had convinced the Tong members that Macky had not been involved, then managed to escape their retribution and faked his death – only to be caught by the police and imprisoned for an earlier misdemeanour.

'You hear the news from home?' Macky asked.

The question startled him. 'No.'

'Two, maybe three week ago. The man you tell me about, Vincent Monaghan. He dead.'

'How?' Lucian stared at Macky, his mind suddenly animated as he thought of Mary, Monaghan's unhappy wife. It was more than twenty years since he'd last held her. Held her, then fled Wisstingham from the family disgrace and her husband Vincent's impending wrath.

'Accident. He involve in something bad. He kill two men.'

'Two *men*?'

'Yes, that's what I say.'

Thank God not Mary. Even so, Lucian's emotions began to run riot. He pictured Vincent, his manipulative and devious cousin, then Mary, whom he'd loved and made love to. Selwyn's face now loomed large, the brother whom Lucian had deserted. And then there was the child Mary had insisted was Vincent's, whom he knew nothing about – assuming it had been born. 'Who was killed?'

'No worry, it not your brother. Men from his village.'

Lucian closed his eyes in gratitude. He was so glad he'd confided in Macky about his past; how else would he ever have known about this? He pondered for a few moments. 'I think I need to go back home.'

'I knew you say that,' said Macky, who grinned at him once more.

***

10TH JANUARY

Striding down the corridor to the mayor's parlour, Amanda recalled her last visit to see her ultimate boss.

She suspected that this latest summons was related. The same mousy secretary rang to inform the mayor of her arrival then asked her go in.

Councillor Cheyney was again seated behind her desk, but this time she rose and even smiled as she led Amanda to the conference table. That she should actually offer refreshments was a further departure but, once these had been served, the mayor wasted no time in getting down to business.

'The last time you came to my office, Miss Sheppard, you told me you'd brought documents that related to Wisstingham Hall.'

'Yes.' Amanda was impressed that the woman had at least remembered her name this time, though she remained apprehensive about the way the conversation was heading. 'You told me to do what I thought best with them.'

'What were they?'

The query sounded so exaggeratedly casual that alarm bells started to ring. Had Marcia, her bitch of a boss, somehow found out and compromised her? 'It was a map and a land transfer deed relating to the Wisstingham estate.'

'And what did you do with them exactly?' Miriam casualness appeared to be failing her.

'I returned them to their rightful owner, Commander Fitzgerald.'

'Miss Sheppard, I understand that you have a certain acquaintanceship with the commander because you're in a relationship with his nephew, but did you appreciate the significance of those documents and their importance to the council?'

Oh, the gloves are coming off now, aren't they just? 'I did.'

'Then why on earth did you not pressure me to take note of them? I realise I might have been somewhat dismissive on that occasion, but you could have sent me an email, which I'd have been obliged to read.'

Somewhat dismissive? Amanda seethed. Councillor Cheyney had been overbearing, hostile and bloody rude. 'You gave me authority to do what I thought was best. What would you have done if you *had* seen them?'

Miriam sniffed. 'Handed them back to the commander, of course, and then I'd have begun a search for the council's own set and alerted my colleagues to their existence.'

What? Pull the other one. Amanda gave the mayor a smile that she hoped would relay the message. 'Perhaps, under the prevailing circumstances, you might have been glad to be spared having to make such a decision.'

Miriam glared at her in silence for a long moment. 'Be that as it may, you had no right to deny the council that information. It was a dereliction of duty on your part, and I'm now obliged to consider what action needs to be taken.' She rose, Amanda's signal to do the same. The meeting was evidently at an end. 'I shall let you know in the next few days whether or not I'll be taking the matter up with Miss Pincher. Goodbye.'

Amanda turned and headed to the door, determined she'd not go down without a fight. *God help us all if mindless Marcia gets to stick her fumbling fingers into the pie.* She couldn't imagine how her boss had found out about those documents. And even if the mayor decided to let things slide, the question of who – or what – had alerted the mayor to their existence would plague her for days.

***.

'So, what'll you do when you get back, Clifford?' Sebastian asked as he swung the Jaguar onto the rue de Baume and headed for the airport.

'Suppose I'll get myself signed back to work and climb back on the treadmill again, teaching the little oiks.' Caines flicked his cigarette stub out of the window and scratched his thick head of hair. He stared out of the window in the ensuing silence. 'I hope you find the papers and loot,' he said eventually. 'I still feel mortified that I had a hand in causing all this trouble for you and Selwyn.'

'Don't beat yourself up about it too much, mate. It wasn't voluntary on your part, and if you hadn't turned up and offered to help us, we wouldn't have had a clue about it, let alone where to start looking. Anyway, it's the missing money from the estate that's the real issue, and you didn't have a hand in that. If we don't find it, God only knows what the commander's going to do to keep afloat.'

'Well, let's hope you do. He's a good old boy. What do you make of our Maurice Fox?'

'Seems a good sort.'

'The commander seems to have taken to him.'

Sebastian chuckled. 'What do you expect? Similar ages, Oxford University, a love of horse racing and a passion for cricket… They could almost be twins. Mind you, his advice on *notaires*, the bureaucracy and his translation's already been helpful. I don't think either of us appreciated how difficult it would be. These buggers really won't try to speak English, even when they can.'

'Tell me about it!'

To Sebastian's dismay, Caines lit another cigarette.

At the airport, Sebastian shouldered Clifford's bag as

the teacher, who had now been able to dispense with the walking sticks, carefully and slowly made his way to the terminal building. Across the car park, beyond the runway, a thin band of morning mist still hugged the ground; above it, parasol conifers rose like spectres, their tops bathed in the golden glow of the newly risen sun.

'Are you sure you'll be OK at the other end?' Sebastian asked, when they reached departures.

'Yes, I'll be fine. I'll just take it steady. I really would have stayed on if I could have been of use.'

'Thanks, but you've done all you can. It's down to us now.'

'So when do you think you'll be coming back?'

Sebastian shrugged. 'No idea. I've managed to get another two weeks off from the company. Old man Fellowes is very understanding, though I hope it won't take that long. I'm not sure my finances would stretch to it. I told Amanda about the extension and she wasn't best pleased.'

Further conversation was drowned out by the tannoy call for Clifford's flight. They shook hands and he made his way to the security check in.

By the time Caines' flight was en route to Stansted, Sebastian had already picked up Selwyn and Maurice from the village square for the appointment with the *notaire*. Selwyn and Sebastian had deliberated at length whether to invite Maurice to join them at the meeting. They'd finally concluded that their paltry smattering of French needed his input if they were to make any progress, though they'd been at pains to divulge only the bare essentials.

'We'd have been really stuck without Caines,' remarked

Selwyn. 'And he sorted out that surly brute Xavier.'

'Except we're still no nearer to finding what we came for,' Sebastian grumbled.

'Cheer up, my dear chap,' chirped Maurice from the back seat. 'There's got to be a garage somewhere that your man Monaghan used. I'll make some enquiries.'

By the time they went back to the car park, Sebastian was fuming. 'It's bureaucracy gone mad. They've got copies of the passports *and* the birth, marriage and death certificates, as well as the probate. Why the hell do they have to do their own investigations?'

'C'est la France, mon ami, c'est la France,' commented Maurice with irritating cheerfulness.

'It's gonna take forever.'

'I have to say, Maurice, if it wasn't for you being there I don't think we'd have made any headway at all,' added Selwyn. 'We're obliged to you.'

Sebastian nodded his agreement, a little embarrassed at having been so surly.

'Don't mention it, my dear fellow, it's all part of the service. Listen, things look pretty dismal at the moment but they have a way of suddenly coming right. What do you say to a beer and council of war back in Versain, then I'll look into the garage situation?' Receiving unanimous agreement to this proposal, Maurice gave Sebastian a reassuring pat on the back and they made their way to the car.

***

At the sound of voices, Mac Bilton came to a halt in the dark recess of the passageway that led to the hall's side entrance and cellars. From the shadows, he could safely look across through the open doorway into the kitchen. There, Mrs Soames was seated at the table across from a young woman Bilton recognised as Amanda Sheppard.

As the housekeeper started to pour the tea, Amanda excitedly fished out a piece of paper from her bag and spread it flat on the table. Mrs Soames lowered the teapot and scrutinised the document. 'So it's the thirteenth you're flyin'. Good job it's not a Friday. Are you sure this is wise, dearie?'

'Of course it is. I might commit a murder unless I take a break from work, and it'll be a lovely surprise for Sebastian.'

'I only 'ope as 'ow it will be.' The housekeeper sounded totally unconvinced by the prediction. 'Wot if 'e changes his plans, or shoots off somewhere, or gets tied up in that there red tape? Them French 'ave an awful lot of that, you know. What if… ?' Fortunately, the dear lady had temporarily run out of disaster options.

'It'll be alright,' Amanda tried to reassure her. 'If anything does change, I'll know in advance and I can let him know I'm coming.'

'What about accommodation?' Mrs Soames asked, with a resurgence of negative thought. She glanced hesitantly across the table. 'Oh, I'm not prying, dear.'

Amanda broke into a smile that Bilton rather liked. 'Well, that shouldn't be a problem. Sebastian's just dropped Caines off at the airport, so there's bound to be enough accommodation, whatever arrangements there are.'

'So it's just the two of 'em there now?'

'If it's not, I, for one, will be most interested to learn why.' The two ladies looked at one another in silent agreement on that particular point.

When Amanda declined a second cup of tea, Bilton took the opportunity to slip quietly from the shadows and creep out of the building. Having miserably failed to find the filing cabinet, he was hugely relieved to have some news to pass onto Ronnie.

Chapter 5

Amanda stared in surprise and relief at the email that flashed up on her screen.

Hello, Miss Sheppard

With regard to yesterday's meeting concerning the Wisstingham Hall documents you originally brought to me, I have considered the matter and decided that there is no further action to be taken.

I should like to take this opportunity of expressing my regret at any abruptness I might have afforded you at that meeting. Your work as librarian and contribution to the council is, and always has been, much appreciated, and I look forward to continuing to work with you in the future.

Regards

Miriam Cheyney

Councillor

The change of tone was rather startling, not so much an olive branch, more of a bush. Why the apparent change of heart? Was it because of Amanda's connection with Sebastian and hence the commander? And how far could the woman be trusted?

'Or perhaps I've just misjudged her?' she murmured. Nevertheless, she'd proceed with caution in her future dealings with the woman. In the meantime, she'd relax and enjoy her holiday.

**

DI Stone put down the receiver, stared at it then looked over to the window. He slowly shook his head in a mixture of disbelief and despair. McBride had seemed to take a delight in informing him that they now had a new missing person's case, namely a Fred Ferris from the Wisstingham estate. From past experience, Stone knew it would only be a matter of minutes before he'd receive a call from DCI Nelson. How the man found out so quickly about things, Stone could never fathom. Even worse, they were always issues that spelled trouble, one way or another.

The phone rang. Stone sighed and picked up. 'Yes, I've heard.'

'I thought you'd got that kettle of fish sorted out.' Nelson's tone sounded ominous. 'I don't want that estate running away with our resources like last time. If it does, I won't be able to draw the flak from you again. You hear me, Roger?'

'Loud and clear. I'm no happier about this than you are, believe me.'

'Well, for God's sake, don't come up with a body. And tread gently with the commander, eh? Remember, he's got friends in high places.'

'How do I avoid coming up with a body?'

'Don't be pedantic. But if you do, move fast and carefully. We don't want the man complaining.'

You want results, but if I start getting tough with him and his mob, you'll be running around your office like Henny Penny. 'He never has complained that I know of.'

'What?'

Embarrassed at having thought out loud, Stone cleared his throat. 'I said I don't think he *has* ever complained.'

'Just make sure you don't give him a reason to.' Nelson rang off.

'I'm damned if I do and damned if I don't,' Stone complained.

Much as this closet republican resented the landed gentry, particularly in the form of the commander, and dearly wished to see charges brought against him for something or other, Stone's retirement and pension were too tantalisingly close to upset the apple cart. For now, softly-softly would have to be the order of the day.

Though if he *could* legitimately get the boot into the commander, he wouldn't hesitate to do so.

***

Armed with Harry's advice, a French dictionary, phrase book and a hotel booking at Les Trois Clefs, Ronnie finally arrived in Versain exhausted after a manic journey. The unhappiness his car had shown while clattering off the Channel-tunnel train at Calais had graduated during the journey south to positive distress by the time it came to a wheezing stop outside its final destination in the rue de Porche.

The enforcer wearily carried his bags into the hotel and

embarked on the first of what was to be many skirmishes to make himself understood.

'Bleedin' 'ell,' he murmured, once the bedroom door had been finally closed on the confused but well-meaning host.

He took out the bottle of scotch and went in search of a glass, only to emerge moments later from the bathroom with a flimsy plastic cup. He was almost tempted to go and demand a more suitable vessel, but the anticipated pain and aggravation to achieve this, coupled with his tiredness, was sufficient to deter him. Accordingly, he sat on the edge of the bed, poured out an unprofessional measure of whisky and stared at faded floral wallpaper, which looked old enough to have graced the room in Napoleon's era.

Ronnie had been annoyed enough that he'd been despatched to France to intercept and kidnap some bird from the airport before she could so much as set foot in Frogland. He was even more annoyed to find that the hotel proprietor didn't know of Xavier Dumas. He'd expected everyone would know everyone else in such a village, but evidently not.

'Firstly, whatever you do, keep your head down,' had been Harry's first instruction. 'Then, to find this Xavier guy, the first place to try is the bread shop. Every fucker buys bread every bleedin' day, and they all know each other's business. If that fails, try the tobacconist's. If that's no good, try the grocer's. Lastly, try the town hall – but for Christ's sake don't go near the bloody gendarmes.'

After another drink, Ronnie's rumbling stomach dictated his next move: a stroll back down the street to the pizzeria he'd spotted on his way in. Then he'd settle for an early night.

On his return from the restaurant, Ronnie poured himself a stiff measure and sat on the edge of the bed to ponder. What the hell was he doing there?

His dislike of Vincent Monaghan had intensified. It galled him that he was here to pick up the pieces left by the man who'd stolen from Harry and got away with it because his stupid shirt-lifter of a boss had loved him.

If I'd done that, I'd be lyin' at the bottom of the Straits of Dover, bumping into Taylor or what's left of 'im.

Ronnie knew he was getting too old for all this. You needed to be nimble of body and mind to dodge the bullets, the blows and the Old Bill. But there was no pension in this game. Nor could he trust Harry, merciless bastard that he was, to do the right thing by him when the time came to quit.

One way or another, Ronnie had managed to put a bit by – it had always been his dream to have a little place by the seaside – but he needed more, so he'd have to go on smacking people about, cracking skulls, doing Harry's bidding and grabbing everything he could for some time yet.

Then there was that bastard Jock, always after his job. The Scotsman would stop at nothing to get one over on him and worm his way into Harry's favour. It was the only reason Ronnie had agreed to come out to this god-forsaken village to grab that Sheppard bird as collateral – to remind Harry who could be trusted to see a job through.

The Hammer let out a little growl, determined to keep Jock in his place. He'd see that twat out.

***

Under his new identity of Jack Cavannagh, provided by Macky and his Hong Kong associates, Lucian stepped off the train at Hopestanding station. Outside on the concourse, he stood and blinked at the changes that had taken place since his last hasty departure. As he made for the taxi rank, he wondered how many more changes he'd find in the town and in Wisstingham.

The monosyllabic driver deposited him at the car park above Frogsham Bay harbour. Jack shouldered his rucksack and trundled his case towards the Tasty Crab café, which had changed very little over the years. Inside sat a solitary customer, an elderly woman who wore a tam-o'-shanter hat, a green tweed coat and sensible brown shoes.

Could be straight out of Brigadoon, Jack thought, as he approached the table where the woman was now standing up.

'I'm assuming you're Mr Cavannagh,' she greeted him in a soft Scottish brogue.

'I am indeed.' Jack proffered her a smile and his outstretched hand. 'Mrs Dunbar the estate agent, isn't it?'

'Miss,' she corrected.

Jack gave an apologetic nod. The proprietor approached, wiping her hands on her long white apron. Since Miss Dunbar had hardly started her coffee, Jack ordered a cappuccino and sat opposite her.

She reached down, withdrew a folder from her briefcase and opened it on the table. 'We received your bank transfer. Thank you.' The agent passed across some forms and papers. 'If you would please read through these and sign them… Then, when we've finished our coffees, we can proceed to Osprey Cottage and conclude the lease arrangements.'

From the café, Miss Dunbar led him through a ginnel and down a narrow cobbled street, past a double-fronted, grey-walled house, towards a terrace of smaller fisherman's cottages. One boasted a red mailbox set into white stone. The wall opposite was draped with a fishing net and some ropes. Jack watched as two fishermen hauled laden crates from a boat beached on the foreshore. As he walked, a small lifeboat station came into view.

At the red doorway to the end cottage, Miss Dunbar opened up and let them in. Jack glanced up at the sash windows, which sat between stone sills and an undulating tiled roof. It was a pretty place to stay for however long he'd be there.

The joint inspection and letting arrangements finalised, Miss Dunbar hastened away leaving Jack free to search out a glass and his hip flask. Thus armed, he wandered about the building on a closer inspection before he started to unpack and move in properly.

He'd been relieved that the busty, business-like Miss Dunbar had shown no interest whatsoever in himself or his background. He felt like a spy who needed to bone up even more on his assumed identity and background, about which he was not yet word perfect. But he'd need to be, and very soon indeed.

Before him lay the task of searching out information about his brother Selwyn and Mary's child, while avoiding recognition by any of Wisstingham's stalwarts.

***

'Do you ever get that feeling of *déjà vu*?' the smirking DS McBride asked his colleague as they stood yet again at the front door to Wisstingham Hall.

DI Stone rolled his eyes and pursed his lips. However, if he'd placed a bet on the sort of reception he'd receive from Mrs Soames, based on previous experience, he'd sadly have been parted from those coins in his pocket that rarely saw the light of day.

Only too keen to see some action in the search for Fred Ferris, Mrs Soames welcomed the DI and was extremely cooperative. 'You'll be needin' Mac Bilton to show you round.' she advised, as she shuffled ahead of the officers to the drawing room, which was to be set up as a temporary ops room.

When, over her shoulder, the housekeeper actually offered them refreshments, Stone shot a look of amazement at McBride. 'We really are in the good books,' he muttered after she had waddled out of the room.

For Bilton, the short guided tour became the longest twenty minutes of his life.

It was Sergeant McBride who found Ferris's body, minus one shoe, at the foot of the stable-block stairs. The DI let out a world-weary sigh, then bent to take a closer look at the corpse. His lips compressed in exasperation as McBride called in the discovery.

'Right, sergeant,' Stone muttered some time later, as the small flock of SOCOs arrived to carry out their grisly work. 'You'd best take chummy elsewhere and get his statement while I search the rest of the building.' He went to see if there was another way of getting to the offices on the first floor.

'Did you search all these buildings?' McBride asked Bilton, as he indicated the other buildings round the yard and Monaghan's old cottage.

Bilton felt positively sick. 'Well, er… Well, no. Not the

cottage. He'd have had no reason to go in there. I did try the door when I went past and it was locked. He wouldn't have the key, nor did I, so I left it.'

'So where is the key?'

'It's kept in the kitchen.'

'We need to inspect the place,' the sergeant insisted.

Bilton sighed and trudged off to the hall. On his return, the perpetually disapproving DI Stone had joined the DS in lurking outside the cottage. Trying not to let his hands shake too obviously, Bilton unlocked the cottage door and they entered.

'Hello, what's this doing here?' asked Stone, once in the hallway. He gestured to a shoe on the floor.

Bilton stared, transfixed. 'I d-d-dunno,' he eventually managed to stutter. 'It's probably one of Vincent's that should have been thrown out.'

Stone stared at him for a moment. 'I think we'd better have you out of here.' He put on a pair of latex gloves that he'd fished out of his pocket. 'Don't touch anything as you leave.'

Bilton paced restlessly in the courtyard as two of the forensic officers split off from the inspection of the body and joined the DI and DS in the cottage. He didn't know what would be worse – having to respond to further police questioning or having to face Harry's wrath when he learned of this blunder.

***

Stone's sense of gloom deepened as the estate once again became a hive of police activity. Despite the patholo-gist's preliminary thoughts that the cause of death was possibly heart failure that had induced a fatal fall, the shoe rendered the death suspicious. Furthermore, a check of Ferris's pockets had yielded no key to fit the front door to the cottage.

At the hall, the task of taking the tearful housekeeper's statement fell to WPC Pelman. Over tea and biscuits, she sat with Mrs Soames in the kitchen and tried hard to comfort the woman, who continually mangled her handkerchief when it was not being applied to her eyes.

Stone paced the floor in the drawing room, jingling the change in his pocket for comfort and giving voice to his thoughts, while McBride sat precariously on the edge of a Chesterfield. 'So Ferris is in Monaghan's cottage in the middle of the night with no electricity, since it was switched off at the mains. Oh, make sure the fuse box and switch are checked for fingerprints. He didn't have a key, so either he was taken there, or he found the door open, or something drew his attention to the place, since it's doubtful he'd check it as a routine precaution. After all, apparently he was only at the stables because of Conrad's attention to the horse.'

McBride looked up from his rapid note-taking. 'So he either disturbed someone in the cottage, or he died in there and was found later.'

'Indeed, and the body was taken to the stables to make it look like he'd died there. Check if his clothes bear out that theory. If he was dragged, there might only have been one person involved. If he was carried, it's likely there were at least two of them.'

McBride nodded. 'I'll ask the doc about lividit—'

'And check with the pathologist what sort of bruising there was,' Stone interrupted, causing McBride to glance heavenwards. 'That should tell us one way or another.

Oh, and check to see if anything looks disturbed. There must be something in the cottage our mystery man was looking for.'

'Person.' McBride's correction drew a dirty look from the DI.

'Unless, of course, this mystery "person" is looking for something amongst the stuff we're still holding at the station from the last time.' Stone stopped pacing and his pocket went silent. 'OK, so if SOCO uncover any new prints at the cottage, check them against Ferris's, and make sure you get some from Bilton. When Pelman's finished with the housekeeper, you'd better go with her to break the news to Mrs Ferris and get her statement.'

And just what the hell will you be doing while I'm chasing around like a blue-arsed fly? McBride merely nodded and got up.

'Oh, McBride,' added Stone, when the DS reached the door. 'When you get back to the station, dig out the evidence we secured from the cottage after Monaghan's death. Let's see if there's anything our mystery caller might have been searching for.'

Hoo-bloody-ray. McBride gave his boss a long stare before he left.

Chapter 6

'Are you alright? Is something wrong?' Sebastian asked as he joined Selwyn at the breakfast table and saw the expression on his face.

Selwyn stopped buttering his croissant and gave his nephew a perfunctory smile. 'Bit of a bad show. Things we need to talk about.'

'Fire away then.'

'I had a call from Mrs S. She's completely distraught. The police found Fred Ferris's body in the stables yesterday, so I've got get back.'

'Oh jeez. What happened?'

Feeling terribly tired, Selwyn shrugged. 'I really don't know. He was found at the bottom of the stairs. It could have been an accident, but Stone's involved so my gut feeling is that there's more to it. He wants to talk to me as soon as possible. I've booked a flight from Montpellier tomorrow afternoon.'

'God, that's all we need. Do you want me to come with you?'

Selwyn shook his head. 'No, there's nothing you can do. Besides, you need to get this lot sorted out, if you reckon you can manage without me.'

'I'll be OK. I'm sure Maurice'll help, if I need it. Will you be coming back?'

'Yes. That's the intention.' Selwyn resumed the buttery

attack on his breakfast. 'However, there's something else I need to follow up while I'm there. Geoffrey Hirst's now badgering me to sell him that piece of land on the edge of the estate – the area I told you about.'

'I thought you were going to leave that on ice in case we found the money?'

'I was, but he's given me an ultimatum. If I don't agree to sell within the next seven days, he's withdrawing the offer. Blasted man. I can't afford to lose the cash, much as I don't want to sell. I've run out of ideas for getting in money and cutting costs. I've also run out of things to sell – it'll be some of the furniture next. The wolves are really clawing at the back door.'

Sebastian put a consoling hand on Selwyn's slumped shoulder. 'We'll get through this, don't worry.'

Selwyn turned to face him and managed a smile. 'Of course we will. Just a bit tricky at the moment, eh?'

***

As he'd expected, the day proved a busy one for Jack Cavannagh. After an early breakfast, accompanied by a trawl through the *Hopestanding Gazette* to bone up on the local news, he stepped from Osprey Cottage into the bright morning sunshine. His sunglasses added to the disguise of deliberately close-cropped hair, grey beard and a bushy moustache, in sharp contrast to the younger and fuller appearance of his earlier years when he'd resided at the hall. These changes were further accentuated by how much he'd aged and his slightly bent, gaunt frame. Even his accent had changed during the time he'd lived in the Far East.

Nevertheless, Jack still felt some trepidation at the

encounters that would inevitably take place with people he'd known before.

By late morning, he was the proud owner of an elderly Ford Focus, yet to be delivered, and the driver of a much more modern courtesy car the garage had kindly provided. He'd also set up an account at the small branch of Hadwin's bank, for which he could expect to receive the cards within a few days. Until then, he'd manage with the account that had been opened in Hong Kong and the wad of cash Macky had handed to him before he'd left.

He decided to lunch in Wisstingham to see if he could glean any news of Mary, her child or the estate.

As the door to the Mazawat café swung open and the bell rang, Gwen Chase looked up from her weekly task of topping up the cruet sets and noted the arrival of a distinguished, if middle-aged, man. He stopped for a moment at the door, slowly removed his sunglasses and scanned the virtually empty room. As their eyes met, Gwen smiled and swept her hand in an arc, inviting him to sit where he wished. The man chose a table at the back of the café, divested himself of his scarf and coat, then scrutinised the menu.

'Good morning, sir,' Gwen greeted him cheerily. 'What can I get you on this sunny day?'

'Sunny, but a touch chilly. I'll have a cappuccino, please.'

Jack watched as the waitress returned to the counter and slipped behind to froth the milk. 'Is it always as quiet as this?' he asked, on her return.

'It's market day. Give it another half hour and our regulars will be flocking in. You're not from round here, then?'

'No, just passing through. But if I find what I'm looking

for, I'll probably stay for a while.'

'Oh?'

'I'm doing some research into the local area.'

'For a book?'

'Maybe, but at the moment it's for a possible documentary.' Jack had deliberated as to what line of work he should be in. This approach appeared to offer the greatest latitude for enquiries whilst not pinning him down to a particular profession or company.

Her eyes lit up. 'Ooh, that sounds interesting. For television?'

'If I could pitch it right. I want to focus on a typical English village with some history and a stately home, or something similar.'

'I reckon you've come to the right place, here. We've got Wisstingham Hall. That's centuries old, with a family that goes back yonks.'

'Really?' Jack feigned surprise and hoped he did a good job of it. 'Tell me more. That's if I'm not dragging you away from your work.'

'Not a problem. I'm Gwen, by the way.' She promptly sat and proceeded to tell him about the hall, the village and some of its more distinguished and interesting inhabitants. There were a couple of intermissions when she reluctantly broke off to serve customers, but she was always quick to return.

'Would this be the place where there was some trouble over a chap who … um … ran a side line, shall we say?' asked Jack.

'Yes, that was the estate manager, Victor Monaghan. A really evil man. Came to a bad end.' Gwen paused for effect. 'It made the national papers.'

'And his family?' Jack tried to sound as nonchalant as he could. 'How did they get on?'

'Well, the wife had died a few years earlier, but the son, Sebastian, poor lamb… He's had a real rough time of it.'

Jack's coffee spilled. He replaced the cup unsteadily in its saucer. Gwen frowned and looked closely at him 'You OK? You've gone quite pale. I'll go and fetch a cloth.'

His breathing laboured, Jack simply stared as Gwen hastened away. *Mary's gone. Gone?*

By the time Gwen had wiped up the spill, he'd pulled himself together. 'I just get these funny turns from time to time. It's nothing serious. You were saying about the wife's death?'

'Cancer, it was.'

Jack closed his eyes momentarily. 'And… And the son? Is he still here?'

'Oh yes. He's still at the hall. Engaged to our librarian.' Gwen sniffed disdainfully. Her eyes narrowed. 'You seem very interested in the family.'

'Well, er… It'd be an unusual angle to bring out in a documentary. A wider perspective on a cosy village.'

'Oh, I see. Well, if you want to meet the owner of the hall, I'm sure it could be arranged. I happen to know Sebastian very well, and he'd certainly be able to get you in with Commander Fitzgerald.'

They both looked up as the bell rang and an elegantly dressed woman walked in. 'That's the mayor,' Gwen whispered. 'She's got a great interest in the hall and the village's history. She'd be a good person to talk to. Shall I have a word with her?'

Still struggling with the anguish of Mary's death, Jack was tempted to say no, but this was an opportunity he couldn't afford to miss. Much of what he'd learned pained him and he needed to know more. He nodded, tried to smile. 'No time like the present.'

Gwen went off to approach the mayor, who was now sitting at a table in the bay window. Jack watched as Gwen spoke and the elegant lady turned to observe him. As Gwen disappeared with her order, the mayor waved Jack over.

'I hope I'm not intruding,' he said, as he stood by her table.

'No, not at all. Do please join me. I understand you're interested in making a documentary about our village. I'm Miriam Cheyney, Wisstingham's mayor.'

'Jack Cavannagh.' They shook hands. 'I'll go and fetch my things.' Once seated, Jack repeated what he'd told Gwen. All the while, Miriam watched him with a slightly quizzical look.

'I'm sorry,' she said, when he'd finished, 'I know we've not met before, but your face looks terribly familiar.' She appeared to ponder this for a moment then dismissed it with a shrug. 'Sorry, I'm staring rather. Anyway, I'm sure we'd want to do everything we could to assist you, if it meant your documentary would put Wisstingham in the public gaze.'

'It's early days and only exploratory at this stage.'

'Nevertheless, whatever we can do to help.' Miriam fished out a business card from her handbag and gave it to him. 'Please don't hesitate to contact me if there's anything I can help you with. I hold the council's portfolio for leisure and tourism, so the entire department could be brought to bear behind the right initiative if it would help Wisstingham.'

'That's very kind of you. I'll look forward to taking you up on your offer and meeting you again. Now, I'm afraid I do have to make a move.' His legs barely cooperated as he left the café.

***

Jack sat in the car and stared through the windscreen, the steering wheel clasped in both hands. He let out a huge sigh at the cruel blow he'd been dealt. Through all these years, he'd lived in the hope of being reunited with the woman he'd always loved. At times, engulfed in the misery and loneliness of prison, that had been the only thing that kept him going. And now, having at last been given the opportunity to find her again because of Vincent's death, he'd travelled in hope – only to find she'd been dead all along.

Were it not for her son, Sebastian, who Jack believed was *his* son, he'd have left immediately and forever, without any attempt to seek reconciliation with the brother he'd deserted without so much as a goodbye. Selwyn believed him dead; there seemed little point in rocking the boat.

***

Across the English Channel, the start of the day found a dismayed Ronnie gazing glumly at the breakfast offering of some cut pieces of baguette and a limited selection of cold meats and cheeses, coupled with jams and a croissant. In the face of the proprietor's confusion and rising exasperation, he'd eventually abandoned his attempt to determine if the hotel could provide a full English.

Ronnie's enquiries at the *boulangerie* and *tabac* had met with no success and many baffled looks. Now, with growing concern, he approached what appeared to be the only grocer's shop, near the Place de la Concorde.

Inside Gaston le Gourmand was an Aladdin's cave of goods. The walls were lined with shelving units, some utilitarian and basic while others looked as if they'd been salvaged from the library of a grand château. The wall behind the vast chiller cabinet was filled with a painted alpine panorama, complete with snow-covered mountains, trees, chalets and pastures dotted with delirious-looking cows. The whole place was crammed with produce, fixtures, and refrigerated cabinets of all shapes and sizes.

Ronnie threaded his way towards the counter and waited for the customer in front of him to be served. An old lady, who totally obscured the chair in which she was sitting, leaned forward on her walking stick as she chatted with Gaston. He was clad in a long green apron, sported thick-rimmed glasses, and seemed in no hurry whatsoever. The lady paused to give Ronnie the once-over, then gestured that Gaston should serve him.

Ronnie smiled his thanks and then, in that typical British manner of speaking to a person who doesn't understand English, he slowly and loudly enquired if the proprietor could help him to find Xavier Dumas.

'*Mais oui,* I can 'elp you.' Gaston disappeared into the bowels of the shop and returned with pen and paper.

With elaborate 'thank yous' and bows of the head to both Gaston and the old lady, Ronnie departed with Xavier's address and directions, together with a fairly large measure of relief.

Whereas Gaston had been a pleasant Frenchman, the shifty Xavier posed a stark contrast. His squint did nothing to endear him to anyone, his brow was beetled in suspicion, his mouth downturned, and one corner of his lip raised to expose yellowed teeth, as if he were about to break into a snarl.

Ronnie tried to explain how he and Vincent had been business partners, but it was only when he produced a photo taken on a sea-fishing trip of himself and a smiling Vincent, and then a wad of money, that Xavier's expression and attitude suddenly improved.

Laboriously, Ronnie explained he was staying at Les Trois Clefs, whereupon Xavier adopted an expression as if he'd just hit his thumb with a hammer.

'*Non*, I az a 'ouse zat you can stay. It was home to a *vigneron*, a wine grower. More cheap *et* private. A special price only for you.'

Ronnie felt if he were being propositioned by Blackbeard.

The deal done on the accommodation, Ronnie explained that his car needed the attention of a mechanic. By now, the Frenchman appeared transformed.

'I take you now to ze garage de service of *mon ami,* Quentin, ze finest mechanic in le Midi. If your car is not finish tomorrow, I 'as a car you can use for 'alf what you pay to rent.'

Ronnie began to feel he was dealing with a slot machine. Every sentence seemed to involve some form of payment to Xavier. And the car would have to be cash and no questions asked. However, much as he wanted to slap the man around a bit, Ronnie knew he couldn't afford to antagonise him.

By the time Ronnie's car had limped into the yard of a dubious-looking back-street garage in the nearby town, and Xavier had driven him back to Versain, Ronnie had learned a great deal about the visitors from Wisstingham. The decrepit French villain had wittered incomprehensibly all the way around the local *hypermarché*, where Ronnie had picked up some basic provisions for a few days.

When the battered Clio eventually halted outside the *vigneron*'s home, Dumas tapped the side of his nose. 'These *Anglais*, zey don't know about the garage of Vincent.'

Which was no doubt where he was supposed to pick up this borrowed car, Ronnie thought darkly. At least the borrowed home was decent. The *vigneron*'s house was stone-built and set in its own grounds a short distance from the nearest neighbour along a country road flanked by plane trees. With tall stone walls, mature trees and a gravel drive, it had a huge integral garage with massive wooden doors that once would have housed the wine-grower's machinery and equipment.

Having extracted an assurance that Dumas would return the next day with news of his car, Ronnie turned on the water and electricity then went in search of his depleted bottle of scotch to help him take stock of the situation and formulate his plans to deal with the Wisstingham contingent.

It was later, when he'd unpacked his bags in the bedroom and was on his way downstairs, that Ronnie missed his footing on the narrow, winding staircase and plunged with a cry to the terrazzo-tiled floor below.

***

Fred's death, coupled with Miriam's repeated refusal to

answer Selwyn's calls, had plunged the commander into a gloom from which Sebastian and Maurice could not lift him.

Over a dinner of *carpaccio du boeuf* at La Panouille restaurant, followed by one of Gustave's large, wafer-thin pizzas and a dessert of *coupe colonel* – lime sorbet in vodka with lime zest – the three men formulated a plan of action for Sebastian during Selwyn's absence. Although Maurice hadn't been taken fully into their confidence, he was clearly aware that they were searching for Vincent's elusive possessions and documents.

'Don't you worry about Sebastian, my dear fellow. I'll make sure he comes to no harm,' Maurice assured as he puffed on a cigarillo.

'I'm grateful for all you've done for us,' replied Selwyn. 'We'd have been on a pretty sticky wicket without you.'

Maurice dismissed the compliment with a shake of his head and reached for one of the complimentary digestifs that Gustave had brought over. 'It'd be a pretty rotten sort of chap who wouldn't come to the aid of a fellow countryman, especially when abroad and dealing with Johnny Foreigner.'

As Fox looked down at the cigar ash that had fallen onto his waistcoat and started to brush it off, Selwyn caught Sebastian suppressing a smile as he had done on the numerous occasions they'd witnessed this. He felt relieved that at least he was leaving young Sebastian with a friend.

'If it turns out that I can't get back before you're ready to leave, Sebastian, you'll have to drive home on your own. Can you handle that?' he asked.

'I reckon so.'

His lack of conviction made Selwyn glance at Maurice.

'Sorry, old boy, can't really help you out on that one. I need to stick around here for a while.'

'I quite understand, but if should you change your mind there's an open invitation for you to stay at the hall.'

'Any other time, Selwyn, I'd be delighted.'

'Of course I'll be alright,' Sebastian rallied. 'What time's your flight tomorrow?'

'I have to be at the airport for one-thirty.'

'So we'll need to set off from here by eleven-thirty, to be safe,' suggested Maurice.

'Are you coming too?' Sebastian sounded relieved at the prospect.

'Of course, my dear chap. Got to see you're alright and that Selwyn gets off safely.'

'I'm much obliged, to be sure,' said Selwyn.

***

Maurice and Sebastian managed to persuade Selwyn to join them in a nightcap back at the hotel, where Maurice eventually steered the conversation round to horse racing. When he enquired about the stables and horses on the estate, Selwyn became quite animated and barely remembered to wave off Sebastian as he bade them goodnight and retired.

Later still, when the proprietor came to advise them that the bar was closed, Selwyn was on the verge of calling it a night.

'Oh no, my dear fellow,' Maurice protested. 'The night's still young, and I thought to bring along a bottle of malt. Let's knock the top off it and chat a while. I'm intrigued by your grand abode. And anyway, I may not see you again.' He reached down into the bag that had accompanied him all evening.

As the level in the bottle gradually fell, Selwyn waxed lyrical about the estate, the family, stables, clients, his horses and their successes.

Maurice appeared quite content to let him do most of the talking. 'So I imagine there's a tremendous history to the estate itself,' he commented during a lull in the conversation. 'Antique furniture, family heirlooms and the like, eh?'

'History, yes. As for possessions, there's quite a bit of furniture, furnishings, *objets d'art* and paintings, but the actual family treasure went missing way back during the English Civil War. I've been searching for it since I was first able to use a spade.'

Maurice leaned in closer. 'By Jove, that sounds exciting. What kind of treasure?'

'Very possibly some chalices, silver plate, jewellery, coins, maybe even some gold. So far, it's eluded me. There was a recent survey carried out on some of our land that's currently leased to the council. The results looked promising.' Selwyn hiccupped. 'I'd negotiated access to excavate the land, but the whole shooting match got bogged down with some sinister goings-on, and my murderous estate manager embezzled much of the estate's funds.'

'How dreadful.'

'He subsequently died, so it wasn't all bad.'

'Was it this Monaghan fella I've heard mentioned? Is that why you're here? To rescue the cash?'

Selwyn hesitated, feeling sheepish about how much he'd allowed himself to blather on. Some things were best kept to oneself. He glanced at his glass. 'I reckon I've said more than I should have done… '

'Don't worry, dear boy. It's all safe with me. You can trust Maurice.'

Selwyn gave him an embarrassed smile. 'I'm sure I can. Well, I really must turn in now. Can't be late on parade tomorrow. There's a plane to catch and a garage to find, so… ' He finished off his drink and bade goodnight to his companion.

Chapter 7

On their return from the airport, Sebastian immediately headed to the café bar for some refreshment while Maurice went off to pursue a possible lead on Monaghan's elusive garage.

'Great news, my dear fellow,' he exclaimed when he joined Sebastian later, followed closely by a somewhat wary Frenchman.

To Sebastian, despite the man having pulled his Breton hat from his head, he still looked every inch a fisherman. His thinning curly hair, grey at the temples, was matched by a full moustache. The face was expressive and the eyes, which darted around the room, had a mischievous sparkle about them behind the thick-framed glasses.

'Sebastian, meet Jean-Louis, a chap I've known for a little while. Jean-Louis, Sebastian.'

The Frenchman moved forward and shook hands vigorously as Maurice motioned him to sit down, took their drinks order and moved off to the bar.

Sebastian and Jean-Louis smiled at one another across the table in that embarrassed, polite silence a lack of common language inspires. Each racked his brain how best to start the conversation. Eventually the Frenchman took the plunge. 'I think I 'ave a resolve for your problem,' Jean-Louis ventured. 'Maurice tell me you have a *clef*. A ... 'ow you say... ?' He rotated his closed wrist.

'A key?'

'*Oui, oui*, a key,' Jean-Louis cantered on. 'I think I know the garage for it.'

'Brilliant!'

'What's brilliant?' asked Maurice, back with the drinks.

'He reckons he knows where Vincent's garage is.'

'Yes, I reckon it's a lucky break, my dear chap. The drinks are on the tab and I forgot to bring my wallet out with me. Sebastian, can you cover it?' At Jean-Louis' querying frown, Maurice rubbed his thumb and forefingers and shook his head. '*Pas d'argent, mon ami*,' he added regretfully.

'*Putain*! Capitalist,' Jean-Louis teased. He turned to Sebastian and wagged his forefinger. 'Always "*pas d'argent*", zis man. You 'ave to see 'im like ze okk.'

Sebastian frowned. 'An okk?'

'I think he means hawk,' Maurice explained. 'And the chap's a defaming bounder.' Nevertheless, he gave Jean-Louis a genial smile.

'A question,' Jean-Louis said suddenly, aiming it at Sebastian. 'You are friends of Xavier?'

'No, no,' Maurice replied quickly, before Sebastian could get a word in. Between them, they managed to explain that they'd had to deal with Xavier Dumas because he looked after the house of someone who'd died, and that they were trying to sort out the belongings.

'Aaaaaah.' Jean-Louis's frown eased, but it soon returned as he shot a glance around the room. '*Soyez prudent*,' he cautioned in a low voice. 'Zat *connard* is no correct.' He gave an emphatic nod.

'OK, *merci,* Jean-Louis.' Maurice tapped the side of his nose.

This appeared to put the Frenchman at ease. He promptly finished his drink and rose. '*Allez*, we must go.'

Their glasses drained, Sebastian settled the bill and Jean-Louis led them to their destination. Vincent's garage was located on a quiet road about ten minutes' walk from the bar. Sebastian tried one of the keys in the lock; though stiff, it turned. The door creaked as he tilted it upwards.

'Eh *voilà*,' Jean-Louis proudly exclaimed with a wave of his hand and triumphant smile. '*Mes amis, a votre service.*' He gave a slight bow.

'*Merci bien*, Jean-Louis,' said Maurice.

Although his job was done, the Frenchman seemed reluctant to depart. He reached into his pocket, pulled out a torch and offered it to Sebastian. The gloomy garage housed a battered CV6 with very little room for anything else. On the end wall was a shelf on which lay a toolbox and some tins.

Sebastian tried the car door, found it locked and selected a key. Once inside, he tried the ignition but the engine wouldn't even cough.

Jean-Louis promptly came forward, unceremoniously shooed Sebastian out of the seat and tried the ignition himself, to no avail. '*Merde!*' He released the bonnet, grabbed the torch and, with a withering frown, peered into the engine compartment. '*La batterie est debranchée*,' came the announcement.

'Flat?' queried Sebastian.

'Disconnected,' Maurice replied.

Jean-Louis started to rummage through the toolbox and pulled out an adjustable spanner. With a constant stream of muttering interspersed with the odd oath, he reconnected the battery then tried the ignition once more.

The starter gave a few whines and the engine spluttered into life. The Frenchman emerged from the garage with a grin that would have put the Cheshire Cat to shame. He patted the roof of the car and swaggered towards Sebastian. 'Is French *savoir-faire*. I 'ave finish here and I am late for my *dodo*.'

'Afternoon nap,' Maurice mouthed.

Sebastian thanked Jean-Louis, who set off for home wishing them a '*bon après-midi*' over his shoulder.

Sebastian studied the vibrating car as it chugged away in the garage. 'One battered Citroën, a shelf with not much on it and bugger-all else, by the looks of things,' he observed, sourly. 'I suppose we might as well get it out of the garage and give it a going over.'

'Not often you see a carpeted garage,' Maurice observed, once the car was removed.

They searched the car but found nothing of note other than the insurance documents, a *carte grise* and a few old garage invoices. Despondent, Sebastian was about to drive the car back in when Maurice frowned as he ran his sole over a section of carpet he'd just trodden on. He bent to roll it up. Underneath, in the centre of the concrete floor, was an inspection pit covered over with a flush-fitting board. Recessed into one edge of it was a handle.

Indulging in a little hope, Sebastian lifted the board and propped it against the wall. Maurice manoeuvred the car to the entrance and switched on the headlights to provide light and screen off visibility from passers-by.

As Sebastian crouched to look into the pit, Maurice joined him and let out a low whistle. 'Crikey!' His eyes roved the boxes and numerous packages crammed into the space, on top of which lay a battered briefcase. 'What's all this, then?'

'It's what my father left behind.' For a split second he'd been tempted to disown Monaghan but thought better of it, at least for the moment.

'Most intriguing.'

Sebastian hauled out one of the boxes and opened it to reveal neatly wrapped packages. He selected and opened one to find a silver chalice. Another yielded a pair of silver-framed miniature portraits. They felt heavy. Expensive. Treasured.

'Good grief, it looks to be something of a treasure trove,' said Maurice as he scrutinised the chalice. 'Where's this all come from?'

'It's a long story. I'll tell you over dinner.' Sebastian glanced beyond the open door and silhouetted car. A bank of ominous grey cloud had gathered, heralding the rain forecast for the afternoon. 'I think we'd better leave all this for now and pick it up tomorrow.' He re-wrapped the chalice and portraits but set aside the briefcase before they replaced the cover and rolled back the carpet.

'No wonder the car battery was disconnected,' said Maurice, when the car was back in the garage. 'A safety precaution, eh?'

Sebastian nodded. His impatience to explore the contents of the briefcase mounted as they walked back to the hotel. Maurice was quite animated as he held forth on the chalice and expanded on its likely origins, such that Sebastian marvelled at how knowledgeable the man sounded.

'One of my pet subjects,' Maurice confessed. 'I did once think of specialising in antiques, but I ended up just dabbling.'

At the hotel, Sebastian retired to his room and delved into the briefcase. Inside was another treasure trove of a different sort. He found a copy of Vincent's passport, a notaire's contract of sale for the house, letters from a bank and just about everything he assumed he'd need, alongside his own documents, to pursue the acquisition of Vincent's estate. There was also a large wad of money in euros and sterling.

As he leafed through the paperwork, Sebastian realised that, yet again, he'd need to call on Maurice's services to better understand just what he'd laid his hands on.

He waited a couple of hours before calling Selwyn.

'Thank goodness for that. We could do with some good news. It's all a bit bloody here, I'm afraid. Mrs Soames is in a bind over Fred's death, the police aren't ruling out foul play and have been quizzing the life out of everyone, and, of course, I'm once more in bad odour with our friend Stone.'

'Sorry to hear that. Do you want me to come back?'

'Good lord, no! There's nothing you could do. Anyway, it's vital you get things sorted out with the *notaire*. How are things with Maurice?'

'He's been very helpful. I think I'm going to have to explain the background to all this. He's seen some of the stolen goods anyway, and I need his opinion on the paperwork I've found.'

There was a pregnant pause. 'Well, if you have to, do so.'

Sebastian frowned. His uncle sounded awkward, almost embarrassed. 'Is there a problem? I thought you were hoping he'd help.'

'Oh, not at all, dear boy. I've just got the old guard up. Try not to tell him any more than is absolutely necessary.

I'm sure he's totally trustworthy, but it's as well to exercise caution.'

**

Miriam huffed a sigh at finding the entrance to the estate's drive almost entirely blocked by parked cars and vans, round which the media's finest bloodhounds were milling and making a general nuisance of themselves. The wretched paparazzi seemed to have descended in droves. She was hardly surprised, given the headline in the morning's paper, calling Wisstingham 'The Murder Estate'.

Beyond the gates, further up the drive, the steps to the hall were besieged by more newshounds who watched, waited and smoked their way through the sunny morning. No doubt poor Mrs Soames, who'd called Amanda in desperation, had been pacing the hall. Amanda, equally desperate to get her flight to Montpellier, had called Miriam, who felt compelled to leap to the housekeeper's aid.

As the gates opened, Miriam negotiated her way through the mêlée, refused to wind down her window or speak, then sped down the drive. Another gaggle descended on her as she got out of the car. Once she'd made it up the steps to the front door, she turned. 'Right, what's all this fuss about?'

She was assailed by a barrage of microphones and questions, everyone wanting to know who she was, what she was doing at the hall, and what she thought about the murder on the estate.

She gave one reporter a particularly quelling look. 'How do you know it's murder?'

'The police think so,' yelled another. 'Who are you?'

'A close friend of the family. Have the police issued a statement saying it's murder?'

'What friend?' queried a young hack. 'Where's the commander?'

'Not here,' Miriam confirmed.

'When will he be back? We need a statement from someone in authority.'

'I'll give you a statement,' Miriam offered. The hubbub suddenly subsided and the press shuffled even closer. 'This is private property, none of you are invited or welcome on it, and therefore you are trespassing. You will make your way immediately beyond the drive and front gates. I suggest you do so before the dogs are released to patrol the grounds. You have been duly warned.'

As the protests continued, she turned to the partially open front door, at which an extremely nervous but grateful Mrs Soames had been listening. Once inside the hallway, the housekeeper clasped Miriam's hand in hers. 'You was just m-marvellous. Them 'orrors 'ave been hounding me all mornin'.'

'I'm only too glad to help. Amanda called to tell me you were under siege, so I said I'd step in.' It seemed best not to draw attention to her main reason for being there: to minimise any adverse publicity for Wisstingham. 'Amanda told me you're expecting the commander back later today. Is there someone who can lock the front gates? And do you actually have any guard dogs?'

'Well, there's Mac Bilton, he can lock up. But as for dogs, we've only got Young Mustard.'

Miriam gave her a puzzled frown.

'He's a puppy. Same kennels as Mustard came from,

poor ol' boy. I miss him somethin' chronic.' Mrs Soames gave a sniff. 'He 'ad to be put down, he was so badly. But he was a good age. The commander's still not over it. Calls all 'is dogs Mustard.'

'Oh dear. How terribly sad. I didn't know Mustard had gone, poor thing. So, a puppy's our only deterrent?'

As if on cue, the hall's newest resident romped friskily into the kitchen. Miriam exchanged a smile with Mrs Soames at the thought of the beagle being passed off as a guard dog. 'I suppose he'd probably pee on their legs in excitement. Perhaps we should content ourselves with just locking the gates,' she suggested.

'Right you are, your worship. You make yerself comfortable in the drawin' room and I'll be right in with a cup of Rosie and some cake after I've rung Mac.'

Delighted that she appeared to be in Mrs S's good books once more after her previous break with Selwyn, Miriam made her way slowly down the hallway, taking in as always (though this time with sadness) the exquisite furnishings and ornaments on display. It pained her to realise she'd no longer share the joy of them or any other happy occasions with their owner, whom she was still unable to expel from her thoughts, mind and heart.

***

The queue shuffled its way slowly round the snake of barriers, the passengers' lively chatter blending with the sound of trundled hand baggage. After several minutes, it was Amanda's turn to approach the surly-looking customs officer who mechanically held out his hand for the passport, scanned it and its owner, then nodded for her to proceed.

Fortunately, hers was one of the first bags to arrive on the carousel. She hoisted it off the belt and aimed for the glass exit door, which slid open silently on her approach. Beyond were several groups of people. Some were anxiously watching for a first glance of their expected arrivals, while others embraced and eagerly chatted to those who'd already joined them.

With no expectation of any such greeting, Amanda was about to head outside when, to her surprise, she spied a short, stocky man holding up a hand-written sign with her name. She approached him with some uncertainty. 'I'm Amanda Sheppard. I wasn't expecting anyone. Who are you?'

The man broke into a smile and offered his hand. 'Wally Clark. Sebastian would've been here 'imself but he's tied up like, wiv a meetin'. I said I'd pick you up as I was already droppin' someone off.'

'But he didn't know I was coming.'

'I'm afraid Mrs Soames let the cat out of the bag. Here, let me get yer case.'

Although still slightly puzzled, Amanda surrendered it and followed Wally as he limped out of the building and across the road to the car park. 'How do you know Sebastian?' she asked as they arrived at a Renault Twingo.

'Met 'im in the local bar. Got chattin' and I said I'd show 'em the ropes. After all, we Brits have got to stick together, right?'

'I suppose so.' Amanda automatically made for the wrong side of the car as Wally approached the passenger side. Realising their mistakes, they smiled and changed places. Amanda felt a sudden unease. 'Do you live out here?'

'Yeah. I've 'ad to borrow this for a few days cos mine's in dock. It's an English one an' I never get used to the steering wheel on the wrong side.'

'But surely you can only keep an English car here for a limited period?'

Clark glared momentarily. 'It's registered 'ere.'

Despite her attempts to continue the dialogue, there was very little further conversation on the way to Versain. By the time they arrived, the light was fading and there were lengthy shadows across the gravel drive.

'I said you could wait here until Sebastian returns.' Wally opened the front door and placed Amanda's luggage in the hallway. 'Come in and make yerself at 'ome.'

Hesitantly, Amanda entered and looked around. 'Is this your place, then?'

'Yeah, it is. Would you like a coffee or tea?'

'Yes, please. Coffee will be fine. Milk, no sugar.'

'Take a seat.' Wally disappeared, presumably to the kitchen.

As Amanda sat down, she spied a pile of *Vogue* magazines on the lower shelf of the coffee table. 'Do you live here on your own?' she called out.

'Yeah,' came the reply.

Amanda glanced around at the furniture and ornaments. She rose to join her host and stopped at the doorway as she heard him speak. 'Yeah, I picked her up OK. We've just arrived at the villa.'

Must be Sebastian, thought Amanda, and relief blew away the billows of doubt and suspicion. She returned to the settee, shortly to be joined by Wally with two mugs of coffee.

'He shouldn't be long, I expect,' he said, as if he'd read Amanda's mind.

She reached for the coffee and sipped at it. Wally watched her, smiled when she looked at him, then reached for his own drink. They sat in silence. Amanda put her empty cup down, glanced at her watch and took in the room again. Her gaze involuntarily shifted from the magazines under the coffee table to her host, whose smile instantly faded when he saw she'd spotted them. It was the fact that he forced another smile that set alarm bells ringing in Amanda's head.

She consulted her watch again then rose. 'What's keeping him?' Her pulse raced; it was difficult to focus. Panic took over. 'I think I'll just step outside for a breath of fresh air.' She sneaked a glance at her baggage in the hallway.

Wally merely smiled and gestured to the door. 'Be my guest.'

As Amanda started forward, her vision clouded. She staggered and when she reached the door, she was unable to open it. 'It's locked!'

Those were the last words she uttered. Her eyes closed, her legs buckled and she slumped to the floor.

***

Waiting at the bar to be served, Jack Cavannagh looked back across the room and returned Miriam's smile. His exterior calmness gave the lie to his conflicting emotions. While eager to learn anything about Selwyn, and in particular Sebastian, he dreaded the revelation of any more bad news and feared how he might react.

'I hope you didn't mind meeting here, but I thought it'd be more private than the café,' he said, returning with the drinks.

'Not at all.' She raised her glass and gave a toast. 'To your research.' They chinked glasses.

'Yes, to the research.'

There followed an exchange of pleasantries until Jack eventually said, 'So tell me a bit about the Wisstingham of today and its main movers and shakers.'

'Now there's a challenge! Where would you like to start?'

'How about the Wisstingham estate?'

Miriam stared at him for a moment; she seemed suddenly distracted. 'Well, the hall dates back to before the English Civil War. A beautiful place with exquisite furniture and décor. Its owner is Commander Selwyn Fitzgerald, who had a half-brother, Lucian, but he died abroad. It did appear that the commander was amenable to the hall being opened to the public, but some rather shady events put paid to that, which is a great shame.' She gave a sad shrug. 'I've since wondered if he ever really intended to do so.'

'And what about the rest of the family?'

'There isn't anyone else, now. Selwyn's son was killed in a road accident about seven years ago and his wife died shortly after.'

'Oh no,' Jack murmured, just managing to stop short of uttering their names. He stared at Miriam for a moment then let his gaze fall to the table as he tried to take it all in. It was a struggle to retain his composure. *Felix and Georgina both dead? What sort of hell must Selwyn have gone through?* He felt ashamed at not having known, and not having been there to support his brother.

Apparently his distress did not escape Miriam. With a look of concern, she gently placed her hand on his arm. 'Are you alright?'

'Yes, yes, I'm fine. It all sounds such a tragedy.'

'Yes, it certainly was.'

Jack inhaled deeply and swallowed hard. He offered a weak smile. 'And what were those shady events you referred to?'

'Monaghan, the estate manager, turned out to be a real villain. He carried out a stolen goods' racket right under the commander's nose. To add insult to injury, he embezzled a lot of the estate money and implicated Selwyn and his nephew. As if that weren't enough, he also murdered at least two people to cover his tracks. At least he had the decency to die before the police could arrest him. Selwyn was there at the time, but *he* didn't kill the man. That whole nightmare would make a television series on its own.'

Jack frowned. 'You said nephew?'

Miriam appeared puzzled, but only for a moment. 'Oh, sorry. I should explain. Sebastian was supposed to be Monaghan's son, but it turned out he was really Lucian's.'

Jack's heart raced at this confirmation that Selwyn knew of Sebastian's paternity – one less hurdle to get over – but his surge of elation was quickly tempered by foreboding. How would Selwyn and Sebastian receive him? Their opinions of him, formed so long ago, would be well entrenched. How could he hope to gain their acceptance after all this? 'Good God! How totally sad,' he murmured.

'Indeed.' Miriam put her head on one side and her face puckered as she studied him. 'Do you know, I'm sure I've seen you somewhere before.'

'I doubt that very much. I can't think how our paths can have crossed.' There was something in her gaze that suggested regret, but he ploughed on. He needed to know more about his son. 'What happened to Sebastian?'

'He lives in a little place on the estate, though he's been staying up at the hall for a while now. And recently he's been in France with the commander.'

'Do you know when they'll return?'

'I don't know about Sebastian, but Selwyn was due back at some point today. Is it just the estate and family you're interested in for your research?'

'No, indeed not. I'm very interested in knowing about you. And the council, of course,' he added quickly, as Miriam raised her eyebrows and smiled. 'But let's discuss that over our meal.' He reached for the menus.

Miriam gave a slight shake of her head, troubled by how much she was enjoying Jack's company. She tried to dismiss images of Selwyn, which vied with thoughts about her distinguished-looking and likeable dining companion, a man who'd shown such compassion for the tribulations of strangers.

***

Over dinner, without any elaboration on the stolen antiques' racket Vincent had been involved in, or mentioning that Vincent was not really his father, Sebastian enlightened Maurice. He explained how Monaghan had embezzled the estate's funds, murdered his partner in crime, Jez Fellowes, and nearly killed Caines. 'And,' Sebastian added, almost running out of steam, 'when he was alive, it seems that Vincent dubiously acquired numerous items of value.'

Maurice continued to gaze at him for several moments then let out a low whistle. 'You mean the stuff's stolen?'

'I reckon at least some of it is. Selwyn will need to see

if he recognises any of it. So, I'll quite understand if you don't want to get any more involved.'

'Oh, don't worry about that.' Maurice gave a dismissive wave of his hand. 'I'll do all I can to help you. What'll happen to the stuff?'

'We've racked our brains about that. Obviously, we'd like to restore it to the rightful owners if possible. The main aim is to get the missing estate money back, but it's likely there'll be more than that. The problem is that if we declare that we've found the stolen goods, the police may want to claim *all* the money as the proceeds of crime. If so, the commander may never get his portion back.'

'Hmm, tricky. So presumably the priority is to get Selwyn's money home and dry, then sort out what's left, eh? Well, whatever happens, you can count on my help and absolute discretion.'

'Spoken like a gentleman, Maurice. I'm glad I can count on you.'

***

The honey-hued stone façade of Versain's *mairie* glowed under the floodlight's glare. At the top of the building, the red, white and blue of the tricolour was picked out by more lights. Otherwise, apart from the few streetlights dotted around the square and the spotlights trained on the monument to the war dead, all was in darkness. The café bar had long since closed, and the only signs of activity were the occasional comings and goings of diners at La Panouille.

A couple of youths broke the quiet with the drone of their *mobilette* engines, but after some animated conversation they were soon off again at high speed amid a volley of noise to disturb another neighbourhood.

As silence descended once more, a black Mercedes purred into *la place* and stopped. Berensen got out, looked around then walked slowly towards the restaurant. About to enter and have a meal, he hesitated just outside the doorway. Facing him through the window, occupied with his menu, was a man he thought he recognised as Archie Fox. He withdrew to a bench under the thick canopy of the *plantane mourier* trees and lit a cigarette.

From across the square, he looked through the restaurant window at the only occupied table. A youngish man sat with his back to the door opposite the older man, who'd now abandoned his menu. At this distance, Berensen figured they would not make out his presence in the darkness. He pulled out Cutler's photograph from his leather jacket, studied it and pocketed it again, delighted that he'd found his quarry so quickly and easily.

***

Later that night, as he lay awake and stared through the bedroom window at the silver, moonlit wisps of cloud that were drifting across the sky, Archie pondered his predicament and the opportunity that now presented itself. His intention had been to lie low in France using his brother's identity, but here was the temptation to find a bolthole closer to home. After all, he'd been given an open invitation from the commander and there was, perhaps, the opportunity of money and valuables to exploit. Sebastian and Selwyn would be no match for him, he was certain.

'Follow the money, Archie, follow the money,' he

muttered. He turned over to go to sleep. He'd give the matter more serious thought the next day.

Chapter 8

With the promise of sunshine, Maurice donned his lightweight jacket, plonked the battered straw hat on his head and sallied forth to catch up with Sebastian, who was already waiting outside number 27. Maurice's eyes closed almost to slits as he closed the door and savoured the aroma of at least three Sunday dinners wafting down the street, enough to tantalise the nostrils of any passer-by. He paused to light a cigarillo. 'All set, dear boy,' he announced and jingled his car keys as evidence of his readiness.

They laboured up the hill and arrived in the open *place*, devoid of traffic other than a black Mercedes. Behind its tinted windows, Berensen looked up from his newspaper.

As the men approached the car park by the *mairie*, Berensen set aside the paper, reached into the glove compartment and withdrew a black leather case. From this he took out a gun, screwed a silencer in place and placed it under the newspaper. By now, Fox's car had emerged from the car park. Berensen set off to follow at a distance.

At the garage, Maurice rummaged in the glove compartment. 'Put these on, dear boy,' he told Sebastian and handed him a pair of latex gloves. 'I don't know what you're intending to do with the stuff, but since it's probably not kosher it'd be as well not to leave any fingerprints.'

Seemingly impressed by the forethought, Sebastian acquiesced.

When the CV6 was manoeuvred onto the road and Maurice's car was parked adjacent to the garage, there was still enough space for a passing vehicle. The garage door was swung open, the carpet removed and the board to the inspection pit lifted.

Maurice was barely able to suppress his excitement at what met their eyes in the brighter light. They quickly started to load the goods into the boot of the car, lowering the lid each time to obscure the hoard from passing pedestrians.

Having halted further up the road, Berensen watched the two men. He decided to get closer and drove past the garage but couldn't find anywhere to park. He swore as his mobile rang. From a glance at the screen, he saw it was Cutler. He drove on and eventually found an open area in which to stop. By now a message had registered, but the reception was so poor he couldn't listen to it or call back.

So began a hunt through the narrow winding streets of the old quarter for a place where he might both park and return the call. Infuriated to find he'd driven what seemed like miles only to find that Cutler was merely checking on what progress had been made, Berensen tossed the mobile onto the passenger seat and returned to a convoluted search through the labyrinth of streets to find his way back to the garage.

***

Amanda awoke to blackness feeling drowsy and sick. Her head ached, as did her limbs. Her mouth stopped with sticky tape, she began to panic. Eventually, she managed to overcome her terror and force herself to breathe regularly through her nose. Her arms and feet were trussed with gaffer tape, and she sensed she was lying on thin material on a cold, solid floor.

After several minutes, the door was unlocked and there was a grating sound as it slowly opened. The light almost blinded her. In the doorway stood Wally, wearing the same pained expression she'd seen at the airport.

He stared at her for a few moments, then hobbled over and squatted down with a grimace. He ripped away the tape, making her cry out. This brought a sneer of satisfaction to her captor. 'Ain't no good shoutin' down 'ere. No fucker'll hear yer.'

Then why put me through that hell, you sadist? Amanda looked about her. She shuddered to see she was in an old wine cellar, its walls lined with dusty, empty racks thick with cobwebs. In one corner stood a heap of old wine boxes, and on a battered wooden table a rusty metal bin. A single, discoloured lightbulb hung from the ceiling, its light dimming as Amanda's sight adjusted.

'What do you want with me? Who are you? Where's Sebastian? I need some water.'

'Ain't no good givin' you food and drink, you'll not be around long enough to benefit from 'em. Unless you tell me where yer feller is.'

Amanda struggled to fight down her rising terror. 'I've no idea.'

'Then you'd better get yer phone working on the fuckin' answer, and bleedin' quick.'

Anger now started to combat her fear. 'So you can go after him as well? Not likely.'

'You're givin' me the right 'ump.' Clark slapped her across the face.

Amanda cried out and grimaced.

'If you don't cooperate, it's gonna be an 'ole lot worse for you *and* a load of other people. We'll go through the whole fuckin' household at Wisstingham.' He leered. 'Who knows, I might just have some fun with you into the bargain before I top yer.'

Amanda shuddered and her eyes started to mist over. She wanted to scratch out his eyes and kick him in the bollocks but, until she was in a position to try, it wouldn't help to make things worse. 'What do you want me to do?'

'Ring yer feller and find out exactly where 'e is. And not a word about where you are, or me.' Clark produced her mobile, gave it to her, then took out a stiletto. He flicked it open and pointed it against her throat.

***

Maurice watched from behind the car as Sebastian answered his mobile. The boot was now fully loaded and Maurice's mind was alive with speculation on the value of the items he'd seen.

'Where are you?'

Maurice looked up at Sebastian's terse, puzzled question.

'How did you get here? Why didn't you warn me you were com— Please don't cry. What's the matter, Amanda?' He glanced across to Maurice as he listened. 'We're at the garage.' Sebastian's face drained. A muscle jumped under his ear. 'Who are you? What have you done to her?'

Maurice waited until Sebastian miserably ended the call with the information that they were at the garage at the rue des Pommes. He didn't like the sound of this. The fewer people who knew about their bounty, the better. 'What's the matter, dear boy?'

'Someone's got Amanda. He's coming here.'

'What? From England?'

Sebastian gave an exasperated sigh. 'No, she's *here*. It was supposed to be a surprise visit.'

'Well, she's certainly achieved that. What should we do?'

Sebastian peered helplessly up and down the street. 'There's nothing we can do.'

***

Ronnie stared down at his terrified captive, who lay helplessly trussed on the floor. 'Don't worry, you'll see yer boyfriend again before I do him in. Then it'll be you an' me, eh, lady?'

He chuckled as he plunged Amanda into darkness and desolation once more, not giving two shits that she'd spent a night in the cellar already. Upstairs, he consulted the street plan and got into the Renault, which refused to start. If it hadn't been for his bad leg, he'd have aimed a kick at it.

After several oaths, he set off on foot, only realising after he'd got into the open that he'd forgotten his jacket. Unwilling to go back, he pressed on.

Within five minutes he arrived in rue des Pommes and spotted a short, stocky man in a straw hat standing by the rear of a car. At the front stood a younger man, whom Ronnie recognised as Sebastian.

Ronnie looked round to see the coast was clear, then approached. 'You two, in the garage, now,' he ordered.

The older man looked as if he were about to challenge him but Sebastian said, 'Do as he says, Maurice,' and they reluctantly obliged. 'What have you done with Amanda?' he demanded.

Ronnie screwed a silencer onto the gun he'd taken from his pocket. 'You do as yer told and she'll be alright. What's in the car?'

'Nothing much,' Maurice retorted.

Ronnie checked out the contents of the boot and couldn't help grinning. 'Nothing much?' He closed in on Maurice until they were face to face. 'You're a fuckin' joker, ain't yer?' he said, then butted him in the face.

Maurice cried out and staggered back, clutching a hand against his bleeding nose.

'Leave him alone!' Sebastian started forward but stopped in his tracks as Ronnie levelled the gun at him. 'Take the stuff if you want, just release Amanda. Please!'

'Fuckin' right I'll take it, but you're coming with me too.' Now in full-on Hammer mode, he kept the gun levelled at Sebastian whilst glaring at Maurice, who now had a handkerchief at his nose. 'You're staying here. Where are the car keys?'

Maurice delved into his pocket and quickly handed them over.

Deciding to snaffle a little camouflage, Ronnie demanded Maurice's hat and jacket. Anyone who'd seen these two would probably be fooled. As Maurice handed them over, Ronnie spied the Rolex. 'And I'll have that watch,' he added.

Maurice glared at him as he reluctantly parted with it.

Ronnie grinned as he took off his own Timex, stuffed it in his pocket and put on the Rolex. At the open garage door, he addressed the rattled Maurice. 'Keep yer fuckin' trap shut and it'll all be OK. If you make any sound, or I find anything's happened when I return, him and the girl will be toast. You, too. You understand?'

Maurice nodded, then Ronnie swung the garage door shut and locked it. Sebastian stood helplessly by the car.

Once I've done the bastard and the bird, I'll bring the other one back and do him. Ronnie grinned as he climbed into the car. That way, it'd look like the older bloke had done them both in then killed himself. Harry would get the goods and his revenge, and there'd be a Rolex and maybe one or two of the trinkets for keepers. *Happiness!*

Berensen brought the black Mercedes to a halt a short distance up the street, just in time to see Sebastian and his straw-hatted colleague get into the car and drive off.

***

'And what can I do for you today?' asked Selwyn, when DI Stone was shown into the drawing room. 'I assume it's about Fred Ferris.'

'Correct. Now I'm sure you'll appreciate, commander, that this place is getting a very bad reputation with our force and, I suspect, the Wisstingham community, because of the number of incidents we've been called to investigate. I'm increasingly inclined to believe that either this estate is disaster prone, or that there are still some pretty nasty forces at work.'

Although he took the message seriously, Selwyn couldn't resist an inward smile when he noticed that the DI was not adopting his customary stance of hands in the pockets jingling his change. Either the man had acquired a hole in the lining or he'd been seriously pressured by a charity collector.

'Did you hear me, Commander Fitzgerald?'

'No one regrets these occurrence more than me. And let me remind you that *I* was on the very unpleasant receiving end of the villainy associated with them.' *So stick that in your pipe and smoke it.*

'Be that as it may, I have to tell you that we're treating the death of Mr Ferris as suspicious. I understand you were in France with Sebastian Monaghan when the body was discovered. Why was that?'

'Not that it has any bearing on the matter, but it was a business lead.'

'I see.' Stone waited, but Selwyn did not amplify. 'Let me explain our dilemma. We have the body found in the stables with one shoe missing, which was discovered in the locked cottage that Vincent Monaghan used to live in. And I understand that no one's been in residence there since Monaghan disappeared. Would Ferris typically have had access to the cottage? And if so, what might he have gone in there for?'

'As acting estate manager, he had access to the majority of buildings, although a key to the cottage is kept in the kitchen here. As to why he went in there, I haven't a clue – unless he came across something that needed looking into.'

'Indeed. But one problem we have is that the key was not found on Ferris's body, nor in the stables. We've confirmed that the kitchen key is still in place, so we need to account for all other copies. Who else would have access to the key?'

'Anyone working here, I suppose. There's Mrs Soames and Mac Bilton, who live in the grounds. All the other staff travel in daily, but as a rule they don't enter the hall, except for the four cleaners. As for the keys, I have a full set. I assume Sebastian still has his. I'll look into it and check my set.'

'Thank you. We've checked the cottage for fingerprints. There's no trace of Bilton's or Ferris's. In fact, the whole banister rail's been wiped clean. Is there anyone, other than Bilton, the housekeeper, Sebastian and yourself, who's been in the cottage since it was closed up?'

'Not that I know of. Mrs Soames would have a better idea.'

'We've already checked with her.'

Selwyn was starting to feel very tired. 'Then I suspect it's something to do with the criminals Vincent associated with.'

'I think you're probably right. Which begs the question, what were they after?'

Selwyn felt uncomfortable about the direction the conversation was taking in relation to the search for Vincent's stolen goods. If he hadn't done so already, was Stone about to make the connection?

'I'm inclined to suspect there was inside involvement,' Stone said.

Though initially put on edge by the oblique accusation, Selwyn realised that Stone wasn't even looking at him, let alone giving his trademark glare. 'You suspect Bilton?'

Stone nodded. 'We've already interviewed him. He gave nothing away, though I reckon he was shaken. We're going to bring him in again tomorrow – but not a word about this.'

Selwyn pondered the request. 'He's a member of my staff and I'm bound to do everything I can to support him. Unless it transpires that he really was involved. But no, I won't say anything to him.'

'Good. I know we've had our differences in the past, commander, but I'm sure you'll want to get to the bottom of this as much as we do.'

'Absolutely.' This mellower approach made Selwyn wonder if the DI was trying to sneak under his defence radar. Yes he'd cooperate, but with the utmost caution.

'Well, I don't think there's much more to be said at this stage.'

As Selwyn escorted him down the hallway, the DI glanced about him at the furniture and ornaments. 'It's quite a place you've got here,' he observed, as they reached the front door. 'Do you think any of the cleaners you mentioned could be involved?'

Selwyn let out a chuckle. 'I really don't think so. One's just a young girl, and the other three are on the church flower-arranging committee and just about every other committee in the village. Pillars of society. If you so much as broke wind in their hearing, they'd probably have the vapours.'

The commander stood at the entrance and watched as the DI's car disappeared from view. He reflected on the interview and wondered why he hadn't heard from Sebastian. Perhaps he was too occupied with Amanda's surprise visit. 'Probably having a whale of a time,' he muttered with a smile as he went back inside.

In the hallway, he stopped to gaze at the large mahogany bureau. He'd just moved closer to examine it in more detail when Mrs Soames sallied forth from the kitchen. 'Anything wrong?' she asked

Selwyn straightened. 'No, not really. I was just wondering how much this would fetch.'

Alarm spread on her apple-cheeked face. She scuttled up to the bureau and stood with her back to it, her arms spread protectively. 'You're not thinkin' of sellin' this, surely?'

'Well, I've got to get some money from somewhere. Things are bad, you know.'

'I know, but not this. I've spent half me life polishing and lookin' after it,' she begged. 'You can flog that there armour. Clanking monstrosities. They're a dust trap, them are.'

Selwyn set his chin resolutely. 'Not the armour. That's the family heritage.'

'Promise me you'll not sell anything without talkin' to me first,' Mrs Soames pleaded.

Selwyn let out a tired sigh of resignation as she turned to give the bureau a loving polish with the underside of her apron. 'Very well, Mrs S, but *something*'s going to have to go.'

He turned and walked huffily off to the library, shaking his head. He was now resolved to resume his desperate search through the old documents to find the land-transfer deeds bestowing land to the estate. He had to come up with something, and quickly.

**

Parked with a view of the courtyard into which the Renault had driven, Berensen watched as the driver got out, limped to the house and unlocked the ornately carved wooden front door. The younger man was ushered in and the door left slightly ajar. Tempted though he was to follow them, Berensen waited several minutes, his hand on the gun that lay on the passenger seat.

Eventually the limping man returned, opened the boot of the car and stared at the contents. He started to ferry them into the house, then finally slammed the boot and went inside.

Having put on latex gloves, Berensen got out of the Mercedes, checked to see that all was clear, and walked quickly to the building. By the time he reached the threshold, the man had emerged from a room near the front door and started to limp down the corridor. He was a silhouette with a hammer in his hand, but that didn't put Berensen off his aim one little bit. Before the man had gone four paces, Berensen fired.

A popping sound was followed by a grunt as his quarry was propelled forward amidst a starburst of bone, blood and other fluids. The hammer clattered to the marble-tiled floor, followed immediately by the body, a neat hole bored in the back of the skull.

After another quick look round for any witnesses, Berensen entered the house and closed the door. He refrained from putting on the lights as he watched and listened for any sign of the man's colleague. There was none.

He walked up to the body, from which blood now seeped. The blood-patched face and beard lay sideways, the eyes staring. Berensen smiled, reached over to the right wrist, found the watch and took it off to check the inscription on the back. Definitely Cutler's Rolex.

He rose and looked into the room from which the victim had appeared in case his companion was quaking in a corner. There was no one. He briefly examined the packages, boxes and other items heaped on the room's central table but left them be, just as he'd leave the missing companion. His contract was only for Archie Fox and he'd fulfilled it.

Within minutes, his Mercedes was headed on the road out of Versain.

***

A clatter and thump could just be made out in the cellar's damp, dark confines. Amanda's start and gasp made Sebastian pull her closer towards him. 'A bit like the babes in the wood, without the moon or even the gingerbread house,' she murmured in an attempt to lift their spirits.

'They had it cushy.' He stared at the cellar's ceiling, keeping his ears pricked for the next noise. 'At least they had some soft ground to lie on.'

'I wish I'd not said that,' Amanda whispered.

'What? About the babes?'

'No, the gingerbread house. I'm famished.'

Sebastian sniggered and they subsided back into the quietness of shared anxiety.

Chapter 9

Roused from his afternoon siesta, Xavier winked open one eye and raised his head to squint at the ormolu clock on the marble table by the window. He rubbed his face, farted, then rose to sit on the edge of the bed. From downstairs he could hear the clatter of pans being put away by his wife, Amelie, who would shortly retire to their sitting room to watch television and inevitably fall asleep.

Xavier contemplated what he might do for the rest of the day. Certainly nothing that involved any exertion. He thought wistfully of their Sunday afternoon ritual of lovemaking, a thing of the past for a long time now. He decided he'd visit the *anglais*. No doubt he'd have some whisky to offer him. The walk would wear off the extra portion he'd eaten at lunch, then he'd return for his pastis at *apéro* time.

As he passed Jean-Louis' house, he glanced up at the balcony where his neighbour was brushing down an object he'd probably bought at that morning's flea market, held weekly on derelict land at the edge of the village. '*Bonjour*,' he shouted up to Jean-Louis, who dutifully returned the greeting.

Slightly out of breath, Xavier arrived at the *vigneron*'s house, rang the bell and waited. After a minute he rang again, then skulked round the building to see if he could spy the *anglais* through the windows. Unsuccessful, he returned to the front door, turned the handle and found it unlocked.

'*Bonjour, monsieur, c'est moi*, Xavier,' he called. After there was still no reply, he entered cautiously. By now it was nearly dusk. Nevertheless, he crept in – then froze at the shadowy sight of a form lying on the passageway floor. '*Mon Dieu!*' he exclaimed and fumbled for the light switch.

Now with full view of the corpse and pool of blood, he thought he might puke but managed to keep control. Panicking, hands shaking, he lurched out of the door, which he still had the presence of mind to close, then sped unsteadily home.

Having witnessed Xavier's frantic arrival, Jean-Louis reluctantly decided he'd have to do the neighbourly thing and investigate what was wrong. It took two raps and a shout to persuade the ashen-faced Dumas to open the door a crack and peer out. On seeing who it was, Dumas pulled the door wide open, glanced nervously up and down the street, then caught hold of Jean-Louis's arm and hauled him inside.

'Jean-Louis, *sacre bleu*,' he repeated, over and over again. His hand, which clung to his neighbour's arm, still shook.

After several moments and much persuasion to calm down, Xavier would only indicate that he needed Jean-Louis to go with him to see something terrible. With mounting trepidation, Gaudin accompanied the distraught Dumas back to a house just outside the village.

There, though shocking, the sight of the body yielded a less histrionic reaction from Jean-Louis. 'Don't touch anything,' he instructed Dumas. He immediately thought of the English group and suspected their involvement.

Xavier began to explain his connection with the dead

man but was cut short as Jean-Louis frogmarched him to the rear of the house and ordered him to sit there until he returned. That took some persuasion and Jean-Louis' insistence that, if he were to put his neck out to help the idiot, Xavier would do what he was told, like it or not.

There followed something of a dark pantomime. On a hunch, Jean-Louis made his way to the garage to try to find Maurice and the *anglais*. He discovered the parked Citroën and the locked door, on which he banged. Having learned what had happened from the relieved Maurice, Gaudin hurried back to the house. He gingerly searched through the dead man's pockets and found some keys, one of which he assumed was for the garage, the others presumably for the rest of the house.

A search through the other rooms yielded no trace of Sebastian, so he looked for the *cave*. Thankfully, it took only a moment to find a door and stairs. The door at the bottom was locked. '*Sebastian, vous êtes là? C'est moi, Jean-Louis.*'

'Jean-Louis!' came the welcome reply. After Gaudin had tried several keys, two weary but thankful prisoners were released into their own personal *entente cordiale*.

Once their eyes were accustomed to the light, Jean-Louis told them they were to touch nothing and avert their eyes in the corridor. He led them upstairs, and naturally they failed to look away. When he saw the body, Sebastian went ashen. The girl gasped, almost retched, and grasped at Sebastian for support. He steadied her and they crept past warily, still led by their rescuer.

'I get you some water,' Jean-Louis offered.

Sebastian took the proffered bottle a moment later and passed it first to Amanda. She drained half before handing it back, still avoiding any further eye contact with the corpse.

Sebastian had just taken his fill when she bombarded him with frantic questions. 'Who is it? Is it him? Who killed him?'

Sebastian pulled her towards him, held her tightly and planted a kiss on her forehead. 'Yes, it's the man who brought me here – but I haven't a clue who killed him. I suppose they've gone.'

'I bloody hope so.'

'*Attention, mes amis! Allons vite!*' Jean-Louis summoned them from the doorway into the lounge.

Sebastian saw Amanda's eyes light on the stolen goods piled on the table. 'Blimey O'Reilly!' she exclaimed, as she stared wide-eyed at the hoard. 'You really know how to surprise a girl, Sebastian. There's never a dull moment with *you.*'

'Monaghan's loot.' Sebastian's mind was still on who might have killed their captor.

'And there's my mobile.' Amanda retrieved it from the table. 'What on earth are you going to do with all this?'

Sebastian stared at the goods and lapsed into thoughtful silence. Jean-Louis signalled they should go but Sebastian waved a hand at him. 'Two minutes, Jean-Louis. It's important.'

The Frenchman threw up his hands, grunted in exasperation and went outside.

'I'd be tempted to leave it where it is,' Sebastian said eventually. 'But if Interpol gets involved and it gets into the hands of the British police, it's bound to lead them straight back to the estate. Not only would Selwyn and I be in the dwang, but we could say goodbye to all the money here. Also, I might end up being extradited to be tried for murder. And remember, here you're guilty until proven innocent.'

'Gee, that's scary!' Amanda gently stroked his cheek. 'Don't worry, I won't let them get their garlicky hands on you, munchkin. We'd better get it out quickly, hadn't we?'

By now, the Frenchmen had reappeared. While Xavier hovered nervously by the front door, Jean-Louis handed the garage key to Sebastian to go and release Maurice. It took just minutes for Sebastian to collect him and return to the grim hallway, where Maurice blanched at the sight of the corpse.

He picked up and nervously fingered the straw hat Ronnie had discarded when he'd walked through the front door, then stared at his bloodstained jacket, which was still on the corpse. It was a while before he was in a fit state to be introduced briefly to Amanda. All the while, the exasperated Jean-Louis hovered, clearly on tenterhooks.

Sebastian, Amanda and Maurice began to reload the car with the stolen goods while Jean-Louis watched on disapprovingly, having refused to help or touch anything. They continued to work under his stern gaze while Xavier observed the proceedings covetously.

'What about the jacket?' Sebastian asked, once everything was on board. 'We're going to have to take it with us. It'll have Maurice's DNA on it.' They all stared at the corpse, but no one moved until Amanda hurried off into the kitchen and returned with a pair of scissors.

Hesitantly, she approached the corpse and grimaced before stooping to cut along the sleeves and the back. Using only thumbs and forefingers, she delicately wrapped the pieces to best enclose the bloodied sections, then turned to the impressed but embarrassed men, the bundle held at arm's length.

Jean-Louis disappeared into the kitchen and returned with a shopping bag, which he opened for Amanda. She gave a sigh of relief at being able to let go of the sticky mess. 'Oh, thank you.'

'I burn,' he said, then told the three of them to go while he removed any incriminating fingerprints from the cellar and the ground floor. Dumas was ordered to remain outside until he and Jean-Louis had agreed their story for the inevitable police interrogation once the body was found in the house under Xavier's care.

Amanda was about to follow Maurice and Sebastian to the car when Jean-Louis caught hold of her arm and pulled her aside. 'Monsieur Maurice, I think maybe 'e is no correct.'

She frowned. 'How so?'

'*Il est avide…* ' Jean-Louis shook his head at the lapse into his mother tongue. 'I sink 'e is greedy. *Prenez garde!*'

***

15TH JANUARY

The following morning, it didn't take long for Selwyn to learn that Mac Bilton hadn't shown up for work at the quarry so, as a deviation from his usual walk with Mustard, he called round at Bilton's cottage. His precaution to take a spare key proved unnecessary as he found the front door unlocked after no response to his knock.

The commander poked his head round the door. 'Mac, are you there? It's Selwyn.' After a few moments of silence, he entered.

Everything ship-shape and Bristol-fashion, he thought, as he passed through the small living room into the kitchen; no doubt a reflection of Bilton's army training in the Sappers.

He moved on to the bedroom and rapped at the door. There was no reply, so Selwyn peeped in. The curtains were closed and the bed hadn't been slept in, though it looked to have been sat on. On the bedside table Selwyn spied Mac's watch, a couple of pills alongside a full glass of water, and a full cup of drinking chocolate, now stone cold. *Seems as if he was about to go to bed.*

Somewhat puzzled, and fearful about what might have happened to the man, he quickly checked out the other rooms, locked the cottage, untied Mustard's lead from the lamp post and set off in search of Bilton's car, which was in its usual parking space.

From there, Selwyn strode towards the quarry office and building. He didn't have to go far to find poor Bilton. At the deserted quarry pit, he saw a body floating face down in the water, a dark patch on the back and the bald head glinting in the sun.

Tempted as he was to try to retrieve the corpse, he knew to secure the access to the pit from any further traffic and personnel, then to alert the police – the implications of which he dreaded to consider.

***

If DI Stone had been exasperated at the discovery of Fred Ferris's body, he was positively incandescent when he learned that Mac Bilton had been found dead. Such was the vigour of his change-jingling as he stormed back and forth in his office letting off steam to his subordinate that the friction must surely have knocked ten per cent off the value of the coins.

'That blasted commander and his bloody estate's become the bane of my ruddy life,' he fumed. 'You'd better get yourself over there and interview the man. I'd probably lose my temper with him.'

McBride's response, that he didn't expect the commander had been personally responsible for the death, was met with a glacial scowl, so the DS quickly made himself scarce.

Accordingly, after the pathologist had confirmed that the probable cause of death was a stab wound that had pierced the heart, the grilling Selwyn received from DS McBride was of moderated severity. From the commander's initial observations at Bilton's cottage, coupled with McBride's own observations, the likely scenario was that Bilton had been disturbed by someone who'd led him away and murdered him at the quarry.

After the police had gone, Selwyn sat alone in the drawing room and nursed a large scotch as he reflected on the day's events and brooded once more about Miriam and how she'd so determinedly ended their relationship. The previous day, armed with a bouquet of flowers, he'd called at her house. His ring on the doorbell had remained unanswered, though her car was on the drive. Similarly, his mobile call to her had won no response. He'd left the flowers on the doorstep with a scribbled message on the back of the card.

He put the glass down and tried to call her yet again. His spirits soared as he heard her voice. 'Selwyn,' came the cold greeting.

'Miriam, at last. I came round yesterday evening. You

didn't answer.'

'No. I don't feel I have anything more to say to you. The flowers were a kind thought but unnecessary. They won't resolve anything.'

'They were there to say that I still love you. I always will. I need you in my life.' There was silence. At least she hadn't hung up – at least, he didn't think she had. He took a deep breath. 'Miriam, are you still there?'

'I'm here.' Her voice was shaky. She sounded subdued.

'Won't you at least see me and talk about things?'

'What is there to say that's not already been said? You've hurt me, Selwyn, and I won't give you the opportunity to do it again. Please don't try to see me or ring again. Goodbye.' Without giving him the chance to reply, she hung up.

He barely had a moment to feel despondent before Sebastian called and gave him the full, horrifying rundown of the past two days' events in Versain, throughout which Selwyn sipped liberally at his whisky and repeatedly apologised for not being there to protect the couple.

'At least we've now got the documents, bank details and the house deeds.' Sebastian sounded as if he hoped this more optimistic news would cheer Selwyn up.

'Yes, I suppose that's a step forward. So what's left to do? You must get out as quickly as possible.'

'Don't I know it. Jean-Louis says he's got the other chap firmly under control and briefed for when the police finally call round. The meetings are set up with the *notaire* and bank, so we have to stay for those. Maurice reckons everything will stall while they check the paperwork I give them, so we'll leg it home.'

'I expect he's right. What about the dead man? Any idea

who he was and who could have killed him?'

'None whatsoever.'

'God, it's a rum do! For goodness' sake be careful, my boy. Is Maurice looking out for you?'

'He's been great. I think he might have changed his mind about coming to Wisstingham.'

'Capital! That makes me feel much better. Just get yourselves back as soon as you can and tell him he'll be most welcome. And look after that girl of yours.'

A further unpleasant surprise was brought to him by Mrs Soames, who waddled into the drawing room bearing a pot of tea and two rich-tea biscuits, to which Selwyn afforded a scornful glance. 'No shortbreads?' he asked.

'Seein' as 'ow someone's seen fit to start raidin' my pantry and making off with things of high-calorific content, it's struck me as 'ow I need to introduce a bit of dietary discipline.' Her tone uncompromising, she fixed such a stare on the commander that he decided not to challenge the insinuation.

'Well, maybe the odd biscuit now and then,' he mumbled, while he simultaneously attempted in vain to nudge the whisky bottle by his chair out of sight with his foot. Mrs Soames spotted the move and glanced meaningfully at her watch, the usual time for aperitifs being still some way off.

'It might not be a bad thing for Sebastian to set up one of them there security cameras in the kitchen,' she threatened, but then softened. 'The 'ead of the council called.'

He groaned and subsided in his seat. 'But it's Saturday, dash it! Does bureaucracy never rest?' Without really listening to the rest of what Mrs Soames had to say, he grumpily took the number she'd scribbled on a scrap of paper, promised to call for an appointment and sank further into his seat.

*** .

On the journey back to England, the nervous tension in Selwyn's Jaguar was almost palpable as it headed along the French autoroutes. The boot was laden with the stolen goods, hidden beneath their cases and coats, Amanda sat in the front passenger seat next to Sebastian while Maurice's generous frame lolled across the rear seats.

Amanda's unusually prolonged silence made Sebastian wonder whether it was due to her concern for what they were carrying or their passenger. Certainly, Maurice's conversation was almost invariably directed to him, interspersed with lengthy silences where he appeared to be plunged in thought.

On the eve of their departure from Versain, they'd dined at the Panouille restaurant. Throughout the meal, Maurice had expressed a great deal of sympathy to Amanda over her ordeal and complimented her several times on how well she'd borne it. His comments, however, were received with polite indifference so the rest of the meal had continued somewhat starved of further conversation.

It was not until they'd booked into their first overnight stop at the Hôtel de la Poste in Langres that matters came to a head.

While Sebastian unpacked his travel case, Amanda stood abstracted at the window and stared out across the square. 'What's up?' he asked, after he'd lifted the overnight cases off the bed and stowed them away.

She turned to face him, wearing a worried expression that he'd seen a lot recently. She walked up to him and took hold of his hands. 'I reckon we are up to no good. We should have left those goods in that horrendous house where they belonged. I feel we're tainted by them. They're a part of Vincent's past. Not yours.'

'I explained – it's not as simple as that. Apart from fingerprints, which would at least tie Monaghan to the stuff, those items belong to people who deserve to be reunited with them. I reckon Selwyn and I have an obligation to try to make that happen. Anyway, you agreed.'

Amanda looked down. 'I know, but I've been having second thoughts. Monaghan aside, just think of all the people who've been involved in the loss of those goods in the first place. It's all very well taking them back with good intentions, but I think we're running a big risk of being landed in the soup without a *crouton* to cling onto. Why don't we just dump it somewhere? We're already on our way home, and for all we know the French police haven't found the body yet.'

'It was a calculated risk that they wouldn't, at least not before we arrive safely back home. Maurice told me the Versain police are pretty laid back. Mind you, I wouldn't bet on that weasel Xavier keeping mum for long once the gendarmes go calling, Jean-Louis or no Jean-Louis. Anyway, the dice are cast now.' He smiled and bent to kiss her.

Amanda's response was so far the only enthusiastic high point of the day, one which he didn't hesitate to take advantage of.

Later, after he'd uncorked the bottle of wine they'd brought and poured some into the flimsy plastic cups

Amanda found in the bathroom, they sat side by side on the edge of the crumpled bed.

'Are the stolen stuff and our dodgy situation the only things bothering you?' he asked.

'I can't say I'm delirious about our passenger.'

'Why? What's wrong with him?'

'I don't trust him, or his motives.'

'Why the hell not? He's a great bloke. What's he done to you?'

Amanda fell silent and stared at the floor.

'Well?'

'Nothing. He's done nothing.'

Sebastian frowned. 'Well, then—'

'There's just something about him. He's never once offered to share the driving with you. Just lolls in the back, yawning like a monkey.'

'Oh, come on! He's been a fantastic help. What's more, I reckon he's in a bit of a precarious situation.'

Amanda spluttered. 'Precarious? He's about as precarious as a swallow on a tightrope. I reckon he's got some ulterior motive in coming to the hall other than to see us safely home.'

Sebastian shrugged. 'He was invited. Anyway, how's he worse than the shady Frenchmen who helped us back there?'

To his relief, Amanda chuckled. 'Now Jean-Louis, I just love. He could be anyone from a pimp to a pirate, but he'd always be lovable. Talk about playing to the gallery! That man's a total performer in everything he does.'

'Well, I think you're wrong about Maurice. When you get to know him, you'll change your mind.'

'I'm quite happy with the one I've got, thanks. I think

I'd prefer to get to know Maurice's tailor – *he* must have a great sense of humour. Let's just agree to disagree. Hit me again with the vino-collapso, my good man.'

Sebastian smiled away his irritation, gave her a lingering kiss and reached for the bottle. Much as he loved the woman, he certainly wasn't looking forward to what was likely to be a strained journey home.

**

Archie lay on his bed. Having drained the last dregs of his hip flask, he'd moved on to the whisky bottle, the only other resident of his case to have seen the light of day. He stared at the undulations in the ceiling and recalled his thoughts immediately after the events at the French house.

The dead man had only seemed interested in Sebastian and the girl. Either her captor and his murderer had been villains who'd fallen out, or the second guy had been a hitman. That he hadn't touched any of the loot seemed to support that possibility. What's more, it struck Archie that, from behind, the dead man must have closely resembled him. If it was a case of mistaken identity, he'd had a lucky escape.

Now convinced that Cutler had taken out a contract on him, it was imperative that he moved on, and quickly. What with the Hillingden police after him, returning to England would be like going back into the lion's den. However, staying in Versain was clearly impossible. The gullible commander's offer to let him stay at the hall seemed his best option, particularly as that was where all that delicious loot was bound. At present, it was his *only* option.

His main agenda was threefold: to lie low; to ingratiate

himself with Fitzgerald and Sebastian, and to find a way to relieve them of as much of the spoils as he could. Both men appeared to have a good opinion of him – but the girl was a different kettle of fish.

Either he'd have to find a way of getting her onside, or deal with her in another way.

***

17TH JANUARY

On a grey and miserable Monday morning, Selwyn found himself being ushered into the council leader's office.

Tyson rose from his desk and smiled. 'Commander Fitzgerald, how delightful to meet you. I've heard so much about you, and Wisstingham Hall. All good, I hasten to add.' He shook Selwyn's hand vigorously and guided him to the conference table, papers clutched in his other hand.

As he sat, his generous smile evaporated and was replaced by an expression of mild concern. 'I've also been hearing one or two interesting stories about some documents relating to your estate.' He peered at Selwyn over his half-moon glasses.

'Oh, really? What would they be?'

Tyson's thin lips broke into a knowing smile. He glanced at the notes on his lap. 'Well, let me see. I understand you recently came into possession of a map and document that indicate certain estate land was deeded to the people of the village, as it was then and as it remains now.'

'In exchange for other land transferred to the estate by the authority of the day.' Selwyn kept his eyes firmly fixed on his adversary's.

'And which land would that be?'

'As yet, I've not located the deed in question. Perhaps you've retrieved it from your archives?'

'Sadly not that document, if indeed it exists at all,' Tyson said.

'It exists.'

'What interests us particularly is the deed you already have to hand. I understand the land not only includes the recreational park area currently leased to the council but further land within the estate boundary. Elusive reciprocal document notwithstanding, our legal expert is of the opinion that the deed transferring estate land to the village constitutes a gift and stands in its own right.'

Selwyn visualised the priceless stretch of the estate he stood to lose: the paddock and part of the stable block. He strove to maintain his composure and the poker face he'd adopted. 'Then clearly we have a divergence of opinion. The transfer is reciprocal. It's all or nothing. None of my land passes from estate ownership until the corresponding land passes into the estate's ownership. I trust that makes my position clear.'

Tyson straightened in his chair and folded his arms. 'I have to warn you that I expect we'll be advised to seek compensation if the council is obliged to take legal action to enforce the terms of the deed. I'm confident an amicable settlement would obviate the need for that – in which case, I'm sure the council would be far more sympathetic in its demands.'

'Good old-fashioned blackmail, eh?'

'Come, come, Commander Fitzgerald, we're both men of the world. It's just a question of being pragmatic.'

'Pragmatic, my arse! I'll see you all in hell before I give

up any land. And if you *do* pursue the matter, I promise that you and your cronies will have a battle royal on your hands. Good day to you, sir.' With that, Selwyn rose and marched out of the office.

***

Tyson checked his office door was closed and reached for his mobile. 'Russell, how are you?' he asked when McKaye, the council's wiry chief engineer and planner, answered. 'How are things proceeding with our mutual friend?'

'Hirst? Och, I've nae heard anything recently, but dinna worry. He's as sound as a bell.'

Tyson pursed his lips and nodded. 'He'll need to get a move on with the acquisition of the Fitzgerald land. Matters are likely to come to a head pretty soon, and we need to get the purchase and planning permission put to bed ASAP.'

'Which matters?'

'A potential dispute between the council and Fitzgerald – but keep that under your hat. It may get pretty messy if it goes to court.'

'Na hold on, Karl, you're beginning to make me nervous. There's a lot of money riding on this, and my job's at stake if things go wrong. Is there something I should know about?'

'Take it easy, Russell,' Tyson soothed. 'There's no need to worry about a thing. We're perfectly safe. You just need to nudge things along a bit.'

'OK, I'll have a word with the laddie.'

'There's a good fellow.'

***

Selwyn strode from the council offices towards the high street in a dogged frame of mind. He hadn't gone far before his equanimity was further disturbed by the sight of Miriam walking ahead of him. He immediately increased his pace to catch up, but the distance between them was too great. By the time she stopped outside the Mazawat café to greet and talk to a man who was evidently waiting for her, Selwyn was too far away to call out to her.

He stopped in his tracks and stared at his rival, who had now opened the café door for her. Just before he followed her in, he glanced in Selwyn's direction. The sight of the man's face came as a jolt to the commander, though he couldn't understand why; there was just something about the face that bothered him.

Selwyn grudgingly made his way back to the car park and set off for home. On his arrival, Mrs Soames immediately discerned he was preoccupied and unsettled. 'I reckon you'll be in need of a refreshing cup of Rosie,' she ventured as he hung up his coat and turned to the drawing room.

He stopped and cast a doubtful look at her. 'Rosie?'

'You know, Rosie Lee. Tea.' She looked perplexed. 'I says it often enough.'

'Oh yes, tea. Capital idea, that woman.' He was about to continue down the hallway when it struck him that the housekeeper might have had an innocent natter and cup of 'Rosie' with a few people around the estate at the time of Amanda's trip to France. He turned and asked, 'Mrs S, did you by chance tell anybody about Amanda's plan to surprise Sebastian in Versain?'

Her look of indignation should have been enough to

dispel the notion. 'Certainly not!' she retorted. 'What *do* you take me for to be accusing me of gossipin' like that?'

Selwyn raised his palms. 'I'm sorry—'

'I never heard such a thing!'

'Sorry, it's just that someone clearly knew she was travelling there, and the very day and time she was going to arrive. Amanda's adamant that she told no one apart from yourself, except for her nan, and that was virtually at the last minute. It's most bizarre.'

'Well, it certainly wasn't me,' Mrs Soames insisted, huffily. She turned and shuffled off, enveloped in muttered protestations of innocence.

Selwyn escaped to the drawing room, fearful it would take most of the afternoon and good measures of tact, diplomacy and further apology to restore the dear lady's good humour.

Chapter 10

If Amanda looked relieved to be back home once more, it was nothing compared to how Sebastian felt as the Jaguar finally passed through the gates of Wisstingham Hall. Hardly had he and Maurice reached the top of the steps before the creaky front door opened and Mrs Soames rushed out, as fast as ever she could rush. She flung her arms round Sebastian and crushed him to her ample bosom.

'Oh Sebastian!' she exclaimed shakily. 'The things I've been hearing wot's bin 'appening to you and our Amanda, you poor mites.'

By now, a smiling Selwyn had joined them and was shaking Maurice's hand vigorously. 'I'm delighted you came, my dear fellow. Do come in. Mrs Soames, allow me to introduce you to Maurice Fox, who's going to be our guest for a while and who's been a great help to us.'

The housekeeper released the relieved Sebastian and turned to face Maurice. She smoothed her hands down the sides of her apron. 'Very pleased to meet you, sir.'

Maurice smiled at her and gently shook her small, podgy hand. 'Do call me Maurice.'

She looked quite taken aback. 'Oh I couldn't be a-doin' that, sir. It'd be bein' far too familiar, Mr Fox.'

He beamed at her. 'As you wish, dear lady.'

Mrs Soames simpered, then stood aside as the commander led them into the hall. After Maurice was shown to his room and left to settle in and unpack, Selwyn wasted no time in asking Sebastian when he might expect to hear from the *notaire*.

'There's no firm indication of timescale. It could take weeks.'

It was a reply that Selwyn clearly didn't want to hear. 'Then goodness knows what we're going to do in the meantime. It's going to boil down to selling some of the paintings and furniture, which'll put Mrs Soames in a blue funk, or selling one of the horses, which will reduce our racing revenue. It's all a bit of bad show. Could be a very close-run thing. Let's jolly well hope France comes good, and soon.'

***

Karl Tyson read and re-read the email Marcia Pincher had brought him. It was a thing of beauty, making it entirely clear that his nemesis had been made aware of the coveted documents and chosen to exonerate the librarian, to boot. He broke into a smile. 'I do believe this is what I was looking for. Congratulations, Marcia, you've done an excellent job.'

She coloured slightly and smiled back at him.

Tyson rose from his chair. 'Now, not a word to anyone about this, eh? This is strictly our little secret.'

'Indeed. You can count on me, sir.' The interview over, she made her way to the door.

'I won't forget this, Marcia,' he called after her.

His smile dropped the second the door was shut. Once alone, Tyson scrutinised the email again. He had two birds targeted with one stone: a means of applying pressure to the Fitzgeralds by punishing the feisty librarian, and an opportunity to destroy what was left of

Cheyney's precious mayoral year.

A good day's work, all considered.

***

After a lavish breakfast, during which Mrs Soames danced happy attendance on their new guest, Selwyn and the ever-eager Mustard took Maurice on a stroll round the grounds. When they arrived at the lake garden, they took a seat on the commander's favourite bench. The grass sparkled with droplets of dew. Thin banks of grey cloud hovered below a brightening blue sky. On the lake, ducks busied themselves in search of sustenance. Somewhere, the shrill cry of a curlew pierced the tranquillity.

'I'm really pleased you decided to come here after all, my dear chap,' said Selwyn. 'I'm most grateful for the support you gave Sebastian and Amanda through all that horror.'

'Don't mention it, though it *was* pretty bloody. I'm only too pleased to have helped and to be here. It's kind of you to have me.'

'Nonsense. Now while you're here, I've a car you can use if you want to get about. A Volvo. It was my son's, and I couldn't bear to part with it. I should warn you it's got some age to it. It coughs a touch in first gear, but it still runs well and you'll be covered on the estate's insurance.'

'That's jolly decent of you.'

'Not at all.'

For a while they watched with amusement as Mustard scampered around. For the commander, it brought back fond memories of the puppy's forebear.

'How are things holding up with the estate?' Maurice ventured.

Selwyn grimaced. 'It's touch and go, I'm afraid. I might have to sell one of the horses as well as some of the furniture, though it'll be a tussle winkling any of that out of Mrs Soames' clutches. She's very attached to it all. Everything hinges on Sebastian getting access to Monaghan's account – providing, of course, the missing money's there.'

'Look, my dear fellow, I really shouldn't impose on your hospitality at a time like this. Perhaps I should—'

'Balderdash! Things aren't so bad we can't have a guest stay with us. Anyway, I'll enjoy your company.'

'If you're really sure… '

'I am. You're welcome to stay as long as you like and that's an end of it.'

On their return, Selwyn took Maurice on a tour of the hall. The last room was the library, where his guest's attention was immediately drawn to the old chest nestled in the corner. Piled on top and stacked alongside it were numerous parchments and scrolls.

'So, Maurice, these are the documents and maps that caused all the mayhem when Monaghan tried to get his hands on some of them. I've not seen hide nor hair of the reciprocal transfer documents referenced in the first set that caused all this trouble.' He shrugged, embarrassed. 'Could be right in front of me, of course, but the writing's all double Dutch to me. Oliver Cromwell had probably just sprouted his third wart when this lot was drawn up.'

Maurice stroked his beard and peered at the piles of scrolls. 'Look no further, my dear fellow.'

'You mean you can understand this sort of stuff? Of course, I was forgetting. You read history at Oxford.'

'I'd be only too delighted to have a look at them. It's the

very least I can do in return for your hospitality.'

'That would be fantastic. And, if you could, please also keep your eye out for anything that might have a bearing on the missing family treasure.'

'Leave it all to me. If there's anything here, I'll find it.'

'Excellent!' The commander glanced at his watch. 'Let's go and persuade Mrs Soames to rustle up some refreshments, shall we?'

'Splendid idea. Top hole.'

Archie cast a fleeting, eager glance at the documents as the commander led him from the room, mentally congratulating himself on this unexpected chance to justify his prolonged presence at the hall and possibly benefit from what he might discover.

**

While the council leader had been generous with his smiles for her boss, there were certainly none on offer for Amanda when she was summoned to his office. She had hardly sat down before Tyson cut to the chase. 'Miss Sheppard, I understand you came across a map and document with profound implications for this council.' His narrowed eyes were fixed on hers, his lips tight.

Amanda flushed. She was stunned. Although she'd been apprehensive as to why she'd been summoned, in view of the mayor's assurance, she'd never suspected it might be about the documents. Miriam had betrayed her. Nevertheless, she resolved to stand her ground and appear as unflappable as she could. 'That's correct. They belonged to Commander Fitzgerald of Wisstingham Hall.'

'I'm well aware of who he is and where he comes from,' came the icy reply. 'I believe you made Councillor

Cheyney aware of their existence.'

'No.'

Tyson's eyes narrowed. 'Please explain why not.'

'I intended to make her aware of them, but she said she'd no interest in them, whatever they were. I was to do with them as I thought fit. I think she assumed they were part of some exhibition that had fallen through.'

'And what *did* you do?'

Amanda shifted in her chair. 'I returned them to the commander, from whom they'd been taken without his knowledge.'

'And how were you to know they belonged to him in the first place?'

'Because they were found on *his* land amongst papers that related to *his* estate,' Amanda replied firmly.

'Nevertheless, your failure to alert the council to their existence constitutes a gross dereliction of duty, Miss Sheppard. A betrayal of such magnitude that it would not surprise me if you were dismissed, or at least invited to resign.'

Amanda inhaled deeply, her resolve wavering. 'I assume that would be a matter for my superior and Councillor Cheyney to consider,' she prompted.

'Hardly Councillor Cheyney,' sneered the leader. 'I think *she* has enough problems of her own in relation to this affair.'

'How do you mean?' Needing to learn as much as she could, Amanda remained even-toned. She feared Tyson would cut her short but hoped his vanity and feeling of self-importance would lead him to disclose more.

Tyson gave way to a self-indulgent smile. 'Not that it's any business of yours, Miss Sheppard, but we have a copy of the councillor's email to you, which clearly shows she was aware of the documents albeit after the event.' He handed Amanda a copy. 'So the councillor herself owes an explanation or two.'

Amanda's relief that she'd not been betrayed by the mayor was overshadowed by anger at Ms Pincher, who was surely the instigator of her present dilemma. *That shifty, fat frump. I'll make her life a living hell while I can.*

She met Tyson's gaze. 'I assume you've found the council's own copies of these documents?'

'Not yet. They are being searched for, as we speak.'

'And what of the other papers? The ones granting land back to the estate?'

'I think the location of those is a matter for Commander Fitzgerald to pursue rather than us. He's certainly got no claim if he can't find them. Our legal eagles are quite firm on that.'

'That should make for some interesting reading in the local press,' Amanda commented. '"Local council, unaware of and unable to find its own important documents, sacks librarian for return of documents to their legal owner and seeks to enforce one-sided deal."'

The leader's eyes widened momentarily. 'I don't think that's a line you'd be best advised to pursue, Miss Sheppard.'

Her hackles now up, Amanda leaned forward slightly, her eyes firmly on his. 'Whatever line I decide to take, I shall certainly not go gently into that good night.'

'Very well. I shall instigate the appropriate investigation through the HR department. In the meantime, I strongly advise you to say nothing to anyone and to go about your duties until further notice.'

Thus dismissed, Amanda strode out of the building, her morale low but her determination to fight exceedingly high. By lunchtime, however, her adrenaline had quite abandoned her. She stared at the sandwich she'd hardly touched and brooded on recent events. She was about to lose her job. Her nan was getting steadily worse. Hector's farm was driving her into the ground. She had a fiancé sitting on a horde of illegal booty...

'What else could possibly go wrong?' she murmured. That she'd spoken too soon became evident moments later when her smartphone alerted her to a message from Martin.

> *Hi Amanda, sad news. Aunty Hilda passed*
> *away last night from a stroke. I'm returning*
> *to Wisstingham ASAP. Will stay at Penrose*
> *Cottage in her old spare room. If there's*
> *anything urgent that won't wait till I arrive,*
> *could you please step in?*

'Of course I will,' she whispered through tears that she'd been fighting since the meeting with the leader.

***

'I can't say I'm looking forward to handing all that stuff over to Stone,' Selwyn remarked at the dinner table.

Archie stopped chewing and glanced at him.

'Tell me about it,' agreed Sebastian. 'I'm still worried he'll try and throw the book at us for being complicit.'

'He's got a point,' Archie added. 'Wouldn't it be better to hold fire for a while?'

'No,' Selwyn insisted. 'The longer it's left, the more suspicious it'll seem. That's certainly something the police would home in on. The quicker we hand it over, the sooner we might get some of the reward money.'

'If Stone agrees to it,' Sebastian warned. 'If he puts the kibosh on that, we'll really be struggling. It could be ages before we hear from the *notaire*.'

'We've a better chance of getting the reward if we act responsibly. Anyway, thanks to Wisstingham Prancer's performance and the stables, our heads are still above water. Also, the deal with Hirst for that land should go through pretty soon.' Selwyn turned to their guest. 'Food not to your liking, old boy?'

Archie, who'd been staring silently at his plate, looked up and surrendered a faint smile. 'No, it's fine. I just seem to have lost my appetite.' His thoughts were focused on what time in the early hours he'd try to filch some of the stolen goods before it was too late. Just a few of the smaller items to ensure they'd not be missed.

Chapter 11

The following morning, DI Stone surveyed the pile of goods Sebastian and Selwyn had unloaded from the Jaguar and placed on the interview room table. He scratched his head. 'And you say this lot came from Versain, where Monaghan had stored them?' The stare he gave Sebastian was not to the commander's liking. 'When was this?'

Sebastian told him.

Stone slowly nodded his head. 'Well, well. That's just round the time the French police found one of our well-known London villains dead. A chap called Slade. And in the same village.' He eyeballed the commander, missing the sight of Sebastian's mouth gaping open. 'An all-stations' bulletin. That's how we found out.'

Selwyn noticed that Sebastian was nearly ashen and sought to keep the DI's attention. 'Where did they find him?'

'Some holiday home owned by a Brit. Chap called Stavely. He's already been contacted.'

'Can't say I know of anyone by that name,' said Selwyn.

Stone looked at Sebastian, who shook his head. 'It can only be that the dead villain was connected to Monaghan's operation. It sounds like he might have been on your tail all along.'

'Bloody hell!' exclaimed Sebastian.

Stone looked from one man to the other and then to

the pile of stolen goods. 'I don't believe either of you are assassins, and I suppose you did the right thing in bringing that lot in, but you may have got yourselves into something deep whether you like it or not. If there's anything that you've not already told me, now's the time.'

'There's absolutely nothing,' the commander assured him.

Stone glanced between the two of them again then narrowed his eyes. 'So *this* was the business lead that took you to France, was it?'

'Sebastian had to tie up the loose ends that Monaghan left behind. He's not had an easy time. I wasn't going to land him with more questions from you. We've done what we thought was right.'

Stone stared at him, then closed his eyes and nodded.

Encouraged by the response, Sebastian piped up, 'Since we've effectively recovered the stolen goods, we want to lay claim to any reward that's been offered by the owners when they get their things back.'

The DI gave an incredulous snort. 'Considering how they were lost in the first place, I think you've got more neck than a giraffe in asking that.'

'Nevertheless, the theft was nothing to do with us and the estate's been left in desperate financial straits by Monaghan's actions,' Selwyn argued.

Stone glanced at these two pains in his backside and weighed it all up. Much as he wanted to refuse, a reward would be above board; it might backfire on him if the commander chose to complain to Nelson. Also, if it kept them both on side, he'd have a better chance of getting their further cooperation and information. 'Alright,' he conceded. 'I'll do what I can.'

***

Berensen looked at the caller's number and frowned.

'It's me, Cutler. About the contract you said you'd ful-filled.'

'Yes?' Berensen replied warily.

'The consignment you sent was the right one but from the wrong supplier.'

Berensen went quiet for a moment. 'Are you sure?'

'Absolutely. My friends in high places assure me they know who your actual supplier was. You need to deal with the *right* supplier, as soon as possible.'

The hitman screwed up his eyes and pressed the back of his hand firmly against his mouth. That he'd messed up was bad enough, but his commitment to another contract made things so much worse. He furiously played over in his mind the events of the kill: the appearance of the hit, Fox's hat and jacket. And the limp. The light had been poor, but he should have scrutinised the face more closely. He hadn't because of the watch, which he now realised must have been taken from Fox, who was still alive.

'Berensen, are you still there?' Cutler's voice sounded cold and impatient.

'Yes, I am here. I am apologetic. It will be dealt with immediately.'

'It better had be. Keep me informed of progress or I may need to hand things over to someone else.'

'That will not be necessary.' Mortified, Berensen rang off, fully aware of the chilling consequences of failure.

He dropped into an armchair and softly tapped the mobile against his cheek as he pondered who the dead man might be and his connection with Archie Fox. Where was he to start – France or Britain? If Fox were still alive, it was unlikely he would hang about in Versain; he stood out as a foreigner and it had been his clothing, and thus his DNA, on the dead man. Fox would need to get out of France, and Spain would not be an option. No, it was more likely that he would return to Britain.

Berensen decided he'd check the local French news. Then, if there was nothing about Fox, he'd start at the man's last known address in Cusham.

***

About to abandon the wait and drive away, Jean-Louis had just stubbed out his fifth cigarette when he saw Xavier come out of the *gendarmerie*. He breathed a sigh of relief that the man hadn't been detained.

Once Xavier left the car park, Jean-Louis tailed him into the countryside until they reached a remote spot on the edge of a vineyard. The two men sat in Jean-Louis' Citroën, which was soon engulfed in the smoke from their Gauloises.

'What happened?' Jean-Louis demanded.

'It was as we agreed. I told them I did not know the man, that he just turned up and asked for somewhere to rent for a week. So I let him into the place.'

'Did they ask how he knew to contact you?'

'Yes, and I said I did not know. He must have had a recommendation.'

Jean-Louis spat contemptuously out of his window. 'Did they ask about the payment?'

'Yes, I told them he paid cash—'

'And they want to see it?'

'Yes. I told them I gave most of it to you. That I owed it to you for some work you did at our house.'

'You bastard!'

'I could not think what else to say,' whined Xavier. 'I knew you would think of something. You're clever like that.'

Jean-Louis, now well and truly *en colère*, looked daggers at Dumas as he began to grapple with this new problem. 'You have the cash?'

'Most of it. Except for one hundred euros.' Xavier edged away timorously.

'Cretin! Where is it?'

'At home.'

'Then bring it here. I will make up the difference, go to the bank and deposit it in my account. The police will have nothing to search for fingerprints.'

'And then?' Xavier looked fretful about this new departure.

'Then later, at a suitable date, I will take out half of the money and give it to you. The rest I will keep for the trouble you have caused me. Now go!'

'Thief!' protested Xavier but said nothing more under Jean-Louis' intense glare. Instead, with every possible gesticulation of silent protest, he left the car and set off for home.

***

'I thought it would be more discreet to meet here than in my office,' Karl Tyson said as he passed a glass of tonic water to Gerald Cheyney.

A silk scarf draped casually round his neck, Cheyney was a tall man of slim build. His full head of silver hair was styled immaculately, and his white, near-perfect teeth gleamed. With clear, steel-grey eyes, an aquiline nose and sharp facial features, he merited his position as one of the country's prominent mature models. Alas, his rather high-pitched voice was both a surprise and something of a flaw in his overall image.

'On the phone, you mentioned my ex-wife.' he said guardedly.

'Yes. It's a rather delicate matter.'

'Go on.' Cheyney's brow was knitted in apprehension.

'Well, not to put too fine a point on things, the issue is Mrs Cheyney's behaviour as a councillor.' Tyson noted with satisfaction the flicker of annoyance that crossed the other man's face at the mention of her title. 'The thing is, trouble is brewing for her and I want to ensure that she's given every possible benefit of the doubt. Consequently, I thought it might be useful to have a chat with you.'

Gerald Cheyney's face registered disdain. He took a large drink. 'I'm afraid there's not much you'll get from me that'll be in her favour, and that's putting it mildly.'

Bingo! Tyson raised his eyebrows in question.

'I must warn you, we parted on very bad terms. I hate the bitch. She was determined to pursue her career. I'd expected we'd have children.' He broke off and stared thoughtfully at his glass. 'Well, there were none,' he added bitterly. 'She was just too busy. I felt totally cheated, and the marriage fell apart.'

'A family wasn't an unreasonable expectation, I suppose,' Tyson coaxed.

'You're dead right,' squeaked Cheyney. 'If she's going to get her comeuppance, that's just fine by me.'

'She has a very successful internet business, has she not?'

'Yes, principally selling clothing. Why do you ask?'

Tyson ignored the question. 'Mostly sourced from abroad, I should think.'

'I believe so.'

'With the attendant cheap labour that involves, I imagine.'

Cheyney looked intrigued. 'Go on.'

Tyson leaned in towards him. 'To be perfectly frank, I want to see her gone from the council. What she's been up to fully justifies that, but she's a gutsy woman and I foresee I'll have a battle on my hands.'

Cheyney smiled as realisation finally – and pleasantly – dawned. 'If there's anything I can do to help, you can count on me – but off the record.'

'I thought perhaps a two-pronged attack. Discredit on both a personal and professional basis might serve to weaken her resolve.'

Cheyney grinned. 'Ah, I see what you mean. You go for the council business and I lay in with the slave-labour aspect. I do have one or two contacts who could do a good hatchet job. I must admit, such an angle had never occurred to me.'

Tyson smiled back at him. 'I also have one of our council officers working on another front looking for any irregularities. Between us, I'm sure we can find a happy outcome. I do believe we're ready for another round. After all, we've quite a bit to discuss.' He rose to return to the bar.

***

Archie looked up from the manuscript he'd been engrossed in and gazed out through the stone-mullioned window across the lawn to the mature sycamores on the edge of the wood and the long shadows they cast. He glanced up at the nests silhouetted in the bare, upper-tree branches, from which a crow flew. Below the trees, the pale January sunshine reflected off the carpet of fallen golden and brown leaves. In the distance, Fox could make out the shimmer on the lake beyond the garden he'd taken to sitting in while helping the commander to walk Mustard. He gazed out on the scene for several minutes before he turned his attention back to the desk.

Interesting though the documents were, they shed no light on the transfer of the Wisstingham common land to the Fitzgerald family. His thoughts turned to his plunder from the stolen goods, which was now carefully stowed at the bottom of his valise. He had squirrelled away some very choice pieces, but it certainly didn't look like their absence had been noticed.

He felt safe enough ensconced at the hall. Both Fitzgerald and Sebastian were very much on his side, as indeed was the dragon of a housekeeper, though she'd certainly not breathed any flames in his direction thus far. On the contrary, he had her eating out of the palm of his hand. Accordingly, all seemed fine – other than for the Sheppard girl. She was the chink in the armour, the fly in the ointment, a smart young filly and not afraid to speak her mind, more was the pity. If anything, her hostility towards him appeared to have grown. A solution had to be found.

Archie had witnessed a couple of occasions when she and Sebastian had been at odds at the mention of some chap called Martin. Maybe the answer was to drive a wedge between them over him. Sebastian seemed pliable enough.

Whatever else, Archie recognised he needed to stay close to the commander and remain in his good books. Not difficult, he thought. They had enough in common – or at least Fitzgerald believed so.

***

Selwyn paced slowly along the darkened hallway, which was lit only at intervals by the fading afternoon light that filtered through the leaded windows,. He paused at every painting and item of furniture and studied it to re-assess its potential worth and whether he could part with it. Instead, he found himself drawing memories of earlier times from each item. Memories of his various lives: as a young boy, forever scampering about the hall to the eternal consternation of the frosty housekeeper, Mrs Everett; during his occasional returns home as an Oxford undergraduate and then a naval officer; a few years later as the newly-wed husband of the ravishingly beautiful Georgina; next, the proud father of the scampering Felix, and then…

Where had all those years gone?

His mood grew more sombre as his thoughts drifted to the darker, more recent history of death, betrayal and decay, an apparently steady downward spiral.

At the staircase, he thought of Miriam and how impressed she'd been when she'd first ascended it with him and gazed in awe at the family portraits. As his eyes travelled up the staircase and along the walls, Selwyn found himself drawing comparisons between Miriam and his late wife, which further unsettled him.

He approached one of the suits of armour and ran his finger across the breastplate as he dwelt on the missing family treasure he now doubted he would ever see. Not only the treasure, but possibly the future of the hall, the estate. These, and indeed his own future, hung in the balance and were dependent on Sebastian's success in France. Only that morning Selwyn had agonised over which bills could be deferred for payment, if only for a week or two more.

'I 'opes as how you're not makin' a spot inspection of my cleanin', Commander. Them's on tomorrow's roster.'

Startled, Selwyn quickly withdrew his hand and turned. 'By no means, Mrs S. I was miles away, reminiscing.'

'There's a tray of ginger cake not long out of the oven. Can I tempt you to a slice?' She gave him an appraising look. 'Maybe even a couple, with a cuppa?'

He smiled and nodded. 'First-class idea, Mrs S. That would be very pleasant. I think it's still light enough for the garden room.'

Much relieved, Beatrice Soames gave Selwyn a mock curtsey and bustled off to the kitchen, pleased that she'd lightened his gloom – at least for the moment.

***

'I'm sorry I'm late,' Amanda blustered as she hurried into the room.

Sebastian directed his gaze from the television screen to his flustered fiancée. 'That's alright, dinner's keeping warm in the oven. It might be a bit dried up by now, though.'

Amanda came up and knelt by his leg. 'I'm so, so sorry.' She smiled into his disgruntled face and rubbed her hand along the top of his thigh. 'I was longer at the farm than I thought I'd be.'

'In case you'd forgotten, this was supposed to be a special meal to celebrate moving back into my old cottage. At least you could have rung.'

'Yes, I know. I'm sorry. I got so involved with the paperwork that I lost track of time. Come on, grumpy chops. Give me a smile.'

Sebastian forced one. Amanda rose and kissed him fully on the lips. It was a kiss that would normally have lingered but not on this occasion, as indeed on several previous occasions recently.

Sebastian broke away and rose from the settee. 'I'll go and dish up.'

Amanda shrugged and followed him into the kitchen.

They ate in silence. He ignored her glances as he devoured his food, his concentration focused on the plate and its dwindling contents.

'You do still love me, don't you?' she asked eventually.

Sebastian stopped chewing and stared at her. 'Of course I do. What makes you ask that?'

'Well, you don't seem as interested as you used to be.'

'What do you mean "interested"?'

'Sebastian, are we on the same planet? *Interested*. Kisses and cuddles. How was your day? What would you like to do tonight? If I start taking my clothes off, will you drag me off to the bedroom? *Interested*.'

He gave her exasperation short shrift. 'You're hardly ever here to talk to, let alone to be dragged off anywhere.'

'That's because I've got a lot on. Not only my job, which is pretty pants at the moment, but doing my bit in running the farm and visiting Nan.'

'And?'

'And what?'

'And spending time with dear Martin.' Sebastian almost spat out the words.

Amanda placed her knife and fork neatly on her plate and sat back slowly in her chair. 'So that's what this is all about,' she said softy. 'You're being a jellybags again.'

'No, I'm not,' he snapped. 'You're just never away from the ruddy bloke.'

'As it happens, I'm spending time with him to try and sort out his late aunty's cottage and affairs.'

The last word jarred. 'Quite an *affair* then, is it?'

'Facetiousness does not become you, Sebastian. And if you don't cheer up a bit, I'll make you spell it.'

Sebastian glowered at her for a moment but then couldn't help grinning. She'd always been fast on the draw.

'Thing is… ' Amanda's face contracted into a grimace. 'I said I'd go over this evening to sort through her things for tomorrow's jumble sale.'

Sebastian's shoulders drooped. 'Oh, I don't believe it! When?'

'Well, about now.'

Now it was Sebastian's turn to sit back in his chair, all humour having deserted him. 'Then you'd better go.'

Amanda rose, came over to his side of the table and kissed him on the lips again. At the doorway, she turned. 'For what it's worth, I could think of nothing I'd prefer to do than stay here, drag you upstairs and bonk your brains out.'

'Ditto,' he replied and blew her a kiss, though once the door closed a cloud of resentment smothered the rest of his evening.

Chapter 12

Selwyn put aside the list he'd been compiling as the draw-ing-room door opened and in walked Sebastian and Amanda. Pleasurable though it always was to see them, this particular unannounced visit rankled slightly. It had been a wearing day.

At that morning's inquest into Mac Bilton's death, the coroner had arrived at a verdict of murder by person or persons unknown. This, coupled with the ongoing police investigation into Fred Ferris's death now hampered further by the death of the one person whom DI Stone believed to have been involved, once more focused entirely the wrong kind of attention upon the Wissting-ham estate.

It was with a heavy heart that Selwyn had finally left the court and made his way home. Having arrived back at the hall and pestered Maurice on his progress with the documents, which had yielded zilch, Selwyn had embarked on another thorough search for saleable items. He'd been conscious all of the time of Mrs Soames' eagle eyes following his every move.

'And to what do I owe the pleasure of this visit?' Selwyn asked the young couple who were now sitting across from him.

Amanda glanced at Sebastian then began to speak. 'I have a proposal for you. We all know that things are very

177

tight for the estate at the moment. If Sebastian can get the money back, though, it'll be a different story. For me, running the farm on top of my own job is proving both time-consuming and tedious. The foreman's a great help, but I'm not certain that between us we're doing the best we could. What I'd like to explore with you is the idea of the farm's management being incorporated with that of the estate, at least for a trial period. It would provide some additional income for you and relieve me of a lot of pressure.'

The commander stared at her, overwhelmed by this gesture that could rescue him. He sent off his tongue on one of its oral jaunts to distract himself from the tears he feared might well up.

'Commander?'

'That's an amazingly generous offer, Amanda,' he replied eventually.

'There are a couple of conditions, though. The first is that the foreman, Kevin, retains his job. The second is that I need a modest income to cover Nan's costs at the home.'

'That's only fair and reasonable. Was this all your own idea?'

Amanda looked slightly sheepish. 'It was Sebastian's, really. We had a long chat this morning.'

'It sounds an eminently sensible idea, which will benefit both the farm and the estate. We'll make an estate owner of you yet, my boy.'

'There is one other thing… ' Amanda looked hesitant. 'About Councillor Cheyney.'

Selwyn sat up, his whole being alert at the mention of Miriam's name.

'I've brought a copy of the local rag. There's a scathing article about her and her internet company. It seems that someone's really got it in for her and is accusing her of profiting from foreign sweatshops.' She handed him the paper, opened at the article.

Selwyn fumbled for his reading glasses. It made for horrible reading. 'Good Lord!' he murmured, as he lay aside the paper.

'What's more, the council leader and one or two other councillors also appear to have it in for her over the land transfer documents.'

'Oh crikey!' sighed Selwyn.

'Rumour has it that they're trying to oust her from the council and usher Geoffrey Hirst into her place.'

'Hirst? He's the chap who's buying some land from me for a market garden. Never liked the fellow. Got some dangerous notions that would spoil the village, I reckon. I've only agreed to sell because things are desperate.'

Sebastian looked grim. 'Amanda won't tell you but I will – her job's on the line for not having told the council about the documents.'

'Hell's bells! This gets worse and worse.'

'Never mind about that,' said Amanda. 'The most important issue is that if Tyson succeeds in pushing the mayor aside and getting Hirst on board, he'll have a very strong power base to do just as he likes.'

'Then I'd better see what I can do to help Miriam,' said Selwyn. 'That's if she'll let me.'

'By the way, what's happened to Maurice?' asked Sebastian. 'I haven't seen him for a while.'

The commander brightened. 'He's keeping himself busy going through all those old documents.'

A look of alarm flashed across Amanda's face. 'You're not trusting him with those, are you?'

'Why ever not?'

'Yes, he's a perfectly safe pair of hands,' added Sebastian.

Amanda's uncharacteristic silence unsettled Selwyn. 'Do tell me, Amanda. What makes you say that?'

'I don't feel he's trustworthy, that's all.'

'But why?'

'She's got some bee in her bonnet about him,' Sebastian interjected.

Amanda bristled. 'We don't know anything about him.'

'On the contrary, my dear girl,' insisted Selwyn, 'we know a great deal. An Oxford man, good public school, businessman—'

Amanda's eyes shot skywards.

'Now come on,' badgered Sebastian. 'He's worked for what he's got. At one stage he was reduced to living in a caravan at Frogsham Bay. What's most important is that he helped us out no end in France. We'd have really struggled without him.'

Amanda looked from one to the other as they stared at her and waited for her response. She shrugged. 'Well, I've told you what I think, and I won't change my mind. Not until I hear something far more convincing. Even Jean-Louis thought he was up to no good.'

Sebastian spluttered. 'Jean-Louis? He hardly had a good word to say about anybody, and I wouldn't rate him or Dumas as France's most law-abiding citizens.'

'I think we should draw a line under this topic,' the commander said, somewhat affronted at the apparent challenge to his character-assessment skills. 'As for the farm, I'll have a draft memorandum of understanding drawn up for us to go through to protect your interests as the owner, Amanda.'

She merely nodded.

As the couple said goodbye and departed with hardly a word to each other, Selwyn gave a slight shiver brought on by a chilliness that was not *only* due to the time of year.

***

21ST JANUARY

Selwyn's attempt to contact Miriam once again met with total failure. When his call went through to answerphone, his moment of happiness upon hearing her voice was only fleeting. He knew she wouldn't respond to his message.

His persistent ringing on the doorbell yielded no answer, though his visit did alert a busybody neighbour. Once she'd judged him to be trustworthy, the woman told him that Miriam had left several days earlier without saying where she was going. Nevertheless, he pushed a note through the door. A brief telephone conversation with her secretary informed him that she'd gone away for an unspecified period and wasn't taking any messages.

From there, his next destination was the Mazawat café, which he knew Miriam frequented regularly.

'Can't say I've seen her for a few days now,' Gwen said.

'And her gentleman friend?' Selwyn probed, the question a shot in the dark.

'Oh, Mr Cavannagh. Lovely fella. No, I haven't seen him around, either.'

'You don't by chance know where he lives, do you?'

181

Noting her concern and suspicion, Selwyn added quickly, 'Only the mayor appears to have gone away and there's something important she needs to know. Maybe he knows where she's gone?'

'Have you tried calling her?'

'No joy there, and she's not responded to my messages.'

'Well, I *can* tell you where Mr Cavannagh lives cos he's renting Osprey Cottage, what my uncle owns. Ship Lane, Frogsham harbour. It's got a red door. You can't miss it.'

Selwyn thanked her profusely, hurried back to his car and drove there. When he reached the cottage, he encountered a Scottish lady in tweeds who'd just locked up after an inspection. 'Och, the man left a few days ago, but I've no idea where he went,' she said.

The frustrated commander was a little less generous with his thanks than he'd been earlier in the day.

***

The bunch of flowers Martin presented to Amanda at Penrose Cottage was supposed to raise a smile, but instead the tears began to flow, tears that welled up from the murky depths of growing uncertainty.

Martin looked downright alarmed, as he always did when she was distressed. Rightly so, because here was a man who was kindness and consideration personified. Thoughtful and, although he'd never once referred to it after his first declaration, very probably still in love with her.

On the other hand, there was Sebastian, the man she loved, or at least believed she loved. Of somewhat rougher trade, nevertheless he had the boyish qualities and charm that had captivated her from the start. But he seemed to be tiring of her; certainly, he took her more for granted than she'd like. And if this were happening now, before they were married, what did the future hold for them? Amanda recalled the sight of elderly couples, seated on benches sharing not a word with each other, silent observers of the world around them. Was that all that marriage had to offer?

'I'm sorry, I never intended to upset you,' Martin apologised. 'It's just a small token of my appreciation for all you've done for me and aunty.' Since her waterworks were really turned on now, he fumbled in his pocket and offered a handkerchief, which Amanda put to good use.

'It was a lovely thought,' Amanda said, after she'd recovered, 'but I can't take them home. They'd send Sebastian spare.'

'So where are you living?'

'You tell me. Nan's cottage, the farm, the Monaghan cottage. All I need is the camel, then I'd be a proper nomad.'

'But surely he's not still suspicious of me?'

'He most certainly is.'

'Then he doesn't deserve you.'

'Careless talk, Martin, careless talk,' Amanda warned.

'Sorry. I know – I've got the perfect solution! Take the flowers to your nan. That way there are winners all round.'

'Brilliant idea, Martin. You're not just a charming cartographer after all.'

'Don't get me started.'

They smiled at each other; Amanda's faded first with the discomfort of the warmth that had momentarily passed between them.

Martin cleared his throat. 'You know, I would have

183

taken you out for a Chinese in preference to the flowers. Well, I'd have done both really. I so enjoyed those times at Qwik Qwak, but I suppose it wouldn't be a good idea now.'

'No.' Amanda's head bowed. 'I don't think it would. And yes, I enjoyed them too.' She glanced at him. 'I'd better go. Thanks for the flowers. You really shouldn't have.'

'It was my pleasure.' He followed her to the door and they stood on the threshold. 'Goodbye,' he said. 'Don't let the pressure get to you. You know I'm here for you whenever you need me.'

Amanda walked down the path and impatiently dashed away another tear from the corner of her eye. She got into the car and stared through the windscreen.

There was so much uncertainty in her life, yet no one to confide in. Martin was not the person for that. It would be unfair, and possibly unsafe, to burden him with her problems. She was unsure how much she could now trust her feelings. That was the trouble – there was no one to speak to, confide in, or seek advice from.

Or maybe there was…

***

Cusham is a small village on the outskirts of Hopestanding boasting three hostelries, each of which most pubgoers would give their eye teeth to have as their local. For many years the village was the focus for evening visits by eager diners from the wider locality until the drink-drive laws tempered the public appetite for trips out for pub meals. Nevertheless, two of the hostelries that offered accommodation still managed to attract a substantial clientele. Thus, it was at The Inquisitive Duck that Berensen chose to stay until he'd tracked down the elusive Archie Fox.

'Room five on the first floor,' the receptionist confirmed as she returned his passport, together with the room key. 'Will you be dining with us this evening?'

He nodded and booked a time. Having also ordered a newspaper for the morning, he made his way up the stairs and along the creaky corridor to his room. The morning's activities had met with limited success. Archie Fox's house was empty and had remained so for several weeks according to his enquiries. No one had any idea where Fox had gone or when he might return.

No matter, Berensen decided. He had the meal and the rest of the evening to formulate his plans to locate the fugitive.

***

Amanda didn't have to wait long for Kathy Turnbull to show up at the Ferret and Wardrobe. It seemed that her old friend was dead keen to get out of the office.

'Hello, Mandy. Penny for them,' Kathy said, noting Amanda's disquiet.

Amanda managed a feeble smile. 'I'd save my money, if I were you, though I'm glad you came. What are you having?'

'Better make it a spritzer. I'm on call, though it's been as dead as a dodo for the past few days.'

Amanda rose. 'Peanuts?'

'Is the Pope Catholic?'

Once they were settled, between mouthfuls and crunching Kathy persuaded Amanda to unburden herself. This she did, unfurling Sebastian's inattention and apparent indifference, Martin's charm and contrasting thoughtfulness, the pressures of visits to Nan and provision for her care, and all the uncertainty at work thanks to those bloody land transfer documents. Despite Kathy's insistence, she held back on giving the precise details of how she'd come to be hauled before the mayor and the leader in quick succession.

Everything received Kathy's agony-aunt attention. After all, that was one of her roles as a reporter on the *Hopestanding Chronicle*. 'You'd better be bloody certain that Sebastian's the guy you really want to spend the rest of your life with, Mandy, before you tie the knot.'

'I'm sure he is. It's just that I wonder how much he loves me and wants the commitment.'

'Strikes me you should make him feel there's some competition and see how he reacts.'

Amanda snorted. 'He's already seeing competition where there isn't any – that's half the problem. Besides, I wouldn't want to use Martin that way.'

'Are you sure you're not a bit smitten with him?' Kathy's eyes were questioning.

'Not at all. Well, no.' The lack of conviction in her reply surprised both of them. Amanda shook her head, grateful that Kathy didn't seem determined to pursue the matter further.

'Anyway, about your job situation... Tyson's a nasty piece of work. And dodgy, I reckon.'

'Do you know something I don't?'

Kathy stared thoughtfully at the empty, crumpled peanut packet. 'He features in something I'm currently investigating.'

'Really? Do tell all.'

Kathy scoffed. 'You're asking me that, and you're the one who won't confide in me? No way! I'll show you mine if you show me yours.'

Amanda laughed. 'Mine's better than yours.'

'OK,' said Kathy, 'if I tell you what I have, you *have* to tell me yours. But it's all strictly off the record. How about it?'

That seemed fair enough. Over a second drink, Amanda spilled all the beans. Her news of the transfer documents and description of the interview with Tyson proved so absorbing that Kathy's second packet of peanuts remained unopened in her hand.

'But this is just incredible!' she said finally. 'I'm amazed none of it has seen the light of day before now.'

'So, what about your investigation?' Amanda asked.

Kathy related how, subject to remaining anonymous, Suzie Lathom had provided copies of the photos she'd taken of the leader, the chief engineer and Geoffrey Hirst, some of which clearly showed cash being transferred.

'Hirst? That's the bloke who's supposed to be buying some of the estate land.'

Kathy sat up straighter. 'Is he indeed? That figures. There's a very fishy smell about all of this.'

'What do you plan to do?'

'There's not enough for an exposé yet. It's going to need something more for the paper to go up against the council – but I'd love to do a piece on *you* if the bastard does get you sacked.'

Amanda's attention had wandered off. Maybe … just maybe there was a way round all this on the basis that the enemy of her enemy might prove a friend.

'Hello, hello, is there anyone in?' Kathy prompted.

Amanda gave a quick shake of her head. 'Sorry, I was thinking. Do you know, I reckon there's a great opportunity here, and a bigger story. If you'll trust me, there's something I need to look into. It might take a few days.'

'That's a lifetime in my line of work.'

There was not much Amanda could do about that. She shrugged apologetically. 'I'll keep you involved and ensure the scoop's all yours. Promise.'

'You'd better, kiddo, otherwise I'll never forgive you.' Kathy glanced at her watch. 'I'd better go and show my face at the office.'

Seated alone at the table, Amanda racked her brains as to how she could win Councillor Cheyney over to her plan.

***

22ND JANUARY

It was over breakfast that Berensen got his lucky break. A veteran of hunting people down, he knew he'd eventually home in on his prey, but this was a rare and fortunate occurrence.

As he sipped his coffee, he glanced through the copy of the local paper that he'd picked up at reception. Page six made his week: it featured a photo of a local dignitary at the unveiling of a monument in Hopestanding. There, standing on the dais alongside Hopestanding's mayor, was Sebastian Fitzgerald, the young man he'd seen dining with Archie Fox back in Versain.

Berensen was sure of it. He peered closer and was gratified to have his recognition confirmed by the caption. The other man in the picture was evidently Commander

Selwyn Fitzgerald of Wisstingham Hall, Sebastian's uncle, no less.

That morning, breakfast tasted uncommonly good.

***

The sun shone palely on the bare branches of the elms and chestnut trees, and upon Jack Cavannagh's face. The comings and goings of a robin and a couple of blackbirds had fully occupied his attention as he sat on the bench by Mary's grave, a folded newspaper giving him a little protection from the damp wood.

Mary's gravestone was stained green in places, though the inscription's gold lettering still reflected the light well enough. Immersed in his memories, Jack failed to notice anyone approaching the bench until a shadow fell across his knees. He looked up and made to rise.

'No, please don't get up if you don't mind my joining you,' the young man said.

'Not at all.' Jack was about to offer some of his newspaper but stopped and smiled as the man took a magazine from inside his jacket to place on the bench. 'Great minds,' he observed.

'Yeah.'

There were a few moments' silence as the young man stared at the grave then turned in silent enquiry to Jack. He felt obliged to answer the unspoken question of why he was sitting there in particular. 'It's a lovely spot. I'm here on a visit, looking into the possibility of a documentary. Wherever I go, I always make a point of visiting the graveyard. They can reveal so much history. The name's Jack Cavannagh.'

'Sebastian...' He paused for an instant. 'Fitzgerald.' He

glanced at the gravestone. 'Well, it *was* Monaghan. It's complicated.'

They half-turned to each other and shook hands. 'I'm pleased to meet you.' Jack consciously moderated his voice to hide his enthusiasm.

'Likewise.'

'So is this is your mother's grave?'

Sebastian stared at the headstone. 'Yes. She died of cancer.'

'I'm sorry. And your father?'

Sebastian gave a snort. 'Vincent Monaghan's ashes were scattered elsewhere. It's a long story.'

'I've plenty of time, though I wouldn't want to pry.'

Sebastian stared at him for several moments.

Weighing me up, Jack assumed and gazed back. He wondered if his son would take the leap and confide in him. He felt a sort of bond, which he hoped Sebastian might also sense.

Although he seemed uncertain about doing so, Sebastian gradually opened up, starting with some terrible stories about the way Vincent Monaghan had treated him even when he was a child.

Jack sat silent and absorbed as Sebastian told all. 'My, my,' he said, when Sebastian had finished. 'What a hell of a time you've had of it.'

'Could've been worse, I suppose. I've got Amanda, who's fantastic, and the commander. He's great, just like a father to me.'

Jack swallowed the stab of jealous resentment. What a daunting task it would be to untangle the knotted skein created by his betrayal, lies and misinformation. Where to begin? Who to confide in first? He was so tempted to reveal his true identity, but he needed more time to think. 'So what are your plans for the future?'

'The first priority is to sort things out in France,' Sebastian said, 'but I do need to put the holiday cottage in Alstherham up for sale. It's about a hundred miles away, so it's hardly ever visited. Anyway, it means nothing to me. Just a place with bad memories.'

Having grown up there, Jack was surprised how hurtful he found this intention. 'Never a good thing to sell property if you don't have to.'

'I'm working on the basis that I *will* have to. If France doesn't come up trumps, the estate will need every penny it can get, and pretty damned quickly.'

'I suppose so,' Jack acknowledged reluctantly.

They lapsed into silence until Jack, sensing he might overstay his welcome, rose and picked up his paper. 'I'd better be getting along. It's been a real pleasure to meet you.'

Sebastian also rose. 'Same here. I hope we'll be back from France pretty soon. When we are, you must come and meet my uncle Selwyn and visit the estate – if you're still around, that is. I'm sure it'd be of great interest for your documentary.'

'I'd love to. I've no plans to move away in the foreseeable future. These things take quite a while to put together.'

They exchanged mobile numbers, agreed to keep in touch and shook hands.

***

Back in his new digs, a mobile home on a caravan park outside Hopestanding, Jack sat deep in thought. He'd talked to his son, his real son. Of that, there was now no doubt. But he hadn't had the courage to reveal he was really Lucian Fitzgerald; he was frightened of outright rejection.

He'd not reckoned on coming across Sebastian at Mary's grave, so he'd not been ready for the encounter. His son had to be the first to learn the truth, even before Selwyn, but how best to go about it? And now his old family home was to be sold, the home he and his cousin Vincent had lived in all those years ago.

Jack decided to visit the place one last time. The journey there and back would also give him time to come up with a definite plan of action.

***

23RD JANUARY

Whilst Harry Gaverty was devastated to learn of Ronnie's demise, Jock Cameron certainly wasn't. For years he'd played second fiddle to the Hammer, who'd always ensured that Jock never got access to the boss for a moment. There'd been no love lost between them, despite the mutual respect that came from knowing that the other was as hard and ruthless as himself.

A Glaswegian who'd made his way south when he found himself on the wrong side of a vicious and deadly turf war, Jock was proud of his hard-won toughness. He knew he was strong, so it didn't bother him that he was also thin to the point of gauntness. Nor did it bother him that his head and teeth seemed large in proportion to the rest of him. It added to his intimidation factor. Not that Harry was intimidated, of course.

'You bin around Ronnie and the organisation long

enough to know what's what,' said Harry. 'I expect you to look after my interests like 'e did. Understood?'

'Aye, boss.'

'I want you to go back to Wisstingham.'

At the mention of the place, Jock automatically sensed the presence of the knife strapped into his armpit sheath, its last outing having been at the quarry.

'Find out if Fitzgerald an' the Monaghan boy are there. If they are, they got stuff of mine I want back. *And* we've got a score to settle wiv 'em. Make out yer lookin' up your old friend Mac Bilton. That should get yer under their guard, him being dead an' all.' They both smiled at the irony of the suggestion. 'If they're there, don't hang about or get involved. Call me an' I'll come and join yer. Then we'll pay 'em a visit. Take yer shooter.'

'Aye, I'll do that.'

'I know you fuckin' will. Now go.'

***

Alstherham had changed so little since the last time he'd been there that Lucian had no problem finding his boyhood home, Mole End. The cottage looked tired and in need of much maintenance and care, and the front garden was completely overgrown. What a difference to the days when he'd grown up there with his mother after her divorce from Colonel Fitzgerald.

He remained seated in the car for a while and stared at the place. His mind conjured up memories, good and bad, of the years he'd spent there: mostly good when he'd lived there on his own, but not so much once his cousin Vincent had moved in.

Lucian walked down the path and tried the door, which

was locked. Through the grimy living-room window he could just make out the leatherette suite, similar to one he'd last seen in York's castle museum, many years ago.

Watch what you're getting rid of from here, Sebastian. Some of it's so antique it's probably worth a bob or two. It struck him that, by association, *he* must now be something of an antique, though certainly not so highly saleable.

At the rear of the cottage he peered into the kitchen where, according to Sebastian, Selwyn had endured his ordeal at Vincent's hands. *Why had the lad been so communicative about what had happened here?* The thought of Selwyn reminded Lucian of his failure to come up with a plan of how to reveal himself to him and Sebastian.

Lucian turned to view the back garden, which was also overgrown. So here was where Vincent had met his end, down the well. The same bloody well that, more than forty years earlier, had caused Lucian so much grief when little Kenny Budd had plummeted to his death.

It hadn't been his fault, Lucian had told himself for years. Not his fault, other than that he'd been Vincent's stooge, as always. Stooge, victim, puppet, any position of subservience on which his cousin decided, depending on his mood and circumstances. Lucian cursed the way his weakness had shaped and ruined his life. If only he'd been strong enough to wrest Mary from Vincent's grasp when he'd had the chance. But he'd not even been man enough to do that, much as he'd loved the woman. Instead, at her insistence, he'd fled.

Overcoming his natural inclination to stay away from the well, Lucian started towards it. A stone slab was in place, blocking the cavernous opening. As he stared at it, there came a voice from behind. 'Hey, you. What're you doing there?'

Lucian froze, recognising Sebastian's voice. He turned around slowly.

'Jack, is that you? What the hell are you doing here?'

Lucian tried to make light of things. 'Sebastian, what a surprise and coincidence.' He set off towards him. 'I was passing through and thought I'd call in and see the place you described.'

Sebastian looked perplexed. 'But I didn't tell you where it was. And why would *you* take an interest?'

By now, Lucian was in front of him. 'I made some enquiries. It's no big deal.'

Sebastian stared at him intently, then his eyes widened. The frown receded as recognition and realisation gradually dawned. He started to shake his head slowly, almost imperceptibly. His eyes narrowed. 'It's not that at all, is it? You're not Jack Cavannagh, are you?' He paused, appearing to struggle with his thoughts. 'You're – no, it's not possible.' He paused again, then his mouth slowly opened. 'You're Lucian, aren't you?'

Lucian took a deep breath then exhaled loudly, relieved that the charade was over. 'Yes.' He looked hopefully at Sebastian. 'It's me.'

Sebastian looked away, his eyes darting about as if in search of better comprehension. 'But you're dead.' He paced. 'No, you're bloody not,' he corrected himself. 'Where the hell have you been? Why didn't you tell us you were alive? What are you doing here now?'

The questions flowed thick and fast while Lucian watched his son in mounting anguish. 'I'm your father, Sebastian.'

'Father? What kind of a fucking father vanishes like you did? Not one I want anything to do with. Just get out of here and stay the fuck out of my life.'

Lucian held out his hands in supplication. 'Listen, please.'

'Listen nothing – you've not given me a thought for your whole life. Why the hell should I just welcome you back now? Just bugger off. For good.'

'No, you listen,' Lucian shouted back. 'Your mother sent me away when she found out she was pregnant with you. I had no choice but to go. Then I spent years in a Chinese jail for something that wasn't my fault. I couldn't say anything to anyone.'

'You spent nearly all that time in jail and not a word to anyone to say you were even alive?' Sebastian scoffed. 'Not much of a brother, lover or father, eh?'

'I wanted to write,' Lucian insisted. 'I really did. But before I got caught up in trouble, Selwyn had told me to stay away and communicate with nobody.'

'Your silence was *all* down to you,' Sebastian raged, 'and so was our suffering. None of it was my fault, but it was my mother and I who suffered from Monaghan. It's all too late now. I don't want to know you. Just clear off, for God's sake. Go!'

Lucian bowed his head. 'Alright. You may not want to know me, but there's Selwyn to consider and things to sort out. I need to tell him what happened, but in my own time and in my own way. I've not even figured that out yet.' Sebastian's unsympathetic snort made him flinch. 'Alright, so I've clearly ruined things with you, though I never intended to. I'll stay away – though it's the last thing I want to do – but just promise me you won't say anything to Selwyn till I've had a chance to tell him.'

Still scowling, Sebastian reluctantly nodded his agreement.

'I'll tell you when I'm going to see Selwyn, but please call me anyway. There's still much to talk about.'

***

On his return from Alstherham, Sebastian drove straight to the office to work late. He couldn't rid himself of Lucian's dejected expression and was torn between rage and frustration. How dare that absent sod tug on his heart strings like that?

He couldn't trust himself to hide his emotions, and feared discovery from Selwyn or Amanda. He needed time alone to think and come to terms with the day's encounter and revelation. However, as he opened his inbox, his spirits lifted.

There was an email from the *notaire*. It was coming at the eleventh hour, given that he and Selwyn, desperately trying to force things along, were setting off for France in the morning. Even so, the relief that overcame him once he'd passed the email through Google Translate was total. All the paperwork had passed muster; Monaghan's estate was his for the taking.

By the time Sebastian had returned to the hall, broken the news to Selwyn and made a call to Amanda, who was visiting her nan, the euphoria of the situation proved a sufficient distraction to counter his disquiet.

Chapter 13

Yawing in the crosswind on its final approach, the plane bumped onto the tarmac and taxied to its stand outside the small terminal building. Cabin bags in hand, Selwyn and Sebastian anxiously scanned the security men and gendarmes then joined the queue at passport control. Once successfully through, Sebastian exhaled a big sigh of relief as they went to wait for their luggage at the carousel.

Within the hour, he'd parked their hire car back at the Reynard d'Or.

'Could have done with Maurice being with us,' Selwyn commented, after a linguistic struggle with the owner over their requirements and timing for *le petit déjeuner* the next morning. 'Goodness knows how we're going to get on at the *notaire*'s and the bank. It'll be ruddy difficult dealing with these coves without him.'

'It should be easier if they're not contesting anything.' Sebastian shrugged. 'Shame Maurice wasn't for budging.'

'He reckoned he needed to go and see an old college friend as a matter of urgency. Never mind. He's certainly brightened the place up a bit. I can't fathom why Amanda's taken against him.'

'Me neither. She's had no time for him right from the start. No matter what I say in his defence, she won't have any of it. I've given up trying.'

Selwyn glanced across at him. 'You two are OK, aren't you?'

'I reckon so, though she's not been herself for a while. Worried about her nan – and having that Martin around doesn't help matters. I just wish the guy would bloody well clear off back to Canada and leave her alone.'

'Don't take her for granted, dear boy. Make sure the girl knows you love and care for her. You don't sound up to snuff yourself. Is there something bothering you, apart from the pantomime we've got ahead of us?'

Tempted though he was to open up, Sebastian lied that there wasn't.

***

Mrs Soames opened the door guardedly to a tall, smiling stranger. She'd have found the sheer toothiness of the man alarming had he not looked so amiable.

'Good afternoon, ma'am. Would you be the lady of… of this magnificent residence?'

Flattered, Mrs Soames dropped her guard and smiled. 'Heavens to Betsy, no. Whatever gave you that idea? I'm just the 'ousekeeper.' Ever vigilant, she regathered her natural suspicion. 'You're not selling anythin' are you?'

'Och no. I was in the area, passing through, and thought I'd call in on my old pal Mac Bilton. He does work here, does he not? It's a wee while since I last saw him. We were in the army together.'

Mrs Soames raised her fingers to her mouth. 'You haven't 'eard, then?'

'Heard what?'

She looked the lanky chap up and down, then opened the door wider. This wasn't a conversation to be had on a doorstep. 'You'd better come in. I'll make a cup of Rosie and tell you all about it.'

An hour later, his brain laden with news and his belly full of cake and biscuits, Jock finally managed to escape the generous ministrations of the chattering house-keeper. Outside, he encountered one of the cleaning staff and chatted with her, then made the call he really didn't want to make.

Predictably unhappy to learn that the commander and Sebastian had cleared off to the safety of France for the foreseeable future, Harry told the lanky Glaswegian to get his arse back to London pronto; the business with the Wisstingham estate was now on hold.

This Jock did, feeling he'd been berated unjustly for the frustration to Harry's plans.

***

'It should sell fairly easily,' the estate agent predicted con-fidently. 'It's in excellent decorative condition, a place you could just walk into and put your bags down.'

Miriam smiled at the verdict, feeling the first signs of happiness for several days.

Once the fee had been negotiated, the agent was instructed to put the house on the market without delay, informed that Miriam was going away for a while and given strict instructions that her forwarding address should not be divulged to anyone.

Then Miriam was left alone, seated on the sofa, a copy of the agreement clutched in her hand. *Am I doing the right thing?* she wondered for the umpteenth time that morning as she gazed about the room.

Memories of the good and bad times spent there flooded

back: the first sale on her internet business; her appointment as a councillor; the bitter rows with her husband and his jealousy at her success; finally, his desertion and the eventual divorce, with all the financial wrangling that had involved.

Now it seemed that all Wisstingham was against her. The leader had threatened to have her ousted both as mayor and a councillor over the land transfer documents' episode, and the press were after her blood following the exposé on child-labour claims levelled at one of her internet suppliers. Being ostracised cut her to the quick. The silence that descended when she went into the local shops was almost unbearable.

She'd been tempted to contact Jack Cavannagh for some friendly company, but that was clearly a relationship that would not be going anywhere. She'd convinced herself that it was better to give it all up and move away to make a fresh start.

For now, she'd leave the area and stay in the hotel she'd booked to plan her future. If it came to exposure at the next council meeting, for that was the tack that Tyson would undoubtedly take to ensure she was as publicly humiliated as possible, she'd submit her resignation in writing beforehand to spike his guns.

Her thoughts strayed to Selwyn, and she wondered what he was doing at that moment. Her eyes were drawn once more to the vases holding the bouquets he'd left on the doorstep, with notes that had frayed her resolve. All too little too late, she told herself, though her heart remained unconvinced.

So far, she'd not bumped into him nor responded to his calls, each time having recognised his number and not answered. She dreaded chancing across him in the street, certain she'd capitulate at the sight of him.

No matter; by this evening she'd be well away from Wisstingham. And him.

***

It was late in the afternoon. Amanda and Mrs Soames were on their second cup of tea when Maurice passed the kitchen window, looked in and waved cheerily. Mrs Soames grinned while Amanda forced a lukewarm smile.

'Takes Mustard out the same time every day for a couple of hours, regular as clockwork, no more, no less,' Mrs Soames explained as Amanda eyed the last shortbread on the plate. 'Go on, 'elp yerself, dearie. It'll give me an excuse to do a fresh batch. Maurice just loves 'em.'

Amanda left the biscuit untouched.

'Mind you, he don't go anywhere else. Never been beyond the gates since he got 'ere. Place could be a monkery, as far as he's concerned.'

'Monastery.'

Mrs Soames looked puzzled.

'Where monks live.'

'Yes, well, one of them,' the slightly affronted housekeeper replied.

'So what *does* he do all the time, apart from walking the dog?'

'Shuts 'iself away in the library with all them dusty old papers what the commander found. Sometimes he'll come and 'ave a cuppa with me, but he doesn't let on about 'iself, other than talk about 'is parents, their travel business and living in a caravan. I reckon he must be lonely, pour soul. Mind you, 'e does make me laugh.

Some of the things he says makes me die, you know.' Mrs Soames let out a chuckle.

Thankfully, Amanda's eyeroll went unnoticed as the housekeeper got up to check on the cake in the oven. 'It all seems a bit mysterious. What about his business or job? He's never mentioned anything like that,' Amanda observed.

'He's most likely retired, duckie. Maybe he sold the family business and 'e's now a man of leisure.'

Amanda mustered an 'Hmmm,' and rose. 'I think I'll go and have a quick peek in the library.'

Mrs Soames became flustered. 'I don't know as 'ow he'd like that.'

Amanda was not prepared to abandon the idea.

'Whatever you do, don't mess his things up,' pleaded Mrs Soames.

Amanda gave her arm a reassuring pat and smiled. 'I'll be like a little field mouse. Won't disturb a thing, not even the dust. It'll be our little secret.'

Mrs Soames gave a rueful shake of her head. 'There'll be plenty of that about. Place 'asn't been cleaned in ages. It's disgraceful, but he's such a nice chap.'

As Amanda headed back to the library, she raised two fingers to her open mouth in a mock-vomit. 'He's got the whole ruddy household enchanted,' she muttered.

In the library, what had once looked like a jumble sale of documents had been transformed. Papers and scrolls were neatly arranged in rows along the tables and plan chest, each bearing a sticker giving a dated, explanatory description. Amanda quickly glanced through them. Interesting though some of them appeared, none seemed to relate to the second land transfer. Then again, if Maurice *had* found them, he'd probably keep them hidden somewhere.

Now determined to try and track them down, she searched through every drawer in the room. Finally shaking her head in frustration, she stood in the centre of the room and viewed the library shelves. *Crumbs, they could be anywhere there.*

She felt despondent. Briefly. 'Apply some logic, woman,' she muttered.

They'd probably be hidden out of easy reach. Her eyes travelled to the upper shelves. Also, the documents would be too large to secrete within or between the books without folding them, which would make them very bulky, so they'd probably need to be hidden *behind* the books.

Amanda pulled the library steps into place and started to look systematically along the upper shelves. Maurice was a short bloke, the same height as her, so she discounted the top two rows.

Her hands felt along the row, dipping behind the fat volumes. By the time she was halfway along the next row, her arms were aching, as indeed were her calf muscles as she stretched up.

She froze at the sound of a bark. *Bloody hell, where's the time got to?*

Now she could discern voices. 'Keep him talking. Please, please, keep him talking, dear Mrs S,' she whispered as she scrambled down and put the steps back where they'd been.

With a quick glance round to check she'd left nothing out of place, Amanda went to the door. By the time she'd closed it gently behind her, she could hear footsteps coming from the kitchen. She dashed further down the hallway just in time to pretend she'd come out of the drawing room.

'Amanda, what a pleasant surprise, my dear,' Maurice called out as he caught sight of her. 'What brings you here?'

'Maurice, how are you?' she replied with feigned sincerity. 'I came to look for some exhibition folders I left with the commander a while ago. He last had them in the drawing room, but I can't find any trace of them. Perhaps they're in the library?' She set her eyes on the library door, which Maurice now blocked with his back. The smile had suddenly deserted him.

'I shouldn't think so. Can't say I've seen anything like that. Anyway, the place is in a real mess. Documents strewn everywhere, though I have started to sort through them.'

'Oh, could I see? A librarian's interest.'

Maurice shifted uncomfortably then straightened his frame as if to block out more of the doorway. It was a wonder he didn't go up on tiptoes as well. 'Not just now, I'm afraid. Wait till I've got things sorted out better, then I'll be delighted to give you a full guided tour.'

Pretentious prick! Amanda agreed without a fuss – for the time being. It was best not to spook the fat fraud too much.

***

25TH JANUARY

Timing her next clandestine visit to perfection, Amanda finally found the map and scroll tucked, as she'd deduced, behind a row of books shorter in depth than the tomes that flanked them. Having had the foresight to bring both her camera and iPad, she took multiple photos of exceptional quality, replaced everything exactly as it had been, swore the confused housekeeper to silence then scooted back to Nan's cottage and her computer.

By the time she'd summoned Martin to her office, the shock of what she'd discovered from the map for the Wisstingham land transfer had still not worn off. The size of the land to be granted back to the estate was vast, and its location wouldn't just rock the council's boat – it would capsize it. It was imperative to see the mayor as soon as possible.

As for the commander and Sebastian, she'd have to tread very carefully indeed. Maurice, who'd proved beyond doubt to be the untrustworthy villain she'd suspected him to be, was a slippery customer. His own dated note proved that he'd located the precious missing papers some days earlier, and he had clearly not told Selwyn. However, the cunning toad might well talk his way out of that one if she showed her hand too soon. She'd have to box clever.

Amanda spent the hour waiting for Martin trying to contact Miriam but, to all intents and purposes, the mayor appeared to have deserted both her home and the mayoral parlour. The secretary implied that she'd gone on holiday but Amanda was convinced that the woman simply had no intention of disclosing her boss's whereabouts.

'I've got to find her somehow,' Amanda told Martin when he arrived at the library. She twirled the ends of her hair and gently nibbled on the corner of her lip as she racked her brains.

'If the secretary won't tell you, who else in the council is likely to be in contact with her?' Martin asked. 'There must be someone.'

Amanda's face lit up. 'Of course. What a clever little Marco Polo mint you are. The post room! They'll have to send meeting papers and agendas out to her. What's more, Suzie in there owes me a favour.'

Within minutes, Amanda had scribbled down an address for the mayor's hotel and waved it triumphantly at Martin. 'Llandudno,' she announced. 'We're off to Wales, you and I.'

'Me? Why do you want me there?'

'For moral support *and*—' she raised a finger to silence him '—you have the expertise to interpret the map.'

'But won't Sebastian go ballistic?'

'He's in France, I can't call him back at a moment's notice. This can't wait, and it's far too important to worry about the niceties. Anyway, he probably won't find out.'

'He probably will. There are no flies on him,' warned Martin.

'No, but you can sometimes see where they've been.'

Martin was unable to suppress a grin. 'God, you're a wicked girl.'

'Then the game's afoot, Watson. I'll call the mayor at the hotel and tell her we'll bring the solution to all her problems with the council. She can't help but agree to meet us.'

Having printed off a few copies of the map in various scales from her iPad, she lent Martin her office so he could translate the land boundaries from the digital originals onto a modern OS map and larger-scale plan of the area. She wrote Marcia an email excusing herself from work, then she and Martin took advantage of the last hour before darkness fell to see the land itself. The sheer size of it was even more gob-smacking than the map's initial revelation.

'Gordon Bennett!' Martin exclaimed as they visually plotted the boundaries on site. 'Talk about putting the cat among the pigeons when this gets out!'

'You can say that again.'

***

26TH JANUARY

Amanda was pleased with her hotel room in Llandudno, a single adjoining Martin's. There was a faded, though sustained, elegance to the hotel, a gentle reminder of the Victorian era that had shaped the resort. Her window view took in the pier and bay beyond, with just a glimpse of the promenade. On the mahogany dresser, covered by a lace-edged runner, lay a highly polished tray on which stood a glass and small carafe of medium-dry sherry.

She made good inroads into the sherry before joining Martin in the corridor to make their way to the cosy bar lounge, where the absconded mayor had agreed to give them an audience.

Their meeting with the initially wary and frosty Ms Cheyney soon necessitated an adjournment to the vacant dining room where the maps could be spread out and perused more easily. Miriam was clearly shocked at what she was shown and stared at them thoughtfully and in silence for some time. Then she asked Martin to give her a few minutes alone with Amanda.

'This really will be devastating for the council – and for

Wisstingham. However, I really appreciate that you've brought it to me. What happened at your meeting with the leader?'

When Amanda had finished telling her, Miriam shook her head sadly. 'I've misjudged and mistreated you, Amanda. When all this is over, I promise I'll make it up to you. What you've brought will most certainly help me to put things right.'

'There's one other matter that you may also want to bring into play,' Amanda advised. 'It could very well aid your cause.'

'What's that?'

Amanda described what Kathy had told her.

'And you can actually see Hirst handing over money to Tyson and the chief engineer in the photos?' asked the amazed mayor.

'Apparently.'

'How marvellous.' There was now a positive sparkle in Miriam's eyes. 'I shall do my own discreet digging into that one.'

She confirmed she'd be back in Wisstingham in time to prepare for the accusations and criticism that would undoubtedly be levelled at her during the next council meeting.

***

Sebastian was beside himself with rage. 'She's gone *where* with him?' he bellowed.

Mrs Soames' bottom lip started to tremble and she held the phone further away from her ear. She'd never heard him like this before. 'Llanduderno, but I don't think as 'ow there's anythin' in it, Sebastian.' Her attempt at appease-

209

ment cut no ice. 'Just said she needed 'im to support her with the meetin' with the mayor. She can be a bit of a tartar, yer know, that Mrs Cheyney.'

'I bet she needs his support. As soon as my back's turned, there she goes again, off with *him*. Well, she can bloody well keep him.'

'Don't be like that, Sebastian, please. I'm sure it's not like that at all. Don't be 'ard on the girl. She's a lovely lass an' she does love you.' Mrs Soames was starting to feel resentful that she'd been put in the position of having to tell Sebastian anything at all. 'Anyway, why did you ring here?'

Sebastian sighed. 'Because I couldn't get hold of her anywhere else. I thought she might be with you.'

'I'll tell her you rang when I see 'er.'

'Thank you, Mrs S, but please don't bother. I've nothing to say to her.'

The line went dead. Mrs Soames took the receiver away from her ear and looked at it. 'Naughty boy,' she murmured as she returned it to its cradle. 'I just 'opes as 'ow she's not being a naughty girl, an' all.'

***

27TH JANUARY

Despite the cordial parting with the mayor and the smooth journey home, Amanda's guts were in a fresh knot when she got back to her nan's cottage. Since her discovery of the documents in the library, she had brooded over whether she should have taken them and kept them safe. She could not for one minute believe Maurice would destroy them, otherwise he'd have done so already, and he had nothing to gain by doing that. But suppose he planned to ransom them? Finally, she decided she couldn't leave them at risk any longer, irrespective of how things might turn out in her tug-of-war with Sebastian and the commander over Maurice.

She'd barely dumped her bag in her room before she locked up again and headed for the hall. If she were quick, she'd arrive just as Maurice headed off for his usual morning walk.

She called into the kitchen. Mrs Soames, surprised to see her back so soon, immediately busied herself with the teapot and a lecture about the awkwardness of dealing with irate paramours on the phone.

Amanda accepted these reprimands meekly but very briefly before she begged the housekeeper's pardon for having to sprint to the bathroom. Instead, she hurried to the library. The knot in her tummy tightened even further when she felt behind the books and found nothing there. In a cold sweat, her heart thumping, she felt frantically further along the shelf.

Maybe it's the wrong one. She adjusted the ladder and tried again, but to no avail. Then she heard the concerned housekeeper calling to enquire if everything was alright.

Chapter 14

Maurice quietly opened the door and crept into the room. The exasperated librarian was teetering on the ladder with an armful of books. He couldn't help smiling at her get-up-and-go. 'You won't find them up there,' he said, startling her into dropping the books as she jerked around.

Amanda's cheeks coloured. 'Maurice, I was just looking for a tome on the redemption of sinners. Any idea where I'll find that?'

Maurice regarded her. Her quick-wittedness made him smile. He reached into his pocket, drew out a packet of cigarillos and lit one. 'Probably under B for Beelzebub. A good effort at defending an indefensible position,' he congratulated her, after he'd inhaled and blown out a puff of blue smoke. 'Would you like a hand down?'

She started to descend. 'I'm quite capable of making my own way down, thank you. Mind you, it'd take quite some time to get to your level.' At the bottom of the steps, she met his gaze. 'Where are they? What have you done with them?'

'Do you mean there are two or more volumes on sin?' he teased.

She glared. 'You know what I mean.'

'Ah! The document of promises and the map to the Golden Road to Samarkand.'

'I hope we don't have to go that far. I don't reckon Wisstingham's finest travelled such a distance.'

Maurice nodded in acknowledgement. 'My God, I wish I'd met you in my youth.'

'Don't piss about, Maurice.' Amanda's patience was clearly exhausted. 'Those documents are bloody important for the commander. What have you done with them?'

Maurice took an unhurried puff at the cigarillo. 'Don't worry, they're quite safe. But what does it matter to you?'

'Selwyn and Sebastian are family. Well, *nearly* family. *They* matter to me.'

Maurice snorted. 'The good commander... A first-rate chap, I'll grant you, but you're hardly close. It's young Sebastian that's the prime concern, eh? And what of him, dear girl? You're just engaged and already he's barely giving you the respect or trust you deserve. Am I right?'

Amanda swallowed and glared at him in silence.

Maurice pressed home his advantage. 'At this rate, the two of you aren't going to be hearing wedding bells. Within a year he and the estate will be a thing of the past, other than whatever arrangements you come to with the commander over the farm. And that doesn't bring in much, does it?'

Amanda put a finger to the corner of her eye, making him feel almost sorry for her.

'And on top of that, your nan's fading away in a second-rate care home, which you know you can't afford for too much longer, and your brother's in no position to help because he's been laid off from the cruise liners.'

Amanda gasped. 'How do you know all this?'

Maurice moved in for the kill. He hated messy business, so whatever threats he made had to work before either of them left the room. 'I make it my business to know things. I get people to talk. Both Sebastian and Selwyn get quite chatty when they're primed in the right way. I have many, many contacts – some of them in the leisure industry – and I do my homework. So what I'm offering you, my dear girl, is this. Through those documents, there's the possibility of some real treasure, though I've no idea what or how much. The commander will no doubt recover his lost money from France, Sebastian will manage quite well without you, and you will have the opportunity to share in something that will benefit those dearest to you. The commander will get by. I'm offering you a fifty-fifty share in whatever we find. If it's nothing, there's nothing lost and Selwyn can have his documents – for a fair price that covers my expenses, of course. What do you say?'

Amanda's glare turned into an appraising stare. 'You really are a first-rate shit, Maurice. Do you know that?'

He gazed back at her completely unfazed, took another puff and relaxed as more smoke rose into the air. An animal is always angriest when it knows it's been trapped. 'It has been said, dear girl, it has been said. However, I think I've made you a very fair offer.'

'Since you're the one with a creative mind, I'll leave you to consider where your offer might be inserted,' Amanda snarled.

Maurice's sense of humour deserted him. 'And in turn, I'll leave you to imagine what will happen to your brother when my associates meet up with him if you don't toe the line.'

Amanda paled. 'You wouldn't do that. You can't—'

'Indeed I can and will. Therefore, you will keep your trap shut about the documents and my intentions. And if you're a good girl – after all, I'm not unreasonable – I'll still share some of whatever I find with you. If not – well, I'll leave your fertile imagination to dwell on the possible outcomes. Furthermore, at the first hint of any betrayal on your part, those documents will never again see the light of day and neither will your brother.'

Amanda's hands shot to her mouth. She stared at him then her gaze fell to the ground, at which she stared in silence. After a while, she looked up, her eyes moist and shoulders bowed. 'Alright,' she murmured, looking very frail in defeat.

***

It was only a matter of minutes after Maurice had left the estate in the Volvo that a car made its way down the drive, towards the hall.

'Good afternoon, madam,' the visitor greeted the wary Mrs Soames when she cautiously opened the front door. 'My name is Karl Svensen, attached to the Swedish Embassy. Would it be possible to speak to Commander Fitzgerald, please?'

In the housekeeper's mind, the mention of the embassy instantly chimed a note of respectability, together with some confusion over what the Swedes would want with her boss. 'I'm afraid you can't as 'ow he's not here.'

'Ah, is he likely to be home this evening?'

'No, an' he won't be here tomorrow, nor for a few days. Can't say as I know when he'll be returning.'

The man passed his hand across his mouth then flashed an ingratiating smile. 'I don't suppose *you* might be able to help me, dear lady?'

'Depends on what it is.'

'Well, I am really trying to locate this gentleman who I

understand might have stayed with the commander or who may even still be here.' He withdrew a photo from his inside pocket and offered it to the housekeeper.

Mrs Soames took hold of it uncertainly. She glanced down and recognised Maurice, complete with straw hat. Though determined to give no indication that she'd recognised him, she instinctively glanced up and beyond the caller to the drive, down which Maurice had driven minutes earlier. Then she looked at the visitor. 'Why are you lookin' for 'im?'

'It's a rather delicate matter. He is a possible witness to a car accident in which one of our Swedish diplomats was involved. We are trying to find out what happened as discreetly as possible. The reputation of a senior politician could be at stake. Can you tell me, please, whether you have seen him?'

Mrs Soames glanced at the photo again. Tempted though she was to cooperate, her inclination was to say nothing and wait to tell Mr Fox on his return from his trip to Oxford, then he could decide what, if anything, was to be done. She looked the caller straight in the eye. 'No, I can't say as I've seen 'im. He's not been 'ere.' Unfortunately, her cheeks coloured at the lie.

The man replaced the photo in his pocket and smiled. 'I see. Thank you for your help.' He turned on his heel and made his way back down the steps to the car.

So, Archie Fox *was* here. And, from the woman's reaction on seeing the photo, he'd probably very recently left the estate, Berensen surmised as he drove down the drive. If he'd gone for good, Berensen felt sure the woman would have disclosed that. Why not? To say so would have done no harm to the man.

Discreetly parked outside the entrance gates, he took a case from the boot of the car and from that a remote security camera. After he'd scouted around at the end of the fence, he found a tree branch to secure it to and carefully angled the solar panel. After he'd walked back to check how unobtrusive the set-up was, he reversed the car a little way back up the drive and drove out again. Finally, he checked the resulting recording on his iPad. It was satisfactory for remote monitoring, and it would take a sharp-eyed driver to spot the camera when they entered or left the estate.

Now it was just a matter of time and patience.

***

The two men stared at each other incredulously, then Sebastian shook his fist in triumphant excitement. 'Awesome! We've done it. We've bloody well done it.'

Selwyn let out a huge sigh of relief and patted his nephew on the shoulder. 'I thought we'd never get through all that malarkey.'

'Even the *notaire* said how quickly it all went through was some sort of record. At least, that's what I think he said.' Sebastian looked down at the sheets of bank statements still clutched in his hand, which the bank assistant had printed off for him. They'd need to go through them in more detail back at the hotel, but they'd checked the balance and that was good enough for now. It would take two or three days for the money to be transferred into the new account Sebastian had opened, but what did that matter?

'This calls for a celebratory drink and a slap-up meal this evening – on me,' declared Selwyn.

Back at the Reynard d'Or, after they'd roused the napping landlord to serve them a bottle of chilled Picpoul, his annoyance at the disturbance ill-disguised, Selwyn and Sebastian sat at a table in the empty bar area and pored over the statements. They soon homed in on the transfer of two amounts that corresponded closely to those stolen from the estate accounts, though in each case the amount was minus ten per cent.

'A money-laundering fee, I suppose,' Selwyn grumbled.

'I'll make sure the full amounts are credited back. There'll still be over €80,000 left after that. What do you reckon I should do with the balance? There's no way of knowing how much is legal.'

'You'll just have to go through the statements and look for any regular credits that correspond to debits from his UK account. They at least could be legitimate. I suggest that, for now, you transfer that money and set it aside in a separate UK escrow account as soon as you can. If Stone and his cronies come after you, at least you can show that you've not touched anything other than the estate's recovered money.'

'Good idea, though I can't see how we'll ever be able to decide just what money came from where. Then there's Number 27. I reckon I'll sell it.'

'You don't think you and Amanda might like a holiday home?'

Sebastian's good humour suddenly seemed to desert him. 'I don't think so. There's a lot of water to flow under the bridge before that'd ever be a consideration. Anyway, I wouldn't want to have *this* house with the memories associated with it.'

'I don't blame you.' The sudden change in Sebastian at

the mention of his fiancée had not gone unnoticed. 'You are OK, aren't you?'

Sebastian nodded, a little too vigorously for Selwyn's liking. His experience told him something was not right. 'Come on, Sebastian,' he coaxed. 'You should be over the moon today but suddenly you're not. What is it?'

Sebastian looked at him, then stared down at the table strewn with statements. 'Amanda,' he muttered. 'She and that damned Martin. She's been off to Llandudno with him to see the mayor about goodness knows what.'

Mention of Miriam's title jolted Selwyn. He paused to rein in his thoughts, then looked at Sebastian. 'And you believe they've been up to something?' he asked, though he wanted to ask different questions.

'I don't know.'

'I think you do, and I think you know she wouldn't do anything wrong. She loves you too much for that.'

'I hoped so. I really hoped so but now … I just don't know. She seems to be happier with him than me.'

'Put that out of your mind, my boy. She loves you, I'm totally convinced of that. Don't give way to jealousy. There be dragons! Believe in her, believe in yourself and in your relationship. Treasure her, look after her, and make the most of the time you have together. It soon goes, and you can't bring back either time or people once they're gone.'

'You're right, of course.' Sebastian eyes moistened in gratitude.

Selwyn studied him for a moment. 'But that's not all, is it?'

Sebastian gazed out of the window at the terrace of houses opposite. 'Why do they leave those plastic bottles of water on the doorstep?'

Nonplussed, the commander frowned. 'To stop the cats peeing on the step, apparently. Or so Maurice told me. Well?'

Sebastian sighed. 'Yes, there is something, but I can't tell you. Not right now, anyway.'

'You know I'm always here for you. So what was Miriam doing in Llandudno?'

Sebastian was unable to shed light on exactly where Amanda had found Miriam or why she was there, so Selwyn reached for the Picpoul and topped up their glasses. As he poured, he decided he'd try to phone Miriam yet again, though he was doubtful he'd meet with success. In that case, he'd ring Amanda on the pretext of discussing the farm and try to find out Miriam's whereabouts.

'Let's finish this, get ready and hit the village. What do you say?'

Sebastian nodded his agreement.

Later, alone, Sebastian paced his room. He pondered the commander's advice but did not reach for his mobile, fearful from previous experience that a call before he'd commanded his emotions would lead to acrimony and failure. He'd need to see Amanda in person to try to mend some very broken fences.

***

28TH JANUARY

Somewhat out of breath after their clamber over a dilapidated fence and through shrubs, undergrowth and a stand of mature trees that surrounded and shrouded the site, Archie and his friend from his undergraduate days stood amidst the scant ruins. To the far boundary, a wood of larger trees completed the site's obscurity.

The sheer scale of the tract legendarily promised to the Fitzgeralds took even more of Archie's breath away.

'It was a priory once,' Graham announced.

'I thought so, but there's not much of it left,' observed Archie.

'The buildings would have been left very much as a shell after the dissolution. The stone would have been plundered for other local building needs.' Graham shot Archie a concerned look. 'I say, are you feeling quite the thing? Gone rather purple, you know.'

Archie panted his way back to composure, wishing he'd kept as fit as his oldest friend. 'University life seems to have suited you well.'

'Yes, it has, but I suspect the Dean's thinking of pensioning me off.'

Archie gawped. 'They can't get rid of the infamous Professor Ingrams!'

'Not sure if I'd miss it, to tell you the truth. The undergrads get more stupid and bolshy each year.' Graham nodded in the direction of a couple of the standing pillars. 'It's good to be out and about.' He wandered off a few paces, then turned with a wry grin. 'Don't forget you owe me a good claret for all this crashing about in the undergrowth.'

'That I do,' Archie panted. He sat down on a low wall, all that remained of one of the main walls. Still panting from exertion, he mopped his moist brow with a large handkerchief.

After several minutes Ingrams returned, perplexed. 'There's something not right here.'

'What do you mean?'

'I'd have expected to find a crypt, but there's no trace of one.'

'That's what confused me when I called here before coming to see you,' Archie said.

'According to the records, there were three abbots and each would have been buried within the grounds.' Ingrams scanned the area round them.

'Which I presume are those three graves.' Archie pointed a short way off to where the rough stone ground was interspersed with stone slabs.

Ingrams walked over to them, looked around then started to pace away from them in different directions. 'But they're not right somehow,' he observed on his return. 'An abbot would normally have been interred in a crypt, or at least in a more prominent position within the priory. This place was certainly big enough to warrant a crypt. Anyway, those graves are out of kilter.' He shook his head. 'It's a bloody shame you got sent down in the second year,' he remarked. 'I really missed you. We'd have been a good team.'

Archie hung his head at the memory of his fall from grace, the drunken prank with the moored punts that had gone horribly wrong. He'd remained in Oxford, transferred to dingy lodgings in South Hinksey and eked out a living working in pubs and restaurants, postponing the evil day when he'd have to break the news of his rustication to his parents. 'My dear fellow, there's not a day I don't regret that whole sorry episode. What are your thoughts about the graves?'

Ingrams slowly massaged his mouth as he contemplated them. 'Imagine this. It's the time of the dissolution of the monasteries. Henry VIII's men are rampaging through the country, sacking and looting the holy places. What if the monks here, realising what was going to happen, sealed off their crypt – presumably to safeguard the remains of their dead abbots – then concealed the entrance with those three lowly graves?'

'Wouldn't the men who came to tear the place apart have twigged?'

'Most probably not. The clerics with knowledge of these places would, as a priority, have been sent with the soldiers to the larger monasteries. This was a comparatively small and insignificant place, so would have merited only a detachment of soldiers to remove anything of value.'

'You reckon there's possibly a crypt underneath here?' murmured Archie, starting to understand why this piece of ground could have sufficiently interested the Fitzgerald family to seek to exchange it for some of their land.

'It's a distinct possibility. What's your interest in the place?'

Archie had anticipated the question. 'I'm doing some work for a rather eccentric cove who came across documents his family had hung on to for ages. One of them mentioned this site and he asked if I'd do some research into it.'

'If you like, I'll look into it further when I get back and send my findings on to you. That should be easier with the university's reference resources.'

'What a splendid fellow you are. I'm most grateful, old chap. And it was great to be with you again. I owe you one.'

'Nonsense. It's been a pleasure to see you and spend time together. Don't make it so long next time, d'you hear?'

Archie promised he wouldn't.

After he'd waved off Ingrams, he returned to the site to formulate a plan of action.

***

'What have you got for me?' asked Harry, as Jock slipped into the room. The henchman's face was going off on one of its contortions again, which always made Harry feel a touch queasy. He glared, fearing Jock had brought more bad news.

'I got a call from the wee young cleaning lassie I slipped a few notes to at Wisstingham. The news is the commander's due back Tuesday morning with the other feller.'

'Is he indeed?' Harry consulted the desk calendar and decided that there was no immediate rush to gallop over to Wisstingham. That bloody commander could wait another couple of days; Harry had other fish to fry. We'll pay them a visit on the Thursday. You find a hotel nearby and book us in for the night before. Usual names. We'll drive down in one of the vans.' As Jock nodded, Harry shot him a warning glance. 'Make sure it's had a good clean outside and in. I ain't gonna sit in a pigsty. Understood?'

Jock indicated he had and was dismissed.

'Make sure you're well tooled up,' Harry called as his deputy reached the door.

***

In the council offices, no tea was offered to Amanda or Martin as they sat opposite the grim panel of the unlovely head of HR, Miss Teresa Blanchard, Marcia Pincher and a secretary.

Miss Blanchard was a wizened-looking woman with a small, round mouth; from her permanent expression, one might imagine she was sucking a slice of lemon. Her thin fingers, adorned with numerous rings, drummed the table as she concluded a recital of the negligence charges that had been brought against the librarian. A gold bracelet hung from an equally thin wrist, appearing to be far too heavy for it to bear.

Amanda had never thought she'd be the sort of person to get suspended. Just weeks ago, she'd have been distraught at the prospect. But in the back of her mind she clutched the comforting image of the second set of land transfer documents and anticipated the hell that Miriam would unleash with them on Monday at the meeting that was meant to bring about her professional demise. Amanda was convinced that quite soon everything would be back to normal – at work, at least. She still had no idea what she was going to do about Maurice.

When invited to explain her version of the events, Amanda reiterated the arguments she'd made previously to the leader, Karl Tyson.

Before Miss Blanchard could move on with the agenda, Marcia Pincher leaned towards Amanda and offered her an 'I'm your friend in all this, really' smile. 'Miss Sheppard, you mentioned to the leader that you had in fact offered the documents to Councillor Cheyney, but that she'd refused to see them. Is that correct?'

'I'd rather not say anything about that.'

Martin shot her a glance. Amanda squeezed his hand.

'But this is your chance to defend yourself,' Marcia almost pleaded.

You scheming, transparent bitch. Amanda fixed her

boss with a smouldering stare. Under no circumstances would she help Tyson put a noose around the mayor's neck. There'd be no prizes for guessing who'd play the lead role if this panel were to be cast in *Toad of Toad Hall*. She remained silent.

Marcia shrugged and sat back resignedly in her chair.

'It does strike me,' offered Martin, 'that you're all laying a great deal of blame at Amanda's door. If these are such tremendously important documents for the council, why on earth does no one know where they are?'

Miss Blanchard threw him a look as if she'd found a pip in her mouth. 'Thank you, Mr Brightside. I'm sure every effort is being made to discover their whereabouts.' She turned to Amanda. 'Is there anything further you wish to say at this juncture?'

Amanda shook her head and then breathed serenely as she was suspended from duties on full pay with immediate effect. She was to be escorted to her office under Miss Pincher's supervision to collect her personal possessions.

She rose and headed for the door, contemplating the looks of surprise and horror that would spread across *their* faces when the tsunami of Miriam's news crashed through the council office doors in just a few days' time.

It was when Amanda was collecting her things from the desk drawer that Marcia, who was standing in the doorway, said, 'You should have said more to defend yourself, Amanda. You should have blamed the mayor for not listening to you and telling you to do what you wanted with the documents. She's on her way out.'

Amanda stared at her in silence. *You're really in deep with Tyson, aren't you? Did some digging through my emails and got yourself lined up for a spot of promotion, eh?*

'We will find both those sets of documents,' Marcia assured her.

'As the Chinese say, be careful what you wish for.' Furious at Marcia's treachery, Amanda upended the bag of ten-pence pieces she kept as change for the coffee machine onto her desk, carefully counted out a number of them and placed them in two neat piles on the desk. She turned to Marcia. 'They're for you. There are thirty of them. Not real silver, but they'll do.'

With that, she walked past the red-faced and open-mouthed Ms Pincher and out of the building.

***

After Graham had left, Archie sat for some time on the priory wall to ponder his next move. Time was of the essence if he were to get away with what needed to be done.

He went over to study the gravestones. Lowly they might be compared to an abbot's crypt, but still not something you'd shift in a hurry. You'd need the right tools for the job, and the right people. He remembered the three beefy Irish lads who'd excavated the concrete slab and foundations to the old outhouse back at home. Their card would be in his house in Cusham, but should he risk going to find it?

He studied the terrain again. What if they needed a digger? They'd never get that onto the site. Then again, if originally it had been down to some monks to manhandle everything into place with no modern equipment, surely to God his Irish lads could smash it?

It was in the late hours, after he'd dined in a small, almost deserted roadside pub, that Archie parked up a few streets from his house and stealthily let himself in. The place was freezing but, once he'd found the business card he needed and set his alarm for very early the next morning when he'd slip away quietly, he nestled under the duvet and fell asleep.

Chapter 15

Miriam returned to her house in a totally different frame of mind from that in which she had left it. Gone was the suffocating cloud of defeat and demoralisation, replaced by a thirst for revenge and a bloody good fight with that jumped-up pipsqueak Karl Tyson.

Before she'd left Llandudno, the agenda and papers for the week's forthcoming council meeting had been forwarded to her. In the early part of the agenda was an innocuous item tabled by the leader, listed as: *Wisstingham Hall: documentation regarding land matters pertinent to the council*. This was to be followed by the usual *Planning matters*.

She had much to say with regard to both items.

Miriam dropped her bag and briefcase in the hall and went through to the kitchen, where she made a much-needed cup of tea. Seated once more in the comfort of her living room, she finally acknowledged the presence of the elephant in the room trumpeting a need for action. Although she'd repeatedly avoided contact with Selwyn, she now had to tell him that she was going to disclose the discovery of the second set of land transfer documents at tomorrow's council meeting: precious documents that were awaiting his return from France.

These would have such a profound effect on the council that some official would need to negotiate with him. It certainly couldn't be the leader, who'd do anything to scupper the estate and Selwyn. Anyway, by bringing everything out into the open, she hoped to get rid of that corrupt bastard.

Had she and Selwyn still been an item, she would also have been excluded from any involvement in the negotiations on account of her having a vested interest. However, with their relationship at an end, she might now be the prime candidate for the job.

The thought of being in Selwyn's presence again brought a lump to her throat. How on earth would she have the strength to resist the entreaties he would undoubtedly make to her, and, indeed... would she still want to?

***

31ST JANUARY

The snatched conversations and general buzz as the members filed into the council chamber to their customary seats was different; even allowing for virtually no absences, it was different. There was apprehension in the air and a scent of blood that had set political noses twitching.

Prior to the meeting, Miriam had tried to persuade the leader to refrain from a personal attack on her for the sake of party unity. He'd graciously offered that, if she were prepared to offer her immediate resignation, he'd refrain from mentioning her part in the earlier suppression of the documents. She had refused to do so.

Consequently, the mayor entered the chamber with no undertaking whatsoever, nor did anyone even deign to engage in casual conversation with her. Yes, the blood they could smell was definitely hers.

She took her usual place in the members' tiered semi-circle of seating; as always, the cushions were ineffective in shielding one's rump from the hardwood benches. The deputy leader took his place on the dais that faced the semi-circle, as did the chief executive, followed by the leader himself, who bore a smile that would have done the Cheshire Cat credit.

Once the minutes of the last meeting had been proposed, seconded and approved, Karl Tyson made his way down to the chamber floor. There he stood in front of the gathered councillors, on whom descended an expectant hush.

'Members,' he proclaimed, scanning the assembled throng to gain visual contact with as many as possible. 'It brings me a mixture of great pleasure and sadness to raise this item before you.'

A murmur rustled through the assembly, quickly stifled by a roving, silencing scan of Tyson's narrowed eyes.

'On the one hand, I am delighted to advise you that documents have come to light from our archives that indicate a significant piece of land was gifted many years ago to the village – and hence the council – by the Wisstingham estate. This land encompasses all the recreational park that has hitherto been leased from the estate, and further comprises significant other areas of land currently falling within the current estate boundary. I hardly need to tell you what a dramatic and beneficial impact this will have on the council and the community as a whole.'

A wave of murmurs rolled through the assembled members. Kathy, the sole member of the press, scribbled away furiously in the public gallery.

Tyson cast a triumphant glance at the mayor. He was

surprised to see that she appeared to be unfazed by his performance. Irritated, he raised a hand to silence the room.

'This is the part of today's proceedings that brings me pleasure. However, there is more to be said. The unfortunate matter I am obliged to report to you is that one of our members, namely Councillor Cheyney—' he glared at Miriam '—was offered the opportunity many months ago to acquaint herself with this vital information but declined to do so. Furthermore, it has been disclosed that when she *was* informed of the situation, she decided not to share it with her council colleagues, nor to take action against a certain council employee who was instrumental in covering up this information.'

A murmur flittered through the chamber, augmented by calls of 'shame' and 'resign' from some opposition members. All eyes were now fixed on Miriam, who, to the annoyance of the assembly, sat smiling and composed.

Tyson's gleaming eyes and triumphant smile turned on the mayor like a matador's stare when goading a bull into whose shoulder he was about to plunge his sword. 'Accordingly, I now invite Councillor Cheyney to comment.'

As Tyson nimbly resumed his seat, Miriam rose. A hostile, expectant hush descended as she approached the spot he'd vacated.

'I admit, fellow members, that I did indeed – albeit unwittingly – fail to take the opportunity to avail the council of the information contained in the documents in question. Documents owned by the estate, I would emphasise, relating to the transfer of estate land to the council.'

Murmurs and further demands for her resignation

232

rumbled from the opposition enclave.

'Before I address you further, I would request that since what I have to say is such a sensitive matter for the council, and one to which the councillors are not yet privy, the public gallery be cleared.'

Kathy immediately stopped writing and glowered down at the mayor, while Tyson harrumphed in ridicule.

With the thinnest of smiles he replied, 'This is just the sort of stunt I might have expected from Councillor Cheyney. I hardly think that would be in the public interest. The public and press have every right to know what has happened.'

'Very well, on your head be it.' Miriam went on to explain the reciprocal agreement of transfer of Wisstingham land back to the estate, a critical stipulation mysteriously missing from the leader's own summary of the situation. With relish, she concluded with the pronouncement that she had copies of the documents specifying the transfer of some of Wisstingham's common land to the Fitzgeralds.

The expression of complacency drained instantly from Tyson's face, to be replaced by one of both suspicion and incredulity.

Miriam waited for the noise to die down before continuing. 'Unfortunately for the council and Wisstingham, this basically encompasses the most precious stretch of land the council currently possesses – the Cresthaven industrial estate.'

Expressions of astonishment, horror and dismay erupted from the members.

'Furthermore,' Miriam pressed on, her glance to Tyson one of a bull that would yet gore the matador, 'I regret to advise you that it was only after receiving Councillor Tyson's threat that he'd persuade the council to press its claim on the estate for the recreation land that the current owner, Commander Selwyn Fitzgerald, initiated his search for the reciprocal documents.' She waved said copies in the air, a final taunt at the now-impaled leader.

Kathy's pencil was about to burst into flames, and her expression was a mixture of concentration and glee. Miriam stood in silence, her arm still raised as the hubbub broke out. Tyson, oblivious to the angry stares now aimed at him, was consumed in the venomous glare he cast at the mayor.

As the clamour rose, the deputy leader silenced the room with a sharp bang on his minute book. 'Councillor Tyson,' the deputy invited him, 'may we hear what you have to say on the matter?'

Tyson rose shakily, attempted to trivialise the mayor's claims as biased and unsubstantiated, then called for a motion of no confidence in Councillor Cheyney and her omissions to be tabled. But the chamber was having none of it. He fell back silently into his seat as the deputy shouted to regain control of the meeting.

It was finally agreed that Councillor Cheyney's revelations would be the subject of further urgent consultation by a committee yet to be agreed. A report would be made to an extraordinary meeting of the members that would be convened as soon as possible.

'It's time to move on to the next item,' the deputy announced.

Tyson, still seated and ominously silent, continued to glare at the mayor.

'Next is planning matters, with one item,' the deputy

continued. 'I will ask the council's chief engineer and planner to take us through the proposal.'

McKaye got to his feet and described a project for the creation of a market garden on land within the Wisstingham estate. This matter, which paled into insignificance compared to what had just aroused the chamber, drew little comment until Miriam rose to speak.

'Are we to understand that this proposal has been put forward by the estate's owner?'

McKaye cleared his throat. 'No, it's an application from Mr Geoffrey Hirst, who has agreed to purchase the land from the estate.'

'Solely for the purposes of a market garden?' Miriam pressed.

'Correct.'

'I take it there is no mention or intention of a subsequent application for the land to be used for housing development?'

McKaye's throat appeared to insist upon further clearing. 'That's not something that's been mentioned at this time.'

'And if it were, would such an application be considered favourably by the council?'

'It's not something that's been mooted or even considered,' McKaye stonewalled, with a glance at the leader.

Tyson feigned no interest in the proceedings.

'Of course,' Miriam ploughed on, 'the value of the land for the development of a market garden would be very much less than if it were for housing development, would it not?'

McKaye shifted from one foot to the other. 'Well, yes, of course.'

'Would the leader have any comment to make on this

proposal?'

Tyson shot her a scowl. 'I've no interest in this, or awareness of the project at all.'

An expectant hush had now descended on the room. Kathy jotted furiously about this fresh new gem. Her byline would be splashed all over the paper tomorrow.

'That's most interesting.' Miriam reached into her brief-case and, within moments, efficiently shared incriminating papers around the room.

McKaye turned almost the same colour as the illustrious council leader.

'These photos were taken at Wisstingham estate on the seventh of January. They appear to show Mr Geoffrey Hirst, the current planning applicant, together with the leader and chief engineer. I thought at first that the envelopes contained copies of the planning application but, as you'll see from the photos, they were sharing notes of a monetary nature.'

A Mexican wave of guffaws and expressions of surprise, dismay and disgust rippled through the room.

'Oh hell!' murmured McKaye.

The deputy leader raised a hand to his forehead and glanced sideways at Tyson, whose clenched teeth were barely discernible through his thin-lipped mouth. In the realisation that no explanation was forthcoming, the deputy silenced the room. 'Fellow members, I move that this item be adjourned pending further enquiry.'

This motion received unanimous agreement and much barracking from members of the opposition.

The slow shuffle of the animated and chattering councillors as they filed out of the chamber, one or two pausing to congratulate Miriam or pat her on the shoulder as she remained seated, was in marked contrast to the leader's rapid disappearance and Kathy's racehorse exit.

Miriam was relieved that her ordeal was over. Relieved, and happy for Selwyn that he now possessed the originals of the copied documents that lay in her lap. How she would deal with her further discussions with him and the maelstrom of her emotions was quite another matter.

***

'The bitch, the fucking bitch!' Tyson hissed into his whisky glass as he leaned unsteadily over the table in the bar.

Gerald Cheyney stared at his inebriated partner in crime. His initial misgivings at meeting the man in public had grown into profound regret. 'Steady on. How many of those have you had?'

'Not enough. Not fucking enough.'

'Look, I did all I could to help. I'm not up for any more. I've a reputation and career to think of.'

Tyson looked up and glared at him. 'Yes, so did I. I'm ruined. F-f-fucking ruined,' he slurred. 'Under suspension, can't show my face. That fucking bitch has done for me.'

'So what'll you do?'

The disgraced leader gave a malevolent sneer. 'I'm going to sort her out once and for all.'

Alarmed, Cheyney gave another anxious look around the room. 'What do you mean?'

'What I said.' Karl Tyson prodded the air antagonistically. 'And if you don't have the stomach for anything else, I suggest you clear off right now. You're no further use to me.'

Cheyney wasted no time in making a hasty exit.

***

In the early hours of the morning, the flames had taken hold with frightening rapidity. Within a few minutes, smoke was billowing out of the shattered windows from which flames were licking. The fire teams were scrambled. Residents in dressing gowns stood at doorways or on drives, watching the conflagration and chaotic scene. Miriam's elderly and infirm neighbours viewed the proceedings through their front windows.

Two ambulances were parked nearby, their flashing lights adding to the multi-coloured display offered by the contingent of police cars.

A chorus of gasps went up from the spectators as a fireman appeared at one of the upstairs windows, an inert body slung over his shoulder. This he transferred to his colleague, who stood waiting at the top of the ladder.

'Don't look good, don't look good at all,' murmured one of the fire officers to another, as they watched the mayor's still form being stretchered into the ambulance.

After the brisk emergency ministrations of the paramedics, the ambulance shot away with its siren blaring and lights flashing.

Chapter 16

Selwyn's joy at arriving home with the estate's finances restored was short-lived. He'd just dropped off Sebastian at his cottage and hauled his cases from the Jag's trunk when the heavy door swung open and Mrs Soames waddled out to watch his approach. 'Commander, am I glad to see you 'ome,' she announced.

'And I'm glad to see you, Mrs S,' he replied without glancing up, his attention occupied by his luggage. He looked up and his cheerfulness ebbed as he caught the housekeeper's anxious expression. 'What is it?'

'It's just been on the local radio. It's the mayor. She's badly in 'ospital. There was a dreadful fire at her 'ouse.'

'Oh my God.' He could actually feel the colour draining from his face. 'How bad is she? I must go at once.' He dumped his cases in the hallway and turned back to the car.

'I don't know 'ow she is. Such a to-do, it was. Fire engines, ambulances, police cars.' As she pursued Selwyn down the steps, Mrs Soames continued to recite the lurid details, only stopping when he'd jumped into the car and driven off at speed.

Fortunately for him, once he'd forced his way through the press of reporters and well-wishers at the hospital, the consultant overruled the matron's refusal to let Selwyn see Miriam. He'd called in to check on the patient and happened to be one of the commander's bridge circle. 'Ten minutes, and no more. And don't get her excited, Selwyn,' the medic instructed. 'She's had a very close call.'

Miriam lay with an oxygen tube in her nostrils. Her languid eyes widened at the sight of Selwyn, and her lips parted as if to speak.

'Oh, my love,' Selwyn murmured, and clasped the hand she'd slowly stretched out to him. 'For you *are* my love, no matter what you may think. I've just got back from France and heard. I couldn't bear to have lost you.' The long-pent-up emotion started to flow out of him.

Miriam offered him a gentle smile and attempted to say something, but her face set in a grimace at the pain of trying to speak.

'Hush,' Selwyn coaxed. 'Let me do the talking. I tried so many times to contact you, to say how sorry I was and how much I missed you. Please forgive me.'

Miriam managed a nod and a faint smile.

He sat next to her in silence and caressed her hand as she slipped in and out of sleep. Then her eyes opened fully.

'I'd kneel down to do this,' said Selwyn, 'but I'd be talking to the side of the mattress. Also, I don't have a ring with me. Bit of a bad show, I know, but… Will you marry me, Miriam? Not the best of proposals, but I've wanted to ask you for so long.'

Her eyes widened once more, but the only reply he received was an anxious frown.

'You really will have to leave now, sir,' said the matron, who'd been hovering diligently to ensure that Selwyn got no more than his allotted time. 'This patient needs her rest.'

Reluctantly, the frustrated and crestfallen commander said goodbye and made a promise to return.

Return he did a matter of hours later, this time armed with a bouquet. He peeked about worriedly for any sight of the morning's dragon-matron, but happily her shift appeared to have ended.

'Hello, old thing,' he greeted Miriam tentatively, relieved to find her sitting up in bed looking very much better. And, as she declared, feeling much better too. Her smile of greeting reassured him that their relationship was at least on a better footing.

'The flowers are lovely,' she said, admiring them before she fixed her eyes on his.

'Do you remember much of my earlier visit?' he asked cautiously, after the preliminary exchanges of conversation.

She smiled. 'Yes, especially that you proposed to me.'

'And?'

'Before I answer, there's something I need to say. Have you heard from Amanda? Or about what happened in the council meeting?'

'Yes, to the latter, but that's courtesy of those blighters at the *Chronicle*. Mrs Soames said they'd been badgering her constantly to get hold of me for a comment. Managed to dodge them coming here, but there's been nothing from Amanda. Tried to call her but there's no reply. I've been trying to get my head round it all. Anyway, exciting though it all is, it's your answer that's more important to me right now.'

Miriam reached for his hand. 'I've been desperate without you, even though I could have strangled you for deceiving me.' Selwyn lowered his eyes and only looked up when she squeezed his hand and smiled. 'Over the past few days, I've come to realise you really do love me.'

'And?'

'And, of course, that I love you. However… '

His hopes faded at the word and change of tone.

'If I were to say yes, it would look like I was doing so because of the change in your circumstances after finding the land transfer documents.'

Selwyn snorted. 'Never heard such tommyrot. Don't you think I know you well enough to know you'd never do such a thing?'

'I wouldn't want you to ever think that.'

'Then worry not. It'll never happen.'

Miriam glanced at the flowers again, then back at him. 'Then I'd love to marry you. Mind you, I'll still want to keep my position with the council and my internet business.'

He chuckled. 'Wouldn't have it any other way. Just as long as you can juggle all that with helping me to keep the hordes in order, once the hall's open to the public.'

Surprise and delight lit up Miriam's face. 'That must mean you've got the estate money back!'

'Well said, that woman. I have indeed.' Selwyn was positively beaming now. 'Sebastian finally acquired Vincent's account, and the money was virtually all there.'

'Oh, that's marvellous, Selwyn. I'm so, so pleased for you.'

He surreptitiously took a small box from his pocket and opened it before Miriam's eyes. 'Hope you like it and that it fits, my love, but if not we can change it.'

Miriam sniffed. This was the final straw. The beauty of the ring, his proposal, the stress of the last few days, the joy of Selwyn having retrieved the money, and the news that the hall would indeed be opened to the public...

Tears of joy flowed freely down her cheeks.

***

Having missed a call from Amanda on his way back from France, and having been frustrated in his attempts to return it, Sebastian's determination to sort things out with her took him directly to the library, where he was told only that she was at the council chambers and not expected back for at least an hour, if indeed she returned that day.

Somewhat deflated, he took himself off to the Mazawat café where Gwen was only too keen to dance attendance on him. 'It's been so long since I saw you last,' she complained. 'I really miss you.'

He was guarded in his reply, unwilling to fan any smouldering embers that might still linger for him in her heart.

'Are you and the librarian still an item?' Gwen asked, on her return with his cappuccino. Sebastian nodded. 'Only I've seen her a few times in here with that fella Martin.'

Despite being aware that Gwen was once more stirring things, Sebastian found his jaw tightening at the mention of Martin's name. 'Yes, they're just friends.'

'Hmm.'

'She helped him sort out his Uncle Alexander's affairs, and now she's doing the same for his aunty, who died recently.'

'How very helpful of her.'

Sebastian was in a sour frame of mind when he returned to wait outside Amanda's office. Even the sight of his fiancée's large, almond-shaped eyes as she eventually marched down the corridor towards him failed to arouse his usual excitement. He put this down to tiredness after the long journey home – five-hour nap notwithstanding.

Amanda was still fuming as she went back to work. Her suspension had been lifted, but they might have given her the rest of the day off. She'd already taken all her personal items home and the office looked like an empty warehouse. 'Not the hint of an apology,' she murmured angrily to herself as she approached Sebastian. She was also running late for a meeting with the matron at her nan's care home.

Seeing Sebastian, her thoughts turned immediately to the commander and how she'd avoided answering his calls. She'd felt so guilty at having put off the evil day of telling him about the missing documents, about how she'd had them in her hands and failed to secure them. She dreaded to think how he would react. She hated even more that, to protect her brother, she still couldn't disclose anything. Her heart began to pound with renewed anxiety and thumped all the faster at seeing the expression on Sebastian's face.

'Hello, what brings you here?' she asked.

'Aren't you pleased to see me?' He seemed taken aback by her coolness.

She smiled. 'Of course I am, you ninny. I've just got a lot on my mind at present, and not a lot of time. Come into the office.'

'You never seem to have much of that, these days.'

Amanda frowned, confused.

'Time,' he clarified.

She planted a soft kiss on his lips. 'That's a down-payment. Now, what's all this grumpiness about?' *Please don't let him say that Selwyn wants to see me!*

'I'm not grumpy, it's *you*. You're always busy.'

'Don't be so ridiculous. You're the one who's been absent, gallivanting through France.'

'Hardly gallivanting. There was precious little joy in dealing with all that bureaucracy. What's more, as soon as my back was turned you were off with bloody Martin. Llandudno for a dirty weekend, no less.'

Her hackles now fully risen, Amanda gave him a withering glance. 'Oh, that hoary chestnut again. If you showed me more affection and attention, it would be a different story.' She regretted the words as soon as they'd left her lips. That wasn't what she'd intended to say, nor what she'd meant. She hadn't even rebutted his accusation about the weekend away.

But the die was cast. 'So that's it, is it?' Sebastian glared down at her. 'You prefer his company to mine.'

'No, I don't. It's not that at all. It's just—'

'I don't think this relationship is going anywhere any more.'

The words, which she'd recently heard predicted by Maurice of all people, cut to the quick. Amanda bit her lip to try to hold back her emotions. 'Please, Sebastian.'

He shook his head. She stared at him for any sign of regret or uncertainty, but there was none. Slowly, she slid the engagement ring off her finger and held it out to him. 'Then I suppose you'd better have this back. I wouldn't want to waste any more of your time.' She barely managed to get the words out through the flood of emotion that burst upon her.

He stared at it and then into her moistening eyes before grasping it and storming out of the office.

Amanda collapsed into her chair and burst into tears.

**

Seated in his car opposite the library, Sebastian gripped the steering wheel and stared down at the ring. His shoulders shook as he sobbed uncontrollably, anguished at what had just happened. His acceptance of the ring had been the final and defining slam of the door on their relationship.

He glanced through the side window at the building. Surely, there was still time? It wasn't too late to run back, clasp her in his arms, apologise, say what a big mistake he'd made then smother her in kisses and put the ring back on her finger.

He was about to jump out of the car when the spectre of Martin arose. He stared back at the steering wheel. She hadn't refuted his accusation about Llandudno. His thoughts and logic became clouded in confusion and resentment. He wiped his eyes, gave a deep sigh and started the engine.

**

Once again, having waited some twenty rings for her brother to answer his blasted mobile, Amanda cut her call to Stevie. She paced the pavement outside the Qwik Qwak restaurant, trying to wipe her eyes dry before she returned to Martin.

Her despair knew no bounds. Despite her reinstatement at the library, her inability to contact her brother was too much to take on top of the loss of Sebastian and her predicament over the second set of documents. Since Maurice's threat, her calls had gone unanswered; nor had there been any replies to the messages she'd left.

Not knowing if Miriam had been in contact with the commander, Amanda knew she must speak to him urgently, though she hadn't yet worked out how much she could tell him while concealing the truth. What she really feared was the interrogation that would result from her necessary vagueness. The only person she had left to turn to was Martin.

She went back inside and sat opposite him. Seeming to realise that she didn't need to be told again that Sebastian was a plonker who didn't deserve her, Martin turned the conversation to the land delineated in the Wisstingham set of documents.

'Although the Cresthaven land is worth a small fortune now, when the land was originally gifted it would only have been fields,' Martin explained. 'So I suspect the only interesting part of it, from the Fitzgeralds' point of view, would have been the priory site. That's where I think that subsequently the family treasure might have been buried. Otherwise, why trade land within the estate for it?'

'Maybe that explains why Maurice went off for a few days. For all we know, he could already have found the treasure.'

'And taken it?'

'God, I hope not.'

'I'm assuming you've told the commander about the documents?'

Amanda shook her head and stared down into her lap.

'Oh jeez! You must tell him, and quickly.'

'Yes,' she murmured. 'I know.'

***

The sound of the commander humming 'The Waltz of the Toreadors' as he passed her in the hallway brought a smile to Mrs Soames' face. All was clearly once more well between him and the mayor.

She was, therefore, in an equable mood when she answered the doorbell, and almost friendly to DI Stone as she led him to the drawing-room door. Her brightness was contagious, and Selwyn was happy to make Stone comfy with a cup of tea before he got down to business.

'Our experts have gone through everything we got from the original discovery of Monaghan's operation, what they found listed on the computers at that point, and then the stuff you brought back from France,' Stone said. 'They believe some of the smaller stolen items are missing.'

Baffled, Selwyn stared at him. 'Of course they'll be missing. They were probably sold on.'

Stone wandered over to the window, looked onto the lawn, then turned to face his host. 'I need to be careful what I say, Commander. I believe you're honest and trustworthy, so I'll level with you. Shortly after we broke up Monaghan's operation here, the Met raided a warehouse on a tip-off. They found stolen goods that had been shipped from here before our raid took place. We know this because the items tied in with the files we got from your computer. That left gaps in the records, against which we checked the items you brought back from France. These must have been systematically picked out by Monaghan, either legitimately as part of his reward or, more likely, just filched.

'Now, we would usually assume that he'd tried to sell some of the smaller items from his ill-gotten gains but, under the circumstances of his hasty exit from the estate, we think not. That would have been his nest egg, and I don't think he was ready to hatch it when he met his end. Anyway, smaller items like that are normally fenced as one lot to get a better price and minimise risk.'

Selwyn frowned, his tongue setting off on patrol around his molars. 'What exactly are you saying?'

'We suspect that some of the items have gone missing since they were recovered in France.'

The commander jumped to his feet. 'That's preposterous! You're implying that either Sebastian or I are responsible. I won't have it!'

'Or anyone else who came into contact with them,' Stone countered, clearly unmoved by Selwyn's indignation. 'Was there anyone else who could possibly have had access to these items?'

Selwyn's mouth snapped shut. What if the hitman had stolen the stuff? Or one of the Frenchmen? He couldn't admit to knowing that the stolen goods had been found in the house where the London villain's body had been discovered.

Stone watched the silent commander intently. 'Well?'

'I'll have to quiz Sebastian on that, since I wasn't there.'

'I can do that myself.'

'Yes. Yes, I suppose you can.'

'Please tell him to give me a call as soon as he can.'

'By the way,' said Selwyn, 'what's happened with that chap Tyson? Have you charged him yet? It could only have been him who was responsible for the fire.'

Stone glanced back, stared at him for a moment then

slowly shook his head. 'We've interviewed him at length and carried out tests, but there's no evidence to charge him with, nor any witnesses. Says he was so drunk that night he was completely out of it when the fire took place. We're keeping an eye on him and making further enquiries, but I reckon we've got a very smart and cool customer on our hands.'

Selwyn groaned. 'There's no bloody justice, is there?'

'I'm afraid you're preaching to the converted, Commander,' Stone replied as he turned to leave.

Alone once more, with only the distant sound of the housekeeper's receding muttering, doubtless at another foot-wiping transgression by the departed officer, Selwyn turned his mind to this new development of the missing stolen goods.

***

'Hi.' Sebastian greeted his uncle cheerlessly as he trudged into the drawing room, having been summoned for drinks and a chat. 'What's new?'

Selwyn glanced up at him, looking equally gloomy. 'DI Stone. He wants to speak to you.'

Sebastian breathed out a long sigh. 'What about this time? He's here so often, I don't know why he doesn't just move in and ask Mrs Soames to do his laundry.'

'More likely she'd stuff *him* into the machine.' Selwyn summarised the meeting he'd had with the DI.

'The bloody cheek of the man!' Sebastian fumed when his uncle had finished.

'You don't think the Frenchmen could have been responsible?'

Sebastian thought for a moment as he cast his mind

back. 'No. The small pieces were boxed up and under the pile of larger items. Anyway, I reckon they were in too much of a panic about the dead body to give any thought to them.'

Silence reigned as they pondered further. Then, simultaneously, they glanced at each other. 'You don't think…' started Selwyn.

'Maurice!' They stared at each other as their suspicion grew.

'But when?' Sebastian asked. 'It couldn't have been in France.'

'Then here, before we took the stuff to the police.' Selwyn looked wounded and incredulous. 'I just can't believe it of him.'

'Nor I, but Stone sounded very confident and no one else has been near the stuff. What if Amanda was right all along? By the way, where is she? And more to the point, where's Maurice?'

Sebastian dragged his foot across the rug. 'We've split up.'

'Oh no! What's gone wrong?'

'I'm not sure how it happened. She's been spending so much time with Martin—'

'So jealousy crept in, despite my warnings.'

Sebastian hung his head. 'I suppose it did.'

'I have to say, I don't think you've treated the girl right. It seems to me you've taken her and her affection for granted for a while now. I did warn you.'

Sebastian glanced across but the commander merely shrugged. 'She offered me her ring back and I took it.'

Selwyn groaned. 'And do you love her?'

'Yes.'

'Then you're a bloody fool. She's an absolute gem, and you've let her slip through your fingers. I strongly suggest you get down on your knees and get her back immediately before you lose her for good.'

'I'll go and ring her.' Sebastian made to leave the room.

'No, wait,' said Selwyn. 'I need to talk to her urgently, so I'll ask her to come round. She might be more amenable to that.'

'What do you want to talk to her about?'

'I'll tell you later. Now, what about Maurice?' asked Selwyn. 'Where is he? No doubt Mrs Soames will know.' He went over to the bell pull.

Within minutes the housekeeper had informed him that Maurice had gone off for a few days without saying when he'd return. Despite her confirmation that a few of his belongings remained in his room, both Sebastian and the commander began to fear the man had scarpered.

***

Eight o' clock came and so did Amanda, who sheepishly took her place opposite the commander and nervously nibbled at her bottom lip.

'I was very surprised and disappointed that you didn't take my calls or reply to my messages. I assume you didn't want to tell me that the second set of transfer documents had been found – though goodness only knows why,' said Selwyn.

Amanda, whose eyes had been fixed on the coffee table between them, flashed him a glance. 'I'm sorry.' Her voice was a mere murmur.

Selwyn could wait no longer to fire the question he'd

needed to utter as soon as she'd entered the room. 'Where are they?'

'I don't know. I assume Maurice has them. He found them.'

'But you had them at some stage. You took photos of them.'

She swallowed. 'Yes. He'd hidden them on the library shelves. I found them, then put them back. I wanted to discover what he was going to do.'

'But you must have thought he was up to no good. You've always believed that.'

'And you and Sebastian wouldn't hear a bad word against him,' Amanda retorted.

Now it was Selwyn's head that drooped.

'Not that I could tell you much at the time, you being in France, but I knew that if I called and told you he'd found the papers and was keeping them secret, he'd somehow wriggle his way out of the situation. I'd be berated for continuing to bad mouth your new best friend.'

'Nevertheless, the documents are missing. And so is he, apparently.'

'I know and I'm so, so sorry.'

Amanda looked so desolate and fragile that Selwyn went to sit next to the wretched girl and tried to comfort her. He felt more than a pang of guilt at how both he and Sebastian had refused to give any credence to her misgivings about Maurice. And as if that were not enough, the poor girl's engagement had been broken off.

'I'm sure we'll get them back,' he tried to reassure her. 'After all, they're valuable. And if he really is the person we now believe him to be, he won't dispose of them. He'll try to use them.'

Amanda smiled at Selwyn and wiped her eyes. He was such a good man. She desperately wanted to tell him about the priory site and her suspicion that Maurice might already have investigated it, but Stevie's face loomed large in her mind. In any case, she'd not yet heard from Martin, and much depended on what he might find.

Their meeting concluded, she made to leave – but not before Selwyn asked if she'd see Sebastian. That, she resolutely refused to do.

***

'Tomorrow night at the hall, if you can make it. Around 7.30pm,' Sebastian told Lucian.

'I'll be there. Selwyn doesn't know what it's about, does he?'

'No. I told you when you rang to set this up that I wouldn't tell him. He just thinks I want to have a chat about something.'

'That's fine. I'll see you tomorrow.'

'Yeah.' Sebastian rang off quickly.

***

Harry Gaverty slid the gun into his inside pocket. It had been a good friend to him over the years: got him out of many scrapes; threatened a fair number of people, crippled others, and relieved some of their lives. And in all that time, he'd only taken a couple of bullets himself. As always whenever he handled it, he recalled the highlights of his criminal career.

He glanced down at the photograph he'd removed from the bottom drawer where it had always been kept safe. 'This one's for you, Vincent,' he murmured. He'd have lingered over his memories of Monaghan, but there was a knock at the door. Harry quickly replaced the photo and shouted.

In walked Jock. 'Ready when you are, Harry. The van's outside.'

Harry's narrowed eyes turned to him. 'You sure it's been cleaned out?'

'Aye, it's like a new pin.'

'Got yer shooter?'

Jock tapped his breast pocket.

'Then let's go.'

When they reached the van, Gaverty opened the passenger door, gave the inside a critical once-over, then hauled himself onto the seat. 'Where've you booked?' he asked, several minutes into the journey.

'The Inquisitive Duck, near Hopestanding.'

'Not a doss 'ouse, is it?'

'Och no, it's one of the best in the area.'

'That's alright, then.'

'So we hit them tomorrow, eh?' asked Jock.

'Yeah, tomorrow night. Do the business, then back 'ere sharpish.'

***

Normally a patient man, Berensen was beginning to worry if Fox was already on the estate or, if not, was likely to return to it. He'd not seen a hair of the man, despite almost continuous monitoring through his iPad, and he was painfully aware that he should have already started on his next contract. Not even the splendid dinners at The Inquisitive Duck could distract him from his anxiety.

Casually dressed and seated at his usual table in the

main dining room, Berensen blended in with the sartorial offerings of the other guests except for the jeans-clad couple nearby who, from their overabundance of happiness and preoccupation with each other, were probably newlyweds.

He was pondering whether to make a further visit to the housekeeper, the following day, when two men in dark suits were escorted to a table in the window, which they declined. The hitman watched as the waiter led them to the table they indicated at the rear of the room.

From their body language, Berensen singled out the smaller, wiry man as the boss and the taller, angular one as the henchman. He had little doubt that they both knew how to handle themselves, and that the boss was accustomed to getting just what he wanted without argument. As such, they fitted a profile that Berensen knew only too well.

As the new diners took their seats, they scanned the room and appeared to weigh up each of its occupants. The smaller man's attention lingered on Berensen for seconds longer than it did on the others. Aware of this, the hitman fixed his gaze slightly off from the man as he pondered the possibility that Cutler had sent them for him, Fox – or both of them.

During his meal Berensen darted glances at the duo and concluded he was not their quarry. Nevertheless, he left the table immediately after dessert and headed quickly to his room. He ensured the loaded gun remained by his side throughout the evening, and that a chair was propped under the door handle while he slept with the gun beneath his pillow.

Chapter 17

Archie was most pleased with the progress the Carey brothers had made at the priory site. Though much of the work had been achieved by brawn and brute force, at one stage they'd needed to bring in a small excavator, which meant clearing an access through the bordering vegetation. Once or twice vehicles had passed along the road, but no one had stopped or appeared to show any interest in what was going on.

The removal of two of the tombstones and the underlying earth revealed old timbers laid across a stairwell. This led down into the crypt that Ingrams had believed was there, and which the superstitious Careys refused to enter. Archie, therefore, had undertaken the exploration himself.

With only the borrowed light from the stairwell, the room was in virtual darkness. The air was cold, but not as damp as might have been expected. During a brief search with a flashlight, Archie came across three coffins that cast eerie shadows on the stone walls and barrel-vaulted ceiling. Recesses had been cut into the walls at regular intervals, probably for candles.

The stone coffins were simple, with no ornamentation other than the wording and symbols carved into the lids. Using the Careys' pickaxe, crowbar and scaffold pole, Archie found he could move the lids. He prised them open just far enough to determine whether the coffins were occupied.

To his relief, this was one of Ingrams' predictions that fell short of reality. The monks fleeing from the dissolution must have either taken the remains of their abbots with them or buried them elsewhere on the site in unmarked graves.

That was as far as his initial reconnaissance had gone. The Careys' impatience to be paid and leave prevented any further investigation of the coffins, so Archie decided to continue his search the following day. Satisfied with their remuneration and the price they'd negotiated for the tools, which Archie kept hold of, the Careys drove off in their battered, backfiring van.

Shortly afterwards, Archie replaced the wooden beams. He headed for the car to return to the hall, his plans already laid and well-rehearsed. If Fitzgerald was back and asked about the documents, Archie would present them to him. After all, he'd gleaned all he needed from them. If the commander wanted to know why he'd not left them in the library, he'd simply say he'd taken them to Oxford to have them authenticated but had found no one to do it. Of course, if Fitzgerald hadn't returned or didn't yet know about the documents, he'd keep quiet and hang onto them either for ransom or as a possible bargaining tool. He'd need any money he could gain, in addition to money from the fenced goods, to sustain his continued evasion of the law and Cutler.

The light was fading by the time Archie drove through the estate gates. 'Good evening, my dear Mrs Soames,' he greeted the housekeeper when she admitted him.

'Mr Fox, I thought you'd met with some mishap, all this

time you've been away. Do come in and make yerself at 'ome. Shall I bring you some tea?'

He glanced at his watch. 'I think I'll forego that pleasure, dear lady,' he said, his hopes set on something stronger. 'Has the good commander returned yet?'

'Oh yes, a couple of days ago, but 'e and Sebastian are out. I'm expecting them back around sevenish. Dinner's at eight, and I do believe there's another gentleman joining 'em, accordin' to Sebastian, though we're not to let on to the commander. Something of a surprise. So there'll be the four of you.'

'In which case, I'll go and have a lie down then freshen up, though I must admit a quick livener wouldn't go amiss.'

Mrs Soames face crinkled in a conspiratorial smile. 'You just go and help yourself to some of the whisky, Mr Fox. Not 'is posh stuff, though.'

Archie smiled, gave her a wink and moved off towards the drawing room while the obliging housekeeper took it upon herself to lug his case upstairs.

***

Mrs Soames was both mystified and somewhat put out by the arctic reception the commander gave to her news that Mr Fox had returned. 'Has he, indeed?' was all that Selwyn said.

Sebastian looked no more welcoming. That they'd both greeted her warmly as they walked in indicated that they weren't otherwise in bad humour.

'Very well, Mrs S,' the commander continued eventually, his smile returning. 'I assume you've set a place for Mr Fox, though it's possible he may not be joining us for dinner.' He gave Sebastian an ominous glance.

'Yes, Commander.' Mrs Soames was thankful that Maurice had taken himself upstairs. She decided upon quiet obedience in view of the no-nonsense tone in the commander's voice.

Selwyn watched her retreat to the kitchen, gently shaking her head in bafflement and muttering in a low voice, then propelled his nephew into the drawing room. 'In terms of how we approach the man,' he began, once they were seated over a drink, 'I think I'll just have to come out with it.'

'What about the documents? What if he refuses to hand them over?'

'Assuming they're here, we'll find them.'

'And if they're not?'

Selwyn's tongue went off on a minor reconnoitre. 'Then we'll lock him in the old cell until he does, or until he tells us where we can find them.'

Sebastian grinned. 'That's a bit medieval, isn't it?'

'Needs must. We might still have some of those thumbscrews,' Selwyn said, giving his nod to the black humour of the situation.

'*And* there are the missing stolen goods.'

'Crikey, yes! That'd be the icing on the cake. When we see him, I'll start the proceedings and we'll see which way he jumps. You play good cop and I'll play the bad one.'

***

In his hotel room, Gaverty checked his gun and slipped it back into his pocket. Next door, Jock followed a similar routine then checked the throwing knife, his preferred weapon. He considered himself highly proficient with it after years of practice.

Harry opened his door and glanced up and down the corridor before tapping gently on Jock's door. On the first-floor landing, they passed the man they'd seen in the dining room the previous evening. With the briefest of nods, the three men acknowledged each other and moved on, two of them to reception, the other to his room. After their bills were settled, Harry's van headed in the darkness towards Hopestanding and Wisstingham.

In much better spirits, having seen Fox's borrowed Volvo returning to the hall, Berensen changed into a suit, checked his Ruger and nestled it in his inside pocket. His bag packed, including the packet of latex gloves he always wore while in hotel rooms, he consulted his watch. He'd need to take down the security camera at the Wisstingham gates before driving up to the hall; that meant he'd have to leave in five minutes, allowing time to check out.

***

Seated in a corner of the Ferret and Wardrobe, Amanda looked up from her handkerchief as Kathy returned from the bar with the drinks. Amanda gave her a smile, then blew her nose. Loudly.

'OK, your horn works. Now try your lights,' Kathy quipped.

Amanda gave a slight splutter and a grin. 'Hey, you get your own jokes. That's one of mine.'

'I know, just paying you back. So, tell me. Bare all to Aunty Kathy. It's all strictly off the record, I promise.'

Amanda's smile vanished as quickly as it had appeared. 'I just came from the hospital. Nan was admitted this morning. She's got cancer. Two weeks to live, at the most,' she mumbled through a fresh wave of grief.

Kathy reached for her friend's arm. 'I'm so, so sorry.'

'I knew it would happen one day, but it still comes hard. She doesn't even recognise me.'

'Perhaps it's for the best.'

Amanda shook her drooping head.

'And what's this about Sebastian?' Kathy asked.

'We had a row. He accused me of spending too much time with Martin, and I accused him of not seeming to care any more. I offered him his ring back and he took it.'

'Idiot!' Kathy exclaimed.

'What him?'

'No, you. Well, both of you, really.'

Amanda was disinclined to argue with a viewpoint she'd already come to agree with. 'I miss him like hell.'

'Then go to him. He's a good bloke, Amanda, though he could do with turning down the volume on his shirts a bit. He loves you madly, believe me. And you love him.'

Amanda nodded silently, desperately trying to hold back another flood of tears. Any life had long since been wrung out of her very moist handkerchief.

'Where is he now?'

'At his cottage or at the hall, I assume.'

'Then go there. I'll drive you back home to get your car.'

Amanda stared into the fire. A return to the hall could be fraught with problems. What if Maurice had returned and convinced the commander and Sebastian that there was nothing wrong? How would they react to her, and what hope would there be for her and Sebastian then? She turned back to her friend. 'But what if... ?'

'No buts,' Kathy insisted. 'Just use your unhappiness and charms, and he'll be all over you like a rash. I know it.'

Somewhat cheered, Amanda smiled at her friend. 'Do

you know what it is I love about you?'

'That I always buy the first round?'

Amanda managed a laugh. 'No, that you're so pragmatic and reassuring.'

'I still buy the first round, though,' Kathy insisted as they rose to leave.

Twenty minutes later, a more optimistic Amanda was on her way to Wisstingham Hall.

***

'Selwyn, my dear fellow, how nice to see you back,' Archie gushed as he breezed into the drawing room. He came to an abrupt halt when he observed the uncompromising set of the commander's mouth and Sebastian's stern expression. 'What ho, trouble at the mill?'

The doorbell rang in the distance.

'Trouble indeed, Maurice,' replied the unsmiling commander. 'There are a few things we want to ask you about.'

However, the opportunity to do so did not arise; in fact, for the next half hour all plans were thrown out of the window. In the days to come, all the survivors would struggle to piece together the mêlée that marked the evening of the third of February, 2011.

The confusion began with a shriek from the hall, followed by a commotion that grew louder as those involved approached the room. Suddenly the door burst open and Mrs Soames almost tumbled inside. Behind her were two suited men; one brandished a gun which, though it had been trained initially on the housekeeper, now scanned the room and threatened each of the three men in turn. The other intruder, a tall, thin but muscular man with bared teeth, stood a short distance from his colleague who was clearly in charge.

'What… ?' began Selwyn as the distraught housekeeper took refuge next to him.

'Shut it,' Harry barked, his tongue working between thinned lips. 'Nobody moves a muscle. I ain't known for my patience. You, get over there.' He gestured with the gun for Archie to go closer to Selwyn.

'Didn't even wipe their shoes,' Mrs Soames complained to Selwyn, almost under her breath.

'Fuckin' shut it, I said!' Harry turned narrowed eyes on Archie. 'Who the fuck are you?'

'Maurice Fox.'

Jock's attention darted between his boss and the others, though he hadn't yet drawn his gun. 'All four of them?' he asked, in a low voice.

'Not yet. Things to do,' Harry replied. 'All of you, sit down over there. Close like.'

The four prisoners complied and occupied one of the Chesterfields and an adjacent armchair. 'You!' Harry jabbed the gun at the commander. 'Where's Vincent's stuff and where's the filing cabinet that was in the stables?'

Selwyn raised his eyebrows. 'Stuff?'

Harry gave a low growl. He levelled his gun at Selwyn. 'Don't fuck me about. You know what I mean. The stuff he had from our enterprise.'

Although the gallant housekeeper had adopted a bulldog expression, which she now focused on the intruders, Selwyn could feel her body shaking.

Archie breathed an audible sigh. 'I say, I'm a visitor here and haven't a clue about what's going on. I—'

'Shut the fuck up!' Harry roared, then turned back to Fitzgerald. 'So, where is it? Or do I have to start doing some damage to someone before you tell me?' He glared at Mrs Soames, who bit down on her bottom lip.

Fitzgerald's reply was surprisingly calm. 'You're presumably talking about the stolen goods.'

'Yeah. Where are they?'

'Don't you think *we've* been looking for them?'

'You found Vincent's fuckin' 'ouse and got Ronnie killed into the bargain. You must've found the goods.' Harry's angry breathing was coming harder and faster.

'The guy who killed Ronnie took them,' Sebastian chirped up.

Harry slowly turned a malicious gaze on him. Out of the corner of his eye, he saw Jock's lips draw back fully as if he were about to bite into something – or someone.

'So the bastard's finally got something to say,' Harry sneered. All the pent-up emotions of the loss of Vincent and the adrenaline of the moment kicked in, bringing him to a precipice. The recovery of the stolen goods now paled into insignificance. He eyed Sebastian with all-consuming hatred and an insatiable lust for revenge. 'Here's one piece of filth I think we can dispense with right now.'

He smiled as he aimed the gun at Sebastian's head.

***

It felt so strange for Lucian to be driving up to the hall after all these years. Though surprised by the number of parked vehicles, he didn't dwell on them. Of greater concern was how he was going to start the business of explaining himself to his brother.

He brought his car to a halt next to the Jaguar he'd known so well. So Selwyn had hung onto it. Through all the hardness that had crept into his heart, solidifying like the calcium deposits in the water pipes of the stinking Chinese jail, there rose an upsurge of nostalgia that touched him deeply.

Lucian got out of the car and climbed the steps, wondering what he'd say to the housekeeper. He really hoped it was still Mrs Soames; then again, if it were, how would he keep her response quiet from the rest of the building? Always assuming the dear woman didn't faint on the spot at the sight of him.

He needn't have worried. When he arrived at the front door, it was ajar. He paused to consider whether to ring the bell or just enter. He decided on the latter and headed off in search of Mrs Soames to deal first with that aspect of the grand family reunion.

***

Frowning, Berensen stopped his purring Mercedes alongside the other vehicles on the driveway. The white van he'd observed in the hotel car park registered immediately. Once out of the car, he unholstered his Ruger and cradled it within his jacket as he mounted the steps. To his surprise and relief, he found the door open. He stepped quietly into the hall, looked in all directions, then stealthily headed in the direction of the raised voices.

The sudden distraction of Sebastian's glance to the door as he caught sight of something or someone caused Harry to pause and swing round. He took one glance at the familiar, blond newcomer standing in the doorway and had almost demanded, 'Who the fuck are you?' when a shot rang out. There was a shriek from Mrs Soames, who seemed to fold in the middle before falling to the floor.

In the kitchen, Lucian halted at the sound of the shot.

His mind was instantly transported to Hong Kong and the times of high risk, high profits and high chance of death. In the dim light, he found where the cutlery used to be kept and fumbled through it until he'd selected a long-bladed knife. He crept stealthily towards the door, then headed in the direction of the gunshot.

***

Having been surprised to see almost everybody's car outside the hall except for Sebastian's, Amanda trudged towards the cottage in case he hadn't left to join Selwyn yet. Timekeeping was not always his forte, after all. She hadn't got far when a gunshot rang through the night.

She froze. Dithered. Was Sebastian safe in the cottage? But in that case, he'd come running at the sound. Or was he in the hall?

She had no idea which way to go.

***

Harry stood frozen in time, a look of surprise on his face and a neat hole in his forehead. A split second later, his body lurched backward and fell to the floor. Before Jock could reach into his inside pocket, he suffered a similar fate. The back of his head collided with the corner of an escritoire before his lanky body finally came to rest on the Persian carpet.

Alongside and below the commander's crouched, shielding body, there came a moan as Mrs Soames came to. She lifted her head and gazed in horror at what she saw. 'Oh, the carpet… '

Selwyn stared at the newcomer, who struck him as a very different kettle of fish from the first round of intruders. Since he'd fortunately – or unfortunately, who was to say? – seen a few bodies in his time, the sight of two decidedly dead criminals didn't markedly distress him. He put his arm round Mrs Soames, who stared blankly at the blond hitman.

'You're not working for any Swedish ambassador,' she muttered.

Or at least, that's what Selwyn thought she said. The poor lady was still quite confused and faint.

Relieved that nobody else seemed inclined to pick a fight with him, Berensen turned a smile on Fox who, from the expression on his face, now knew for whom the bell was about to toll. 'I believe we have some business to do, Mr Archie Fox. Please come with me.' He focused on the stern but calm man he assumed was the commander. 'I have no intentions of hurting any of you, but I must insist you remain here for ten minutes. Do not do anything, if you value your lives. Also, I am needing your mobiles, please.'

By now, the moaning Mrs Soames had roused herself and was laboriously trying to get to a kneeling position. 'Do help her. You *are* Commander Fitzgerald, I assume,' said Berensen.

Selwyn took in the assassin's details. Now, here was a real professional, a mercenary, Scandinavian, perhaps, from his accent.

Seated back on the Chesterfield, her gaze steadily fixed away from the two bodies and the mayhem created in the room, Mrs Soames glared at the hitman. 'An' 'ow I thought you was a gentleman.'

'We all have imperfections, madam.'

Selwyn felt a chill at the calm detachment and politeness of this cold-blooded killer. He'd faced a few desperate situations, but this was surreally different.

'The mobiles, please,' the Scandinavian reminded them. 'One at a time, on the table over there. The line to the house is already, how do I say, unavailable.'

Selwyn and Sebastian reluctantly complied.

'Oh, not you, Mr Fox. You can keep yours. You won't need it long, anyway.'

Archie glared at him. 'Cutler?'

'I am professional,' was the only reply he got. The hitman turned to Sebastian. 'You will come with me as insurance.' He glanced at the commander. 'If you do nothing, he will be safe. If not?' He raised the gun and shrugged.

'Take me instead,' Selwyn offered.

His offer was politely declined.

***

Finding the cottage unlocked but no sign of Sebastian anywhere inside, Amanda started to run back towards the hall, almost shaking from the surge of adrenaline.

***

Logic quickly forestalled Lucian's impulse to approach the scene. To dash into the room with only a knife would doom him to failure. He remembered Selwyn's revolver and where he'd always kept it, checked to see the coast was clear, and crept quietly upstairs.

Search as he might, there was no trace of the revolver nor the box of bullets. Clutching the knife tightly, Lucian retraced his steps downstairs. He'd just passed the first landing when Sebastian appeared with an older man both walking slowly towards the front door.

The scene swiftly descended into a state of bewildering mayhem.

Lucian shouted out to Sebastian just as Berensen came into view. It was as Berensen turned to train his gun on Lucian that a panting Amanda burst through the rear door. The split-second distraction of her scream was enough for Berensen's shot to miss its mark. Lucian ducked backward and was obscured by the line of exceptionally solid banister rails.

Adjacent to the open front doorway, Archie saw his chance and hurtled through it.

Berensen ran to the front door and fired a shot into the darkness. He turned to look back at Sebastian, decided against the burden of a hostage and disappeared in pursuit of his mark.

Somewhat hampered by the need to bear Mrs Soames' weight, Selwyn slowly went into the hallway towards Sebastian. Amanda reappeared from where she'd hidden and rushed into Sebastian's arms, while Lucian made his way down the stairs. He'd just reached the ground floor when he came face to face with Selwyn.

Lucian held his brother's gaze as both the commander and housekeeper stared at him in utter astonishment. Selwyn's jowls drooped in slow motion and his eyes widened as realisation and incredulity struck. 'Lucian? No, it can't be.'

'Yes, Selwyn, it's me.'

Selwyn's hand rose slowly, as if to dispel an apparition, then his other arm suddenly drooped under the collapsing weight of Mrs Soames. Amanda dashed over to support the poor woman and help her to the kitchen.

'Selwyn, what do we do now?' Sebastian cut in.

Selwyn dragged his gaze from his brother's face and turned to his nephew. 'I'd let that villain get on with it, but Maurice—'

'The hitman called him Archie.'

'Fine. Archie has our documents. I'm going after them.'

'It's too dangerous.'

'I'll get my revolver.'

Lucian shook his head. 'Selwyn, it's not where you used to keep it. I went to find it just now.'

'That bastard Fox must have it,' Selwyn growled. 'The damned mountebank. I'll have to manage without.'

'I'm coming with you,' said Lucian.

'And me,' added Sebastian.

'Alright. You'd better arm yourselves with something.' Selwyn glanced at Sebastian, then at Lucian. 'You take bloody good care of him, OK?'

Lucian nodded. 'As if I wouldn't.'

'Amanda,' said Selwyn, as he went to rummage through the knife drawer, 'don't go near the drawing room. Lock all the doors after we've gone, get yourself up to speed with Mrs Soames on what's happened, and phone the police. Tell them there's an armed and dangerous man loose on the estate in pursuit of Fox, and that we've gone off to try and find him.'

Amanda sighed. *Nothing new there, then.* She looked at Sebastian. 'For God's sake, take care.'

Each armed with a knife, the men disappeared through the front door leaving Amanda with the prospect of facing DI Stone, which she certainly didn't relish. On balance, she decided as she locked the door, she'd rather be out in the rain hunting deadly criminals.

Chapter 18

'What's the plan?' Lucian asked Selwyn, once they were outside.

'We'd better split up. Fox will want to get off the estate, so he'll make for the Volvo. I'll go and find it. You two drive down to the old quarry road in case he's taken to the woods. If he's headed in that direction, you may be able to intercept him and get him away before the hitman arrives – because I'm certain that's what he is. Just be careful and don't take any chances.'

'You too, Selwyn,' said Lucian.

Selwyn saw no sign of the Volvo where it was normally parked, nor any sign of Fox or the contract killer. Resigning himself to heading into the woods, he glanced down at the knife. He felt very ill-equipped to tackle a killer whose professionalism had been displayed only too well.

***

Terrified, Archie used his one advantage: his knowledge of the terrain. The daily walks with Mustard had taken him almost everywhere within the estate boundary. Nevertheless, he could hear his pursuer close behind and it was nearly impossible to locate familiar landmarks without a torch.

Panting, he stopped to get his bearings. He realised he could go no further into the wood; not only was there the risk of getting lost, but his energy reserves were already low. He really needed to double back to try to reach the Volvo.

After what seemed an age, he stumbled across a hollow in the ground big enough to hide a man. Pausing for a second to wipe the sweat from his brow, he scrambled down, pulled as much of the undergrowth about him as he could, and tried desperately to control his panting as the hitman's approach grew louder and louder.

***

Lucian veered off the Hopestanding road onto the old quarry road and brought his Ford Focus to a halt outside the deserted barn. It was the place that had seen the start of his fall from grace many years earlier, when he'd become involved with Monaghan's illegal racket. He glanced at its black outline silhouetted against the moonlight that cleared the treetops on the edge of the wood.

The thoughts that flooded back to him were interrupted by the unfriendly glance Sebastian gave him. 'Brings back memories, does it?' his son asked, his voice hard and cold.

Lucian looked in vain for a trace of understanding or compassion in Sebastian's eyes. 'Yes, it does. I got involved with Vincent and his racket. Times I'm not proud of and would dearly love to change.'

'Is that why you ran out on everyone? On my mother and me?'

'No, I went because Mary sent me away. I would've fought to keep her, but she told me you were Vincent's child and closed ranks on their marriage. I couldn't fight that.'

Sebastian stared at the barn then at Lucian. 'Did you love her?'

'I adored her and still do. And I would have adored you,

our son.' He fixed his eyes on Sebastian's. 'I would have come back much earlier, but I was stuck in that damned jail.'

'What did you do?'

'I took the rap for someone, but I also went inside to save my own life. It was complicated.'

His words seemed to hit home. 'So ... we mattered?'

'You'll never know how much. I was always convinced you were mine.'

They looked at one another, Sebastian's gaze now softer. Lucian grabbed his hand. Sebastian smiled and squeezed back. 'I suppose we'd better try and find Maurice,' he murmured.

'Perhaps a few more minutes to talk, eh?'

A couple of minutes was all they managed, and they were both too fixated on scanning the woods and road to concentrate on what was being said. Finally Lucian told Sebastian to stay put. He got out of the car and made for the shelter of the side of the barn. Other than nature's eerie noises of the night, there was no sound of any human movement.

***

'I don't believe this. I just don't believe it!' Roger Stone fumed, his knuckles white as he gripped the receiver. 'What sort of a bloody circus is the commander running there?'

'None of this is his fault.'

For some reason, the librarian's calm voice made his blood boil even faster. 'That man leaves a bigger trail of mayhem than Mr Magoo. Alright, you sit tight. Keep all the doors locked and don't answer them to anyone –

unless it's us, of course, or your mob. Lie low with anyone else who's there, preferably in a room without windows. Lock the door or barricade it, if you can. We'll send an armed unit. If the commander or one of yours gets in touch, tell them to abandon the search and return immediately to the hall.'

He hung up before he could add anything inadvisable, then called the armed response unit.

***

Shivering from cold and fear, his face pressed against the wet foliage, Archie lay motionless. He was conscious of the cold dampness and the beat in the vein that furiously throbbed in his forehead. The noise of movements in the undergrowth grew ever louder as his nemesis approached. The killer must surely hear the pounding of his heart.

Archie flinched as an animal's harsh cry burst out of the stillness, then there was silence. He sensed the killer must be slowly and carefully scanning the ground and surroundings for a sign of him. As the few chinks of light faded, presumably as cloud blocked out the moon, the sound of rustling resumed and gradually became fainter.

When all was quiet, Archie painfully shifted position as quietly as he could, raised his head and looked about him. The cloud had passed over and in the returning moonlight he could see no trace of his pursuer.

He lumbered to his feet and, with occasional backward glances, began to stealthily retrace his steps towards the hall. At the stable block he cut across to the lake garden, then to the mound of the folly and from there to the clearing in which he'd parked the Volvo, loaded and ready for escape.

***

Selwyn's search took him to the quarry lake. The moonlight was shimmering on its otherwise dark surface. He shook off memories of finding Bilton's body floating in its waters.

The dark flank of trees to his right marked the boundary of the wood, a useful guideline as he moved along the road. Every so often he stopped and listened. Apart from the odd bark of a fox or the hoot of an owl, all remained silent.

A twig cracked somewhere behind him and Selwyn froze, the knife handle clammy in his palm. He edged into the shadows at the side of the road, watched and waited.

***

Berensen was now completely lost in the denser part of the wood he'd ventured into. His occasional halts to listen for his prey's movement met with nothing more than the sounds of nature's night watch, now on duty.

The going was difficult. Very little moonlight pierced the canopy of the trees to ease his way, and the light from his mobile was almost useless. Now it was more a matter of escape from the wood than a search for his victim.

A car engine started; it sounded so far away that Berensen doubted the vehicle was even on the estate. Nevertheless, he was compelled to turn and follow the direction from whence it came.

***

Selwyn heard the familiar triple-cough of the Volvo growling along in first gear and resisted his first instinct to follow it, much as he wanted to get his hands on the rogue and the documents. Furious though he was, he had no means of pursuing a car. Even if he ran for the Jaguar, the cowardly swine would get clean away.

He seethed as the car engine faded away to silence and pressed on down the road. He was desperate to meet up with Lucian and Sebastian. While the questions he had for his brother were legion, his apprehension at Lucian's return was overridden by the joy of being reunited with him.

Ahead, he could now make out a car and a solitary person alongside it. He hoped it was either Lucian or Sebastian. Unsure, Selwyn hugged the edge of the trees as he advanced.

***

For several minutes, Lucian had kept his eyes trained on the wildflower meadow. In the moonlight, it looked like a badly floodlit football field. He could easily pick out anybody crossing it, but there was no one to be seen. If either Fox or his pursuer had already vanished into the woods, there was little more he could do to aid the chase.

He decided to return to the car and his son. He desperately hoped Sebastian had obeyed his instruction to stay in the car and be ready to drive off at the first sign of danger. He feared, however, that the lad was made of sterner stuff.

Fear brought urgency to his steps.

***

Sebastian was now increasingly worried and impatient. Barely able to see a thing through the windscreen, and completely unable to stay still, he'd done innumerable laps around the car. The only saving grace in the whole drama was that there had been no gunshots. Overhead, patches of cloud scudded across the moon.

As one cloud passed, he thought he saw a shadowy figure approaching along the edge of the trees. Panicked, he darted for the cover of the barn.

***

Berensen had never been so pleased to see a road and a car in his life, even such a dull car as a Ford Focus, but his relief was momentary. Much as he was relieved to be out of the woods, he should have been alone out here.

He drew out his gun, flicked off the safety catch, crept forward and took the risk of finally stepping into the light.

Lucian spotted the killer and Sebastian's fleeting shadow in the same instant. His boy was running right into the line of the killer's gunsight. He started forward. 'No, Sebastian! Get do—'

A shot shattered the silence, followed by another.

Selwyn gaped in horror as a cry rang out and Sebastian dropped to the ground. A figure emerged from the trees and walked steadily towards the car, his gun levelled at the body sprawled on the road.

To Selwyn's relief Sebastian tried to push himself up, but he flattened himself once again as the hitman grew near. Fearing that any sudden motions would surely get Sebastian killed, Selwyn could only watch helplessly.

***

Approaching the outskirts of Wisstingham, Archie considered his options. The Cusham house was unsafe now, but there was still the other bolthole. It was probably safe for only a few days more, but staying there would give him time to come up with somewhere else to go. Spain, France and Britain were blown; maybe he'd head somewhere quiet in Greece, find a small fishing village or town off the beaten track and rent an apartment.

One thing at a time. There was a job to be done.

He'd have to concentrate on that first, then think about longer-term strategies. After all, he still had some of the Tradesail stash he'd siphoned away over the years for times such as these. And, of course, there were the stolen goods to fence.

He pressed down on the accelerator, smiling at his deliverance and congratulating himself on his wiliness.

***

As the young man slowly rose from the ground, his hands in the air, Berensen grabbed him around the neck from behind and levelled the gun at his head. It seemed that he'd recovered his hostage. Now he needed to recover his car, assuming the police hadn't already arrived.

Berensen scanned the darkness as he forced his captive into the driver's seat, took the keys then quickly got in the passenger side. He handed Sebastian the keys. 'Drive to the car parking. Not on the main road. There is a way down here, yes?'

Sebastian merely nodded, started the car and drove off towards the quarry. On Berensen's instruction, they came to a stop at the garage block at the rear of the hall. As yet, there was no sign of any police presence.

'Keys,' Berensen demanded as they got out of the car. Holding the gun to Sebastian's head, he propelled him to the corner of the hall. 'Turn around.'

Sebastian's eyes betrayed his terror.

Berensen regretted needless violence, but he did what had to be done. He left the hostage motionless on the ground before reclaiming his black Mercedes and heading back down the old quarry road towards Hopestanding.

***

Anxious about Sebastian's abduction, all Selwyn could do was track down his brother, Lucian.

There was a faint cry from the woods. 'Keep making a noise,' he called out. There was an agonisingly long silence, then he heard what sounded like a stick being repeatedly banged against a tree.

Selwyn almost stumbled over Lucian's half-prone body. His brother's back was leaning at an uneasy angle against a tree trunk, his mouth working as if he were speaking to some invisible person. Selwyn crouched down.

'Is Sebastian ... alright?' Lucian asked.

'I hope so. The man made him drive away in your car.'

'Bastard!' Lucian panted through gritted teeth.

'How bad is it?' Selwyn gently pulled Lucian's hand away from the wound. Lucian tried to stifle a cry of pain. 'Oh Lord.'

'It's... not too good, I think. He's either a bloody good shot or very lucky.' Lucian let out a groan as he tried to shift position.

'Keep still, if you can.' Selwyn took a handkerchief out of his pocket. 'Here, press this against it as hard as you can. I'll go for help.'

Lucian grabbed Selwyn's arm as he made to rise. 'There's no need for that.' He fixed him with moist eyes. 'Someone will be here before long. Just stay and … let's talk while we still can.'

About to protest, Selwyn caught the look of calm resignation on his brother's pale face. 'Alright.' He sat down and clasped Lucian's hand. Anguish consumed him at the thought of another loved one about to slip from his grasp. Visions of earlier days, when Lucian had lived on the estate and both Felix and Mary had been alive, flooded in. 'What happened, Lucian? What on earth happened?'

'I made mistakes. Got in with the wrong crowd. I really wanted to come home, but things happened. I was in jail for years.'

Selwyn groaned. 'Why the hell didn't you tell us?'

Lucian looked incredulous. 'You told me not to communicate with you. Take the money and stay the hell away, you said.'

'I was angry because of the way you just vanished. One day at home and then weeks later – not a peep in between – you call from the other side of the world asking for money. I was furious at the time, yes, but I never meant you to think that I didn't want to see you again.' Selwyn sighed. 'I missed you so much.'

'It was shame.'

'Hmm?'

'I didn't know how to return. I'd done enough damage here, and was already dead as far as you all knew, so … time just went by. I kept trying to muster the courage to write but couldn't. And then I ended up in prison like the useless bugger I am.'

'No, no, no, don't say that. You're my brother, no matter what.' Selwyn's tears started to flow. He clasped Lucian's hand tightly. 'We'll get you right, don't worry.'

Lucian smiled and slowly shook his head.

Anger and hatred overshadowed Selwyn's grief. The thought of that odious Fox having caused all this was almost too much to bear. He'd strangle him if he got hold of him. Tear him limb from limb.

Lucian's low moan brought Selwyn back to the grim present.

***

It seemed to take the armed response team forever to arrive, having been on another 'shout', but DI Stone had to give them credit; when they did appear, they seemed to sweep the hall in about two seconds flat.

Parked at the far end of the drive, Stone stepped out of his car and went to meet Sergeant Selkirk as he jogged down from the hall.

'All clear so far. We're now ready to cover the grounds.'

'Do you know exactly who's out there?' asked Stone.

Selkirk pulled a face. 'Miss Sheppard tried to explain, but it's a bit of a farce.' He counted the reprobates on his fingers. 'The Scandinavian hitman's still on the loose along with his target, called either Maurice or Archie Fox. Then there's a posse made up of the estate owner, Commander Fitzgerald, Sebastian Monaghan and a third man identified by the housekeeper as Lucian Fitzgerald.'

'It can't be Lucian, he's dead. Jesus, that's all we need. Bloody heroes! Sounds more of a circus than a farce,' groaned the DI. 'Can you communicate with them?'

'No. The Scandinavian apparently took all their mobiles.'

Stone's eyes rolled. 'The evening just keeps on giving.'

'Do you know the terrain?'

'Do I?' Stone replied. 'I almost live here.'

'Any potential hideouts or ambush points?'

'Buildings all over the place. There's a large open area at the back of the hall that fronts onto a wood. Beyond that, there's a road that connects to the quarry and eventually comes out over there, beyond that folly.'

'Then we'd better get on with it.'

Stone walked rather more slowly behind Selkirk, who jogged to re-join and brief his men outside the hall. He could only huff in disbelief and shake his head at what lay ahead. The tedious interviews, endless resources to be fed into this wretched place's maw, and the critical supervision and interference of his superiors.

His precious pension had never looked so far away.

***

In the dark silence two voices, one more pained than the other, shared history, revelations and anguished emotions, each listener in the despairing knowledge that this was their only opportunity.

Lucian described his life in the Far East after he'd fled the estate, the desperate entrapment he'd fallen into with the criminal underworld, and the calamity of imprisonment that had ultimately befallen him. As Lucian spoke, Selwyn's spirits once more plumbed the murky depths of despair experienced after the deaths of his family, depths from which it had taken him so long to surface.

Lucian's hand, still gripped by Selwyn, gradually grew colder; his words became slower and more indistinct. Eventually they faded to mere whispers.

Selwyn shifted his position, put his arms as gently as he could around the stricken man, kissed him on the cheek and told him he loved him. It was not a moment too soon. Lucian's closed eyes drew wearily open and he offered a tired, fleeting smile.

As he sat next to his brother, the cold hand still in his, tears coursed down Selwyn's face. He vowed vengeance on both the killer and Fox. The dream that had suddenly arisen, of sharing life on the estate with the brother he'd thought was gone forever, was now gone. He was furious with himself for having trusted and been so taken in by that bloody fraudster.

The silence was broken by a car purring along the old quarry road away from the estate. Neither the Ford nor the Jaguar, it was quite probably the killer's, but Selwyn had no intention of releasing his grip on his brother in the vague hope of discovering the make and model before it vanished into the blackness.

Just how long it was before the silence was broken again, Selwyn had no idea. The first indication was a faint rustle of vegetation, then the snap of a twig. Selwyn's ears pricked up. Reluctantly, he let go of Lucian's hand and padded the ground around him to try and locate the knife he'd discarded. At last he found and grasped it.

He glanced down at Lucian, whose face, bathed in the moonlight, looked quite serene. He gently stroked his cold cheek then looked back up towards the trees.

'Armed police. Stay perfectly still and low on the ground,' ordered a voice.

'It's Commander Fitzgerald. We're here, up by the edge of the road. I think the other two fugitives have left the area. A car passed by several minutes ago.' Selwyn tossed the knife out of reach. Torch beams picked him out and he flinched away from the light.

'Sergeant Selkirk,' a black-clad figure introduced himself as he crouched by the commander. 'Are you injured?'

'No, but my brother's been shot. He's dead.'

'I'm sorry to hear that, sir. We'll clear the area to the road and call in an ambulance and support vehicle.' Instructing one of his men to remain, he moved off into the shadows.

Chapter 19

Organised chaos appeared to reign at the hall as its bedraggled and weary owner was escorted into the hallway by the armed officer. Several people in white overalls were milling around, some busily dusting for fingerprints while others carried equipment in and out of the main rooms. All bore looks of intense concentration on faces framed by the white hoods of their protective overalls.

Selwyn stared at the activity for a few moments without anyone attempting to engage with him, as if he were an invisible ghost. Then DI Stone appeared in the corridor from the drawing room, saw the commander and strode towards him.

'What the hell's been going on here?' he demanded.

Selwyn watched the approaching figure, whose fierce expression quickly became more deferential once he caught sight of the look on Selwyn's face. 'Commander Fitzgerald, sorry. Bit abrupt of me, I suppose.'

'Where's Sebastian? What's happened to him?' Selwyn asked.

'He's on a couch in the library, unconscious. We're waiting for the ambulance. He was found outside. Must have been knocked out.'

'Then I must go and see him.'

Stone raised his hand. 'The librarian's with him. We've taken her statement and we need to take yours. There's nothing you can do for him at the moment. A senior officer is also on his way. He's been tied up on another incident. Where can we talk?'

'We can use the garden room. No one was in or out of there all evening. I need to clean up first.'

'You'll have to do that upstairs and put on some protective overshoes and gloves before you come down. You'll get them from that officer over there. This whole floor's a crime scene. I'll be waiting for you.'

As Selwyn was about to go upstairs, Mrs Soames appeared from the kitchen where she'd finished giving her statement. She looked comical in her protective overshoes and gloves, though her face was still ashen. She took one look at him and hurried over. Stone looked impatient at this delay in the proceedings. Mrs Soames stared up at Selwyn's eyes for a long moment before throwing her arms about him.

'He's gone now, really gone,' was all the commander could blurt out above her bowed head.

She drew back to look at him. 'Lucian?'

He nodded, tearfully.

Mrs Soames let out a low moan. 'I don't understand what's goin' on.'

Over her shoulder, Selwyn could see the unsmiling DI as he looked on unsympathetically. He gently patted his housekeeper's arms and murmured, 'I'll explain everything later. I'd better get along and tidy myself up. You keep yourself busy, eh?'

As the poor commander departed, Mrs Soames reluctantly headed back to the kitchen, fishing about in her pocket for the handkerchief that had already done sterling service that evening.

'I think he could do with a strong cup of tea,' Stone suggested as she passed him.

Mrs Soames came to an abrupt halt and scowled at him. 'I don't need you or anyone else tellin' me 'ow I should look after my commander,' she retorted.

Several minutes later, Selwyn and Stone settled themselves in the garden room amidst its impressive array of potted ferns and palms.

'I'm still trying to get my head round whether the events of this evening are connected or merely coincidental,' the DI confessed, after Selwyn had described what had happened.

'I can't see there was any connection between the dead chaps… '

'Gaverty and Cameron.'

'… between them and the blighter who came after Maurice. Gaverty was after anything Vincent had left behind, as well as revenge for his death, it appeared.'

'If that's the case, it could wrap things up very neatly. According to your housekeeper, the other chap called your visitor Archie Fox, didn't he? If that's his real name, he may well be the same person who's wanted for questioning in Hillingden.'

'Oh?'

'Fraud and the suspicious death of his colleague.'

Crikey, Selwyn reflected miserably. It really did appear that they'd been seriously conned in France.

'It's imperative you tell us as much as you can remember of what he said to you.'

The commander's jowls sank at the prospect. 'Good Lord, that's asking something. There's been a lot of water under the bridge since then. Sebastian spent more time with him than I did.'

'Well, I'd better start with you, since your nephew is not

in a position to say anything right now.' Stone opened his notebook.

***

Unbeknownst to the DI, Sebastian was fully awake. Amanda had been talking to him at length about the Wisstingham land transfer documents and her mission in Llandudno. Though bleary, he appeared to absorb the fact that she and Martin hadn't disappeared on some seedy tryst.

It was while she was watching him trying to get his head around the fact that the Cresthaven industrial site was owed to the estate that a penny suddenly dropped. 'Oh, good Lord!' she blurted out, right in the middle of describing the priory site to him. She felt so stupid! 'It had all gone out of my head,' she exclaimed, then bolted out of the room and upstairs.

She eventually located Archie's room and began to search through the few belongings he'd left. He hadn't brought the documents or maps back with him from wherever he'd been.

'Bugger!' She sat on the edge of the bed and pulled out her mobile. 'Martin, it's me. Listen. Fox was here at the hall but he's gone. He may be on his way to the priory.'

'Then I'll go there right now.'

'I'll join you. Stay by the road until I get there. Don't put yourself in any danger.'

'I'll see you shortly.'

Amanda crept back downstairs, berating herself for being distracted from making the connection sooner. She couldn't tell Sebastian because the SOCO team had now moved back into the hallway. As for the commander, he was tied up with Stone who would only pose endless questions and then probably be unwilling to divert his resources.

She peeped round the corner to check for more lurking officers. When the coast was clear, she went to the kitchen in search of Mrs Soames. 'I'm going off to meet Martin at the priory to try and stop Maurice in his tracks,' Amanda told her. 'Make sure Sebastian and the commander know.'

Before the bewildered housekeeper could say anything, the librarian ran into the hall, through the front door and rushed to her car.

***

Archie grinned. Despite the onset of steady rain, the job was nearly done. In a few minutes he'd be on his way with his find carefully stowed in the car boot. It was by no means what he'd expected; when he was safely ensconced in his temporary hideaway, daylight would give him a better idea of what he'd found. Not that he could afford to stay there for long because his last bolthole would soon be discovered. He regretted the loss of his billet at the hall. It had been very comfortable, and Fitzgerald had been a generous and interesting host.

All that was needed now was to put out the lamp he'd rigged up, pull the timbers back into place over the entrance and make his getaway. As he closed the boot lid, he caught a flash of light reflected in the rear-view mirror. He turned and made out the steady approach of headlights, still some distance away. He switched on his torch, partially masked its beam and hurried back to the priory to take up a position behind a wall, as close as possible to the steps to the crypt.

The headlights looked awfully close now. There was no time to go down and extinguish the lamp, so he waited in the darkness, revolver in hand, sheltered from the driving rain.

***

For a split second, Martin thought he saw a pinprick of light through the rain-spattered windscreen. He slowed as his headlights picked out a car parked by the side of the road and came to a stop behind it.

Martin Brightside could never have been considered a *Boy's Own* hero, not by a long chalk; the derring-do type he certainly was not. The prospect of creeping around in the pitch dark and pouring rain on the site of an old priory, and possibly being accosted by a man of distinctly dubious character, was not one he relished. However, he was a gentleman. Ignoring Amanda's instructions to stay put, he decided he'd scout around to satisfy himself that the woman he still loved was not about to walk into danger.

He groped around in the glove compartment, found the flashlight then got out of the car. Although he'd previously visited the site with Amanda, any familiarity with it was dispelled by the darkness. He nearly tripped over a fallen branch and instinctively cursed as he stumbled through the rough vegetation, conscious that he could probably be heard a mile off.

Finally, he emerged onto open ground, wiped his wet brow and made for the source of the light a little way ahead of him. He was puzzled that it appeared to come from below ground; when they'd visited before heading to Llandudno, the site had been completely flat.

'Stop right there and don't move a muscle,' came a gravelly voice from behind, which, together with the jab of the cold gun against his neck, produced an involuntary cry. 'Walk slowly down the steps. I won't hesitate to shoot if you try anything.'

'Quite the melodrama,' Martin said, attempting to ease the tension while fighting back the sick feeling in his churning stomach.

'Except that the gun's for real and so's the threat.'

'Other people know I'm here.'

'Let's hope you're right and they find you still alive.'

At the bottom of the stairs the gunman, whom Martin assumed to be Fox, motioned him to stand against a wall that was dimly illuminated by a lamp set on one of the coffin lids. Each coffin lid had been prised out of position sufficiently to allow easy access.

Archie motioned the gun at one of them. 'In there.'

Martin's rising panic began to affect his breathing. 'What are you going to do?'

'You'll find out. Just get in.'

Martin stared at the gun then fixed his gaze on Archie's face to try and discern his intentions. He clambered into the coffin and sat there. He could feel the bile rising.

'Lie down.'

Martin was about to protest but the gun was levelled at his head. With some difficulty, he squeezed into the dusty, rough-hewn space.

'Keep your hands down.' With a grunt, Archie heaved the lid back.

'Oh God no! Please, no! Not this. Let me out, please, PLEASE!'

The villain had left a tiny gap, Martin noticed, which

gave him a moment's hope that he might escape. But, try as he might, he could neither lift nor move the lid from within.

***

Amanda gave a sigh of exasperation as she turned away from Martin's empty car. In front of it was the Volvo, so she had to assume that Archie was also around. She looked fruitlessly into the darkness and listened for any sign of either of them.

'I should have become a nun,' she muttered. 'Men are too much like hard work.' She switched her mobile to torch mode and threaded her way through the under-growth towards the priory.

When she was past the trees, she caught sight of a faint light; she hoped it was courtesy of Martin but feared otherwise. Arriving at the ruin, she was amazed to find steps leading down to what she assumed was a crypt. At the top, she stopped and listened. Sounds of movement came from below, together with a faint muffled noise as if someone were shouting from a long way off.

Amanda tried to control her breathing as she crept carefully down steps made slippery by the rain. At the bottom, she stepped gingerly through the puddle that had formed there. Now the stifled sound was more distinct; it was coming from the nearest of the three rectangular stone blocks that dominated the room. In the dim light she recognised them as coffins.

Oh my God, Martin's in there.

She'd just moved over to the coffin when a dark figure detached itself from the shadows at the far end of the room. Although her first instinct was to flee, she stood her ground and glanced around desperately for a weapon.

'Stop right where you are,' Archie ordered. 'I have a gun.'

'Something else you no doubt stole from the hand that fed you,' Amanda managed to reply.

'I don't imagine the commander will miss it much, dear girl.'

'Nor you. Quite the little kleptomaniac, aren't you?' She called out to the coffin, 'Martin, I'm here. You're going to be alright.'

'And for what exactly *are* you here?' Archie asked. 'Come for your share of the loot?'

'Did you seriously think I'd sell out like that? I only kept quiet because of my brother and your threat.'

Archie snorted. 'And you believed it, you gullible child.'

Amanda glared at the barely visible face and ground her teeth.

'I suppose you believed I'd actually give you a share of the proceeds as well.'

'Not in the least,' she snapped. 'I'd have to be a complete half-wit to believe that a charlatan and failure like you would honour any promise he made.'

Archie's equanimity promptly deserted him. 'Shut up, you cocky little bitch! Get over there to that coffin.'

'Most eloquent, Maurice. Old boy's gentlemanly bowler slipping a bit there, is it?' Despite her challenging tone, Amanda's pounding heart was signalling her fear.

'Get in the coffin.'

Her pulse began to race even faster. 'And if I don't?'

'Then you'll die with a bullet in you, so don't bloody tempt me. At least in there you'll have something of a chance.' As he approached her and the light, Archie's face was clearer now. His composure restored, he assumed a bemused smile that Amanda dearly wanted to wipe off his whiskered face.

She caught his gaze, held it and forced herself to smile back at him. 'What a shabby little man you are.'

'Get in.'

From behind, Martin's muffled shouts continued. Amanda glanced at the coffin, summoned up what little courage remained and climbed in. It was only when Archie finally heaved the lid back into place that her nerve failed her and she cried out.

With a smile at her capitulation, Archie started to remove all traces of his presence. He replaced the timber beams over the entrance and returned to the car, relieved that the desperate cries of the entombed victims could no longer be heard – not even from mere feet away.

***

DI Stone's interview with the commander was interrupted by the arrival of Sergeant Selkirk. Stone was relieved to have a break in a most circular conversation.

'Sorry to interrupt, sir,' Selkirk said, as he entered the room. 'I need to make my report before we withdraw.'

'Certainly, sergeant,' replied Stone, now on his feet.

'We've not found the fugitives. I reckon they've gone. We covered the grounds right up to the southern boundary road and through to the quarry. The front of the hall has also been searched, as well as the paddock, lake area, gardens, garage block, the stables and the buildings around that courtyard.'

Stone turned to look at the commander, who wore a crestfallen expression. 'Does that about cover the estate? Any other places or hidey-holes you can think of?'

'What about the folly?'

'That's also been covered. The lock to the door was still secure.'

'Then that sounds about it. No sign at all of the two men?'

The sergeant shook his head. Selwyn groaned and sat back in his seat.

'Very good,' said Stone. 'You may go. Thanks for the support.'

'Don't mention it, sir. Some of the men have got rather used to this particular area by now.' He threw a telling glance at Fitzgerald, who cleared his throat and looked away.

'He does have a point, Commander.' Stone rubbed in the allegation once Selkirk had gone. 'I dread to think how many police hours have been spent on this estate.'

'I'd remind you, Inspector, that none of this has been of my making. And it's certainly not been a bundle of fun to experience what's happened.'

'Although Archie Fox took up residence at your invitation.'

Selwyn's jowls drooped and his hang-dog expression returned. 'Yes, well, hang it all! A chap can't always get it right in sizing people up. He seemed first rate. How was I to know he was a bounder?'

'Went to the right school and played a straight bat, I suppose.' The words were out before Stone could stop them.

Selwyn glared at him. 'I'd appreciate your keeping a civil tongue in your head.'

Stone knew he'd overstepped the mark. 'Yes, I'm sorry. That was uncalled for and I apologise. I'd better go and check how my men are getting on, and then there'll be a few last details I need to clear up with you.'

'Apology accepted. I'll go and rustle up some tea.'

Stone strode ahead of him down the hallway until he reached door of the library where Sebastian was waiting for the ambulance. 'Have you told him about the death?' he asked Selwyn, quietly.

'No, and I don't intend to until he's been to the hospital.'

As Stone went off, nodding agreement, Selwyn took a deep breath, pursed his lips, and poked his head round the library door. Sebastian sat alone on the couch, focused on his mobile.

'How are you doing, my boy?' the commander asked. 'No sign of the ambulance?'

'I'm fine. No, not yet. It must be a busy night. Have you seen Amanda?'

'No, I thought she was with you.'

'She was. Suddenly rushed off and she's not been back.'

Selwyn walked over to the window and looked out. 'Her car's not there.' He glanced back at the lad's pale face. 'You sure your noddle's OK? Eyesight up to snuff, is it?'

'My head hurts but I can see OK. No double vision. I don't think it's anything serious.' His face turned bleak. 'Selwyn, where's my father?'

The word 'father' stung. Selwyn closed the library door and went to sit next to Sebastian. He stared at the floor as he spoke. 'I wasn't going to tell you until you'd been to the hospital. I'm sorry, my boy. Lucian was shot and passed away in my arms.'

Selwyn's shoulders started to shake. Sobbing, he looked into Sebastian's moistening eyes then clasped and hugged him. They remained like that for some time before

Selwyn drew away and said, 'He was a brave and lovely man. He saved your life.'

Sebastian nodded, dislodging many tears of his own onto his lap.

'We'll talk more, later. For now, I'd better get that tea sorted out and return to Stone.' As Selwyn left the room, his heart went out to his nephew who sat forlornly with his head clasped in his hands.

It took a while for Sebastian to get his breath back. The situation seemed so surreal. Finally, his composure partially restored, he found himself concerned by Amanda's sudden disappearance.

He went to seek out Mrs Soames. Of the SOCO team there was no sign, but she was in the kitchen, staring out of the window.

'You OK, Mrs S?'

She swung round to face him. 'Course I am,' she fibbed, as she hurried over to brew the tea. Once done, she turned to him, her face red and puffy. Sebastian drew her to a chair, sat her down and put his arm round her shoulders.

'It's all been too much,' she moaned, in between dabbing her eyes and wringing the handkerchief. 'If it hadn't been for—' A look of horror came over her face. 'Oh my giddy aunt! Amanda told me to tell you and the commander that she's gone off to a priority!'

Sebastian wrestled with this for a moment before his head started working again. 'Did she say priority or priory? This is important.'

'Oh, priory, I think. She spoke so quick, then vanished.'

'Jesus! On her own?'

'No, Martin was going to be there,'

298

Sebastian was immediately hit with conflicting emotions. He started to pace as he thought through the tactics. 'Look, Mrs S, I need you to get the commander in here right away without the inspector. Amanda could be in danger.'

'Oh my gawd!' Two minutes later, she returned with Selwyn.

'What's going on?' he demanded.

'Haven't time to explain, I'll tell you on the way. We must get after Amanda.'

'What about the ambulance and—?'

'To hell with that, this is far more important. And no, we can't tell Stone. Presumably, you've already told him that Archie's got your revolver, which would mean dragging the armed police out again. There isn't time for all that malarkey.'

Sebastian ushered the confused and reluctant commander towards the front door with Mrs Soames in tow. He stopped for a moment to face her. 'Just stay in the kitchen. When the inspector comes looking for the commander, tell him he had to go away to an emergency. Don't tell him where, though.'

***

In the darkness and deathly silence of the crypt, Amanda managed after some contortions to poke her hand through the narrow gap between the lid and the side of the coffin. However, she just couldn't budge the lid. 'Can you hear me, Martin?' she called out.

'Yes,' came the muffled reply. Then, 'Are you OK?'

'Absolutely. I'm so sorry I got you into this mess.'

'You can make it up with a Chinese when we get out of here.'

'I can't get a signal on my mobile.'

'Neither could I. What the hell do we do now?'

'I don't suppose you can heave the lid off your box?'

'Not a chance.'

'Weakling!' As he failed to laugh, she felt the darkness closing in. 'Neither can I,' she admitted.

'I thought you were supposed to lug heavy books around all day?'

'Not when they're piled on top of me. Martin… we might just be in a spot of trouble here.'

'We'll get out of this.' His words lacked conviction. 'Does anyone know about this place?'

'I told Mrs Soames just before I came here and told her to tell Sebastian and the commander. I couldn't get to them because of the police.'

'Well… that's something. Let's just hope Sebastian puts two and two together.'

'He will. He's good at maths.' Though just when he'd do that was questionable, and the many holes in Amanda's plan were starting to make a mess of her composure. What if he was taken to hospital before he could explain to the commander about the priory? What if Mrs Soames didn't get the chance to tell them because everyone kept telling her to stop fussing?

Amanda was starting to feel mortified for having got the two of them into this mess with such a precarious safety net.

'I'm finding it difficult to breathe. Best not to speak unless we have to,' Martin suggested. 'Better conserve our energy and air as much as possible.'

They both fell silent, Amanda desperately trying to divert her thoughts from the possibility of spiders crawling around in that darkest of spaces.

***

Beatrice Soames braced herself as she heard the sound of approaching footsteps. She put the vegetable knife she'd been using out of harm's way, lest she might be tempted to use it for a purpose it was certainly not intended.

'Where's the commander?' demanded DI Stone, who stood menacingly in the doorway.

She took a deep breath, turned and looked at him. 'He said as 'ow he had an emergency to go to.'

'What? And you didn't think to tell me?'

'I'm tellin' you now.'

'Just what's going on? Where's he gone? No doubt creating bloody mayhem somewhere else before this lot's been cleared up.'

'I 'aven't a clue. It's not for me to pry into his affairs.'

'I could do you both for obstruction, you exasperating woman. There's a senior officer on his way—'

Beatrice Soames took a step forward and squared up to him. 'Now you listen on. I don't really care who's comin' here. You're the most objectionable person what's ever crossed that threshold. You've come in here, throwin' yer weight around – and there's plenty of it.' She darted a pointed glance at his belly. 'My poor commander's gone through hell and back through no fault of his own, so don't you come here threatenin' him and me like that, cos it just won't wash. You show some respect when you're in this buildin' and in his company.'

The DI's eyes bulged in disbelief, his ruddy face almost a match for the tomatoes she'd been slicing moments earlier. His splutter of protest was interrupted by the ring of the doorbell. Mrs Soames glowered as she passed him to answer the door to a bearded paramedic.

Stone looked on as she explained that the patient had been called away on an emergency of his own, whereupon the disgruntled man muttered something uncomplimentary and disappeared into the night.

Still seething, Stone bore down on Mrs Soames and the front door she was about to close. 'So Sebastian's disappeared too, has he? This is just too much. You've not heard the last of this, not by a long chalk, and you can tell the commander that.' He pushed his way past her, presumably to take a breath of fresh air.

Mrs Soames slammed the door shut behind him. 'Good riddance.'

***

'Are you sure you know where it is?' Selwyn asked as they drove past the same spot for the third time.

Sebastian peered through the rain-spattered windscreen as the car slowed. 'It's got to be here. She said it was off a lane at the end of the industrial estate. You'd better turn back. It can't be as far as this.'

'There! What about that?' Selwyn pointed to a junction ahead and immediately veered off the main road. A little further along, their headlights lit up Amanda's parked car. Ahead of it was another car, one they didn't recognise.

'Must be Martin's,' Selwyn murmured. He reached under his seat and pulled out a flashlight. 'Have you got one?'

Sebastian tapped his pocket.

They tried the car doors, looked through the windows,

then set off down the road until their beams picked out an area where the grass and undergrowth had been flattened. Slowly, laboriously, they stumbled through the driving rain and negotiated their way through the bushes and brambles until they reached a clearing. The walls of the ruined priory were now picked out by the torchlight. They scanned the area then split up to look round the site, their shouts for Amanda piercing the night.

'Blast!' exclaimed Selwyn as he tripped and nearly went headlong where the ground suddenly dipped.

Sebastian yelled himself hoarse. Minutes later, he and Selwyn regrouped.

'Not a soul. Nothing.' Sebastian couldn't keep the tremor from his voice. 'Where the hell can she be?' He scanned the site and called Amanda's name yet again.

Selwyn gave a reassuring shake of his arm. 'We'll find her, my boy. Don't worry. Perhaps they've gone off with—'

'I'd thought about that, but how would he keep control of two of them in the car? Oh my God, he might have—'

'Let's keep a cool head. We'll look around for them again, though it's going to be the devil's own job to scour this area in the dark.'

'There's no alternative. I'm not leaving here until we've searched every inch. If that swine's done anything to her—'

'Steady the buffs. Let's get to it. You take a line from this wall in that direction, and I'll cover the other.'

Sebastian had moved perhaps five yards when Selwyn called him back. He was methodically sweeping the ground with his torch where he'd nearly tripped. 'Come and look at this.' He kicked his heel against an old timber that stood somewhat lower than the ground.

Sebastian knelt down, studied it for a moment then attempted to lift it. It came away surprisingly easily. He glanced up at Selwyn, who bent to clear a second timber, and then another. They stared at the exposed steps, dumbstruck for an instant, before descending.

'Crikey,' muttered Selwyn as their lights played on the crypt walls and the three tombs.

Sebastian called Amanda's name. A muffled moan came from one of the coffins.

'Good God!' exclaimed Selwyn.

They hurried forward and pushed at the edge of its covering slab. When the top half was sufficiently open, Sebastian lifted out his shivering love. Her eyes screwed up in the torchlight. She drew in deep lungfuls of air, though she was somewhat hampered by his tight embrace as he repeatedly kissed her forehead.

'Martin's in the other one,' she croaked.

The two men applied themselves to the second slab and pushed it so far that it fell to the ground. Inside the coffin lay Martin's inert form.

***

Berensen watched through the car's darkened windows. A short distance away, the house stood in darkness. A pedestrian crossed its driveway towing a black Labrador that was straining at the lead. The owner pulled up his coat collar, muttered at the dog and yanked on the lead, whereupon the two slowly disappeared from view.

When all was quiet, Berensen slipped out of the car and walked slowly towards the front door. After another glance around, he took out a torch, knelt and looked for the tell-tale paper wedge he'd concealed in the gap between the door and frame a few days earlier. It lay on the floor. Fox had been home.

Berensen pocketed the torch, picked the lock and entered silently. Once inside, he fitted the silencer to his gun and cautiously searched the house. Eventually he returned to the front door, disappointed not to have found his quarry.

He bent to pick up the mail that had arrived since his last visit, having marked the envelope which had previously sat on top of the pile. He carried the few items into the lounge and examined them. Of particular interest was one that bore the stamp of Hollytrees Caravan Park on the back.

He opened it and read the newsletter; its headlines advised caravan owners of a planning application that had been made to re-route the site entry road into Frogsham Bay. There was a slim chance that Fox might be holed up there – but still a chance. Berensen pocketed the newsletter and envelope, placed the remaining mail back on the pile at the front door and quietly let himself out, relocking the door.

It took just under half an hour to drive over to The Inquisitive Duck. 'I didn't expect to see you again so soon,' the receptionist greeted him.

'We couldn't find a resolution to everything, so I stay for another meeting tomorrow.' As he passed the rooms they'd occupied, Berensen's thoughts turned to the two men he'd killed earlier. It was strange how their various agendas had clashed so immediately.

He was sitting on the bed of the same room he'd occupied previously and reaching for the remote control to catch the television news when his mobile rang.

'I've not heard from you for several days now. What's the situation?' Cutler demanded.

Berensen blinked his eyes closed, held the mobile away and exhaled deeply through his nose. 'I am close to a delivery.'

'If it's not here a week from today, I'll be making a contract with someone else. For two items, this time. You understand?'

'I am understanding. I expect delivery before the end of two days.'

'Good. Just make sure it arrives – or else.' Cutler clicked off.

Berensen rubbed his forehead, then switched on the television. Time really was running out. He'd always been one of the best in the business, and he believed he still was, but in this business, alas, someone better always came along eventually.

***

Between the three of them – though Amanda's contribution was mainly solicitous pleas for Martin still to be alive – the prone man was lifted from the coffin and placed on the ground. Sebastian knelt, felt his pulse then prepared to give him CPR. Tears rolled down Amanda's face as she looked on helplessly and wrung her hands, while Selwyn shone his torch on the proceedings.

Just as Sebastian was about to start, Martin suddenly stirred, opened his eyes and panicked at the presence of a face inches from his. Sebastian jerked backward as Martin's hands rose to grapple with his treacherous assailant.

'Martin, it's us! You're safe!' Amanda said.

Her reassurance did the trick and Martin released Sebastian's shirt. His cheeks reddened. 'Sorry, I must have fainted.'

'Yeah, well, er… Glad you're OK.' Sebastian scrambled to his feet, very relieved he'd been spared putting his lips to his rival's.

Martin was helped into a sitting position with his back against a coffin. Selwyn produced the small hip flask that invariably accompanied him on outdoor excursions and offered it to him. Amanda's bewildered, traumatised outpourings were a confusing combination of relief for Martin being alive, gratitude to Sebastian for having been prepared to save him and affection for both men.

When she hugged Martin, Sebastian looked away. Then she hugged Sebastian, to which he raised no objection whatsoever.

'So, the blaggard made off with the goods and the documents and left you both to die, the utter bastard!' Selwyn observed angrily, once Amanda had filled them in on the details.

'God help him when I get hold of him,' Sebastian threatened. 'Where the hell can he have gone? He can't be mad enough to go to his own house, can he?'

'Hardly likely,' said Amanda. 'He may be a bastard but he's not a foolish one.'

'In any event, we must get Martin to hospital to be checked out,' Selwyn suggested. '*And* you, my lad.'

It was agreed that Amanda would drive them there in Martin's car, followed by Selwyn, who would take her back to collect her car before he returned to the hall. No doubt there he would have to face Stone's wrath, provided the irritable DI hadn't already left in a towering rage.

Chapter 20

Archie pulled the net curtain to one side, palmed away the condensation and peered out of the window. At this time of year there was never much to see; most of the other caravans were empty and would remain so until spring. Leaden clouds flitted across the morning sky and the horizon looked dark and forbidding. He watched two magpies swoop to the ground from the tall trees that bounded the park to the south.

He released the curtain, took a mouthful of coffee then looked at the box he'd carried in from the car the previous night. His mind strayed to the two people at the priory. They'd still be alive and should remain so until he called Fitzgerald to tell him where they were. He regretted what he'd had to do, but there had been no option. He certainly couldn't have brought them with him.

'Dog eat dog,' he muttered as he shrugged off any further thoughts of them and turned back to the box.

It took a variety of implements and some time to tease open the lid. Certainly, the contents were nothing like Archie had expected based on what Fitzgerald had suggested when he'd shared his thoughts on the missing family treasure. However, it was beyond question that these items were valuable.

Archie examined them for a while before replacing their protective wrapping and returning them carefully to the box. Fortunately here was something that could be sold virtually anywhere in Europe or America.

That was his next priority: deciding where to go after he'd sold the document and map to Fitzgerald.

***

Miriam sat at her desk, unable to concentrate on the papers in front of her. Amanda Sheppard, now no longer 'the librarian' – far too many things had happened for that to remain her lowly nomenclature – was due shortly.

The mayor's thoughts turned to the council meeting she'd attended the day before. It had been a much more peaceful affair than the previous one. She'd declared a vested interest when the meeting had proposed that she should negotiate with the commander over the two sets of land transfer documents. In the public interest, the council had been bound to accept her self-disqualification for the role, although this had stymied its position. No other councillor or officer was better equipped to take on this new task.

By way of compromise, she'd offered an arrangement that soothed her torn loyalties: they would allow her to work with Commander Fitzgerald on opening the hall to the public and, in turn, she would respond in a purely advisory capacity to any proposals the council received from the commander, and vice versa. It was a wonderful thing not having to choose between the two loves of her life.

Any further thoughts were dispelled by a knock at the door.

'Amanda, do come in,' the mayor greeted her. 'Let's sit at the table. Would you care for a tea or coffee?' She waved to the spare seat and tray of drinks, giving the girl the first genuine smile she'd ever offered her in that room.

Amanda sat, but still looked apprehensive.

'First things first. Since you've been reinstated and exonerated from all allegations brought against you, there are going to be some departmental changes.'

'Oh?'

'You have nothing to fear from these changes. I'll say no more than that at this stage.' Miriam gently placed her hand on Amanda's arm. 'I just want to thank you for the support and help you gave me personally. Without that, I dread to think how matters would have turned out.'

'It was my pleasure. I'm just so relieved at the outcome.' Amanda cast her gaze down to the table, a slight frown on her brow as she appeared to wrestle with something.

Miriam also frowned; she had hoped for a more enthusiastic response to this reversal in the young lady's fortunes. 'Is there a problem?'

Amanda looked up at her. 'Possibly. There is something you might be able to help me with, but it's probably not strictly kosher.'

'Tell me. If there's anything I can reasonably do, I will.'

'I'm trying to find an address. It's to do with either Maurice or Archie Fox and his possible ownership of a local caravan. I'm hoping the finance department's council tax databases may be able to shed some light.'

Miriam stiffened at the name. 'Not a problem. I'll be only too delighted to sort that out for you.'

***

Selwyn glanced up from his book and frowned at the ringing phone. 'Who on earth's that?' he mumbled as he got up to answer it.

'Selwyn, it's George Nelson.'

'Ah, yes, George.' *The walking cure for insomnia.* 'How are you? It's been quite a while.'

'Quite so. I just wanted a word in your shell-like.'

'Ah-ha?'

'I've just had it out with DI Stone about the relentless activity going on at your place. Tactical arms units and so forth. There's some pressure from above to put it all under the microscope and take things further. I've done what I can to smooth things over, but orders are orders and my DI's got the bit between his teeth.'

Selwyn grimaced. 'Which bit is that?'

'Oh, he's been fuming about obstruction of justice, vigilantism and such like. Might have a point, you know, after last night's shenanigans. He's likely to press charges. I'll do what I can to ward off the evil day, but just thought I'd give you the heads up. Off the record, of course.'

'Of course.' Selwyn's mood darkened in parallel with his facial expression. 'Thanks for the call.'

'Not at all. We must have another game when all this has blown over. Cheerio.'

Hardly had Selwyn sunk back into his chair and started to brood when the doorbell rang. Within moments, Miriam swept into the room. Selwyn smiled at this welcome escape from his gloom. Somewhere in his mind, the toreadors were once more on the move.

'Miriam, old thing,' he exclaimed and hurriedly rose to embrace her. 'Tea, coffee, or something stronger?'

'I'd better keep a clear head. Some tea would be fine, please.'

Once it had arrived, Miriam got down to business. 'I

have to warn you, Selwyn, apart from dying to see you I've come to have a chat about the land transfer. Now we're engaged, I won't be involved in the council's negotiations with you. Those will probably be led by the deputy leader and chief executive, no less. From now, I have to be a bit more Switzerland.'

'Neutral, you mean?'

She nodded apologetically.

'I wondered if you'd have to take a back seat. Chief executive got a nice pair of legs, then?' he joked, remembering how Miriam hadn't hesitated to use her feminine charms when they'd first negotiated.

'I wouldn't know. Come on now, Selwyn, be serious. What they *are* happy for me to do is to resume the planning we did for the opening of the hall.'

'Well, at least there'll be some fun.' Selwyn winked.

'I trust you've got the documents and map tucked away somewhere safe.'

Selwyn gulped. Grimaced. 'Ah, well. Not really.'

'What do you mean, "not really"?'

'I don't actually have the originals, only the copies that Amanda gave me. That swine Fox made off with the originals.'

'Oh Lord, I thought you were home and dry. The council won't accept copies of the documents as evidence of your claim.'

Selwyn snorted. 'That's a change of tune. Tyson reckoned they'd proceed against me on the basis of their copies of the estate land transfer documents.'

'He was flying a kite. Anyway, they've now found the originals of those.'

Selwyn slumped into his chair and stared at her in

silence. It seemed so unfair. 'So they can go against me for *my* land, but unless I get hold of my originals for the reciprocity arrangements, I can't go for *their* land.'

'Quite.'

'The bastards! If they want to keep the recreation patch, then they can give me the land that's due to me. I'll fight them on it.'

'What with, Selwyn? What with? If it came to a legal battle, it could cost you a fortune. You've only just got the estate's money back, and things were tight even before it was stolen. The council's got much deeper pockets. Would you be prepared to risk everything?'

Selwyn let out a deep sigh. 'Bugger this neutrality, I'm going to need you on my side, old girl.'

Miriam poked her tongue out at him. 'Less of the "old girl", if you don't mind. And if I did take your side, I'd have to relinquish my position as a councillor – and as mayor.' They stared at one another in silence until Miriam smiled at him. 'If push came to shove, I'd be prepared to do that for you, my love.'

'Thank you. Let's just hope it doesn't come to that. Anyway, it might all get overtaken by my trial.'

Miriam frowned. 'What trial?'

'Murder, when I get my hands on Fox.'

***

A while after Miriam's departure, Mrs Soames went to say goodnight to the commander. She found him staring into the fire, a generous measure of his favourite malt in the glass next to him. Before she even entered the room, Mrs Soames knew what to expect, having heard strains of Bill Evans' 'What Is There to Say' from the hallway.

Selwyn's glance instantly told her she'd get little joy from trying to enter into conversation with him.

As she waddled back to the kitchen, she shook her head. 'That woman's the agony and the ecstasy for the poor man,' she lamented under her breath. She'd need to ring Reggie; it looked like it was going to be a late night. She went off to make the call and find a blanket. The commander would need covering up later, once he'd fallen asleep in the chair.

Her diligent plans were disrupted by the shrill ring of the hallway telephone. She picked up irritably.

'My dear lady,' came a familiar, loathsome voice. 'Might you pop the good commander on the line for me?'

Mrs Soames wanted to call Mr Fox a great many things – a despicable scrub, a worm, a useless ha'porth – but all she could manage through gritted teeth was an assurance that she'd get him directly.

She put the receiver down on the hallway table with a good deal of force and hurried off to find him. Selwyn looked up from his copy of *The Times* as she bustled breathlessly into the drawing room. 'Commander, it's that man on the phone. That there Maurice.'

Selwyn's eyes widened and he stiffened. He discarded his newspaper and hurried towards the door. Mrs Soames stood aside and watched him anxiously as he sailed past her.

'Yes?' Selwyn barked down the receiver and listened with narrowed eyes. 'You're too late with that, we rescued them last night. If that had been left to your information, they'd probably be dead by now, you swine.' His lips tightened as he listened.

Mrs Soames tugged on the hem of her apron as she

watched with a worried frown from a discreet distance down the hall.

'And what do you want for them?' Selwyn's face coloured. 'Ten thousand? You bastard. You utter bastard. No, wait! Give me a moment… ' He lowered the receiver and composed himself. 'Alright. Where and when?' He threw his arm up in despair at the reply. 'Tomorrow night's too soon – I can't get the money that quickly, particularly not in used notes.' He rubbed his brow anxiously as he waited for a reply. 'OK, understood, no police. I'll have the money ready and wait for your call. Now, what about the stuff you took from the priory? Maurice? Maurice!'

Selwyn threw down the phone. Mrs Soames approached him warily.

'Bastard,' he muttered as he replaced the handset. 'Utter fucking bastard!' He looked angrily at her, then his expression softened. 'Sorry, Mrs S. Bad form losing control like that.'

Only momentarily shocked by his language, she forced a smile and nodded. 'I just wish as how I could get *my* 'ands on him,' she murmured. 'I'll fetch you a nice fresh pot of tea, shall I?'

'Just the ticket.'

'Shall I call Sebastian, or—'

'Oh, heavens no. This isn't his problem. And he's been through enough, poor lad. We'll get through this together, Mrs Soames. And mum's the word, eh?'

She zipped her mouth with finger and thumb, then went to press the kettle into action while the commander returned to the dining room deep in thought.

***

The shadows were lengthening when Berensen brought the Mercedes to a stop in the car park. A handful of people were making their way to and from the small shop and clubhouse, which, according to his research on the internet, were due to close shortly.

He turned off the headlights, switched off the engine and got out of the car to sit in the back. There was no safe skulking to be done in the driver's seat, which was caught in the glare of the store's floodlight.

It was when the killer stepped out of the car that he was spotted from the clubhouse doorway. Archie darted back inside and seated himself at the table he'd just vacated. He needed to think quickly about what he was going to do.

***

Amanda leaned across the front seat to fling open the passenger door as Sebastian dashed out of Fellowes House and peered around for her car in the darkness. He smiled as he buckled up. 'Where are we going, and how did you find him?'

'He's at Hollytrees. I remembered that you said he'd once lived in a caravan at Frogsham Bay. If that were permanent, it'd be liable for council tax. It was a bit of a long shot but I asked the mayor to get the finance department to check if there was a caravan listing under his name. And there is – Archibald Fox, no less.'

'You smart cookie. So what's the plan?'

'We go and confront him.'

Sebastian shot her a worried glance. 'But he's got the gun.'

'Maybe he has, but he won't use it. He's not an out-and-out killer, otherwise he'd have put those coffin lids in place and let us suffocate. Anyway, he's not going to go loosing off shots in a residential caravan park. The last thing he wants is to draw attention to himself, not with the hitman still on the loose.'

'You've got it all figured out.'

If only life and love were that simple, Amanda thought.

Fifteen minutes later, she swung into the long drive up to the caravan park. She parked up, got out and Sebastian scanned the area. 'There! That's the Volvo,' he pointed. 'So, he *is* here. What do we do now?'

'I reckon we should—'

There was a loud crack, followed immediately by a tremendous explosion as the darkness was suddenly lit by a flash that became a bright glow. For a second, the couple stood rooted to the spot as they stared at the illumination.

'You stay here, get in the car and be ready to leave,' Sebastian ordered. 'I'll go and see what's happened. What was the number of the caravan?'

'Sixty-two.' As he dashed away, Amanda turned to study the Volvo.

Sebastian sprinted past a couple of small groups of horrified residents who'd emerged to watch the flames. He stopped from time to time to check the numbers on the caravans and finally arrived at the fire.

The caravan was a shell. The roof had been blown off and lay at an angle against one of the burning sides, and black smoke billowed through the flames. If anyone had been inside when the explosion occurred, they'd certainly be dead.

Sebastian dashed back to the car park, drawing curious glances from the spectators. He joined Amanda in her car. 'It was his caravan. It's a burning wreck. If he was in there, he'll be dead.'

Amanda bit on her bottom lip. 'And everything destroyed, including the blasted documents.'

'Completely. What shall we do? The police and fire brigade will be here at any moment. We don't want to get caught up with them, do we?'

'No.' Amanda peered through the windscreen. 'Wait, look.' They could just make out a shadowy figure emerging from the far side of the clubhouse, making its way across the car park straight to the Volvo.

'That's him,' exclaimed Sebastian. 'He's alive and he's going to get away.'

'He bloody well isn't. I've a few scores to settle with him. You try and get round the back and I'll approach him from the front.'

'But… the gun?'

'Get on with it, ninny! He's not going anywhere. Believe me.'

Before Sebastian could protest further, Amanda was out of the car and striding across the car park.

Archie was already behind the wheel of the Volvo and the engine was running. He tried to drive off, but the car stalled. He turned the key again. The car jerked forward and he came to a stop. By the time he'd got out, Amanda was almost upon him. Fortunately, he was too preoccupied with his four flat tyres to notice Sebastian creeping up behind him while Amanda came at him from the front.

'Things getting a bit too hot for you, Archie?' she asked.

He swung round and pulled the gun smoothly from his pocket. He aimed it at her. 'Back off. I'll use it.'

'You'll have to take the safety catch off first.'

Archie frowned and hastily examined the gun.

'You haven't a clue, have you?' Amanda scoffed. 'You're all mouth and no trousers.'

Sebastian stepped up and caught Archie in a reverse stranglehold. 'I think we'll take that.'

Amanda leapt forward, grabbed the gun and stuffed it into her pocket. She approached Archie, who was now grappling with Sebastian's forearm, his face suffused deep pink.

'If you don't mention the gun to the police, we won't. You're in enough trouble as it is, sunbeam,' she said. Archie winced as she jabbed him twice in the ribs with her fingers. 'That's for Martin's coffin and mine.' From the end of the drive came the sound of a siren. 'Hold him there, Sebastian. If he stops breathing, you can let him go.'

Sebastian couldn't help grinning at her ruthlessness.

She leaned into the Volvo to search the back seat, then she opened the boot and pulled out a valise. 'Yabadabadoo!' she exclaimed as she withdrew some familiar documents. She searched further then punched the air as she found what she was looking for – just as two police cars skidded to a halt.

Sebastian released Archie from the stranglehold. The portly villain bent over the boot as he tried to catch his breath. The officers piled out of their vehicles and headed off to the fire, except for one who looked curiously at the trio.

'He's alright,' Amanda called. 'Just a bit of smoke inhalation.'

Sebastian gave him a reassuring wave.

'There's an ambulance on its way,' the officer called, then turned and chased after his colleagues.

'Get in the back seat,' Amanda ordered Archie. 'If you try to get out, Sebastian really will throttle you – if I don't shoot you first. And *I* know how to use this.' She patted her pocket.

As Archie clambered into the Volvo, Amanda transferred the contents of its boot to her own car. All the while, Sebastian stood guard and watched her with admiration.

By now they could hear a fire-engine siren coupled with the sound of another siren. Amanda returned and stood on the opposite side of the car as the fire tender sped into the car park and made its way towards the conflagration. Behind it, an unmarked police car came to a halt and out stepped DI Stone.

'Over here, Inspector,' Amanda called, as he scanned the car park.

'This had better be worth it!' He strode towards her, his face grim.

Before he could say anything, Amanda pointed to the back of the car from whence the morose Archie glared. 'Allow me to introduce Archie Fox. He's all yours. And,' she added, 'in here—' she pointed to the valise '—you'll find the stolen goods the light-fingered little monkey purloined.'

The DI was stumped for words, but only for a moment. 'I suppose it'd be ungracious of me not to thank you, though, heaven knows, you lot have caused me more than enough trouble. So... thanks.' He glanced down at the Volvo wheels. 'What happened?'

'I let them down, just in case he decided to do a bunk.'

'Good thinking.' Stone signalled to DS McBride. 'Put the case in the car and keep him in there while I go and check with uniform what's happened. You two need to stay.' He fixed Amanda and Sebastian with a flinty stare. 'And I really do mean *stay*. I'll need your statements before you go anywhere.' With that, he set off to consult with his colleagues and the fire brigade.

'How could you see the safety catch was on from where you were?' Sebastian asked as they waited in Amanda's car for Stone's return.

'I didn't know if there was one or not.'

'Bloody hell! You could have been killed.'

'He wasn't going to use it. He's all bluff and bluster. He gave himself away when he threatened to have Stevie killed if I said anything about the documents, then later admitted he couldn't have done anything.'

'And what did you take out of the boot?'

'The stolen documents and what he took from the crypt.'

'Which is?'

'I dunno, it's all wrapped up. We'll have to wait till we get back.'

Sebastian returned Amanda's grin and they stared at each other until Amanda glanced away uncertainly. 'I wonder how Martin's getting on,' she blurted out without thinking.

'He should be alright,' Sebastian replied grudgingly, and an uneasy silence descended on the car

Chapter 21

Selwyn rose at six, having snatched a mere two hours' sleep. Sebastian had called from Hollytrees Caravan Park the previous night, just minutes before Selwyn was due to set off and deliver the cheque he'd written for Archie.

The sensible part of him had been apprehensive that the compromise payment would be refused – Archie's ludicrous expectation of ten grand in used notes having been impossible to meet – and that violence would ensue. However, the furious part of him, the part that still felt his brother's cold hand in his palm, the part that grieved for the loss of Sebastian's natural father… *that* part of him had uncovered the old colonel's elephant gun, serviced it thoroughly and slung it into the Jaguar.

In the cold light of the early February morning, Selwyn still wasn't sure whether he was rueful or relieved about his lost opportunity to do that bounder Archie Fox some serious physical damage. Still, he mused, rubbing his weary face, it was best not to give the long arm of the law even more reason to descend upon him.

He crawled out of bed, pleased that he hadn't given into melancholy or tipped himself into a bottle of Jura last night. He'd been ready to fight for the estate, the family name and those dear to him, and that injection of adrenaline and vigour coursed through him even now. In fact, it coursed through him quite violently all morning, to the growing consternation of Mrs Soames.

Having already unsuccessfully tried a variety of distractions to keep his mind off things, at one stage Selwyn wandered into the kitchen, where Mrs Soames eyed him with suspicion as he ambled round the room, peering into cupboards and drawers and generally making an appraisal of the place.

Finally, the exasperated housekeeper rounded on him. 'Just what is it you're after, Commander? Is it something I can get for you?'

'Oh, I'm just familiarising myself with the place and the memories I have of it from when I was young.'

'Well, seein' as 'ow I need to get on with some chores in 'ere and how it's not too spacious, how about your familiarising yourself with the drawing room, and 'appen I can come and familiarise you with a cup of tea or coffee?' Her expression softened. 'Sebastian and Amanda will be 'ere soon, at any rate.'

'Good point, well made. Cup of tea would be just the ticket.'

At the stroke of eleven, Amanda and Sebastian arrived at the hall. 'Get yourselves in there right away,' Mrs Soames greeted them. 'He's been like a cat on an 'ot tin roof all morning. Even left some of 'is breakfast, and it's a full English at weekends. I'll bring you some coffee.'

Selwyn was already outside the drawing room, impatient to greet them as they hurried down the hallway, Sebastian laden with a box. 'Come in and sit down. What on earth's been going on?' He noted sadly that Amanda chose to sit apart from Sebastian, who'd seated himself on the Chesterfield.

Sebastian narrated the events of the previous evening.

Selwyn shifted position in his chair several times as the story unfolded, sometimes placing his hands firmly on his knees, then clasping them in front of him. Throughout, he remained spellbound.

'I tell you, this girl was just amazing,' Sebastian praised Amanda, who merely gave a modest smile.

'Tremendous job. Well done, that woman,' Selwyn congratulated her.

Sebastian passed over the documents on top of the box and Amanda handed them to Selwyn. 'So here's the reciprocal Wisstingham land transfer document and map. Martin and I—' her eyes darted to Sebastian who caught her glance, then looked away '—looked over the site that is shown, which includes the priory and the whole of Cresthaven to the north of it.'

Selwyn nodded.

'Since that entire section is presently leased to the individual industrial units, it represents a serious financial asset for the council.'

Selwyn spread out the documents on the table and sat down to study them. Amanda and Sebastian joined him. After a while, and a great deal of thought, he looked at them. 'I've clearly got the upper hand in terms of value and negotiating position.' He eyed the box.

'Yes.' Amanda brought over the box. 'Here's the other part of the jigsaw. Fox found it in one of the coffins.'

Selwyn studied it with mild disappointment. 'Not very big,' he observed.

He lifted the lid and carefully removed the contents. He withdrew two ancient-looking books from their substantial wrapping of heavy waxed material and carefully set them down in front of him. He turned over the first few pages, staring in amazement at each one.

'They're stunning,' he murmured, then looked up at Amanda. 'But surely this can't be the family treasure, can it?'

'I don't know. They're illuminated manuscripts. I took a peek at them late last night because I didn't want you to be disappointed. They're beautiful books in magnificent condition considering their age, and I reckon they're worth a lot of money. As to whether they are the family treasure, I wouldn't know. Perhaps they were left by the monks at the priory when they fled.'

'But why wouldn't they have taken the books with them?' asked Selwyn. 'They took their abbots' bodies.'

'Perhaps they didn't. Maybe they buried the bodies somewhere in the grounds in unmarked graves, or perhaps they intended to return for the bodies and books once they were settled somewhere.'

'It does strike me these are more likely to have been the monks' treasure rather than the Fitzgeralds,' observed Sebastian. 'So, what do you reckon about the land transfers?'

Selwyn rose, walked to the window and gazed out over the lawn and meadow, pondering how to get the best out of this arrangement. After a while, he returned to the table.

'Right, here's what I think. I don't believe this is the family treasure, so I'm certainly not prepared to give up looking for it. That leaves two possible search areas – the recreation park, which I'd lose if I insisted on completing the transfers, and the industrial land and priory site. It would be impractical to try to excavate at Cresthaven – I wouldn't know where to start, and it'd cost time and oodles of money to terminate the leases, buy the buildings and start digging them up. Furthermore, if I insisted on going ahead with the land transfers, it would be a nightmare keeping hold of easy access to the stables and paddock.

'I reckon my best bet is to leave the land ownership as it is, except for negotiating transfer of the priory site to the estate. I'll seek a financial contribution from the council to compensate for not taking over the industrial land, and permission to excavate the recreation site. This, of course, would then be handed back to the council, providing we don't come across something there of such importance that we need to change the use of the site.'

'That sounds like a plan to me,' said Amanda. 'I suggest your negotiations should include your ownership of the priory site, effective from the date of the transfer document. That way, you'd preserve ownership of these two books.'

'Good point, well made,' acknowledged Selwyn.

'Also, you need to keep quiet about the books until your agreement with the council has been signed.'

Selwyn raised a forefinger in agreement, but made a mental note to show Miriam the books as soon as he could. No more secrets could come between them.

Amanda stooped to retrieve something from her handbag, which she placed on the table in front of the commander. 'I also rescued this, though if there were any bullets with it the police will have already found them.'

'Thank you, my dear.' Selwyn quickly slipped the gun into his pocket. 'Let's hope he didn't leave any of the bullets inside anybody.'

'He wouldn't have had the guts for that,' Amanda reassured him.

'Oh, I nearly forgot.' Sebastian pulled out a mobile from his pocket and handed it to Selwyn. 'Your phone. The police found them all in the hitman's car.'

Further conversation was halted by the arrival of Mrs Soames to ask if the visitors were to stay to lunch. Selwyn was about to agree on their behalf but caught the enquiring look Sebastian gave to Amanda.

She shook her head. 'Sorry, but I've a prior engagement. Thank you anyway.'

'Perhaps another time,' said Selwyn, disappointed.

'Yes, I'll look forward to that.' Amanda rose, gave the briefest of smiles to Sebastian and bade farewell to Selwyn with a kiss on the cheek.

***

7TH FEBRUARY

'Come in,' Amanda shouted, her mood lighting up as Martin walked into the office.

'I don't want to disturb you,' he whispered. 'Just want a quick chat.'

'The library doesn't extend as far as here, so you don't have to whisper. Anyway, you're not disturbing me. Fancy a coffee?'

'That'd be great.'

Amanda returned shortly with two mugs. 'So, what is it?'

'An invitation to dinner at Qwik Qwak's.'

Amanda pursed her lips and deliberated the invitation.

'You did say you'd make things up to me with a Chinese if we got out of the crypt.'

'So I'm paying, am I, you cheeky monkey?' she demanded.

'Your presence will be reward enough.'

She grinned. 'You sweet-talking lounge lizard, you.'

'There are a few things I want to talk to you about.'

'That sounds ominous.'

'Possibly. So is that a yes?'

Amanda nodded and a time was fixed. She got back to work when he left, but had barely checked her emails when she got a call to go and see the mayor.

***

'Selwyn told me the good news about your recovery of the documents and Fox's arrest. Well done,' said Miriam.

Amanda blushed. She still hadn't got the hang of taking compliments from her seniors. 'I suppose what I did wasn't in the best interests of the council.'

'Maybe not, but justice was done. You did the right thing and, what's more,' Miriam leaned forward and whispered, 'it got me off a hook. 'You seem to have a habit of doing that. Anyway, there are two things I want to talk to you about. Firstly, it's been agreed that you will be promoted to head of your department.'

'But that's Marcia's—'

'Was,' interrupted the mayor. 'She's handed in her notice and taken another job away from the area. Your salary will start at the bottom of the pay grade but be backdated to the point of Marcia's departure. I'll send you a full job description. Do I take it you'll accept?'

'Of course.' Amanda's enthusiasm brought a smile to the Miriam's face.

'Good. Now there's something else I want to put to you, to which you need to give some thought before you make a decision. There's no obligation, and if you decline it won't be held against you in any way – though I hope you'll agree. I think it would be a great opportunity for you.'

Amanda goggled as the mayor proceeded to outline an offer of a six-month international cultural exchange of senior council officers. She stared in amazement as the details unfolded and was particularly intrigued by the location. 'Canada?' she double-checked.

'Yes. Fortunately it will be during in their summer, so you wouldn't be plodding around in the snow like Nanook of the North. Give it some thought and let me know your decision as soon as you can.'

***

With that meeting done and dusted, Miriam had lunch then headed over to the hall. 'Selwyn, I was so pleased to hear your news,' she greeted him as she threw her arms around him.

After a lingering kiss, he led her to see the documents, which she eagerly perused. 'So this brings us back to the question of where you want to go from here. If you insist on a straight swap, it will impact severely upon the council's finances and Wisstingham's residents.'

'Spoken like a true official.'

The mayor splayed her hands. 'It's simply a truth. You have the lead now, and the onus is on you to say what you want to do.'

Selwyn gazed at her in silence, glad to be the bearer of a plan that would get what he needed while drawing him and Miriam together. He repeated the proposals he'd outlined to Amanda a couple of days earlier.

Miriam could not hide her delight that the opening of

the hall was firmly back on the agenda amongst his other plans. 'In principle, that all sounds very sensible. If you were to put that to the council, I think they'd be only too happy to accept – subject to the level of contributions you ask for.'

'Yes, that's something I'd need to discuss with your colleagues. You've got the figures from the earlier study we made. They won't have changed very much. However, the maintenance contribution for keeping the hall open would need to be index-linked.'

A slight smile played on Miriam's lips. 'You've really thought this through, haven't you?'

'I hope so.' He took her hand. 'I know you have your loyalty to the council, but do bear in mind that this is not only my future but yours too.'

'I'm only too aware of that. It's a future I want to look forward to and enjoy.'

When they parted, Selwyn could not have felt in a better mood. Almost all the storm clouds of a couple of days ago had lifted one by one. In Miriam he had not only a worthy adversary but also the best of advocates.

***

Mrs Soames waved off the mayor warmly, relieved that Miriam's visit had not punctured the balloon of happiness the commander appeared to be floating on. However, her hackles immediately rose again at the sight of DI Stone pulling up in the drive. Having recently sent him packing, she felt like she could do battle with one of the knights she regularly dusted in the hall and win.

'It's that Inspector Stone,' she announced to Selwyn. 'Should I show 'im in?'

'I think you'd better.' The commander rose from the table and the pile of documents he'd been sorting through and braced himself. *Can't win 'em all, I suppose.*

Mrs Soames showed the DI in, her flint-like gaze on his back as he strode into the room, then closed the door behind her with a little more zeal than usual.

'Commander Fitzgerald.' Stone advanced, his hand outstretched.

Selwyn blinked. This was a new departure from Stone's customary style. Nor did he miss the officer's somewhat conciliatory tone.

'I thought I'd better come round to set matters straight.'

'Do sit down, Inspector. Would you care for some refreshment?'

Stone hastily declined, perhaps fearful of what might be served up to him. 'I did say that further action might be considered and taken,' the DI continued, somewhat hesitantly. 'But in view of recent circumstances, unless anything adverse comes to light, it is our intention to close the file on what's happened here.'

Selwyn breathed a sigh of relief. 'That's good to hear. Much appreciated. What changed your mind about pursuing charges for obstructing justice and whatnot?'

Stone frowned. 'How did you know about that?'

Selwyn grimaced, realising he'd nearly given away George Nelson's warning call. 'That appeared to be your frame of mind last time we spoke,' he dissembled.

Stone looked tired. 'Yes, well, in the name of protecting my reputation, I had the options of coming at you for minor offences with all guns blazing or walking away in a dignified fashion. I'm an easy-going man, Commander Fitzgerald.'

'That you are, DI Stone,' Selwyn lied diplomatically. 'Anyway,' he went on hastily, 'what happened with that blighter Fox?'

'It turns out that Fox spotted the chap who was after him, nipped back to his caravan, turned on the gas and waited. When his pursuer entered the van, he shot into it and blew everything sky high. We didn't recover the gun, nor would Fox come clean as to what happened to it or where he got it from.' He paused to give the commander an appraising stare.

Selwyn raised his eyebrows and stared back.

'We don't intend to pursue that particular line of enquiry any further. The man's in deep enough trouble as it is, and… Well, let's say we need to conserve our resources, eh?'

Selwyn smiled. *So the rogue had a vestige of honour left in him after all.* 'What about the chap in the caravan?'

'They recovered the body, what was left of it. We're checking out his identity through the car, but we reckon it must be the hitman. Fox has given evidence against the bloke who was his backer and whom he believes put out the contract on him.'

'And what'll happen to Fox?'

'He's been charged with fraud, embezzlement, theft and murder – so far. A string of other charges may well follow. Thanks to your librarian, we also have the stolen goods we believe were missing from the French stash you brought into us. I don't know whether there are any other offences that you consider he should be held to account for.'

'What about the Volvo? That belongs to the estate.'

'We'll arrange for you to collect it. Would you want to

add theft of a vehicle to the charge sheet?'

Selwyn shook his head. 'What about the two blokes who were killed here?'

'Harry Gaverty and his crony. He was a London villain who'd long been on the Met's radar, so that was a result by default.'

'So all's well that ends well?'

'It would appear so. I'd better be off now. I'll see myself out.' At the door, he glanced back. 'As long as I don't get my ankles bitten, and I don't mean by your beagle.'

Selwyn smiled.

'Just promise me one thing,' Stone continued, 'that there won't be any more high-jinks going on here.'

'It was never my intention to host quite so much excitement in the first place.'

'Quite. Goodbye, Commander. Let's hope our paths don't cross again.'

'Goodbye, Inspector. That would suit me just fine.'

Chapter 22

It was a crisp, sunny morning. The dew sparkled on the grass. At the far edges of the lawn, hints of yellow stood out in the clumps of daffodil leaves.

Selwyn looked up from *The Times* as Sebastian walked into the dining room. 'Good morning, dear boy. Did you sleep well?'

'Not particularly.' Sebastian took a seat opposite his uncle.

'Me neither.' Selwyn glanced out of the window. 'Lucian's got a good day for it, though.'

Sebastian followed his gaze. Silhouetted against the blue sky, crows rose in the air and flew off to the distant sycamores whose bare branches were stark against the blue sky. 'Yes,' he sighed. 'Can't say I'm looking forward to it.'

'No. It's a day I've been dreading. Still, it has to be done.' A sombre silence fell on the table.

It was interrupted by the appearance of Mrs Soames. 'I take it you'll both be wantin' the full works, seein' as how it's… Well.' Lost for words, she sniffed away threatening tears.

'That'll be fine thanks, Mrs S,' Sebastian replied as Selwyn nodded his agreement.

As she left, Sebastian rose to help himself to cereal. 'I had so little chance to talk to him,' he complained, once back at the dining table. 'I'm going to regret that forever.

334

He gave his life for me in the end.' He stared at the bowl in front of him, tucked in his chin and swallowed deeply.

'He was very proud of you and so happy he got to see you. I'm thankful we had what little time there was before he died.'

'What did you talk about?'

Selwyn set aside the newspaper. 'What had happened to him after he left Wisstingham, about his life in China and the dreams he'd had of returning home and finding your mother again. He really loved her.'

'How did it all go so wrong?'

'He got mixed up with a bad crowd in Hong Kong.' Selwyn passed on every detail he could remember from what Lucian had told him while sitting beneath that tree.

Sebastian sighed. 'What a mess it's all been.'

'All because of Vincent. I hadn't a clue that the man had such a hold over him, like some sort of Svengali. By Jove, Monaghan was a crafty devil. The main thing is that Lucian got to see you. He died a happy man, Sebastian.'

The dining room door swung open as a large tray borne aloft by Mrs Soames entered the room. The housekeeper smiled as they made appreciative noises at the sight of the plates then tucked into them with gusto. 'There'll be more toast on the way,' she promised as she waddled off.

'Do you know who'll be at the funeral?' asked Sebastian, between mouthfuls.

'Just ourselves, Amanda, Mrs Soames and Reggie, the gardener, and Miriam. She got to know Lucian quite well, you know. Oh, and Gwen from the Mazawat. He made her quite a fan, the charmer.'

'I'm glad we got a plot near my mother.'

'I was going to put him in the family vault, but I reckon

he'd be happier if we buried him close to Mary.'

After they'd both done justice to the extra toast and home-made marmalade, Selwyn glanced at his watch. 'I think we should set off from here in a couple of hours. I've no doubt Mrs Soames will do us proud for the wake.'

'Are we coming straight back here?'

'Yes. I'd thought about having a drink at the Phantom Hound, but somehow it didn't seem right. We're only a small group, and I've no doubt we'd have had some busybodies asking questions about Lucian.'

Sebastian frowned at Selwyn. 'You're not ashamed of him, are you?'

'Good lord, no! He was my brother. I just feel that coming back here will give him more dignity, which he rightly deserves.'

***

The funeral passed off without incident but not without tears. However, throughout the service and afterwards when they stood round the grave, the commander sensed a coolness between Amanda and Sebastian, even though they were standing side by side.

When they returned to the hall, Mrs Soames divested herself of her thick winter coat and press-ganged Reggie to collect the other coats and hang them up. Shortly afterwards he reappeared in the role of a waiter, bearing a silver salver with glasses of sherry and port. Mrs Soames followed up with a large tray of canapés, the precursor to a procession of sandwiches, pastries and other delights.

'Is everything alright between those two?' Miriam asked Selwyn.

'I'm not sure. The same question occurred to me during

the funeral. Has Amanda mentioned anything to you?'

Miriam shook her head. 'It's not really for me to say. See if you can persuade her to tell you. She might need some guidance which I'm not in a position to give.'

'Curiouser and curiouser.' Selwyn frowned at her, though Miriam would tell him nothing more. 'I don't suppose you've heard anything more from your colleagues?'

Miriam smiled. 'I wondered when the conversation would get round to that.'

'Are you playing hard to get?'

She smiled slyly. 'I was going to tell you. They're more than delighted with your proposals. No figures have been discussed yet, but I've no doubt you'll be able to negotiate something to your liking.'

'Whose side are you on?'

Miriam bent her head next to his. 'Yours, of course,' she whispered. 'I think you've been more than fair and, as you said, it is *our* future at stake. All the hard work is over, such as it was.'

'I'll let you into a secret when this wake is over.'

'Oh, tell me now,' Miriam coaxed.

'No, you can wait. Anyway, I'll have to take you upstairs for it.'

Miriam's eyes widened and she gave a wicked grin. 'Really?' she exclaimed. 'Promises, promises.'

Further banter was halted by the appearance of glasses of champagne for the speech and the toast that Selwyn was to make to honour his brother. Afterwards, as Mrs Soames, Reggie and Sebastian were clearing away, Miriam caught Selwyn's eye. With a nod she indicated Amanda, who stood forlornly by the window, staring out onto the grounds.

'I'll wait for you in the garden room,' Miriam murmured as he passed her.

Selwyn slowly approached the troubled girl. 'Amanda, are you alright?'

'Commander… '

'I really think it's time you started calling me Selwyn.'

She smiled. 'Selwyn, then. Yes, I'm fine thanks. Those were lovely words you said about Lucian.'

'Thank you. You know, you can talk to me in total confidence if there's anything troubling you.'

She appeared to hesitate. 'Actually… ' She glanced around. 'There is something I'd like to discuss.'

'Come on then. Let's go into the library.'

Amanda sat on the edge of a seat across from him and nibbled at her bottom lip, the fingers of one hand playing nervously with strands of her hair.

The commander leaned forward. 'Come on, tell Uncle Selwyn.'

'I'm not supposed to repeat this, so I can tell you only once,' she quipped, tense because of her uncertainty. She outlined the cultural exchange offer she'd received.

'Well that *is* a turn-up for the books,' Selwyn exclaimed. He rubbed his chin as he thought for a while. 'It's hard to know how Sebastian's going to take this news, but there's a Spanish proverb which goes, "Tell a lie and find the truth." Not that it applies in quite the same way when you're trying to discern a chap's true feelings for you, but there's a similarity to what I'm thinking. I take it you want me to help you?'

Amanda nodded. 'I don't know who else I can turn to. Kathy would just shake Sebastian by the shoulders until his brain turned to mush, which would do me no favours at all.'

'Very well. Let's explore the best way to approach this.'

They sat in discussion for several minutes before a much happier librarian finally thanked the commander and departed.

Selwyn went looking for Miriam. She was in the garden room, pacing in impatient expectation of his arrival and the surprise he had in store. 'I thought you'd never come.' She sidled up and kissed him.

'It's not that sort of a surprise.' She gave him a quick pout. 'Well, maybe later,' he conceded and she laughed.

Upstairs, seated on the edge of the bed, to Miriam's increasing astonishment, Selwyn outlined what had happened at the priory then carefully unwrapped the two illuminated manuscripts. Never before had he seen such a look of amazement on her face.

'They're gorgeous,' she whispered as she delicately turned the pages. 'They must be worth a fortune.' She suddenly looked up. 'I've had a terrific idea. Supposing one of these had pride of place in the hall when it opens to the public, and the other is displayed in a prominent London museum? What a terrific advertising tool it would be to say that its twin can be seen in Wissting-ham or London. Then they could be changed over after a time.'

'That sounds top rate.'

'Who knows about these?'Miraim asked.

'Sebastian, Amanda and Martin. That's all.'

'Good. They need to be kept under wraps until the deal with the council is signed and sealed. It's going to take some time. After all that's done, there's the Land Registry to deal with. That could take forever and a day, consider-ing the documentation.'

'We're one step ahead of you there.'

'If it were any other day than this, I'd ask if you had any other surprises for me.'

'How about a waltz?' In Selwyn's mind, the toreadors once more were taking their places on the dance floor.

Miriam laughed lightly. 'I know how your waltzes end,' she reminded him.

'Hmm, yes, I suppose you're right. Another day then?'

'Yes, and very soon.'

***

5TH MARCH

Selwyn glanced up from his book as Sebastian slouched into the room and threw himself onto the Chesterfield. He twisted round to turn down the music and looked at his nephew. 'Had a bad day?'

Sebastian nodded, his elbows on his knees and his hands clasped in front of him as he stared down at the Persian rug.

Selwyn laid aside his book. 'Tell me about it.'

Sebastian shook his head but, as Selwyn continued to stare at him, finally threw his arms up, his lips pursed. 'It turns out that Amanda was out with Martin last night.'

'How do you know?'

'Jamie saw them in Qwik Qwak. At least, I think it was Martin, judging from the description.'

'No improvement in your relationship with her?'

Sebastian sighed and shook his head. 'I don't know what to do. Nothing's changed since she gave me back the ring. She's been friendly enough. I've tried to make up, but she keeps me at a distance.'

'Maybe you're not trying hard enough. Whatever you do, don't lose that girl. She's one in a million.'

'I know she is, but I don't believe she loves me.'

Selwyn smiled. Much as he hated to torment the boy, he needed to light a rocket under his stubborn backside. 'I can assure you she does. But if she doesn't believe she matters enough to you, you're never going to win her back. Has she told you she's going to Canada?'

Sebastian shot a glance at Selwyn then closed his eyes. His jaw tightened. 'Oh well, that's it then. She's off with *him.*'

'Don't you think she's worth fighting for? I strongly suggest you don't despair until you've actually spoken to her. Now, the sun's well over the yardarm. D'you care for a drink?'

'I'll have a pint of hemlock, please.'

'Not totally lost your sense of humour.'

'It's just about the only thing I haven't lost.'

'Nonsense! I'm telling you, my boy, there's everything to play for. So what'll it be?'

Sebastian pondered for a moment. 'Oh, just something soft. A Coke. I may be driving later.'

Selwyn went to fetch the drinks, his head turned to conceal his smile.

***

7TH MARCH

The commander's increased visits to the hall's library had not gone unnoticed. Mrs Soames often found his usual haunts deserted, only to discover him poring over one of those offending piles of dusty old documents she had to dust around every week.

341

'I only 'opes as how 'e'll finish with 'em, pile up and burn 'em,' she muttered to herself on more than one occasion, unburdened by a love of historical things.

Taking a chance on being right first time this morning, the housekeeper headed with the commander's elevenses straight for the library. Sure enough, there he stood at the plan chest engrossed in a map spread out in front of him.

Looks just like he's planning to invade Europe. She placed the tray on a nearby table.

'Ah, Mrs S! Capital,' Selwyn greeted her, after he'd cast a quick glance for the shortbreads.

'I'm going' to 'ave to give this place a thorough clean one day,' she warned.

Selwyn glanced round the room. 'You do a marvellous job of it as it is.' He gave her an indulgent smile, whereupon she snorted and shuffled out of the room.

Less than ten minutes later, there was a knock at the door and Sebastian entered. Selwyn frowned. Amanda's departure was almost on top of them and, as far as he was concerned, Sebastian was spending his time in quite the wrong places with the wrong people.

'What ho, governor,' he greeted his uncle.

'Not at work?'

'I'm off to York later on. I've got a meeting with a new client tomorrow morning. What are you up to?'

'Just developing a strategy for carrying out the excavation on the recreation area and wondering where best to start.'

'So you're convinced that the manuscripts aren't the Fitzgerald treasure?'

'I'm even more certain now. Amanda did some investigation. It transpires their origins are from the same brotherhood of monks that occupied the priory.' Selwyn noted his reaction to the mention of her name. 'What time are you getting back from York?'

'Why? Do you need me tomorrow?'

This was starting to get rather exasperating. 'You've not seen Amanda then?'

'Nope.'

'Past caring, eh?'

Sebastian sighed.

Selwyn's retort was vehement. 'Don't just sigh at me, you bloody fool. I thought you were made of sterner stuff. You're just letting her slip away. Now for heaven's sake, sit her down, find out what's what and tell her how you feel.'

They eyeballed one other. Sebastian's mouth opened and closed in an impotent sort of way for a few moments, then he turned and strode out of the room without another word.

Selwyn could only hope he was finally going to take matters into his own hands.

***

Sebastian called the hotel in York to let them know that he might be rather later than planned while he waited for Amanda at the bar of the Phantom Hound. He frowned at the shake of his hand as he hung up.

Other than a few regulars, who were propping up the bar as they held animated conversation on the day's news, the pub was quiet. When Amanda walked in, she and Sebastian found a corner table and ordered food. After a few casual, mundane exchanges, they lapsed into an uncomfortable silence.

Gathering his courage, Sebastian decided to bite the

bullet. His opening gambit was to peer ostentatiously around the room.

'What are you looking for?' asked Amanda.

'The elephant.'

'Which elephant would that be?'

'The elephant of omission.'

'Now that's a rarity, an elephant on a mission.' She threw him a cheeky smile.

'Omission,' he mouthed, trying not to return the smile that he always loved to see and had missed for so long. 'I believe you're going away.' His attempt to affect indifference but failed dismally.

'Oh, that. Yes.'

'Canada, I heard.'

'Nothing wrong with your hearing then. Your bowels regular, are they?'

'If you're not going to take this seriously... ' The threat remained unsaid due to the arrival of the food. The second the waiter had gone, Sebastian took a deep breath. 'Are you going with Martin?'

'What made you think that?'

'He lives out there, doesn't he? And you were seen out to dinner with him the other night.'

'Goodness, I'm in the presence of a spymaster.' Amanda looked like she might make another quip then relented. 'Yes, we were saying goodbye. He's taken a job in New Zealand. He left yesterday.'

Sebastian's emotions were instantly jumbled, his soaring spirits muddled with confusion. 'But... So... What's Canada all about, then?'

'It's a six-month exchange that Miriam arranged.' She lowered her voice. 'Personally, I think it's a jolly to thank me, but I wasn't going to pass it up.'

Sebastian fell back in his chair and let out a long sigh. It was almost as draining to realise he'd endured countless pointless nightmares about losing her to Martin as it had been to endure those nightmares in the first place. And yet he could have been spared so much of the agony he'd been through. He gaped at Amanda, who stared back with raised eyebrows. 'Why didn't you tell me any of this?' he eventually asked. 'I was going out of my mind thinking you were going off with *him*.'

Amanda placed her knife and fork carefully on the table next to her plate, her expression serious. 'Sebastian, I love you. I've never stopped loving you. I've told you often enough. But I need to know you love me and for you to show it. I also need to know that you *believe* I love you and that you'll stop this insane, infuriating jealousy.'

'I'm showing you now.' The words felt as lame on his lips as they probably sounded. He felt a complete fool.

Amanda folded her arms indignantly. 'When I told Selwyn about Canada, I knew what conclusion you'd jump to – that I was running off with Martin. I also knew that if *I* told you about it, we'd end up having another row. So Selwyn kindly offered to drop the bomb for me.' She sighed. 'Since Selwyn told you, I've been waiting to see if you felt enough about me to try to get me back. It was like Selwyn's Spanish proverb, "Tell a lie and find the truth." I'm sorry to have given the impression that my feelings lay elsewhere, but I really was running out of options.' Her lips began to tremble.

Sebastian stared at her, his eyes misting over. 'I love you, Amanda. I love you so much.' His voice wavered. He reached for her hands. 'I'm sorry. I'm so sorry I've been such a berk. I got wrapped up with the job and all that stuff in France. And I know I've been stupidly jealous. I promise I'll never be like that again.'

'Never?'

'Never!' he swore. 'Please don't go.'

She squeezed his hands and they kissed.

'I *am* going. It's all set up and it'll be a great experience. As for us, you'll have six months to make sure you really want me. If you're there when I get off that plane in six months' time, I'll expect you to have the ring with you.'

'But what if you meet someone while you're there?'

She shook her head. 'There's only one person for me. You're the one I have my adventures with, my love. I wouldn't want them with anyone else – and I really, really hope there'll be more.'

***

Mrs Soames rushed to the front door and opened it, a look of alarm on her face. Alongside her, the commander was initially nonplussed as they watched from the top of the steps.

Sebastian's car horn beeped continuously as the car careered crazily up the drive to the hall, occasionally veering onto the verge. Out of the driver's open window, an arm waved frantically.

'What on earth's 'e doin'?' the housekeeper asked, her hand clasped over her mouth.

Selwyn smiled. 'Celebrating, I do believe, Mrs S,' and he waved back to Sebastian in greeting.

ACKNOWLEDGEMENTS

I once again wish to express my heartfelt appreciation to Pat, my ever-patient wife; to my friend Ted Rhodes for his input and advice on police matters; to my friends and family for their encouragement and support and to Catherine Cousins and her great team at 2QT.

Printed in Great Britain
by Amazon

24476512R10200